MW00816838

HOMECOMING KING

THREE KINGS SERIES BOOK #1

PENNY REID

WWW.PENNYREID.NINJA/NEWSLETTER/

COPYRIGHT

This book is a work of fiction. Names, characters, places, rants, facts, contrivances, and incidents are either the product of the author's questionable imagination or are used factitiously. Any resemblance to actual persons, living or dead or undead, events, locales is entirely coincidental if not somewhat disturbing/concerning.

Copyright © 2021 by Penny Reid; All rights reserved.

No part of this book may be reproduced, scanned, photographed, instagrammed, tweeted, twittered, twatted, tumbled, or distributed in any printed or electronic form without explicit written permission from the author.

Made in the United States of America

ISBN: 978-1-942874-82-9

DEDICATION

For Iveta.
Thanks for sticking with me.

CHAPTER 1

"The moment you doubt whether you can fly, you cease for ever to be able to do it."

— J. M. BARRIE, *PETER PAN*

"To bang, or not to bang? That is the question." Kaylee peered at me from behind her black-rimmed glasses and set a briefcase on the stool to her left. She'd just walked in, and instead of saying hi like a normal person, this was how she greeted me.

Frowning at the empty highball glass I'd just finished drying, I debated how to best respond to my good friend's noteworthy dilemma. "Are we talking about a guy? If so, I recommend making a pro-con list."

"No, Abby. My hair. I love your bangs."

"Oh. Thank you, it has pockets." I'd taken to saying *Thank you, it has pockets* as a means of dealing with the discomfort caused by unexpected compliments.

Picking up a second highball glass, I wiped it clean of watery residue and checked my watch. Kaylee was an hour early, not that I minded. She usually shuffled in ten minutes before closing on the nights she had custody of our car, already wearing her pajamas and a silk bonnet on her head. By then Walker, my boss, would be playing "Never Gonna Give You Up" by Rick Astley over the bar's speakers. He had this automated to happen every night, four times in a row, even when he wasn't here. His way of driving out the stragglers.

Currently, "Monster Mash" reverberated from overhead, a herald of the season, with Halloween just around the corner. The end of October to January 1 was my favorite time of the year for so many reasons, not the least of which were all the decorating opportunities. Orange lights zigzagged across the bar shelves behind me, and I'd covered every tealight on the dining tables and bartop with ceramic ghost covers. I'd also set up a creepy, black Halloween tree—like a Christmas tree, only a spooky and leafless fake willow instead of a lush and vibrant evergreen—in the corner of the dining area, complete with cobwebs, strings of spiders, an eyeball, finger, and miniature ceramic doll head ornaments.

More doll heads—larger ones, fifty or so—were strung back and forth high above the entire bar. They hung from fishing line, which gave them the appearance of floating midair. I'd spent all spring and summer cackling in hilarity while making the heads at my pottery studio via slip cast molds procured for fifty cents each at Goodwill. Their freakishness did not disappoint, and I'd loved watching some of the customers cringe, smile, and then laugh uncomfortably while drinking under the doll head canopy.

"I'm tired of this haircut." Kaylee tossed her long braid over her shoulder, curls straining against and protesting the tidy style. She slid onto the stool adjacent to the one holding her briefcase.

I gave Kaylee's hair a quick once-over. I liked her hair, and she'd mentioned before that cutting bangs would require her to chemically remove the natural curl.

So I said, "I like your haircut and the curls."

"I knew you'd say that. But thank you. I like it too."

The bell over the front door jingled, announcing one or more new customers just as the song switched to Frank Sinatra's version of "Have Yourself a Merry Little Christmas." I liked Frank, but I'd always considered it an impertinent and bossy song; who was he to tell me how to spend my Christmas? Plus, late October was entirely too early for Christmas music.

"Be with you in a sec," I called without looking toward the sound, keeping my eyes on Kaylee as I reached for a few drink menus and cocktail napkins. "I don't understand wanting to change something about yourself you already like. If you like your hair, don't change it. If you don't like your hair, have at it."

"See, I knew you'd say that too." She leaned forward, lowering her voice. "Your statements are unsurprising, and I am unsurprised by your unsurprisingness."

I frowned. Kaylee was obviously in a sassy mood tonight. Maybe her court date hadn't gone well.

"Gee. Thanks," I said, sending her a disgruntled look, knowing better than to argue with a lawyer.

"You're in a rut, Abby." Her eyes turned soft. "You do the same thing every day. You wear the same thing every day. You eat the same thing every day. The only things you change are the color of your nail polish and your hair cut."

"And look how happy I am." I glanced toward the door to count the newcomers but found only a solitary man, already sitting on a stool at the far end of the bar closest to the door.

A huge, enormous, colossal mammoth of a man. He was so big and tall, the rest of the bar seemed to shrink in comparison. Great. *Just . . . great.*

"Who is that? Is he a regular? Why do you look so irritated?" Kaylee glanced between my face and the man, keeping her tone hushed even though we were too far away for him to overhear our conversation, especially with Frank Sinatra crooning at us over the radio, telling us our Christmas will be merry and little this year.

Even so, I also lowered my voice. "It's just, we're less than an hour until closing and he's not a regular. Convincing non-regulars to finish up and head out can be . . . annoying." And he was big. And he was male.

This wasn't always the case, but in my experience—maybe nine times out of ten—a big, burly guy coming into the bar so close to closing didn't typically want a quick drink.

Her gaze stayed on him, assessing. “He’s handsome though, right?”

“Is he?” I grumbled, putting back all but one drink menu and one cocktail napkin.

“Uh, yeah. Very. And he looks familiar. . .” She placed her elbow on the bar, narrowing her eyes as she leaned an inch toward him, as though to see him better in the dim light. “I thought you had owl vision. Who does he look like?”

The truth was, other than noting this person’s size and a general impression of his clothes, my eyes were blurry with visions of tonight’s likely unpleasant conclusion: my coworker Ingrid and I coaxing him to leave, failing, and then having to either call Walker at home or the security company.

I didn’t care if this stranger was objectively the best-looking guy in the world. After tonight I had three days off. Anyone making me work late tonight was a blobfish.

“Whatever.”

My voice must've hinted at my thoughts because Kaylee tore her attention from the man, her eyebrows raised expectantly. "Why do you always sound so irritated when there’s a hot guy? Why do you dislike hot guys?"

“You have to admit, hot guys have hot guy problems, which are like first world problems on steroids.”

“Come on, everyone likes hot guys. It's biological. There's nothing you can do about it. You have no choice.”

I would've argued with her, told her that I had nothing against hot guys in general, but she made a sound of protest before I could speak.

“Abby.” Her eyes were full of sympathy. “Eventually you're going to have to date someone.”

Ugh. Dear. *Lord. Not this again!*

“Do I, though?” I’d tried dating. In fact, I’d even tried marriage. Everything about it was a horrific disaster, on so many levels. This topic was why Kaylee and I currently shared just a car instead of a car and an apartment.

“Yes.” She looked entirely earnest and concerned. That just made her pushing worse. “You can't let one bad experience—what, eight, nine years ago?—dictate the rest of your life."

"Can't I, though?" I tucked a drink menu under my arm.

Albert Einstein defined insanity as doing the same thing over and over and expecting different results, but I'd never been one of those people who needed to learn a lesson more than once. One and done, that was my motto, especially when the "one bad experience" had ended in jail time.

"You must get back on the horse, Abby."

"Must I, though?" I tapped my chin.

"Yes you—" Finally recognizing my attempt at deflection, she snapped her mouth shut and gave me a flat look. "Your dense barrier of sass notwithstanding, you know getting out there, putting yourself out there, would be healthy."

Kaylee hadn't been there for my marriage, but she'd witnessed the aftermath. She'd watched me struggle under the mountain of debt and sorrow and anger and helplessness. Why couldn't she just drop this? And even if I hadn't barely survived my divorce, I'd heard and seen enough sad stories from bitter and depressed bar patrons to convince me that desire was a scam, soul mates were a lie, and the only thing romantic love did to your heart was break it.

And then send it to bankruptcy court and jail for your ex's massive —I mean impressively colossal—debts and Ponzi scheme that you had NO IDEA about when you'd gotten married at an impressionable eighteen years old.

"Why can't you let me live my best life, Kaylee? Maybe my best life is eating scrambled eggs every day and never dating." Legit, I loved both scrambled eggs and never dating.

She scowled, but her words were teasing, "This is a good time to tell you. I, and others, consider your perpetual contentment with life a personal attack."

I laughed. "Here, let me go serve this hot guy real fast and then you can continue to beat this dead horse that you insist I take for a ride."

Utilizing her ninja skills, she grabbed my wrist before I could move away. "Wait. Wait." Her eyes darted to the end of the bar and then back to me, whispering, "What if, instead, you flirt with the hot guy?" Kaylee indicated to the man with her chin, like I wouldn't know to whom she referred. The man's presence seemed to inhabit one tenth of the available space in the bar, there was no missing him.

I blinked at her. "Why would I do that?"

She searched my face. "If you flirt with him, I won't bring up dating again for—for . . . a month."

Typical Kaylee. Life was one big bargaining opportunity. She was only happy when she was negotiating or arguing.

"One flirting encounter buys me a month?"

"I promise." She drew a finger in the shape of a cross over her heart.

"Make it three months and we have a deal."

"Deal," she said quickly, her eyes brighter, happier, like my agreement was a victory for her. "Three months. And maybe unbutton the top button of your—"

I twisted my arm from her grip. "I can flirt without showing my boobs."

"Yeah, but you have really nice boobs, and they deserve to be admired by someone other than me."

"So noted."

"And take off that ring!" she loud-whispered.

Grunting, I did remove my grandmother's ring from my left ring finger, my shield against handsy and aggressive patrons, but I did not adjust the buttons of my shirt. I slipped the antique ring onto the middle finger of my right hand and walked down the long galley to the giant stranger. Obviously, if I got any creeper vibes from him—any at all, even a smidgen—the bet was off. Better to be safe than sorry.

If he was perturbed by my lack of attentiveness thus far, he showed no outward signs. The man's eyes were on the screen of his phone, his arms braced on top of the bar, shirtsleeves rolled up, broadcasting some seriously tantalizing forearm action.

Hmm. Maybe I should've undone the first few buttons of my shirt.

Exposed male forearms, in my opinion, were the equivalent of exposed female cleavage. Tits for that, *er, tat*. I meant, tit for tat.

"Hey, what can I get you?" I asked, placing a drink menu and the square napkin on the bar while studying what I could see of his features.

Dark blue or dark gray dress shirt, top three buttons undone, tie loose and slightly askew, a bright white undershirt beneath. He'd pulled off a heavy coat and it hung haphazardly on the back of his stool. His hair was short on the sides, longer on the top, and either light brown or dark blond. The color was impossible to tell given the dimness of the room and the orange glow of the Halloween lights decorating the liquor shelf behind me.

He had a nice forehead, what I could see of it, but his face and focus remained fastened to the screen of his phone as he responded in a monotone, "Beer. Whatever amber you've got on tap, please."

"Sure thing. You want a pint or—"

"Pint is fine, thanks."

Polite. I'd say he had a nice voice except it had remained monotone.

Stepping to the side, I grabbed a pint glass and positioned it under the tap of our most popular amber.

Somewhere to my right I heard the distinct and obnoxious sound of Kaylee clearing her throat. Sliding my gaze to the side, I found her eyes wide with meaning. Sensing her dissatisfaction with my lack of flirting, I shrugged, like *What can I do?*

She waved an exasperated hand toward her chest, then at the big guy, her eyebrows high arches, and then tugged at the neck of her top, mouthing a word that looked like *buttons* but it might have been *boobs*.

I pressed my lips together, removing my eyes from hers. Again, what could I do? The guy was into his phone way more than the idea of flirting with a female bartender. I wasn't currently, and never had been, in the habit of forcing men to pay attention to me. Live and let live, I say!

The glass filled, I placed it on the napkin near his elbow. "Hey, you want to start a tab?"

"Please." Still without looking up, he set down his phone, pulled out his wallet, and placed a credit card and his driver's license on top of the bar. I swiped up both, my brain telling me to look at his birthdate even as my eyes strayed to his photo and the name beneath it.

"Be right b—ba—ack." My mouth fell open as I stuttered, ending my sentence with a silent gasp, my eyes bolting to the stranger who wasn't a stranger at all. Gaping and caught within a snare I'd fashioned years and years ago, I was quite literally stupefied.

Oh dear Lord in heaven.

Rex.

I gaped. I gaped and gaped and gaped, stared and stared and stared, my mind reeling. *But how? And when? And how? And—*

"Uh ahem, ahem, *AHEM.*"

Kaylee's obnoxious throat clearing snapped me out of my stupor, and I quickly turned before Rex spotted my shock-trance. I stared blankly, not sure what to do next, not remembering whether I was coming or going, my breath tight in my lungs, my heart racing.

Hells bells.

Rex McMurtry.

CHAPTER 2

"You'd rather make up a fantasy version of somebody in your head than be with a real person."

— JENNY HAN, *TO ALL THE BOYS I'VE LOVED BEFORE*

Yes, before you ask, he was *that* Rex McMurtry, the star defensive end for the Chicago Squalls, philanthropist, and sexiest man alive according to all the lists. Here. In my bar. Technically, it wasn't my bar, but it kinda was my bar because I'd worked here since my junior year of high school as a dishwasher, then busser, then server, now bartender. Therefore, I liked to think of it as my bar.

I wasn't dumbfounded because I'd just come face-to-forehead with a bona fide A-list celebrity. I was shooketh because I'd just come face-to-forehead with my elementary, middle, and high school crush. And it had been a brutal crush in the same way the cocktail of teenage hormones, being the tallest girl—by far—since preschool, shyness, and inexperience are brutal.

Rex was the only boy's name I'd ever doodled next to mine in notebooks, the only guy I'd ever had sex dreams about—sorry if that's TMI, but it is what it is—and the sole reason I'd gone to football games or any other optional school related event.

I'd joined Girl Scouts in sixth grade because his aunt was the troop leader. I'd started drinking coffee my freshman year so I could sit in the diner across from where he washed and detailed cars during his spring and summer after-school job. Recalling those actions did not fill me with nostalgia.

I hadn't been boy crazy. I'd been Rex crazy. And now here he was.

Presently, long dormant embarrassment tinted by an unflattering shade of shame spurred my movements. I stepped to the register and tapped the screen, waking up the payment system. Unable to help myself, I hazarded a hurried glance over my shoulder, gobbling up the sight of Rex in the flesh even as I did my best to redirect my thoughts.

I was the bartender, he was the customer, he wanted to start a tab, and so that's what I would do.

But first, one more look at those forearms.

No. No! *If you look at his forearms, you will drool all over your buttoned up shirt!*

Wresting my attention away, I slammed my eyes shut and willed the fogginess in my head to clear. I watched Rex's televised pro football games whenever I could, but I hadn't seen him in person since graduation. He'd been slated to sit right next to me, since our last names were so close, but I'd done Rachel McQuaid a solid and let her take my spot.

First, she'd also liked him since forever. Second, she was kind and funny. And third—truthfully—she'd had a better chance of snagging his attention than I did. They'd had classes together because they were both smart, so he already knew her. Also, she wasn't freakishly tall like *moi.*

Currently, I stared at my cash register like it was the control panel of an alien spaceship while giving most of my attention to Rex's license photo which, apparently, I'd been absentmindedly caressing with my thumb.

Yeah. Gonna stop doing that right now.

Gathering a deep breath, mostly to breathe in some sanity and breathe out a whole tornado of tangled creeper instincts and emotions, I ceased my weirdo thumb caress and ran his credit card.

No wonder he hadn't looked up from his phone. The guy probably couldn't go anywhere without being recognized and ogled. What I remembered of Rex was that first and foremost the dude didn't enjoy attention. I suspected this was still true now. You could just tell when he gave interviews after a game, he only wanted to discuss the game. If a sports broadcaster asked him about his personal life, he'd give them a bored stare, and then change the subject back to the game. Sometimes, if they persisted, he'd add a muttered, *Fuck off,* and then walk away.

But when or if he did deign to speak, he was so nice. So, so, so nice. Like, the anti-bully. He'd been a hefty kid in elementary school, big for his age. "Solid" as my Uncle Mac would've said. Most folks thought he was taciturn and aloof, but when it mattered, and if you were paying close attention, he could be such a gentle giant. A wistful sigh escaped me at a memory of kid Rex picking class rejects for his kickball team during PE, me included.

Ugh, I needed to step back from the ledge of my obsessive admiration and just give the poor man his cards back. Then I needed to leave him alone, let him finish his drink, get him another if he so chose, and leave him alone some more.

Pivoting on my heel, I faced him and stretched the rest of the distance to deposit his license and credit card on the bar. "Here you go. Signal if you need a refill," I said on a rush, hoping my voice had emerged just as monotone as his had moments earlier.

I grabbed a bar towel to needlessly wipe my jittery hands and strolled down the length of the galley . . . to Kaylee . . . who I definitely hadn't forgotten was still there.

Damn.

Kaylee watched my approach. When I drew even with her, she pounced forward, whispering, "What did he say? Did you—"

"Nothing!" I squeaked. Closing my eyes, I took another brain-cleansing breath and leaned my hands on the bar. "Nothing," I said much slower, calmer, quieter, and opened my eyes, arranging my face to feign nonchalance. "He, uh, just asked for a beer. I gave him one. And there you go."

Her suspicion was as plain as the lack of bangs on her forehead. "Um, nope. Tell me what really happened."

"Nothing happened with him." *Y'all, the story of my life in four words.*

Her gaze narrowed, flicked over me. "Then why do you look so skittish?"

"Do I?" I shrugged, frowning like I didn't know what she was talking about.

"Yes." Her gaze continued its pensive assessment, and I understood why.

I'd always been exceptionally gifted at concealing my feelings, even more so now. When I'm distressed or faced with a jarring situation, I wasn't usually one of those people who got clumsy or jittery. Clumsy bartenders do not exist because they don't stay bartenders for very long. I'd learned how to redirect chaos and unpleasant emotions inward, burying everything until I could unpack it all later, while my exterior radiated coolness, calm, indifference.

As a bartender, this skill came in quite handy. But as a person who can't stand upheaval in any form—as in my whole being rejects it on a cellular level—this was a coping strategy, one that had served me well during my twenty-eight years. Which was likely why my looking skittish at present concerned my friend.

Doing my best to keep my attention on Kaylee and *not* on the star of all—literally ALL—my fantasies, I forced an unconcerned smile. "So, anyway, are you—"

"Do you know him?" she guessed, watching me carefully. Before I could think of a way to deflect, she sucked in a breath. "You know him."

Aaaaaahhhh!

"How do you know him?"

"Kaylee—"

"How?"

"I went to high school with him," I said, deciding this truth was best. Better she didn't realize *him* was Rex McMurtry. Even though Kaylee was a good friend and we often watched his games together, I'd never told her about my past—or lack of a past—with him. If she realized the big guy was Rex "TW" McMurtry, she'd go over and ask for an autograph.

"*Ohhh.*" She leaned back, her chin lifting as her gaze grew sympathetic. "Well then, you're off the hook."

"Off the hook?"

"Yeah. I'm not going to force you to flirt with some a-hole from high school."

I angled my head to the side. "But you'd force me to flirt with a stranger?"

"Absolutely. A-holes from high school are the worst. Ask me how I know."

"Uh, okay. How do you know?"

"I don't want to discuss it. See? That's how bad high school a-holes are. Even I don't wish to talk about it, and I want to talk about everything. Blah. How disappointing." She craned her neck, glancing at Rex again and giving him a look of judgy disappointment. "Did he recognize you?"

"No." I cleared my throat, wiping at the bar with the towel in my hand. I felt certain he would have no idea who I was even if he'd looked at me square in the face. I also felt certain—given what I knew of his temperament—he would have zero interest in dealing with some unknown admiring-from-afar fan from his hometown. We may have gone to school together, but we'd never moved within the same social circles.

"But you recognize him. He must've been awful," she lamented. "Oh well, that sucks. I might as well have a drink."

"What'll it be?" I reached for a martini glass because I knew what it would be.

"I suppose a vodka martini will do." Her eyes moved to my right, to where we kept the cherries.

"Got it." I readied myself to defend the condiment tray—Kaylee was always snatching cherries—and reached for the vodka. But then Kaylee's phone chimed.

"Belay that order. This might be Nash." She grabbed her bag.

"Nash? Is he meeting you here?"

"Yes. He's picking me up." Whipping her phone out, she scanned the screen.

"He's picking you up?" After midnight? Midweek?

"Yep. Sorry, did I forget to mention that?" She jumped off her stool, tapping out a message on her phone. "You have your car keys? I'm really just here to drop the car off."

"Yes. I have my keys." I was all sorts of confused. "Are you and Nash back together?"

"Of course not." She lifted her briefcase from the stool, her phone chiming again. She smiled down at something she read on the screen. "Okay, I'm leaving. See you later, gator."

"Say hey to Nash for me."

"I will. And—" she shot a meaningful look toward Rex at the end of the bar "—let me know if you need us to come back at closing and help you with high school trash."

"Sure thing."

Giving me a quick, sympathetic smile, Kaylee dashed out of the bar. I watched her go, my traitorous eyes settling on Rex as the door closed behind her. No longer staring at his phone, his large hand encircled the half-full pint of amber ale which he seemed to find engrossing.

My heart gave a stupid, weak flutter, something it hadn't done in ages. More than just Rex's forehead was now visible. His eyes were mostly in shadow but, yep. He still looked fine as hell. More breathtaking in person than he was on TV, visceral masculinity, raw charisma, *magnetic*. Even the grumpy set of his mouth did it for me.

The weak flutter in my heart became a gallop. *He's so gorgeous.*

The dark stubble on his square jaw, cheeks, and chin framed his lips. Even in a grim line, like now, they were lovely and luscious. I'm unhappy to report that, as a teenager, I'd kissed my pillow more than once, wishing the cotton blend of my pillowcase were those lips.

I sensed him stir and I flinched, turning my back to him as another scorching wave of embarrassment climbed up my neck. Pretending to be busy, I faced the liquor shelf, picked up random bottles, set them down again, and strained my ears. Wishing and not wishing Rex would ask for another beer, I successfully resisted the urge to rush over and offer him a refill. Instead, I forced my brain to run through the list of tasks I needed to finish before closing.

With any luck, the next time he waved me over it would be to close his tab. Then he'd leave, my contented life would go on, and I'd watch his Thanksgiving Day game while he continued to be blissfully ignorant of my existence.

I refilled the napkin dispensers at each of the empty tables and contemplated the irony of my predicament.

Sharing the same space as Rex McMurtry for—I glanced at my watch—the last fifty-three minutes would've sent teenage Abby into raptures. This was noteworthy because teenage Abby didn't go into raptures for much—extra time in the high school pottery studio, free concert tickets, free yarn—but she would've been over the moon tonight. My sophomore year of high school revolved around Mr. Peterson's shop class, during which I'd try not to stare at Rex. He'd sat three tables in front of me, and it was the first time I'd discovered male backsides could be attractive.

Whereas adult Abby did not feel rapturous at Rex's loitering. I felt impatient. His presence felt like a big fat interruption in my lovely, quiet, calm existence, a bone in my salmon fillet, a large seed in my seedless watermelon, a pebble of indeterminate origin in my shoe.

Rex had nursed his first pint for a full half hour before gesturing to me, again without looking up, and ordering another. I was happy to provide a refill as it was a timely opportunity to (avoid his eyes and breathlessly) say, "We close in about twenty minutes. Are you sure you want another?"

"Yes, please."

"I'll just close you out, then."

"Okay. Thank you."

He hadn't moved his credit card from where I'd set it earlier, so I grabbed it and cashed out his tab. Swiftly, I placed the receipt and the pen on the counter along with his card, hopeful he'd sign, finish his beer, and leave, and then I could forget about the jarring disruption and pretend it had never happened.

But that is not what occurred.

Each table, one by one, cashed out. Even the Larsons, who typically sipped their one drink for six hours and dawdled until they were Rickrolled out of the place. They'd left at least ten minutes ago.

In high school, I hadn't minded how Rex's presence seemed to draw all my attention, distracted me from whatever I was doing and whoever I was with. But now I found the distraction bothersome. Unwillingly, I'd kept one eye on Rex while I cleaned, put away glasses, checked the liquor levels, and retrieved new bottles from the back. Never willing to actually look directly at him, nevertheless, I'd been acutely aware of his lack of movement.

I mean, he'd moved a little. He'd finished half his second beer but hadn't touched the pen or the paper or his card. He definitely made no move to put on his coat or walk to the door. Nerves built inside of me, weaving a tapestry of anxious dread.

What if he did recognize me? I'd convinced myself I didn't think it would happen, but we'd gone to school together for thirteen years, and I had been exceptionally tall, my one defining trait as far as my classmates were concerned. Maybe, instead of just "tall girl," he did know my name. Would I then be expected to speak to him? I didn't want to speak to him. I wanted to continue admiring him from afar, as I'd done forever. I didn't want anything to change.

I'd twisted myself so tightly, frustrated at my lack of calm, that when the lights flipped on, the abrupt intro of Rick Astley's "Never Gonna Give You Up" made me jump. I almost dropped the napkin dispenser I'd been wrestling.

Pressing a hand to my sternum, I ceased fighting with the napkins and blinked against the sudden brightness, blowing out a long breath. *I need a drink and my bed and three days off.*

"You okay there, hon?" Ingrid bumped my hip as she walked past, splitting her attention between me and the mess I was making with the napkins.

"Peachy."

Facts were facts: I couldn't concentrate while the one guy I'd compared all other men to—nay, all other humans—sat just thirty feet away. And he still hadn't sheathed those forearms.

Why won't he leave? Doesn't he have to get home? Or, you know, wherever he's sleeping?

Rex lived in Chicago from preseason until after the playoffs, of that I was sure. I had no idea what he was doing down here in Texas during the middle of the regular season.

"I'm cashing out table six." Ingrid held up a credit card, talking over the loud song. "And I did all my side-work already. Do you need any help?"

"Nope. I'm almost finished. Everything is prepped for tomorrow."

Ingrid looked relieved, but then she dipped her head toward the bar. "What about the big guy?"

I glanced at Rex, my throat dry, my eyes moving over his broad shoulders and back. He seemed to be having difficulty adjusting to the sudden brightness of the room as it looked like he'd shielded his eyes with a hand.

"I'll encourage him to finish up."

She continued to contemplate him. "Should I call the security guys? Or Walker? Just in case?"

All the businesses in the shopping area surrounding the bar shared a security team. They watched over the storefronts at night and occasionally helped us with customers who were reluctant to leave at closing. Rarely, they had to call the police for backup.

I shook my head. "Nah. I'm sure it'll be fine."

She shot me a disbelieving look. "He's huge. Once table six leaves, it's just you and me. Are you sure?"

"He'll go, no problem."

"What makes you think so?"

"I know him. We—uh—went to high school together."

"Ohhh. Good." Ingrid gave me a nod and practically skipped to the register. She didn't have three days off like me, but we'd both pulled a double shift and were equally anxious to get home and off our feet.

As I abandoned the half-filled dispenser, I wondered if perhaps Rex's presence was an allegory for my life. He'd walked into my bar still just as untouchable as he'd been in high school. He was right there, *right there,* but it made no difference. I would always like Rex, admire him like I admired fancy vacation destinations, but—given who he was and who I was, and my limitations and/or lack of ambition—I could never do anything about it or change my currently comfortable, minimal-stress existence.

Presently, however, I had no choice but to speak with him. I could no longer wait for him to leave on his own. Chin held high, I marched to the bar with every intention of continuing down the galley. At the last minute, I turned to the back office and decided to double-check inventory, hoping against hope he'd be gone by the time I emerged.

I skimmed the shelves, recounting all the supplies I'd tallied a few minutes prior. I checked my numbers against what I'd written down, feeling validated when I found one less bag of single-serve potato chips than last time.

"Good thing I did that," I muttered, changing my chip bag count from 102 to 101, then checked my watch. We were on the third repeat of "Never Gonna Give You Up," and I'd given Rex an additional ten minutes.

Replacing the clipboard, I peeked my head around the doorframe, looking toward the end of the bar and . . . there he was. Sitting in the same position, his hand over his eyes, leaning forward, elbows on the bar.

Hells BALLS.

I rubbed my forehead, frowning with every ounce of my being. Now I really had no choice. Drawing in a fortifying breath, I strolled down the galley, clinking bottles and glasses together purposefully as I passed them, and then tapping the surface of the bar noisily with my nails when I drew even with his hunched figure.

He didn't move.

I reached under the bar to the volume of the speaker and lowered it manually so I wouldn't have to shout over Rick Astley promising to never let me down. We still had one more full Rickroll to go.

Clearing my throat very loudly, I asked, "Can I get you anything else?"

He still didn't move, made no sign or sound that he'd heard my question. Ignoring the siren call of his forearms, I debated whether or not to nudge his shoulder, chaos brewing within me at the thought of touching him.

We'd touched before. In kindergarten, he'd passed me glue and our fingers had brushed. In third grade, I'd collided into him on the playground while failing at somersaults. In seventh grade, another finger brush when he'd handed me a plate of pizza during a Girl Scout meeting at his aunt's house. Our junior year of high school, he accidentally bumped my chair in the cafeteria and put his hand on my shoulder to brace himself.

But there'd never been any *purposeful* touching.

I opened my mouth, uncertain what to say.

But he spoke before I could translate my plans into action. "Did we go to high school together?"

CHAPTER 3

"On the whole, human beings want to be good, but not too good, and not quite all the time."

— GEORGE ORWELL, ALL ART IS PROPAGANDA: CRITICAL ESSAYS

I snapped my mouth shut, my spine stiffening, caught, a jolt of adrenaline pulsing from my chest to my toes.

Rex removed his hand from his face and blinked at me with hazy—but still so amazingly handsome—hazel eyes, bleary and red. "Where'd you go to high school?" he slurred like his tongue was heavy, his head lolling to the side.

My shock at his initial question was quickly replaced by new shock, this time heavily flavored with panic. *Balls.*

BALLS!

"You're drunk?" It was a rhetorical question. He was drunk, anyone could see that. Very drunk. Commode-hugging, knee-walking drunk, and I'd served him two beers! Which meant— "You were drunk when you came in." My stomach plummeted.

He gave me a sloppy nod which transformed into a sloppy head shake. "Don't-don't change the subject. You. I know you." He pointed in my direction, his head lolling again, giving me the impression he was having trouble keeping it upright. "But I don't remember, and I should."

"Lord, help me over the fence," I mumbled, covering my mouth with my palm, panic now a beating drum of doom between my ears.

I'd served a drunk person.

"That waitress said we went to high school together." He tossed his thumb over his shoulder; the movement would've sent him careening backward had he not been sitting on the stool. His eyes moved over me. "I don't member you," he said, squinting. "Are you married?"

"Am I what?"

"We didn't date, if we'd dated, you'd be married."

"Excuse me?"

"Training wheels," he muttered, breathing out a weird laugh, like something was both really funny and sad. He closed his eyes and pointed to himself, his tone anguished. "I'm Training Wheels."

I knew his nickname, everyone did. He'd been dubbed TW, or Training Wheels, in high school because he used to help incoming freshman football players find their footing. It was a sweet nickname, at least I'd always thought so. But now the moniker appeared to cause him frustration, and I supposed I knew why.

Over the last year in particular, a fair number of his friends had gotten married, and they had all married Rex's former girlfriends or women he'd dated. A sports announcer named Clarence O'Dea had thought it would be funny to repurpose Rex's nickname and apply it to his—*ahem*—training of women for male friends, or that the women had used him as training wheels.

Gross and misogynistic? Yes. But it had stuck like glitter and had become a running joke during his games, brought up often by the sportscaster who'd coined the perversion of the nickname and had used it to remind people how clever he supposedly was. I couldn't stand that guy.

Rex had always acted like it didn't faze him, but obviously it did.

Otherwise, he wouldn't have just said, *We didn't date, if we'd dated, you'd be married.*

"Listen, I—uh—can I call you a cab?" I winced, wishing I could take back the thoughtless words as soon as they'd left my mouth.

Since I followed Rex's career, I knew he'd had a bad experience with a cab driver in Seattle a few months ago. The guy had tried to kidnap him at gunpoint. It had been all over the news.

Rex shook his head as it fell to his hands, then he kept on shaking it. "Please don't call a taxi."

"You definitely shouldn't drive." Guilt plucked at me and was soon joined by a chord of remorse. I'd never served a drunk person before. Ever. I'd had plenty of drunk folks come in here and try to order, but this was the first time I hadn't denied service.

Because you were too busy being flustered by lust, stalker!

"They all know me," he said, cutting into my tumultuous thoughts.

I rubbed my forehead, trying to think, find my usual calm, and responded on autopilot, "Who knows you?" I needed to keep him talking. If he talked, then he'd stay awake and that would buy me time to figure out a solution to this insane problem.

"Everyone." He said this to his beer, which was when I noticed he still had alcohol in front of him.

Deftly, I snatched the pint glass and poured the remainder down the drain. "You mean, all the taxicab drivers know you?"

"There is only one season in Texas: football season." He laughed again, a Texas twang making its first appearance.

I think I understood: if I put him in a cab, then he'd be recognized, and that might not turn out well for him, like in Seattle.

"Can I call someone?" I asked, wondering if I should brew coffee as my gaze skated over his handsome features. He was drunk, but he also looked absolutely exhausted. Compassion squeezed my heart.

"Nope. No one." He chuckled, and the chuckle picked up speed in that way it often does with the intoxicated. Soon he was laughing. Hard. Soundlessly.

Waiting for his laughter to subside, I continued to study him, at a loss for the hundredth time that night. My guilt at having served alcohol to a drunk Rex felt like a boulder, heavy on my chest.

When his hilarity tapered, I asked gently, "What about your brother?"

"Lives in New York."

"Your sister?"

"Bahamas."

"Your dad?"

"Don't call him."

I chewed on my lip, debating. "You have so many friends. Surely—"

"No," he said firmly, his smile falling suddenly, his eyes cloudy with what looked like misery. "Unless you want to get married . . .?"

I made a face to hide the strange tightening in my throat. Because, *whaaaa?* Drunk Rex wanted to marry me? Is that what he meant? Come on. That'd be crazy and predatory on my part, even if I did know of a 24-hour drive-through marriage barn not more than five miles from—

NOPE.

Really, Abby? Really? Can we discuss this?

GASP! You rapacious bitch, how dare you! Drunks can't consent, and no way he actually wanted to marry me.

Or, and hear me out, you could always just do it and, if he regretted the decision once sober, he could divor—

Absolutely. Not.

Rex's hand covered mine, yanking me from my guilty thoughts and sending a rush of spiky alertness up my arm.

And by "alertness," I meant: ALERT! WE HAVE PURPOSEFUL TOUCHING!

"Hey, you know what?" He lowered his voice, and I did my darndest to focus on his words and not the feel of his hand covering mine, warm and strong. Rex leaned in, his hazel eyes intent. "We could get married. You could marry me. If I were married, then it would stop."

Breathless—both from arguing with the astonishingly irrational, sinister, and selfish devil on my shoulder and the way he was currently looking at me, so hopeful, vulnerable—I slowly pulled my hand away, folded my arms, and tried to reason with us both. "Rex, you're drunk. It's fifteen minutes past closing time. Who do I call to pick you up?"

His jaw ticked, his gaze turning to an icy glare. "No. One. Just. . ." His eyes seemed to thaw and then warm the longer they held mine, his forehead wrinkling, and abruptly he looked distinctly despairing. "You are—"

I held my breath as seconds ticked by, the moment officially becoming prolonged.

Then he finally finished his thought with, "—very beautiful for a bartender."

Ingrid and the couple from table six helped me load Rex into my car. Yes, moving him required all four of us. He'd been a big, muscly guy in high school, but now he was like a wall of concrete and had grown at least two inches since our senior year. Luckily, miracle of miracles, neither Ingrid nor the couple had seemed to recognize him.

"Where are you taking me?" he mumbled as soon as I slid into the driver's seat and closed my door.

"Alenbach, to your dad's house." I eyed the seat belt on his right, he made no move to fasten it. "You should put your belt on."

"Or we could go somewhere else." He shifted, presumably trying to face me, but my car was just too small. Even with the seat all the way back, Rex's knees hit the dash.

"Like where? Are you feeling okay? Should I take you to the hospital?"

"Like your place." His voice was barely more than a rumbly whisper, and he punctuated the suggestiveness of his words with an absent-minded lick of his lips.

I huff-chuckled, shaking my head, refusing to entertain the suggestion even though I *really* wanted to entertain the suggestion. I wanted to entertain the suggestion *so hard.*

But no.

His dad's house in Alenbach was the safest place for him. "Do you need help with your seat belt?"

Rex blinked slowly, his bleary eyes lowering to my mouth. "Yes."

Gritting my teeth against the ruckus of fluttery nerves in my stomach, I silently cursed myself. I hadn't really meant the offer. In Texas, sometimes when folks make an offer, it's really just a not-so-subtle hint for the other person to do something.

Do you want me to get the door? really means *Go answer the damn door.*

Do you need help getting your shoes on? really means *Why haven't you put your damn shoes on yet?*

He was from Texas, he knew the code! And yet he didn't move, just kept staring at my mouth while our breaths increasingly fogged the interior glass.

Swallowing thickly, I rolled my eyes for no reason and ground out a terse, "Fine."

I unfastened my seat belt before I could think better of it, reached over Rex's barrel of a chest and tried to grab the passenger-side seat belt. This, of course, brought our faces within inches and the entirety of my torso flush against his. The ruckus in my stomach became a hullabaloo, and I snatched the belt, pulling it too quickly and tripping the stop mechanism.

"Dad gum it," I swore, shaking my head at myself, and held my breath. I needed to slow my movements. Coaxing the belt forward, I felt a whisper of a touch on my back and I stiffened, my eyes cutting to his.

Drunk Rex's gaze was still focused—or rather, unfocused—on my lips, his eyes hooded. "You are very, very beautiful," he whispered in that same rumbly tone.

"So you mentioned earlier. And you are very drunk." My voice hitched as I leaned away, bringing the belt to the fastener at his hip. "I've been a bartender long enough to know all people look like supermodels after one too many beers or whiskeys. Lean all the way back, please."

The windows were now completely fogged, my hands were shaking, and I fumbled to fit the pieces of his seat belt together. And then, out of absolutely nowhere and without any warning, his fingers pushed into my hair at my temple, fisted, and pulled, exposing my neck.

I sucked in a startled breath, flinched, and let go of the seat belt. The metal piece boomeranged, smacked him in the face so hard I heard it hit bone, which forced him to release my hair. I covered my mouth, and he covered his cheek where he'd been belted. Literally.

"Ow!"

"Oh my God, I'm sorry!" I reached forward but then snatched my hands back, balling them into fists in front of me. "I'm so sorry."

"No. I'm sorry." His head fell back against the headrest, and he rubbed at his cheek, a gruff laugh tumbling from his luscious lips. "Your hair is so . . . it looked soft, and I . . . But I'm sorry," he slurred. "I shouldn't have done that." He shook his head fiercely. "I *never* do that."

We sat in silence for a minute while I worked to bridle all the various involuntary and confused tremblings and twistings and poundings within my body. Rex closed his eyes, gathering several deep breaths.

"Rex." I broke the silence, eyeballing the seat belt on his right once more. "Do you think, maybe, you could buckle your own seat belt?"

He nodded, swallowing, his eyes still closed. Grateful for the reprieve, I buckled myself in and turned the engine while I watched him reach to his right with clumsy movements. Eventually, he managed to bring the strap over his chest and hips, but his fingers kept slipping and missing the buckle.

"Here. Let me help." Readying myself for more touching, I covered his hands and helped him guide the latch together, breathing out a huge sigh of relief when it finally clicked.

"There," I said, turning back to the windshield, sweaty, breathing hard, feeling like I'd just navigated a Ninja Warrior obstacle course. "Okay, let's—"

"Oh—oh no." Rex's hands came back to the buckle, his movements suddenly frantic.

I stiffened. "What? What's wrong?"

"I—I need—" He turned away, grabbing for the door latch, yanking it so hard the metal piece broke clear off.

I gasped and then recoiled, pressing myself as far from him as I could and against the driver's-side door because Rex McMurtry—the man of my dreams—had just thrown up.

All over himself.

And me.
And my car.

CHAPTER 4

"'Do you think we can be friends? ' I asked

He stared up at the ceiling. 'Probably not, but we can pretend. '"

— PRIYA ARDIS, *EVER MY MERLIN*

I didn't think I'd be able to sleep—what with a mostly naked Rex sleeping on an air mattress just inches from where I'd collapsed on my futon—but I'd zonked out the moment my head had hit the pillow. That said, I didn't sleep very long.

Perhaps if the prior evening's (and early morning's) events hadn't floated into my consciousness the moment I cracked an eye open, I would've been able to flip my pillow, turn, and return to blissful slumber. But the memory of hosing off a fully clothed Rex on my patio, then hosing off myself, then undressing him in the dark and wrapping him in a sheet, and then brushing his teeth while he sloppily told me how beautiful I was and called me an angel, had my eyes flying open and inspecting the floor next to me.

Nope. Not a dream.

There he was. The dude. The man. The Rex. The guy who'd asked me to marry him and then barfed all over my car last night, sprawled out on the bed I'd made for him, wearing nothing but his underwear, a sheet, and a comforter. He slept peacefully at present, like he hadn't a care in the world. Midafternoon Texas sunshine kissed his tan profile, his bulging bicep where he hugged the pillow, and the top half of his impressive back not covered by the comforter.

I frowned, doing a scan of my internal organs. Nary a flutter or surge of excitement. *Huh.*

But then he stretched, and the butterflies in my stomach went from zero to red alert in no seconds. Staring wide-eyed at the rippling muscles of his back, I held my breath and waited, my brain frantic. *What will I say?*

I batted that thought away, the answer obvious. I'd tell him the truth: I'd served him while he'd been drunk, that was entirely my fault, and when he couldn't give me the name of anyone who could take him off my hands—and after I'd ascertained he wasn't in danger of alcohol poisoning—I'd brought him here to sleep it off. Easy.

But what if he—

I batted *that* thought away before it fully formed. I wasn't a soothsayer. I didn't take note of the ides of March. I couldn't predict the future.

And if life had taught me anything, it was to avoid tying myself in knots by worrying about a future I had no control over. I lived—quietly, sedately, conservatively—in the present, which typically meant minimal turmoil or disruption.

Rex would wake up and I'd deal with it, and then I'd take him wherever, and that was that. End of this bizarre story.

After stretching, Rex didn't wake up. He turned to his other side, hugged the pillow tighter, and kept on sleeping. I covered my eyes with an arm, thankful for the reprieve. I wanted to be up and dressed and ready to go by the time he woke up.

I'd had big plans for today. Well, big plans relative to what I considered big plans, none of which had included me hosing out and shampooing the interior of my car as the sun rose behind me, and then sleeping until—I turned my head and squinted at my alarm clock—just past noon. I had things to do, holiday markets to prepare for, cauldron mug special orders to make and ship before Halloween, Christmas tree ornaments to glaze and fire and so on.

But first, another shower. And breakfast. And coffee.

It is my hypothesis that a proper hot shower—proper meaning excellent water pressure and temperature near scalding—equated to a bonus hour of sleep in terms of refreshing one's mind and spirit. And good coffee makes everything better.

Mindful to grab a change of clothes before heading to the bathroom, I stole another glance at Rex, debating whether or not to leave him a note. He would be disoriented when he woke up, and I didn't want him worrying about where he was. Ultimately, I decided against it. Writing out a note would take me just as long as the shower. But I did leave him a glass of water and two pain relievers next to his mattress. Just in case.

Once inside the bathroom, I eyeballed the toothbrush I'd used on him last night, wondering if I should throw it away now or later. *He'll want to brush his teeth again when he wakes up, I think.* And maybe he could take it with him? It was new from the package, and it seemed a shame to waste four dollars on a toothbrush only used once.

Unsurprisingly, the shower was divine, and I likely took longer than necessary, but the indulgence helped clear the cobwebs from my brain. As I dressed, I reordered my mental to-do list, prioritizing the custom orders from my Etsy shop over the holiday market inventory and calculating how much sleep I could miss over the next three days to make up the studio time I'd lost this morning.

Leaving the bathroom, I tossed my dirty clothes in the hamper by the closet containing my efficiency washer and dryer. But then, just as my stomach gave a grumble, I heard the rustle of sheets. Peeking at Rex, I watched as he stretched again, his big body flexing and shifting on the too-small air mattress. I held my breath, certain he would wake up now. I waited. And I waited. And I waited some more.

False alarm. He didn't wake up.

Hmm.

I started the coffee, retrieved the newspaper from outside, and then returned to the kitchen to cook breakfast. After a brief debate, I decided to splurge and use my celebration/commiseration bacon.

Some people celebrate an event or good fortune with a nice bottle of wine. Similarly, they commiserate bad fortune over a nice bottle of wine. I celebrated/commiserated with fancy bacon from the farmers' market. I had no reason to celebrate this afternoon—what with my car stinking like puke and my morning plans ruined—but Rex would definitely wake up hungover. Greasy foods like bacon, fried eggs, hash browns, sausage, and buttered toast were all excellent for hangovers. If it made him feel even a little bit better, twenty-one dollars in bacon was a sacrifice I was willing to make.

Food made—everything but our eggs, because there's nothing worse than cold eggs—I put his plate in the oven set on warm and ate my hash browns, toast, and sausage. Then I read the paper, frowning at the clock at intervals. An hour passed, then another. He stretched a few more times, all false alarms. *Should I wake him up?*

I couldn't go to the studio until he left my apartment. Pacing to the kitchen and bringing my paper with me, I leaned against the countertop and tried to focus on reading the fine newsprint, but restlessness plagued me. *How long is he going to sleep?*

But then, just as I was about to resort to making loud noises with pots and pans, he stretched, and this time it was followed by a grunt.

Straightening away from the countertop and lowering the newspaper I hadn't actually been reading, I lifted my chin so I could see him over the midcentury lounge chair in the living room between us. A second later, he grunted again. I stiffened. He was rousing. I exhaled relief and inhaled mild trepidation.

"What time is it?" The deliciously deep, sleep-roughened question made lovely heat bloom in my stomach, but I shoved the sensation away. I would *not* ogle the man. He was in my charge and deserved patience and kindness, not objectification.

Erecting a nurturing-focused force field to block my lusty instincts, I studied him. He blinked several times. Clearly, he was doing his darndest to keep his eyes open against the stinging afternoon brightness of the room.

"It's two . . . ish, 2:11 in the afternoon, if you want to be precise." I turned my back to him, picking up my spatula and flipping on the stovetop. Cracking four eggs, then another, then a sixth because he was a huge giant of a man, I scrambled the yolks and whites in the pan.

He grunted again but then silence stretched, long enough for me to finish cooking the scrambled eggs and add a fair amount of shredded cheddar cheese on top. I resisted the urge to turn around. My apartment was small, and if I'd been in his situation, I would want some privacy during the first painful moments of sobriety.

"Did you . . ." he started haltingly.

When he didn't finish the thought, I prompted, "Yes?" careful to keep my words light and soft, knowing he must be suffering a terrible headache. Likewise, I was careful to make as little noise as possible as I removed the skillet from the burner and spooned the eggs onto two waiting plates, loading his up. *See? Even in a hurry, I can nurture.*

"Never mind," he muttered.

"Are you hungry?" I set the plates down on my tiny table by the glass door which led out to the patio, where I'd hosed him off last night. Careful to keep my eyes averted—wanting to give him as much privacy as possible—I hurried back to the kitchen on bare feet, debating whether I should take the rest of his breakfast out of the oven now or later. "I made eggs, bacon, sausage, hash browns, and toast. Greasy is good for hangovers." *Feed him, drive him . . . wherever, get to the studio, and get to work.*

Sheets rustled. "You . . . feel okay?" he asked. The question wasn't odd, but there was an odd note in his voice as he asked it.

I paused before giving him the truth. "I feel fine, thanks."

I felt tired, sore from a double shift yesterday, plus supporting his weight as I prepped him for bed, plus cleaning out the car and not going to sleep until after sunrise. But I was, in general—all things considered—fine. I would feel better once I finished making those cauldron mugs at the studio, but I didn't share that either.

My brain preoccupied with rushing through the next half hour as quickly as possible, I glanced at him. Rex had sat up and the sheet had pooled around his waist. His chest was bare because, after he'd thrown up all over my car, I couldn't let him sleep in pukey clothes.

Presently ignoring his scandalously sexy forearms, I focused on his pale features. His eyes closed, his face drawn, Rex seemed to be in pain. Poor guy.

A pang of guilt had my chest feeling tight. I needed to stop rushing him. Open studio hours were over at ten tonight, but I could bring some of my projects home, work on slip casting here, cleaning up leather hard bisqueware. No biggie.

"You don't have to eat if you don't want to." I gentled my voice further. "There's pain relievers next to the bed if you want to go back to sleep."

He opened his eyes but didn't look at me. In fact, as I watched him cast his attention all over the room, I felt certain he was pointedly *not* looking at me.

Hmm. Is he embarrassed? A burst of compassion and care warmed me.

But then, in a tone that felt like a verbal slap across the face, he demanded, "Just give me my things."

I straightened my spine.

Wait.

Wait a minute. Was he . . .?

Is he angry?

Yes. He was angry. Angry and not looking at me.

I knew Rex. I'd basically been his stalker for thirteen years. In all that time I'd cataloged the various shades of his taciturn tones. Ninety percent of the time he sounded just plain grumpy to the untrained ear. Whereas I knew the difference between a deadpan, dispassionate delivery and an angry, seething setdown. He'd just employed the latter.

My stomach and heart switched places, the realization leaving me cold and, quite frankly, stunned. It took me a moment—studying the irritated glint in his eyes and the way his jaw ticked—before finally managing to parrot, "Your things?"

"Yes. My things. Now."

He's mad. At me. Really, really mad. I exhaled a silent breath that burned in my chest and throat. *What a spoiled brat!*

I mean, yes. I'd served him one-and-a-half beers while he'd been drunk. Fine. Yeah. I could understand him being upset about that. But he'd barfed all over my car! Had I complained? No. I'd told him it was no big deal, begged him not to feel bad, then I'd taken care of his sloppy, drunk ass. I'd brushed his teeth and sacrificed twenty-one dollars in bacon this morning to help him feel better. The blobfish.

He wanted to leave now? Fine by me. He could call a cab or an Uber to deal with his ungrateful no-longer-sexy forearms. I'd wasted enough of my day waiting around for him to wake up.

Sliding my teeth to the side, I glared at his stupid handsome face where he still sat on the air mattress I'd blown up without a pump, using only the air in my lungs. I watched as he frowned at my futon—where I'd slept—and then back at his place on the floor.

No use prolonging the inevitable, I crossed to the closet where my washer and dryer were stored, yanked back the curtain, and pulled out his freshly laundered clothes. Then, pushing down all my ridiculous, hot, erratic feelings of disappointment—I really had no right to the feelings in any case—walked to him and held out his clothes.

"Here you go," I said, wiping all emotion from my expression.

"Thanks," he snapped, wearing a scowl as he snatched the laundry from my fingers. Bored, bleary eyes flickered to my face for the first time since he'd awoken. Almost immediately, he reared back, doing a double take as his hand holding the clothes slowly lowered to his lap.

When he left, I was going to eat all that bacon. *No bacon for Rex!*

He blinked at me, staring. I stared right on back. The angry lines around his mouth, eyes, and on his forehead smoothed, his gaze seeming to grow in confusion and shrink in ire. He stared for so long, I couldn't help but feel uncomfortable under his poking perusal.

I shifted my weight from one foot to the other, an acute urge to fill the silence pushing thoughtless words from my mouth. "Sorry they're wrinkled," I said, crossing my arms and removing myself a few steps. I gestured to the bundle of laundry on his lap. "I don't have any outfits that require an iron, so I don't own one."

Rex continued staring at me, like I was something strange, or I might explode, or I'd spoken in tongues.

But then he blurted, "Who *are* you?"

CHAPTER 5

"What's terrible is to pretend that second-rate is first-rate. To pretend that you don't need love when you do; or you like your work when you know quite well you're capable of better."

— DORIS LESSING, *THE GOLDEN NOTEBOOK*

Oh sigh.

I pressed my lips together, irritated with myself that—even after everything last night and so far today—I still felt a modicum of disappointment upon receiving irrefutable proof that Rex McMurtry had no idea who I was—not drunk, not sober, not in a bar, not in a car, not in my apartment in the middle of the day with excellent lighting.

Abruptly tired, I rubbed my forehead and asked, "How much do you remember about last night?"

His eyes, still hooked on my face, narrowed. "You brushed my teeth and hosed me down."

That pulled an exhausted smile out of me. "Yes." I gestured to the sheet and comforter covering his bottom half. "I had to preserve your modesty."

"My . . .?" He looked at his lap and then his chest, the wrinkles on his forehead deepening. "We"—he motioned between us—"didn't sleep together?"

WHAT THE—?

"What? No!" I lifted my hands to ward off the offending suggestion. "God no. You passed out on the air mattress, and I slept on my futon." I turned and ducked my head, moving back to the kitchen and scratching my suddenly itchy neck. "What kind of person sleeps with someone who is incapacitated? Or even contemplates that?" I realized I was muttering out loud and slammed my mouth shut, hoping he hadn't heard me.

I sensed his eyes on my back following me as I moved around the kitchen and prayed my cheeks didn't look as red as they felt. It took a lot for me to be scandalized, and I'd just been officially scandalized.

"I know you," he said, still sounding hostile. "We know each other. How do I know you?"

In my peripheral vision, I saw Rex begin to stand, and I fought the urge to cover my eyes with my hands. He didn't stand, thank goodness, but instead peeked under the sheet as though to confirm he still wore underwear.

His bare chest was one thing—and what a glorious thing it was—but I'd taken great pains last night to not see anything else. However, all this delaying on my part to tell him how we knew each other was verging on ridiculous. I needed to fill him in so he'd stop wondering and asking.

I paced back over to him, stared him straight in the eye, and said plainly, "Yes. We know each other."

He continued to eye me speculatively. "What's your name?"

"Abigail. Or Gail. But people call me Abby these days."

My name seemed to give him no answers.

"How do we know each other? Why don't I remember you? Did I hit my head?"

I opened my mouth, not immediately speaking as I sorted through what to tell him first: that I'd been his bartender last night or that we'd known each other since we were five. Rex's intelligent stare, now sharp with wakefulness, scoured me, probably looking for clues as to my identity.

Surrendering to the fact that I should just tell him the whole truth and get it over with, his eyes abruptly cut to mine, wide and filled with some emotion I couldn't name.

"Hold up, hold up." He licked his lips and croaked, "Are we engaged?"

Did he say *Are we engaged?* Or did he say *Are wheat outraged?*

. . . *Hmm.* That's a hard one. I could do nothing but stare at him as I pondered alternatives to what I'd heard, the question so ludicrous I was certain I'd gotten it wrong.

Bar knee assuaged?

Lars sees a train?

Far we upstaged?

While I debated the potential alternatives, Rex's eyes lowered to my midsection. I followed his line of sight. Ah! *My grandmother's ring.* I wore it on my left ring finger.

"I asked you to marry me, didn't I?" He gaped, his brain clearly working overtime.

"No take-backsies," I singsonged before I could catch myself, wagging a finger, and turned to my little kitchen table.

The part of me who'd cleaned up his vomit this morning just to have to deal with his rudeness—a devil on my shoulder, if you will—had no problem playing along and playing tricks. Whereas another part of me wanted to apologize and immediately clarify his technically true, misleading recollection of last night.

My gaze flickered to him, and I saw his eyes were still on me, shell-shocked. Settling my elbow on the table and tapping my chin, I couldn't resist adding, "I think I'd like a spring wedding."

I ignored the strings of guilt plucked by my conscience, the devil pointing out that Rex hadn't been very nice either. *Real mature. Maybe someone will do the same thing to you one day, and how will you like that?* I squirmed. Sometimes my conscience was a real killjoy.

Rex's mouth dropped open, his eyebrows inching higher, and it was everything I could do to hold in the laughter, unkind though it was. But then I couldn't, and I laughed. It was clear he actually believed me and was frantically trying to figure out how to extract himself from this situation.

"Oh my goodness, you should see your face." I wiped at my tears of hilarity, and damn—after the last twelve hours—it felt good to laugh. "Come on now. Relax! I'm kidding, okay? You and I are not engaged. You can stop freaking out."

Grinning, I watched him, waiting for his relief. He didn't look relieved.

"So . . . we're not engaged?"

"No." I wrinkled my nose at the preposterous thought. "We're not engaged."

He nodded, his frown persisting. Rex looked distracted but, strangely, not at all relieved as far as I could tell. My smile waned as I studied him. Despite my past as a Rex stalker, I couldn't make heads or tails of his current expression and had absolutely no idea what he was thinking.

But it has been over ten years.

He averted his eyes, a strange, stiff-looking sorta smile on his face. "I reckon—" he started, cleared his throat, and started again. "I reckon I'm a little turned around, after drinking so much last night." Rex breathed a shaky laugh and, if I wasn't mistaken, he sounded contrite.

My irritation and indignation suddenly dissolved. *Poor guy.* I shouldn't have teased him. *You didn't get enough sleep and you don't like upheaval,* my brain reminded me. I pushed the excuses away, determined to be more patient with the poor, hungover colossus.

"Go change." I pointed to the bathroom door behind him. "And then eat something. I'll tell you what happened, but you really should eat something."

Once more, he wouldn't meet my eyes in a way that felt purposeful, but this time it also struck me as embarrassed. Now he looked embarrassed, and that just made me feel worse for him all over again.

That's what you get for listening to devils on shoulders. Have classic Disney cartoons taught you nothing?

Wanting to ease his discomfort, I ate a bit of bacon like I hadn't a care in the world. I drank a drop of coffee. I picked up the newspaper and pretended to read it while he loitered in the center of my living room wearing almost nothing but a sheet. I felt his eyes on me, but I just let him look. Maybe he wouldn't stay for breakfast, and that was fine. Maybe he would, and that was also fine. I told myself that whatever he wanted was fine.

Except, his stare persisted. He remained immobile for a full minute, and I grew uncomfortable under the doggedness of his gaze. So I sent him a quick look and frown, like *Come on man, snap out of it. Go get dressed and stop staring at me in my own apartment.*

Finally, he seemed to shake himself, tearing his eyes away and moving to stand. Not wanting to take a chance that I'd be treated to more skin than his chest and back, I lifted the newspaper higher, blocking him from view. I suspected last night had mostly cured me of my lifelong Rex obsession. The last thing I needed was a lusty eyeful of Rex's gorgeous body rekindling anything.

I heard nothing for a bit, no sound of him moving or crossing to the bathroom, and I told myself again not to look at him. *But please Lord, don't let him notice the massive, leaning tower of ugly quilts in the corner.*

Then he asked, "Who undressed me?"

My fingers tightened on the paper. "I did."

"You did." He didn't sound angry, more like disbelieving. "Just you? By yourself?"

"Yes, but I didn't see anything." I kept my tone light and airy. It wasn't a big deal because I'd made sure it wasn't a big deal. Even so, undressing someone *is* a big deal, no matter how many prophylactic measures one takes to ensure it's not.

"You didn't see anything?" He spoke around a yawn.

"I kept my eyes closed, and it was dark." I lowered the newspaper so I could reach for my coffee. "I walked you over there and leaned you against the counter." I lifted my coffee mug toward the kitchen before taking a sip. "Then I turned off all the lights, closed my eyes, and took your clothes off."

"In the dark," he repeated flatly, but I detected the note of incredulity.

Another rush of heat surged up my neck and cheeks, so I lifted the newspaper again. "Yes, in the dark. And don't worry, I wore gloves."

"Gloves."

"Yes."

"You wore gloves when you touched me? When you took my clothes off?" Now his deadpan delivery was laced with amusement.

The amusement only served to fluster me further, and I was so, so grateful for the newspaper blocking me from view. "Yes."

"What kind of gloves?"

"Oven gloves. They're like oven mittens, but they have holes for your, uh . . . fingers." *Ugh! Abby!* I sunk lower in my chair, rolling my eyes at myself.

I don't usually say all the wrong things and make things awkward, but when I do, it's with the former man of my dreams.

Finally, *finally*! I heard the rustle of fabric and his padding footsteps as he walked away. A moment later, the sound of a door snicking shut met my ears and I heaved a giant, silent sigh of relief. He was finally gone. I mean, he was in my bathroom, but at least he wasn't right here.

I used the time Rex dressed in the bathroom to regain my composure and give myself a pep talk. I also added his eggs to the warm plate in the oven that contained the bacon, sausage, toast, and hash browns.

When he exited the bathroom, I didn't look up, keeping my eyes affixed to the paper, but I could detect in my peripheral vision that he was now fully clothed. He loitered by the bathroom door and folded the sheet that had preserved his modesty.

Rex said nothing, and I was acutely aware of him inspecting the interior of my tiny apartment. What did he see, I wondered? *It doesn't matter. He's leaving soon and you'll never see him again.*

That wasn't necessarily true. I'd see him again—on TV and in magazines—just never in person. Like before, his staring went on and on, and I began squirming in my seat, again growing uncomfortable in the silence.

So I broke it. "Do you want coffee? I also have orange juice if you're interested." Restless, I stood from the table and walked the short distance to the kitchen. Reaching inside a cabinet while also grabbing the coffee pot, I pulled out a mug and let the carafe hover over it.

"I can't have either," he said evenly, now normal terse instead of angry terse, his voice just *freakin'* lovely. "Water, please."

I turned away to hide my mild surprise. First of all, he'd said "please," so I supposed that meant polite Rex had returned. Secondly, he couldn't have coffee or OJ? But he could drink enough alcohol to make himself sick? That seemed . . . odd.

Regardless, I grabbed him a glass and filled it with water from the tap while he did whatever he was doing. When I turned, expecting him to still be loitering by the bathroom or hovering next to the kitchen table, he stood directly behind me.

"Oh!" Giving a little start, I blinked furiously, took a step back, and shoved the water glass at his chest. "Here."

"Thank you." He must've picked up the two pain relievers I'd left next to his bed because he now popped them in his mouth. He then drank the water, every last drop of the large glass.

I couldn't help but watch him with bemusement. "Thirsty?" I asked.

He nodded.

I held out my hand for the glass. "More water?"

"Yes, please." He passed it over.

His hand was so big, it was impossible to accept the cup normally without touching him. The Rex spell wasn't exactly broken, and I wasn't willing to reignite the smoldering fire, mostly snuffed out by last night's vomit dousing. Thus, I accepted the cup by the bottom, careful not to touch him, and turned for the sink.

"Sorry I assumed the worst," he said to my profile.

I knew Rex to be a genuine person, so it was easy to accept his apology. "Don't worry about it. I'm sorry I tricked you about being engaged. That wasn't very nice. If I woke up in a stranger's apartment, I'd be freaking out. I think you're handling it quite well."

"How do we know each other?"

My shoulders felt heavy. "We went to school together."

"Really?" Once more, he sounded disbelieving.

If my crush-flame had still been an inferno, his reaction might've singed. "That's right."

"When?"

"When what?" I flipped off the faucet and held out the refilled cup.

He accepted the water but didn't drink it. "College? High school?"

"Oh." I walked around him and returned to the table. "Elementary, middle, and high school."

He coughed, like he was choking on this information. "Are you serious?"

"Mm-hmm." Luckily, I'd already stuffed down the disappointment at not being recognized—at being so entirely forgettable to this man—thus, I felt no upheaval now, just a numb sort of acceptance. Later, I would feel sad. Perhaps I'd wallow, throw myself a bacon pity party. But not now.

I lifted the paper and turned to the events section, scanning for the Christmas market calendar. I'd signed up for a number of Holiday Homecraft markets.

"You don't sound like you're from Texas."

"I lost most of my accent when I moved to Austin from Alenbach." In the events calendar section of the newspaper, I found the three markets I'd signed up for and made a mental note to add two more listed that I'd never heard of before.

"We ever talk?"

"Once or twice." I refolded the paper, picked up my coffee, and took a sip. It was no longer hot. Briefly, I considered heating it back up in the microwave but then ultimately decided to set it back down. I wasn't one of those people who tossed cool coffee. Coffee is expensive, microwaving it for thirty seconds is cheap.

"Once or twice? In thirteen years?"

His tone pulled a smile out of me. He sounded bothered by this news, and I could guess why. Rex was the egalitarian sort, liked to think he treated everyone the same no matter who they were. I suspected this news likely made him question his perception of himself. I suppressed the smile, not wanting him to think I was laughing at him.

"We didn't, uh, move in the same circles," I said, hopefully communicating that it wasn't a big deal.

A spark of something flashed behind his eyes, making me think I'd said exactly the wrong thing.

"Did we have classes together?" A touch of frustration entered his voice.

"A few," I answered honestly, studying the frown lines between his eyebrows. For Rex, who rarely lost his cool, he looked pretty darn upset. "We were in Mrs. Gold's kindergarten class together, and third grade and fourth, a few classes in seventh. I think just shop class, third period, sophomore year in high school, but I was really quiet."

His eyes narrowed. "Were you the only girl? In shop class?"

"No. There were four of us. Becky, Tamara, Mary, and me."

His forehead cleared and I realized—until this moment—he hadn't believed me about us going to school together.

"I remember Becky and Tamara," he said thoughtfully. "What did Mary look like?"

"Short blond hair. She was on the—"

"Soccer team. That's right." Holding the water, he meandered over to the table and pulled out the only other chair, his eyes never leaving mine as he sat. But then he frowned all over again, tilting to the side to inspect my wee little table. "Is this table tall?"

He noticed my table!

"Yes. It is." I smiled, sitting straighter. I loved this table. As someone with long legs, it had been a splurge but so worth it. No one had ever noticed before, and if there was one thing I loved talking about, it was all the cool gadgets, furniture, and fixtures I'd found to make my life as a woman giant easier. "You can get tall tables from the Netherlands. They're a very tall people." I leaned back in my chair. "It drives me crazy when my legs hit—"

"The underside of the table," he finished.

"Exactly." My smile widened. Very few people had this problem, but it was a problem. I was forever vigilant and careful when sitting at a restaurant or at a friend's house not to bump the top of the table. It was an exercise in coordination I did not possess naturally.

Rex also reclined, his eyes dipping to my mouth and then up again. "How tall are you?"

"Six foot one," I said on a sigh, feeling my smile drop on one side with the admission. I'd been six one since seventh grade.

"Six foot one?" Rex wrinkled his nose and cast me a sidelong glance. "Shorty."

That pulled a surprised laugh out of me, and I picked up my coffee cup again. "I can honestly say, no one has ever called me shorty before."

"Maybe you should—should—uh—" Rex's attention returned to the tabletop. He seemed to both frown and smile before giving his head a little shake.

Greedily, I memorized the shape of the almost-smile. He didn't wear smiles often, not even as a kid. As such, I couldn't read his smiles at all. "Maybe I should what?"

Rex cleared his throat. "How tall is your fiancé?"

It took me a few seconds to process his words and reject the alternative *Bow fall wiz boar Beyoncé?*

"My what?"

"Your fiancé. Does he live here?" He grabbed his water cup from the table and gestured to my lap.

Frowning, I glanced down to where his eyes focused. "Oh. This." I slipped my grandmother's ring off my left ring finger and pushed it on the middle finger of my right hand. "Occupational hazard. It's my mom's. I mean, *was* my mom's. And it was her mother's too. I wear it to work to, you know, discourage people from . . ." I waved my hand in front of me, hoping he'd catch my drift.

"You're not engaged?"

I couldn't say, *Nothing on earth or in the universe or in any alternate reality or dimension would ever or could ever convince me to enter into the chains of wedlock ever again. HELL. NO. AS LONG AS I BREATHE AND EAT CHEESE, NEVER AGAIN!*

Instead I chuckled softly and said, "No. That's *never* going to happen."

"Why not?"

"I don't—I just . . ." I flung my fingers around in the air, hoping once more he'd catch my drift.

"Just what?"

I huffed, mock-glaring at him. I did not remember Rex ever talking this much or asking so many questions. Perchance I did not know him as well as I thought? Or perhaps he'd grown chatty in his late twenties?

Regardless, I had no desire to confess the truth, so I offered a perfunctory, "People."

"People." His face didn't seem to know whether it wanted to frown or smile, and I couldn't read him at all.

"I don't think those kinds of relationships are for me," I confessed, squirming again.

I didn't even ask my *friends* the kinds of questions he currently asked me. I was more of a let-folks-volunteer-what-they-want-and-don't-push kind of person, which was probably why I made such an excellent bartender.

"What kind of relationships? Married relationships?"

"Any of those types of relationships," I said under my breath, scanning the newspaper for a distraction.

"So you're not in a relationship?"

My gaze cut to his and I found him examining me while he sipped his water, his expression not grumpy and therefore—to me—inscrutable.

"I'm in plenty of relationships with plenty of people—friend relationships, business relationships, working relationships—and they all suit me better than the kind of relationship you're referring to." Yeah, I was being weird and sensitive about the whole thing, but I was just so freakin' tired of everyone I knew—not just Kaylee, but all my friends and acquaintances—pushing me to date, setting me up when I'd specifically told them I had no interest.

"Do any of those people own that toothbrush in there?" He inclined his head toward the bathroom while a wee little smile curved his lips. "I'm just asking 'cause I want to be prepared for any jealousy-prone significant others who might let themselves in and discover us sitting together at your tall table."

Yeah, right. No one had ever felt enough about me to be jealous, not that I would want someone to be jealous. But—bah! *You know what I mean.*

"No. That's your toothbrush from last night," I responded flatly.

He watched me for a long moment, sipping more of his water, and the silence settled between us for another uncomfortable stretch. I didn't care. He was sitting in my apartment, I refused to feel a pressing need to fill it this time.

Except. . .

"What about you?" I blurted the question, grabbing my mug to take a sip of coffee. I then remembered it was cold. Blech.

"What about me?"

"Are you engaged? Men aren't marked when it happens like women are, so you could be sitting here, engaged to someone, and I'd have no idea. If that's the case, I charged your phone while you were asleep. It was dead when we got here, so I think it's still off. But you should call her and let her know you're okay."

On a whim, I decided to punctuate my statements by drinking my cool coffee and glaring at him over the rim of my cup. *Take that, Nosey McNoserton.*

He returned my glare with a guileless expression. "I am not engaged, and there's no one to call."

I felt myself soften again. "That's what you said last night."

"Pardon?"

"You said there was no one to call, last night, when you were drunk."

The introspection within his stare intensified and it felt weighty somehow. "Why don't you tell me what happened last night."

Pulling my legs under me, I considered where to start. "Um, well, let's see. You walked into my bar and—"

"Your bar?"

"I'm a bartender. You walked in, and I served you, not realizing you were drunk."

I should've realized, but I'd been acting so stupid, I was ashamed of myself. So as I told the story, I tried to stick only to the facts, not wanting to editorialize my actions or make excuses for myself. Nor did I mention his drunken marriage proposal or that he'd called me beautiful. But I did explain how much he'd had to drink and that it had taken four people to load him into my car.

Almost finished with the hard part, I tucked my hair behind my ear and said, "Once you were all buckled up in the car, I was going to drive you to your parents' house, but then you threw up."

Rex's eyes bugged out of his head. "Pardon me?"

He seemed genuinely surprised, and I cringed inwardly. I didn't want him feeling guilty about this, and I should've relayed this part a bit better. "You threw up, in the car, all over yourself. But it was honestly no big deal and probably my fault for serving you while you were already drunk."

His face slackened with plain surprise and he set the glass down on the table, his forehead coming to his hand. I'd never seen him so disconcerted.

I twisted my fingers as my stomach twisted all on its own. "It's fine. I wiped it down last night, left the doors open for it to air out."

Rex gave me an unguarded look loaded with dismay.

I smiled to show how unperturbed I was, adding lightly, "Don't worry about it. Most of it landed on the window and dash. And, you know, your pants. Which was why I had to hose you off, undress you, and wash your clothes."

"So that's why you undressed me."

"I couldn't let you sleep in pukey clothes." I cringed at the thought. "But like I said, I undressed you in the dark, with my eyes closed, and while wearing gloves. It was honestly not a big deal at all."

He nodded grimly, his chest expanding. "First, thank you so much. Thank you for bringing me here, hosing me off, letting me sleep on your floor. Thank you. Second, please, let me cover the cost of the detailing."

I was shaking my head and waving away his offer as soon as he started making it.

Before I could formally reject him, he squinted at me and said, "I have to insist."

"I think it's going to be okay."

"Abby. We go back a long time."

My right eyebrow arched in surprise. "Excuse me?"

"Good friends like us shouldn't argue."

Staring at him and his deadpan delivery, an inexplicable smile tried to invade my features, but I held it off. "You don't remember me, we're basically strangers."

"After all we've been through, after all we've meant to each other—"

I reared back. "This is the most we've talked to each other. Ever."

"You're going to throw my offer back in my face?" He shook his head, pressing his hand to his chest as though my behavior appalled him, an action that oddly made him look like his Aunt Sally, my Girl Scout leader in middle school.

If it weren't for the mischievous—and completely foreign looking—tilt to his lips, I might've thought he was serious.

Wait. What is happening? Is Rex McMurtry . . . teasing me? A pulse of something hot, pleasurable, and unnerving drove me to my feet.

"Okay. Fine." I collected my coffee cup and plate, turning so he wouldn't see my involuntary smile or the blush I felt crawling up my cheeks. In all my stalkery stalking, I'd never seen him be playful with anyone. I wasn't sure how I felt about this new facet of his personality other than I found it irresistible.

"Glad that's settled." His tone returned to normal, no longer judgmental. Or teasing.

I turned from the sink where I left my dishes and crossed my arms.

He gazed at me with wide, innocent eyes. "Tell me what happened next."

"I already told you. I drove you back here, but you—we—were both covered in . . . it. So I hosed us down outside, then walked you inside."

"How'd you manage that?" He inspected my body, obviously sizing me up and likely doubting I could lift him by myself.

He was correct. I might lift fifty-pound bags of clay on the regular, but Rex was way out of my weight class.

"You could walk by the time I got you here."

"I could?"

"Not on your own. You needed some help steering, but I didn't have to hold much of your weight."

"I see. And that's when you undressed me in the dark."

A weird little shiver raced up my spine and I turned to wash my discarded dishes. "Yes. I wrapped you in a sheet and left you on the floor in the bathroom because you said you were still feeling sick." Finished with the dishes, I placed them on the rack. I then grabbed a towel to dry my hands as I faced him. "Then I cleaned up the mess in the car, and—"

"While we're on the topic, let's agree never to mention that again." Pointing all the fingers of one hand at his neck, he moved his hand back and forth quickly in the universal sign for *stop talking about that.* It made me smile. "I'll get some guys over here in hazmat suits and it'll be like it never happened. So you came back here, and?"

"I hosed myself down again."

His focus dropped to the table and he frowned. "Okay. Makes sense," he said, his voice oddly gruff.

"Then I changed into clean pajamas, started the washing machine, blew up the air mattress, and made a bed for you." I returned to the table and sat. "When I checked on you in the bathroom, you seemed better, just mostly tired. You asked to brush your teeth, so I got you a toothbrush, but then you couldn't—" I mimed brushing one's teeth "—you couldn't seem to do it right and your sheet kept slipping, so I did it for you."

"I couldn't brush my own teeth?" Rex covered his face and peeked at me between his fingers.

It was as unexpected as it was completely disarming, and a laugh bubbled out of me. This guy was not known for his expressiveness. At best, he was brusque. At worst—like on the field—people called him ruthless and terrifying.

So this simple, human, relaxed, adorable action coming from the six-foot-six behemoth cracked me up. I realized a bit too late that I'd been laughing for a while, and he was still peering at me from behind his hand.

Ah, darn it. I didn't want him to feel weird or bad about it. Helping him out last night had honestly been the very least I could do considering I'd served him when I shouldn't have.

My instinct was to reach over the table and pull his hand from his face, squeeze it, and comfort him, but I hesitated. I'd done a really good job of not touching him at all so far, not even accidental touches. But in order to comfort him, I would have to touch him. On purpose.

Get over it, Abby! You'll never see him again after today. Being a good person is more important than your level of comfort. Or discomfort.

Putting my plan into action, I removed his fingers from his face and held them between us on the table, leaning forward. "It wasn't like that. Like I said, you were really tired and out of it."

"And drunk." He twisted his hand around and tangled his fingers with mine.

My stomach tried to give a little flutter, but I issued a quick smackdown. "Mostly you were tired. I helped, that's it. That's all that happened."

"And I didn't say anything else to you? During all this, I didn't speak?"

Uhhhh. . . . Trying not to grimace at the memory of what he'd said last night at the bar and in my car and how my body / heart / mind had been conspiring against me, I slipped my hand out of his. "You may have . . . said . . . a few things."

"Such as?"

"It was drunk nonsense. Nothing important." I wrinkled my nose.

He glared at me. "You always were a terrible liar."

I smiled at his odd teasing. "Believe me, I've been a bartender for a long time. You didn't say anything compared to what I've heard from other folks."

"So men ask you to marry them all the time?"

Aaah. Crap. "You remember that from last night, do you?"

"I do." He seemed to think better of his words, and added, "I mean, I remember. That."

"Actually, yes. I have been proposed to on a number of occasions by drunk people from all walks of life. So you shouldn't feel weird about it."

"I'm just one of many, then?" he teased. Again.

I held off more tummy butterflies by scoffing. And then snorting. *WHO IS THIS GUY?*

But I couldn't stop my smile. "It's nothing. You were drunk. No harm, no foul. I'm just glad . . ." I didn't know how to finish that sentence without admitting too much. Taking a deep breath, and having every intention of finishing the thought, I stared at Rex's face. *He has such a kind face.*

Most people would say it was gruff, or ruthless, or stern, but I didn't think so. I'd never been intimidated by the frowns and scowls he typically wore. Which was likely why his behavior today after realizing I hadn't laid a finger on him last night— the stares, the playfulness, being relaxed, all of it—had struck me as so odd.

Maybe he was lonely?

I knew what that was like. All his friends were getting married, the news always loved to point out how they were marrying his ex-girlfriends; he lived in Chicago for most of the year, so far away from our hometown; he had so much pressure on him as a pro athlete.

Maybe he was loitering in my apartment and conversing with me, asking so many questions because he simply missed home? *Maybe he—*

Rex's stomach grumbled.

I flinched, stiffening, and realized I'd been staring at Rex this whole time. I affixed my eyes to my lap as the epic strength of my embarrassed flush spread up my chest, to my neck, and cheeks.

"Sorry. You must be hungry." I shook my head, willing my wits to make a reappearance.

"I am." The softness in his tone only served to deepen my mortification. "But first tell me what you're glad about."

My mouth hooked to the side as I wrestled my feelings into submission. Stuffing them down, all of them, I shrugged. "Oh, just that I'm glad I could be there last night. That's all."

Rex seemed to contemplate my statement before saying, "I'm not used to waking up and not knowing where I am. This morning was a first for me. I usually don't drink at all."

"Me too." I leaned forward to set my elbows on the table. "I mean, I do drink. But this was a first for me too. I'm not in the habit of serving drunk customers or bringing them to my home and hosing them off."

"But you brush everyone's teeth?"

"Yes. Obviously." I smiled, grateful he'd chosen to lighten the mood rather than point out what a weirdo I'd been staring at his face.

He returned my smile, his soft and warm.

See? He's not gruff. He's wonderful!

. . . Uh oh.

I shot up from the table again, casting aside that last thought.

"Okay, let me get your breakfast. I left it warming." Happy to be moving and distracted by a task, I walked over to the oven and pulled on my oven mitts. It wasn't until I reached inside the oven that I remembered these were the very same mitts I'd used to undress Rex last night.

My stomach misbehaved again, and this time it would not be denied. I tried my best, but it just kept on flittering and twisting and tightening until the crush broke free from the box where I'd stuffed it. It didn't even need to be dusted off.

Apparently, though he'd thrown up all over my car and I'd seen him at his worst, Rex's worst was light years ahead of most people's best. And there was nothing I could do about that. *Drat.*

Oh well. I could think of worse things than spending another twenty-three years crushing on Rex McMurtry from afar.

CHAPTER 6

"I used to believe in forever, but forever's too good to be true"

— A.A. MILNE, *WINNIE-THE-POOH*

"Hey you." Walker's friendly drawl greeted me not five seconds after I walked into the Boozy Rancher. "I'm not supposed to see you until Sunday, am I?"

"Under normal circumstances, that would be correct." I pulled off my jacket, noting that the bar was vacant of customers except Owen. Owen, a dentist and a regular, worked a half day every Friday and liked to end his week here with buffalo wings and amaretto sours. I'd tried the combination once. *Just once.*

"You here to eat? Or pick up a Friday shift?"

"Eat," I grumbled, walking down the length of the bar to the stool at the end. "I have a fly problem."

"A what?" Walker placed a cocktail napkin in front of me and then spread his hands to lean against the bar.

"A. Fly. Problem. A fly has taken up residence in my apartment, and it is driving me insane."

After I'd returned from driving Rex McMurtry to his hotel and out of my life yesterday late afternoon, the fly dive-bombed me while I ate dinner. When I attempted to work on my greenware cauldron mugs, it crashed into my hands like it wanted to live inside my veins. And it liked my feet—which I tried really hard not to take personally—continually wanting to sit on them and rub its poopy tentacles together.

Yes, I know flies don't have tentacles. Just go with it.

Walker looked at me out of the corner of his eye like my words were code. "What's that mean?"

"There's a fly in my apartment and it won't die." I hung my jacket over the back of the stool. "But it likes to circle my head and seems to have an obsession with my feet. Nothing helps. I wear socks, it lands on the socks. I wear shoes, it dances on my shoelaces."

"Is that so?" His lips pressed together while his gray-blue eyes danced as they took in my clay-spattered smock and jeans. They danced like that fly had done on my shoelaces. "Where are you coming from?"

"The studio."

"You have to go home eventually. How are you going to kill it?"

"Any ideas?" My elbow on the bar, my chin in my palm, I made no attempt to hide my desperation from my boss. Even if I hadn't been desperate—and I was desperate—I would've asked him for advice.

When I'd initially started working at the Boozy Rancher, he would say things like "Whatever you think is best" or "You'll figure it out."

Then, over time—and especially when I was going through my divorce—he'd started offering his opinion when asked, but always with a caveat, like "You don't need to listen to me, but this is what I'd do" or "I'm probably not the best person to ask, but I suppose I'd do this."

Now, he didn't give caveats or qualifiers or wait for me to ask. We were waaay past that.

"You tried the wine trap?" he asked.

"Yes." I'd made a wine trap with rotten fruit, red wine, and plastic wrap. The evil little bastard remained unimpressed, never even hovering near the lure. *Maybe I should've used my socks?*

Walker narrowed his eyes, then scratched the stubble on his cheek.

The song over the speaker switched from "Thriller" to "Baby, It's Cold Outside."

"You have a fly swatter?" he asked.

"Correct. But the bugger is fast and wily. I almost sprained my ankle last night, jumping off a chair." Stalking the pestilence around my apartment with a fly swatter in the middle of the night after it tried to jettison up my nose did no good other than giving me an intense workout. The insect's evasive maneuvers were Captain Picard-worthy.

Walker nodded, taking this news in stride. "Fly paper?"

"Fly paper!" I made a fist. "No. I haven't tried that."

"I have some in the back. Take it with you when you leave. Now, what can I get you?" He paired these words with his trademark crooked smile, the one that usually made customers swoon.

I, however, had been inoculated against its powers long ago. Firstly, when I'd started working here, I only had heart-eyes for Rex.

Who am I kidding? I still had heart-eyes for Rex.

Secondly, my first year at the bar had basically been a front row seat to the beginning of Walker and Ramona's love story.

And thirdly, I thought of my boss like an older brother and felt confident he thought of me like a little sister. He looked out for me, and I looked out for him.

Other than my apartment, the bar remained my cheapest option for lunch because Walker fed me for free. I didn't accept this generosity often, not wanting to take advantage.

I returned Walker's crooked smile with my straight one. "I want a grilled cheese sandwich and tomato soup, please."

Walker's smile faltered, gray-blue eyes turning flinty. "That's not on the menu anymore."

"But I know we have bread, cheese, and butter. And I left a jar of my tomato soup in the freezer."

He crossed his arms. "Yeah, but when you order soup on a cold day, other people see it and want the same thing."

"Why'd you take it off the menu, then?" I tugged a full bowl of pretzels closer. "At least keep it seasonal."

"You know we want folks coming in here to drink, not just eat." He picked up a towel and motioned to the back room. "Appetizers are one thing—mozzarella sticks, sliders, chili fries, stuff that pairs well with beer—but your soup clogs the place with nondrinkers and health nuts. I can't have people taking up space eating fancy soup and sipping on water, looking down their noses at paying customers. If I wanted to run a hipster restaurant, this place would be called the Bourgeoisie Bistro."

I'd heard this rant before, just days prior to him removing the soup from the menu.

I gave him a beseeching smile. "What if I promise to hide while I eat the soup? I'll face the wall. Or you can put it in a glass and I'll pretend like it's a Bloody Mary."

He grunted, but I could see I'd won. "Fine." He lifted a finger between us. "But only because we just opened and it's still quiet. Once folks start coming in, no more soup."

"After three, no soup for me. Got it, boss."

His left eyebrow ticked a scant millimeter and he turned toward the back, giving me one last warning glare before disappearing. As soon as he left, I chuckled to myself at the name Bourgeoisie Bistro and popped a pretzel in my mouth.

I had a friend who used bougie (pronounced "boo-Zhe") as an adjective, like "I don't want to go to that bougie party" or "Tell me this sofa isn't the most bougie thing you've ever seen." I wasn't quite sure how to apply it correctly, and I was pretty surprised to discover it was a real word, but—as I munched on my second pretzel—I thought maybe the name Bougie Bistro would actually be a good one for a restaurant.

The bell over the door rang just as I plucked a third pretzel from the dish, but the salty snack never made it past my lips even though my mouth now hung wide open.

There, once again, out of nowhere and scattering all my neatly ordered thoughts to the four corners of chaos and heart palpitations (which is a sentence that doesn't make sense and that's the point) stood Rex McMurtry. In my bar, in the flesh, but also in an illuminating pair of snug blue jeans and a cable-knit sweater that instigated a plethora of dirty thoughts, none of which were bougie.

Snapping my mouth shut and wiping my chin, I twisted in my stool, facing the wall, giving him my back. He hadn't seemed to spot me yet, so I used the borrowed time to collect my thoughts.

What is he doing here?

I'd taken care of him without surrendering to the temptation of impropriety or criminal behavior, hadn't I? I'd successfully maintained my composure and moral fortitude while the embodiment of my ideal man slept and then lounged in my apartment, shirtless, hair askew, jaw stubbled.

It's not like I wanted a cookie for being a decent human, but *less* temptation would be nice!

After our late breakfast, I'd dropped sexy Rex off at his hotel, opened the passenger-side door for him since it could no longer be opened from the inside, and then I'd said goodbye. Yes, it had been a rushed goodbye, administered with a quick wave as I dashed back to the driver's seat, but I'd meant it. Good. Bye. Time for me to get back to my uncomplicated, comfortable life and time for him to return to his ivory stadium.

In retrospect, the afternoon had been a singularity, a love note from a higher power. All Rex's adorable and rare smiles, his teasing—I must've done something supremely good in my past to deserve such a gift that required minimal effort on my part. The vomit-mobile had been worth what came after, for *sure.*

But then, the afternoon had ended, and that was totally fine. Great, even! I'd been happy. Content. At peace with our moment lasting only *a moment.*

So why, for the love of pretzels, was Rex McMurtry suddenly here again one day later?

"Abby?"

A jolt of nerves—spiky, tingly electricity—rushed from the base of my neck outward, to every limb and appendage. I inhaled a deep, silent breath, steadying myself. I pasted a smile on my face, shoving away the clutter of self-consciousness. Rotating the stool 180 degrees, I faced him.

"Oh. Hey, Rex. Long time no see. What are you doing here?" I could do this. I'd spent a full two hours in my apartment with him yesterday, having conversations, *not* being a staring, stalkery, simpering weirdo. Heck, I'd even relaxed, forgotten who he was, settled into the conversation. I'd *enjoyed* his company and myself.

I'd brushed his teeth for hootenanny's sake! That was me. Another short conversation should be a cakewalk. *I. Can. Do. This.*

"Are you on the clock?"

Glancing at my watch, I forced a lightness I didn't fully feel. "I have a minute. What's going on? Did you leave something at my place?" *That's probably why he's here.*

"No," he responded easily, bursting my theory bubble and sauntering forward to the stool next to mine while emanating serious BSE (Big Sweater Energy). He looked at me like he knew me, like we were friends and he felt completely at ease in my presence. "I wanted to talk to you."

"Is that so?" My stupid stomach swirled with heat.

His hand braced on the back of the stool, but he didn't sit. "I'm in town for a few more days, until Sunday. Do you have any time off?"

I stared at him, saying nothing, trying to keep my thoughts ordered and my breathing under control, because *WHAT THE HECK IS HAPPENING?!*

Was he . . .

Is he . . .?

Fantasies?!

Naaaaah.

No, Abigail, Rex McMurtry is not here to read quietly next to you on a couch, kiss your face off, and have sex on every surface of your apartment. *This is not a high school musical porno, and you can't sing for shit.*

The inane direction of my thoughts made me laugh—at myself. In what universe did any super famous pro athlete, who could have anyone they wanted, come looking for Abigail McNerny and fulfill her teenage wish list? No. Not happening.

If my life had taught me one lesson exceptionally well it was that nothing too good to be true was ever real. If it felt like a dream, it would—without fail—eventually turn into a nightmare.

Watching me closely, Rex tapped his finger on the seatback of the stool. "So you have no time off?"

"It's just—" I covered my face with my hands, my shoulders still shaking with the remnants of laughter. "I'm sorry. I didn't get much sleep last night."

"Why didn't you sleep? Did something happen?" His shoulders seemed to relax at my words and the confusion around his eyes dissolved into what looked like genuine concern.

Unfortunately, this change completely disarmed me. "Oh. There's this fly that won't die, and I'm really hungry. Sometimes I get goofy when I don't sleep or eat. I get gangry instead of hangry. But gangry sounds like gangrene, which is not what I mean."

"Hunoofy?" he tried. "Hungry plus goofy."

"Seems about right. Anyway, I have a fly in my apartment, and it kept waking me up."

"It woke you up? A fly?" Now Rex looked like he was trying not to laugh, surprising me with another unexpected smile.

"Yes," I grumbled, disgruntled for some reason by the appearance of his smile—maybe Rex was a person who smiles now?—and shoved my index finger upward in front of my face. "It must've thought my nose was a portal to the promised land, a wonderous world filled with poop and dump trucks."

Now he covered his mouth, his eyes bright.

"It also seemed enamored with my feet," I admitted sadly. "Not sure what that says about my feet."

"Oh my God. Abby, stop." Rex covered his whole face with one hand while gripping the leather at the back of the stool with his other, his laughter now uncontainable.

"I wish I could make it stop, truly I do. But I almost killed myself trying to murder it last night and now I'm so tired."

His hilarity tapered and he sighed, the sound drawing my eyes to his magnificent hazel ones, and that's when I remembered who I'd been speaking to about my nose and feet and fly problem. Embarrassment descended like rainfall.

"I really just said all that out loud, didn't I?" I peeked at him.

He nodded, still smiling.

That was a good sign, right? The smile?

Before I could make up my mind, Walker's voice boomed from the back, "Here's your soup." A second later, my boss emerged, holding a tray of food. "And it's even in a bowl, that's how you can tell I like you." He glanced at me, then Rex, then me, then drew up short.

Without putting the food down, my boss straightened and said, "You're—you are TW. Rex McMurtry."

The change in Rex was instantaneous. One second, he was the same Rex from yesterday and in the next moment, a marble-like quality seemed to possess him. He grew still, stiff, his eyes distant, cold, and hard. He didn't look unfriendly, but he didn't look friendly either. He looked guarded, more like the version of himself I'd gone to school with.

Huh. Interesting.

"That's right, sir. Nice to meet you." Rex "Training Wheels" McMurtry issued Walker a tight smile and nod.

"Well, I'll be." Walker returned the smile with one of his own, unleashing the unabashed power of his crooked grin, an unchecked and completely genuine sunbeam of disarming handsomeness and charm.

I squinted at the rare spectacle. It was the kind of smile my boss typically reserved only for his wife and son. But Rex seemed to stiffen further at the impact and blinked twice, like the unexpected sight dazzled.

"You made me a lot of money eight years ago, when you were playing for Texas at Ohio. What can I get you? On the house."

Rex glanced at me, at the food-laden tray, then back at my boss. "I'll have what she's having."

I braced myself for Walker to slide me the stink eye. He hadn't wanted to serve me soup because he didn't want other folks ordering it, and now Rex had just ordered it. But to my surprise—nay, horror and shock—Walker put my lunch down in front of Rex's stool.

"Sure thing." Walker unloaded the tray, a perfect grilled cheese and a piping hot bowl of tomato soup with parmesan croutons.

My mouth watered, and my hunoofy turned into hangry. "Hey! That's my food!"

Both men looked at me, Walker rocking back on his heels. "Simmer down, Abigail. I don't think this fine gentleman was planning to flee with your food."

"It's not Rex I'm worried about." I tugged the bowl toward me, glaring at Walker, then at Rex for good measure before I realized what I was doing.

Man, I must've been really hungry.

Rex held his hands up, a smile playing over his lips. "I'll sit right here and wait for mine."

"See that you do," I mumbled. To evade a renewed bloom of embarrassment, I focused on my lunch, reaching over the bar to grab a roll of silverware.

"Y'all know each other?" Walker didn't leave to get Rex's order. Instead, he brought the tray to his chest, folding his arms over it.

Rex—to my surprise—answered with authority, "We went to school together."

"Oh yeah? High school?"

"All school." Rex pulled out the stool next to mine, his knee bumping my thigh as he slid into place. "Elementary, middle, and high school."

"How about that." Walker rocked back on his heels again, like he needed to absorb this information. "Abby never said anything."

I took a huge bite of my grilled cheese so I wouldn't have to respond and soon regretted the decision. Both Walker and Rex spent the next few seconds in contemplative silence, looking me over, as though seeing me anew while I chewed my food.

I swallowed quickly and said, "It's not like we knew each other. I went to high school with a guy named Dave Hall too. Do you want a list of everyone I went to school with?"

"Just those that made pro ball, please," came Walker's dry reply. Then to Rex he asked, "Anyone else as famous as you go to school with y'all?"

Some of Rex's façade had dissipated in the face of Walker's easy manner, his tone now slightly less stiff and formal. "Do you know who Cyrus Malcom is?"

Cyrus Malcom.

I wiped all expression from my face. Cyrus and I had been good friends in middle school and part of high school, the kind who shared secrets, dreams, and sorrows. Our sophomore year he joined the football team and asked me out—which had blindsided me since he'd known I pined for Rex with the blind devotion of a BTS stan. When I turned him down, things grew awkward between us, and our interactions never felt natural again. We eventually drifted apart and lost touch.

We'd had just two interactions since high school—once at my mother's funeral and once during the early days of my divorce—both of which I wanted to forget and neither of which had anything to do with Cyrus. He'd always been sweet, funny, and I supposed one could call him a movie star now. I hadn't thought about or seen him in years and then, bam. He's on the big screen.

Good for him. He had the looks for it, and the talent.

Walker's gaze narrowed, lifted to someplace behind us. "You mean the actor from that astronaut movie?"

I felt Rex inspect me quickly before confirming, "That's the one. We went to school with him too."

My boss placed a hand on his hip. "Really?"

"Really." Rex nodded, shifting in his seat, which incidentally pressed the length of his muscular thigh against mine.

I swallowed thickly at the contact, abruptly hot and no longer interested in warm food.

"So what happened to you, Abby?" Walker teased, his grayish blue eyes twinkling like mischievous sparklers. "Why aren't you famous?"

Pushing the soup away, I shrugged and wiped my mouth with a napkin. "You know me. I'm just biding my time for that Nobel Prize in knitting."

Both Rex and Walker seemed to think this was highly amusing.

"You are very funny, Abby." Walker pointed the tray at me and repeated a statement he'd said often enough for it to become an inside joke between us, "Funny like a clown with no pants."

"Exactly." I nodded, agreeing with my usual line, "It's criminal how funny I am."

They both laughed harder.

"Listen, I'll be back with your lunch." My boss rapped his knuckles on the bartop in front of Rex. "Anything to drink?"

"I'll take a water, with ice," I interjected.

"I'll have the same, no ice," Rex added, the weight of his eyes on me.

I glanced at him and discovered him watching me with a trace of a smile. And, just like yesterday, his gaze soon became a stare.

I faced forward, giving him my profile, and reached for a pretzel. I didn't dare eat it. I'd probably end up needing the Heimlich maneuver.

"Soooo, Rex." I fiddled with the pretzel, tapping it against the surface of the bar and clearing my throat. "What are you really doing here?"

I sensed him move, and I glanced at him again. The smile had vacated his features and his eyebrows pulled together. "I have—" Rex hesitated, like he was looking for the right words "—a strange question."

"A strange question," I parroted. Sometimes, repeating a person's statement is the safest choice in an unanticipated conversation. I'd just said something, nothing of consequence, and now it was his turn to speak.

He grinned, an inescapable, magnetic event. *God. He's so beautiful. Why did you make him this beautiful?* One would think I'd be less enamored with the guy who'd defiled my car, couldn't brush his own teeth, and had been rude to me upon waking. But here I was, still enamored.

"It's an unorthodox request rather than a question."

Whatever it was, whatever he needed, I felt certain I would say yes. And that certainty scared the crap out of me.

Surely this hold he had—this place of prominence and importance I'd handed over to him years ago even though he'd never sought it or worked to earn it—pointed to hugely wackadoodle choices and questionable mental health on my part. Furthermore, it wasn't fair to him. Here he was, wasting his time with an uber fan and he had no idea.

But it's not supposed to matter whether my admiration-fueled wackadoodle behavior is fair to him! He's supposed to be admired from afar. Why is he not afar? Get thee afar, Rex.

Rex leaned an arm on the bar and faced me, his hazel eyes holding mine while he (likely inadvertently) crowded my space. "This will sound completely crazy."

"Okay."

He visibly hesitated again, his attention moving to my hair. "I appreciated your help yesterday."

I waited for him to voice his request while instructing my heart to chill the eff out. When he didn't speak, I said, "That doesn't sound crazy, and you already thanked me yesterday."

"I know. But it's part of the reason I'm here."

Was he being confusing on purpose? Or was my brain overpowered by the aura of his BSE? "What's part of what?"

"You don't want anything from me," he said, the candid words taking me completely by surprise.

I blinked. Unsure what to say, I glanced over his head, eventually managing a confused, "Okay."

"In my experience, especially since I started playing pro ball, it seems like . . ."

"People always want something from you."

He nodded, his lips forming something between a wry smile and a brittle frown. "Before I know them, before I even talk to them, they have a plan for me, a wish list."

"That seems like it would be very frustrating." I leaned back on my stool, crossing my arms against the twinge of guilt behind my rib cage because I had a Rex McMurtry wish list, most of which involved us naked.

"It is. When I meet someone with no ulterior motives, it's rare."

We traded stares while the twinge of guilt became heartburn. He was wrong about me. I was not rare. I was common. And I couldn't let him continue believing I was something I wasn't.

"Rex, listen. I'm not who—I don't—"

"Abby, I get it. I know you don't date, and I respect that."

"I don't date," I repeated dumbly. Instead of sounding like an echo, as I'd intended, it sounded like a confirmation. But since the statement happened to be an entirely accurate one, I didn't seek to clarify any portion of it.

He nodded. "That's good," he said, then made a face, shaking his head. "I mean—that's fine. Rather, it is what it is and it's your decision and it's good if it's what you want. And it is what you want." Abruptly, he turned to the bartop, a rumbly chuckle tumbling out of him. "I'm messing this up."

Breathless curiosity eclipsed my shame. "What are you messing up?"

"I'll just say it." He rubbed his forehead as he said this, like he was trying to psyche himself up, talk himself into the completion of a daunting task.

Meanwhile, I was on the edge of my seat.

Finally, he faced me again, but some of the granite-like Rex "Training Wheels" McMurtry came with him. "I don't date either, not anymore, not for years. And I have no plans to date anyone anytime soon. I needed a break from all that, and all the . . . all that stuff."

"O-okay." *Why would he tell me this?*

Holding my eyes, he gathered a deep breath, then said, "So, my strange request."

I sat perfectly still, resisting the urge to repeat *strange request* just to say something. My mind darted all over the place, in every direction, working overtime trying to figure out what he could possibly have in mind, when he blurted—

"I want to hire you to marry me."

CHAPTER 7

"The more you struggle to live, the less you live. Give up the notion that you must be sure of what you are doing. Instead, surrender to what is real within you, for that alone is sure."

— SPINOZA

Hire me? "Hire me," I echoed on autopilot because . . . what?

"To marry me."

"Uh." I looked to my right and then my left. "Say what?"

"I need a wife."

I was in an alternate dimension. *No, you're dreaming.* "Am I asleep? Is this a dream?" I moved to pinch myself but then stopped.

Wait, let's just see where this dream goes.

His eyes seemed to spark with amusement, but his mouth persisted in its grim line. "A business arrangement. I need you to come with me to places, events, and act as my wife."

"Places? What places?"

"Weddings." His stare became something both interested and detached, like he was looking at me through a fish tank.

"Weddings."

"Weddings, rehearsal dinners, parties, work events. We wouldn't really be together, but everyone would believe you are my wife. They'd believe we"—he pointed to me and then to himself—"are married in truth."

We wouldn't really be together.

Everyone would believe you are my wife.

They'd believe we are married in truth.

I continued staring at him as I processed this riddle he'd presented and, quite suddenly, I got it. I understood what he was asking. What I didn't understand was why.

An uncomfortable chuckle bubbled out of me. "Uhh. . ." I shook my head and turned back to my now lukewarm soup.

He wants to hire me, to escort him to parties, and pretend we're married. This is bonkers.

I sensed Rex's restless energy, his discomfort, but I didn't seem to care about his comfort right now, or lack thereof, or who he was, or that I should be nervous, or that I should still be ashamed because I had a sexy Rex McMurtry wish list. Truth was, I didn't know what to feel.

"Abby?"

I looked up, finding Walker standing on the other side of the bar holding two glasses of water, his attention narrowed on Rex.

"Everything okay?" Walker ground out, looking less than friendly.

I nodded and reached out to accept the water. "Thanks."

Suspicion clouded Walker's eyes, turning them stormy and distrustful as they moved between us. He opened his mouth, likely to question Rex, but I gave my head a quick shake. *Please. Don't.*

Frowning, he set Rex's glass down with a *thunk,* grumbled something about the soup almost being ready, and strolled down the length of the bar to the other end. My boss loitered, looking over his shoulder at us, watchful.

Looking out for me.

"I've upset you."

"Hmm?" I glanced at Rex.

"Did I upset you?" His expression and voice were gruff, restrained.

"What? Upset me?"

"With my offer?"

"No," I answered honestly, an unforced smile curving my lips. "No. I'm not upset. But I'm not sure why you would want to—why you would need to—you know."

"Pay someone to marry me?"

I nodded, picking up and fiddling with a pretzel again, breaking off the little pieces of salt and rubbing them between my fingers. "Why not just marry someone for real?"

The question seemed to pain and exhaust him, and he inhaled deeply before responding. "I haven't dated anyone in over two years."

I sat up straighter, this news a surprise. I watched Rex's games on TV whenever I could. Sometimes I'd catch a photo of him with some fancy, accomplished lady on his arm in a magazine or on TV. But unless details of his personal life were splattered all over the place—like the attempted kidnapping in Miami or the fact that his ex-girlfriends were marrying his guy friends—I didn't follow his private affairs. I had been a kid, tween, and teen stalker, but I wasn't a stalker as an adult.

Two years?

"But"—I broke the pretzel in half—"I'm sure if you asked, certainly there's someone who—"

"I don't want to," he said simply. "It's one thing to have a relationship when it's just me and her, just the two of us. But when it's me, and her, and football, and the press, and the fans, it doesn't work. Dating me is a big ask, a time commitment, a hassle."

This all sounded like nonsense to me. Dating Rex was a big ask? A hassle? In what universe?

"Part of my contract with the Squalls dictates the number of events I have to attend each year, which includes public appearances like movie premieres, charity fundraisers." Rex slid his eyes to the side, studying me before asking, "You hate the idea?"

I considered the question, taking my time, turning it over in my mind. Did I hate the idea?

His request had disappointed me for some reason, but my disappointment was entirely my fault. The loud, squealing with glee part of me had just received a major blow, and I had no one to blame but myself.

If it seems too good to be true, it is. I knew this. I knew this intimately.

But, if I considered things from his perspective, the request—jarring and unconventional as it was—made a lot of sense. Maybe he wanted to focus on his career and couldn't spare the energy necessary to foster a real relationship. I supposed I understood that. After my father died, my mother didn't have time or energy for a new partner either.

Spouses, she'd said more than once, *take a lot of effort in life, and then when they die, the funeral is expensive.* She'd run a funeral home, so her statement made more sense in that context. For so many years after my ex left me buried under his debt and my idiotic, naïve, foolish choices, I had wished I'd listened to her and never married.

And yet, on the other hand, and specifically in Rex's case, always going to Chicago Squall events and such without a date probably took its toll too. In high school, he'd been quietly kind but not extroverted. Pro ball shindigs didn't seem like his style.

I shook my head. "No. I don't hate the idea. It's an unconventional request, but I understand your perspective, why you'd want to hire someone."

"Really?" He inched closer, the impervious façade version of Rex "Training Wheels" McMurtry fading as visible relief took its place.

"Yes. Really. But why not just ask a friend? Ask a friend to do it as a favor?"

"This can't be just a favor, that would be unfair. You will have to fly places, stay the night in hotels, go to boring events. It'll be time-consuming, and you'd probably miss work here. I understand that if you agreed, not only would I be paying you for your time, but you would also be doing me a favor. I reckon it's a bit of both, a job and a favor."

"Okay. It's time-consuming, I suppose I understand the reimbursing for time and expenses part. But—" *How do I put this?*

"But?"

"But why me?" I peered at him.

"A fair question." He pressed his palms together, as though in prayer, and pointed them at me. "I know you."

"You don't know me."

"I do. I remember you now. You're Abigail McNerny, and in elementary school you always beat everyone in the timed mile, boys and girls. You used to wear your hair real short and dyed black. My aunt was your Girl Scout leader."

Listening to Rex McMurtry list all the details he recalled about me and having none of them be relevant to who I was—then or now—made me feel like the subject of a bad book report. But yes. Technically, he did remember Abigail McNerny.

I breathed out an irritable sigh. "Fine. You remember me. But you know lots of people. Why me?"

"You're perfect. Pragmatically, you couldn't be any more perfect: we already know each other and have since we were kids, you're an only child, both parents gone, no family members nearby."

Discomfort had me crossing my arms over my stomach. Virtually everything that made me perfect for Rex's scheme had also made me perfect for my ex-husband's—a young woman apparently alone in the world—except Rex was being upfront about it. Also, now I wasn't alone. Walker and I were close, he looked out for me. So did Kaylee. I didn't have much in the way of family—my Uncle Mac up in Michigan, a few cousins in other states I didn't speak to often—but I did have friends.

Rex added, "But it's really because I know you *and* I trust you."

"You trust me? Why?"

The corner of his mouth hitched. "You undressed me in the dark using oven gloves when I couldn't even brush my teeth and let me sleep off a hangover in your apartment. I think, if I required a litmus test as to your trustworthiness, that'd be a pretty solid one."

Hmm. "Okay. I see your point there."

"I also thought you might be open to earning some extra money."

Leaning back, I rolled my lips between my teeth to keep from frowning, knowing he didn't mean the words as an insult. Even so, they felt insulting.

"And you're . . ." he started, then stopped, and his lips remained parted even though he didn't seem inclined to finish the thought.

"I'm what?" I asked.

"You're steady."

"Steady."

"That's right."

"Like a boat?"

Another eye twinkle. "Something like that. Reliable. Calm. You have good judgment and don't freak out in stressful situations."

I studied him and his explanations. It seemed he'd thought this through. However! "Who would believe it, though?"

"Why wouldn't people believe it?" He grabbed a pretzel and popped it in his mouth.

I squirmed, not wanting to ask the question, but if he was serious—and it seemed like he was—then it was a question that needed to be asked. "Do you think people would actually buy it? You and me?"

"Yes." His forehead wrinkled, and his tone told me this was a nonissue.

"I'm a hick bartender and you're the star defensive end for the Chicago Squalls."

His frown was severe. "You're not a hick."

"I am a hick. I'm an uneducated hick. I'll embarrass you."

Now he scowled, visibly angered by my words. "Abby."

"Don't you people date actresses and models?"

He made a sound that was half scoff, half laugh. "No. Most of *us people* are with their high school and college sweethearts, who are anything and everything. We've known each other since preschool. Doesn't have anything to do with your job. And you *are not* a hick."

I frowned, and it wasn't just about my job or how we'd gone to school together. I shopped at thrift stores and Walmart. I didn't dress how I thought a pro ball girlfriend would. Also, I didn't know things, and I didn't know what I didn't know. I wasn't cultured. I wasn't fancy.

Finally, I decided on, "I don't look the part."

"Easy to fix." He shrugged, his acquiescence on *this* point made me dislike him a little.

Easy to fix. What a jerk! Like I was some door handle he'd broken off a car. *But you said it, Abby. You're the one who said you don't look the part. Not him.*

Yes, but he agreed with me!

I slouched, pushing my fingers into my hair at my forehead, my disappointment swelling to elephant size. Yesterday, despite all that had happened the night before, I'd dropped Rex off at his hotel with his crown of perfection still mostly intact. But now? It had tarnished.

"Listen, Abby. I don't want to push you into this, but I'm not going to talk you out of it. Goes without saying, you couldn't tell anyone about it. No one could know."

Sigh. "So I'd be lying?"

"Yes," he said plainly, his gaze stark. "I'd be lying, you'd be lying. But we'd also stick to the truth as much as possible."

"How so?" I couldn't wait to hear this.

"We went to school together. We ran into each other here, at your work, while I was in town. We started seeing each other after that. If you agree, we'll marry this week. All of that's true, no need to volunteer the time line." He frowned as he said this, like the words tasted bad in his mouth. "And we'd leave out the part about me paying you."

"And then there'd be the pretending part," I muttered.

"You'd never have to do anything you don't want to do. Nothing that makes you uncomfortable."

I gulped around something solid in my throat, not able to meet his eyes. Despite the tumble he'd just taken off the pedestal of my making, I suspected any touching requirement would be a nonissue. He hadn't ever been demonstrative with his girlfriends in high school, and the times I'd seen him photographed with a woman—in the paper, in a magazine, on TV—they'd never been kissing or anything like that.

If I'm being honest, I wouldn't mind if kissing was part of the deal. The crown was tarnished, but Rex was one of the nicest guys I'd ever known, and so incredibly smart and talented. Yeah, he exuded grumpiness and irritability—or he used to—but he loved and took care of his family despite their craziness, and he was hotter now than he'd been in high school. We're talking plasma levels, people!

Also, I hadn't been kissed in years. Physical stuff was the one thing I missed about being in a relationship. Assuming he was good at it, kissing would be a bonus. Maybe some embracing. Groping would also be on the table. BUT! I would refrain from any of that if he didn't ask. He was safe from me.

To prove my good intentions, I said, "I wouldn't want to make you uncomfortable either. So if we do this, you have to let me know if I, uh, cross any boundaries in our quest to make it appear authentic."

He gave me a side-eye, one that made me wonder if I'd said something crazy. "Uh . . . suuure."

"Good," I said earnestly.

Rex rubbed his eyes. "It's a big ask. Think of this as a job and accept a paycheck because I'll keep you busy. Movie premieres, charity galas, destination weddings."

My stomach swirled, and for once it had nothing to do with Rex. *Destination weddings?* That sounded . . . *FANTASTIC.* I'd always wanted to travel but—

"You'll have to buy an iron," he added, and the way his eyes twinkled, I surmised this was more of his teasing.

"Dresses." My stomach sunk.

"Yep."

Breathing in through my nose, I stared at the broken pretzel in my hands.

"You don't like dresses," he guessed.

"I like dresses fine. But dresses don't like me." I gestured to my legs and torso. "Either they make me look like a hooker or folks think I'm Amish. Everything is too short, even when it's long." I marveled at my admission and realized imperfect Rex was easier to talk to than perfect Rex.

He bit his lip thoughtfully, like he was doing his best to consider my dilemma while also trying not to laugh. "Amish, huh?"

"Nothing against the Amish, but floral prints are a big no."

Rex grinned again, leaning back as though to survey my legs and torso. "You need custom clothes, stuff that's made specifically for your, uh, body. I have to do it too."

"Are you telling me you're going to send me tailor-made clothes? Dictate what I wear?"

"No. You'll get the clothes yourself, whatever you want, and send me the bill. I'll pay you for time spent shopping, or at the tailor's too. Think of the clothes as a uniform. They'd come with the job."

Well. When he put it like that . . .

I set the two pieces of pretzel on the bartop, absentmindedly trying to fit them together. "But, Rex, even with the right clothes, what makes you think I can do this? Movie premieres? *Galas*? I'm just a—"

"Don't call yourself a hick again." His voice dropped, his eyelids lowered by half, and the gruff demand made goose bumps rise on my arms.

"Fine." I threw my hands up. "I'm just a *country girl* from the middle of Texas, more comfortable in bars and barns than at soirees." I knew my place. Once, I'd tried to step out of it and paid the price for years. In fact, I was still paying.

"So what? I'm a country boy from the same place. We can be country together."

I looked him over, his impeccably styled hair, his BSE, his designer jeans. He may have been a country boy once, but now he looked sophisticated, worldly.

He seemed to understand what my perusal meant because he said, "They're just clothes. Part of the job."

"But—" I shook my head, at a loss.

"Are you worried about the time commitment? Your job here? I can work with your schedule. You don't have to go to every single event."

"I'm not worried about that. Walker won't mind. I trust I'll always have a place here even if I needed to take a break." Walker had hired me back once, no questions asked. I knew there'd always be a home for me at the Boozy Rancher. But I didn't like the idea of lying to Walker.

"If you want to give it a go on a trial basis, I have a rehearsal dinner tonight and wedding tomorrow in town. You're welcome to attend and see what it'd be like."

I scratched my chin, considering the offer. "Tonight?"

"Are you working?"

"No."

"Do you have plans?"

"Just with a fly." That wasn't precisely true. I still had a few orders to finish for my Etsy shop and a crap ton of inventory to make for the holiday shows.

He grinned and then dipped his chin to his chest, like he didn't want to share his smile. "I'll write down the address for you, and you still have my number, right?"

"Yes. I have it." He'd insisted on giving me his cell phone number and personal email address yesterday before leaving my apartment, writing them down on a sticky note. I'd put the square between the pages of my inherited copy of Edgar Allen Poe's complete works because I didn't plan to use either of them, but I didn't want to throw away the slip of paper either.

Rex lifted his eyes to mine again, the grin mostly gone, now just a twist of luscious lips. "No pressure. If you want to come, give it a try with no strings attached, I'll pay you . . . I don't know, a thousand?"

"ONE THOUSA—" I started to yell but then caught the words. Forgetting myself, I leaned closer and whispered harshly, "One thousand dollars?! For two dates?"

"No. One thousand per date. So, two thousand for tonight and tomorrow."

I was stunned. And my ears were ringing. And I couldn't catch my breath. I could really, *really* use two thousand dollars. "Are you kidding?"

"No. Plus whatever clothes you buy, if you want to buy any."

I gaped at him, doubly dumbfounded. One thousand dollars for one night? For me to show up and eat free food? For me to hang on his arm and wear new clothes? *What is this life?* Nothing about it was my fantasy, except maybe the free food and money part, but the whole setup certainly sounded like *someone's* fantasy.

And I really, REALLLY need that money.

A voice in the back of my head reminded me of the hard-earned lesson, *If it seems too good to be true, it is,* and I swallowed against a rising trepidation. There had to be a catch.

He studied me while I grappled with his offer, eventually asking softly, "Why the hesitation? Is it me?"

"No. You're—I mean, it's not you. It's—" I gave my head several firm shakes to clear it, feeling like I was forgetting something important "—how would this work in the long run? Would it be one thousand per event? Hourly? Would there be a contract? Is there dental?"

"Do you need dental?" He glanced at my teeth.

"Not necessarily. I'm just trying to understand how it'll work. This is a lot." And it felt like there had to be a catch, a shoe that would drop at the very worst moment, a hidden footnote spelling doom.

And yet, though I was certain this deal could not possibly be as straightforward as he made it sound, I *was* considering his offer. It felt overwhelming. I knew it would be a disruption to the quiet existence I'd carved out, so maybe that was the catch?

Maybe the disruption to my orderly life was the catch.

"If you agreed, you could write your own ticket," he said. "I'll put it into the prenup, whatever you want. I promise."

This promise didn't put me at ease. In fact, it had the opposite effect. It made me feel like maybe I was taking advantage of him.

"Have you really thought about this? I mean, marriage?" I blurted, feeling agitated and restless. "Lying to your family?"

"I have and I'm fine with it."

His statement surprised me, especially how quickly and simply he said the words.

"Really?" I asked, disbelieving. "Would they come to the wedding? What about holidays? Will we attend every Thanksgiving and Christmas, pretending like we're married? How is that going to work?"

"Even if it—this—were real, I wouldn't invite them to the wedding. I have to work Thanksgivings, and I haven't spent a Christmas with my dad or siblings since before college." Rex's tone was flat and hard, as were his eyes.

I frowned, considering what I knew about him and his somewhat tangled family tree. Rex's brother and sister were significantly older than him and the product of his father's first marriage. Rex was the only child of his father's second marriage, which had been short and resulted in a messy divorce. To my knowledge, Rex had never been close with his older siblings. Before his mother had passed away, I knew Rex was more like the parent in that relationship.

Same with his father. Rex had been the responsible, serious child to his father's gregarious, fun-loving personality. I liked Rex's dad, everyone in Alenbach did. But Rex's father was now on his fourth marriage, or maybe fifth. His current wife had been a flight attendant before marrying Rex's dad and—what little I knew about her from my high school friends who still lived in our hometown—seemed really nice.

"What about your Aunt Sally?" I supposed I could understand Rex's antipathy toward his half-siblings and maybe even his father, but Rex's Aunt Sally was a different story.

From all outward appearances, Rex's aunt on his father's side had been the only constant and steady adult influence in his life.

The hard lines around his mouth and eyes softened. I thought I detected a smidge of regret. "She wants me settled. This should make her happy."

"But why get married at all? Why not just—why not just get engaged?"

He shook his head stubbornly. "Engagements are broken. Marriage is supposed to be permanent. I want a permanent fix, I want to end the speculation and attention. Even when we divorce—whenever you've had enough—the situation will still be permanently resolved because we were married."

"You're telling me I can end this whenever I want?"

"Yes. Absolutely. I'll write that into the prenup. The moment you want to stop, we stop."

I couldn't quite draw a full breath. "Rex—"

"No, listen a second. It would be such a *relief*, to not have to think about it anymore." His voice roughened and my heart squeezed. "You would be doing me a favor. To stop the pundits. To have someone I trust there, with me, at these events, someone who isn't going to make me look like a fool after the fact."

Ugh. He needed me.

Unable to help myself, I placed my hand on Rex's shoulder and rubbed a comforting circle on his back. I forgot for a moment who he was and saw only his sadness, his frustration, someone who needed help.

"You could never look like a fool," I tried to soothe, then regretted the words immediately because they were inane. Of course he could look like a fool. Anyone alive or dead could look like a fool, the only requirement for looking like a fool was being human.

And you've never really thought of Rex as a human until yesterday, did you?

The realization and the associated surge of guilt gave me a stomachache. Why are people built this way? Why do we give power to those we admire regardless of whether we know them personally? Our admiration turns them into a thing, a two-dimensional representation of our hopes and expectations rather than a living, breathing person. Shame on you, Abby.

Great. Now I'm back to shame.

"You have no idea," he said, chuckling again, the sound bitter.

"Okay. You're right. Anyone can be a fool, or look like a fool, or act like a fool." I withdrew my hand from his back and leaned my elbows on the bar, staring forward at the orange Halloween lights zigzagging across the shelves. "But, if it's any consolation, at least you don't have a fly obsessed with your feet."

He breathed a surprised laugh—this one sounded genuinely amused, which had been my goal—and I felt his eyes on my profile. "You're good at that."

"It's a natural gift. I didn't do anything to my feet and the fly is obsessed."

"No." He laughed again, elbowing my arm in a move that would've sent me into an apocalyptic fit as a teenager, but which merely caused a warm burst in my stomach at present. "You're good at distracting folks from self-pity, lifting their spirits."

"All bartenders are." I twisted to look at him, leaving just one elbow on the bar and cupping my cheek in my palm. "At least, good bartenders are. A good bartender will let you know when it's time to stop drinking without ever saying a thing. Sometimes people just need an ear, a placeholder for—for . . ."

That's it! *A placeholder.* That's what he was asking for. *I already know how to do that, I do it every time I go to work, right here.*

But did I want to be Rex's placeholder? Keeping the bench warm for the woman who would eventually have his heart?

Why not? You don't really know him. Given how disastrous my first marriage was, it wasn't like I wanted his heart—or anyone else's—for myself. *And even if you did want it, and somehow through divine intervention won it, think of all the pressure, the changes, THE UPHEAVAL!*

But this business proposition would have an end date. I would decide when it ended, and then I could go back to my normal life.

"A placeholder for what?" Rex drummed his fingers on the bar to get my attention and suddenly he refilled my vision.

I must've spaced out. "Sorry. I was just thinking."

"Good. Think about it. Take your time. No rush." He grabbed another pretzel, adding, "There's no harm in thinking."

CHAPTER 8

"Those who don't believe in magic will never find it."

— ROALD DAHL

"What am I doing?" I muttered to myself, swallowing the tangle of nerves in my throat and gripping the steering wheel too tight.

A gate already decked out in Christmas garlands, lights, and red bows as well as a guard looking anything but cheerful loomed before me. I didn't have the mental energy to judge the preemptive seasonal decorations, though I usually would. Decorating for Christmas before Halloween was akin to buying a wedding dress before having a fiancé. . . is my opinion. Not that you asked.

But enough about my festive biases. In order to get through the gate, I had to get through the guard, and I wasn't 100 percent sure I was at the right place. My car's GPS had led me astray plenty of times in the past.

I wasn't even sure I wanted to be here.

Rex had left the Boozy Rancher without eating soup or a sandwich, likely because Walker no longer looked inclined to make him either.

But he did write down the address for the rehearsal dinner tonight. He also told me he'd arranged for a mobile detailing service to clean my car tomorrow morning and would be in touch about getting the door handle fixed before he left on Sunday, no matter what I decided about his proposal.

The news about the car was timely because Kaylee cornered me as soon as I'd arrived home, lying in wait outside my apartment and wanting to know *why in holy hell* the car had smelled like a vomitorium.

I didn't ask how she'd know what a vomitorium smelled like, I think we can all agree it would smell something like the inside of our car. I'd told her the truth.

"I drove a drunk friend home and he threw up in the car. But don't worry because he's sending a mobile unit to have it washed and detailed in the morning. By the way, can I borrow the car tonight?"

She'd agreed immediately. "Go for it. I'm not driving that pukemobile again until after it's been cleaned." She hadn't noticed the passenger-side door handle, but I pointed it out, promising it would be fixed soon.

Presently, I didn't have to roll down the window as I approached the prematurely festive gate and the sullen guard because it was already open.

Smiling as he approached my stinky car, I said, "Hi there."

He did not smile. "Name?"

My smile fell. "Abby—uh—Abigail McNerny." I squirmed in my seat as he peered at me and then lowered his eyes to the tablet in his hands, scanning the screen. I had no idea whether or not I was on any guest list, even if this was the right place. Not wanting him to think I was a party crasher, I blurted, "I'm not sure if I'm on the list, I was just invited this afternoon by my, uh, friend. He—"

"You have ID?" he asked without looking up.

"My name is there?"

He nodded, still not looking up. "ID, please."

With relieved fingertips, I pulled my driver's license out of my wallet and handed it over. He took it, read it, looked at me, then examined my car before saying, "When I open the gate, keep going straight until you get to the circle drive. There's valet for your car. Leave the keys on the dash."

"Oh. Okay. Thanks."

He'd already turned and was walking back to the little gatehouse. He must've pressed a button because the gate swung open not a second later. Giving him a little wave for no reason other than it seemed like the polite thing to do, I followed the winding road. Sure enough, a little ways down the driveway became a circle, and beyond that was the biggest house I'd ever seen.

It was, legit, a mansion. It reminded me of something out of a Jane Austen movie, just with Texas sensibilities. Turrets lit from below stretched into the night sky, and it appeared to be built entirely of some kind of pale stone, currently shadowed except where the ground lights made it glow white. The entrance was framed by a big arch and the single, ginormous wooden door looked like it belonged on a castle. *The glazing on the windows alone must've cost a fortune! And the chimney piece!*

"What am I doing?" I murmured, marking maybe the hundredth time I'd whispered the words to myself since leaving my apartment.

Rolling up the window, I cut the engine and placed the keys on the dash. I glanced down at my puffy black winter coat and dress. I owned two dresses, this black one I had on, which I wore to funerals, formal occasions at night, and Christmas service, and a pink one for Easter, afternoon weddings, and bridal showers. They were almost exactly the same except for their color: A hemline that fell just below the knee, a flowy skirt, a wide, fitted waist, a scoop neck that was what my mother would've called mildly immodest, and no sleeves. A serviceable black dress that could be dressed up or down with a wrap or sweater or jewelry or a pushup bra or heels.

I wore the pushup bra, glad I'd done so as I watched a woman in a sexy, gold, backless dress disappear inside on the arm of a man in a tux. I'd also opted for high heels, a pair of three-and-a-half-inch black spiked pumps with red soles—basically new in the box—I'd found at a Goodwill store just after Christmas last year.

I never had the chance to wear them anywhere, and I reasoned that it didn't matter if I towered over almost everyone else, Rex was six six.

And if he were five six, what difference did it make? I never went anywhere fancy, and the shoes wanted to be worn!

And yet, thinking about the woman's stylish gold dress just now, I wondered if serviceable plus cleavage plus second-hand heels would be enough. I'd spent the later part of the afternoon trying to argue myself out of taking Rex up on his generous, too-good-to-be-true offer. I wanted to help him, and the money would definitely help me.

Here I was, twenty-eight, no family, no security, no savings, still burdened with tons of debt left over from my divorce. I was just two years away from paying off the court-ordered amount, but I still hadn't paid back Walker and Kaylee the money they'd loaned me to claw out of the hole my ex-husband and my stupidity had left me in.

Even if Rex were a loathsome slag and I didn't want to do him any favors, the money he offered for one fake date was insane for a single night's work. Two thousand dollars for two nights of standing around would make a huge difference to my peace of mind. I'd finally be able to start paying back Walker.

So why hadn't I jumped at the chance even if it was too good to be true? Studying the McMansion, now I knew the answer.

"I don't belong here," I whispered.

Heaving an audible breath, I reached for my keys, intent on leaving, but then flinched back, yelping inelegantly as a series of quick knocks rapped on my window, surprising the bejeezus out of me.

I pressed a hand to my chest and turned wide eyes out my window, finding a man just suddenly *there*. A man in a black wool coat and dark suit with his hand moving toward the outside handle of the door.

"Gail McNerny, open this door," a man's voice demanded. In the next second, he'd bent at the waist, his arm along the roof as he braced himself and peeked in the window.

I gaped, blinking at the face of a man who resembled a boy I used to know. "Cyrus?"

"Abigail," he drawled, lifting a black eyebrow over an emerald-colored eye. "Why are you just sitting there? Are you getting out or what?"

I laughed in wonder, unclicking my seat belt and opening the door.

He stepped back, giving me room to exit but not waiting until I'd closed the door to wrap me in a hug.

"What are you doing here?" I returned his hug, still laughing. Disbelief had me pulling away so I could look at him again.

He held my hands out and looked me over. "Woman. Look at you, you're gorgeous."

"Well, look at yourself. You're gorgeous." And he was. He looked like the movie star he'd become, with his dark hair styled so elegantly, green eyes glittering under starlight, and square jaw with the little cleft at the chin. The black stubble dotting his cheeks only lent him extra swagger, like a pirate.

So I said, "You look like a pirate."

"Thank you." He grinned, as though I'd given him the most superlative compliment ever imagined and dropped my hands while offering his elbow. "And did you notice? I'm finally taller than you."

Straightening my back, I said, "If I weren't in heels, maybe by a half inch."

"Two. At least."

I laughed, shaking my head, unable to believe Cyrus was just suddenly *here*. I supposed time really did change people, or maybe time gave past events less importance and weight.

"What are you doing here? Did Rex invite you too?" I asked.

"Uh, no. *Rex* didn't invite me." He cast me a sidelong look. "I'm part of the wedding party. We just got back from the church and everyone is supposed to be inside mingling before dinner. I was walking in before you pulled up."

"You're part of the wedding party?" All at once, I recalled why I was here and what tonight was—a rehearsal dinner—and without me noticing, we were walking toward the house. Cyrus had led me away from my car and now we were almost to the big castle door.

And then I remembered what I'd just said about Rex inviting Cyrus too, which implied that Rex had invited me, which meant—

"Do you know who's getting married tomorrow?" he asked. "Whose rehearsal dinner this is?"

I ducked my head and admitted, "I do not. I was invited just this afternoon, and I didn't ask."

"And Rex invited you, I know."

"You know?"

"Oh yes. I *know.*"

I stared straight ahead, working to squash my skipping heart. Something about his tone had me wondering if he really did know. Rex had said I couldn't tell anyone, but had he told Cyrus? Before I could debate how best to respond, the castle door opened and a man in a black suit, black tie, and white shirt motioned us forward. He held a tablet similar to the guard at the gate.

"Names, please?"

I opened my mouth to answer, but Cyrus covered my hand on his elbow, speaking for both of us. "Cyrus Malcom and Abigail McNerny, Rex McMurtry's plus one."

Not sparing me a glance, the man smiled at Cyrus. "Of course. Mr. McMurtry has just arrived. Champagne and caviar on the heated terrace, right through those doors. Gift bags will be placed in your car before you depart. Please leave your coats with the attendant. Thank you, Mr. Malcom. Have a pleasant evening."

Cyrus gave the man a nod while I swallowed around a renewed bubble of nerves. Champagne? Caviar? Heated terraces and attendants for coats? *What the heck am I doing here?*

I allowed myself to be led to a woman dressed in a black suit, black tie, and white shirt who must've been the attendant as she took my coat and passed me a ticket. I placed it in my black wrist zipper bag while she *attended to* Cyrus. Like the fella at the door, she only seemed to have eyes for him, and that suited me just fine. Being invisible helped me relax a little.

If walking around with Rex was anything like walking around with Cyrus, I'd basically just be a warm, faceless body. A placeholder. My confidence grew. *I can do placeholder!*

I turned in the direction of the promised heated terrace and craned my neck to sneak a peek, trying not to take note of the massive, arching, glossy marble entryway I currently stood within or the arrangements of fresh winter blossoms lining the hall. Looking straight ahead would keep me from appearing like an overwhelmed hic—I mean, a country bumpkin.

"May I?" Cyrus, standing at my left side, offered his elbow again.

I gave him my best serene smile and nodded, slipping my hand over the fine material of his suit.

After a few steps, he leaned to my ear and whispered, "You remember Jason Kepler? From high school?"

"Uh. . . yes." It took a moment, but I remembered him.

Jason Kepler had been on the football team with Cyrus and Rex, but I couldn't recall much else about him other than he seemed to be a nice enough guy and his grandfather had been buried in a Lincoln Spruce midnight blue casket with white velvet interior. My mother had been exceedingly proud of upselling his surviving family on the casket.

"This is his engagement party. He's marrying Amy Arensberg, the singer. This is her house."

I nodded once, keeping my eyes forward while I processed this information. I barely remembered Jason, but everyone knew who Amy Arensberg was. Her last three albums had been huge all over the world.

Cyrus's gaze seemed to inspect my profile as we navigated around a giant arrangement of poinsettias and evergreen garlands. When I said nothing, he whispered, "You don't seem surprised."

I sent him a quick glance. "I am surprised. How'd they even meet?"

He chuckled, drawing my attention again. I found him watching me with a sorta sly look. "Rex, of course. Everyone meets the woman they're going to marry through Rex."

Giving nothing of my thoughts away—since my thoughts were presently tripping all over themselves—I faced forward again as we approached a staircase leading down to the terrace. The noise of conversation reached a crescendo and was entwined with classical music while I found myself looking slightly down at the promised heated terrace. Maybe a hundred or more people, all dressed in formal attire, milled around the space, forming little groups sipping on champagne.

Like the rest of the entry, the six-step staircase and the terrace floor were polished marble, but instead of black and white checkerboard, everything was crisp white—the walls, the long sheer drapes, even the window frames. Decorations, food, and people were the only source of color. A few big and tall fellas were scattered in with the crowd, but I spotted Rex immediately, a jolt of warmth weaving itself into a tight ball in my stomach. His back was to us, and his brown head rose above almost everyone else, his wide shoulders and back straight beneath an elegantly cut dark suit jacket.

"I see Rex, over there." Cyrus lifted his chin. "Shall we?"

Breathing in through my nose, I inclined my head and super-glued on an aloof expression. "I'll follow you."

Ignoring Cyrus's frequent glances while he steered us toward Rex, I reminded myself that it didn't matter if I belonged here with all these fancy people because I wasn't really here. I was a placeholder, a stand-in, a fact firmly cemented as Cyrus was frequently stopped, hugged, smiled at, and talked to while I might as well have been furniture (which suited me just fine). By the time we made it to Rex twenty or so minutes later, Cyrus's smile looked forced, and I was almost fully at ease.

He glanced at me one more time, placing his hand over mine on his elbow and whispering, "Wow. You did great."

I fought the urge to laugh, whispering back, "I didn't do anything but smile politely and say nothing."

"And look stunning. Here we are."

Cyrus reached up and tapped Rex on the shoulder, smoothly insinuating both of us into the circle of people gathered around Rex as the big guy turned. My lungs tightened with a surge of . . . something. Like if anticipation and nausea and excitement and fear had an orgy, giving birth to a baby, and that baby had cold hands that could reach into your chest and squeeze your lungs. Yeah. Like that.

As Rex faced us, what I noticed first was how this here was the granite version of Rex from high school. Rex "TW" McMurtry, slightly removed, intensity behind his hazel eyes replaced with a disinterested gruffness.

But then, as his attention settled on Cyrus, a crack formed. Recognition gave way to a glimmer of relief and sardonic humor peeked through, the faintest hint of the Rex from my apartment and the guy who'd propositioned me earlier in the day. *Human Rex.*

He placed a hand on Cyrus's shoulder, the corner of his luscious lips angling upward by scant millimeters. "You get lost?"

Ugh. I loved his voice. It was so deep. *Baritone.*

"Took us forever to get across the room," Cyrus grumbled, curling his fingers around mine and lowering his arm so that we held hands.

The movement had Rex glancing at me—he was *the first* person to spare me even a glance since we'd walked in. Immediately, he stood straighter, the mask of affability slipping away. His eyes widened as they moved over me.

"Abby." My name sounded a little winded and Rex stepped forward, his hand coming to my arm as he turned his back on the circle of people. On autopilot, I dropped Cyrus's hand and allowed Rex to steer me to the side.

Pulling me in front of him such that we faced each other and only each other, he stared at me, his mouth open like words were on the tip of his tongue. I waited for him to speak. He didn't.

One would think, after all the epic stare downs he'd administered over the last two days during our short time together, his prolonged looking wouldn't affect me, but it did. I couldn't place these stares. I didn't know what they meant, what he was thinking.

He looked absorbed, deep in thought, and yet completely focused. As usual, the longer he persisted in silence, the more uncomfortable I felt. Faintly, I heard Cyrus clear his throat.

Unable to bear it any longer, I said, "Fancy meeting you here."

A whisper of a smile lit behind his eyes and he bent toward me, stepping into my space. I sucked in a spiky breath as his warm body brushed against my front and his lips found my ear.

"I'm so glad you came," he whispered. The words elicited a shiver. He then pulled away and said to Cyrus, "Thank you."

I didn't hear if Cyrus made any response, I was too busy working to recover from the pinprickly sensation of his hot breath falling on my neck. Nor did he give me time to fully recover before deftly wrapping an arm around my waist and pressing me to his side. I fit perfectly, and the arm was the only reason I didn't melt into a pile of goo on the floor.

"You don't have champagne," he said, his hazel eyes warmly

inspecting me. Lowering his voice, he bent to my ear again and said, "Something for me to remedy."

I shivered again, my heart going crazy, and I tumbled headfirst into a hot flash when the loud minority wackadoodle part of my personality made a list of all the other items I wouldn't mind Rex remedying. But then the silent majority brain stakeholder tugged on the proverbial reins before the list grew too long (or illicit).

Stop it, Abby. Get yourself together.

What the heck was wrong with me? I was an adult woman for hootenanny's sake. *Not* a lust-sick teenager. So he'd pressed me to his side with his big, muscly, scrumptious arm. So what? So he was good at sounding sexy without meaning to. So what? So he smelled fantastic. So what?

So you're doing a favor for Rex, being paid to be here and play a part, that's what. Don't make selfish lists or lose your wits.

I'd barely managed to force down the rising blush when Rex used his leverage on me to turn us both away from his circle and toward the tables in the center of the long room.

Inhaling a steadying breath, I followed where he led, the room parting for us. Unlike Cyrus, people didn't stop Rex to engage in chitchat. Looking up at his face, the reason was obvious. His eyes were slightly narrowed, and he wore an expression I'd called the *fuck-off-not-now* face when we were in middle school. Eventually, we stopped next to a tall table covered in full champagne glasses. Releasing me, he plucked one from the table and held it out.

"I didn't think you'd come," he murmured, placing the drink in my hand. His eyes moved over my face.

The effect of his pointed attentions, plus the previous placement of his arm, had my stomach swirling all over again, so I brain-chanted, *It's an act, Abby. Pretend. Play your part.*

"It seemed like a low-risk way to give this a try." I smiled, working to shake off the whirlwind of hot and cold racing through my system.

His eyebrows pulled together slightly. "Give this a try?"

I widened my eyes with meaning. When his confusion persisted, I stepped forward, successfully resisted the urge to sniff him, and whispered, "You know. The fake date thing."

Leaning away, I found he'd dropped his eyes to the floor, his smile waxy as it waned. "Ah yes. That thing."

Rex nodded. He took a deep breath. He nodded again.

Inspecting his ticking jaw, I frowned. "Is there anything wrong?"

"No. Not at all," he said lightly and lifted his attention to someplace over my head. "Your timing was impeccable."

"Was it?" I sipped the champagne. Liking the taste, I took another drink.

"Yes. It was." His slipped his hand into mine and kept us connected by threading our fingers together.

"How so?" I licked my lips and then took another drink, surveying Rex's face.

His marble exterior I knew so well had returned. I supposed he was also playing a part, and the thought helped settle the remainder of my jitters. We could pretend together. I found Gruff Rex much easier to navigate as Fake Date Abby than New Rex. New Rex made me want to be Real Abby, and Real Abby had no business getting real with any Rex.

His gaze settled on me, a caustic-looking curve on his lips. "People always want to set me up."

"Set you up?"

"With their sisters, cousins, nieces, friends."

"But no mothers? What's wrong with their mothers?" I went to take another drink of my champagne and found the glass empty. *When did that happen?*

"That's a great question." His mouth tugged to one side, the curve no longer caustic, and he chuckled. "I'm glad you came, Abby."

"Me too." I placed my empty flute on the tray with the full ones and scooped up a second glass. "This shit—uh, sorry—this champagne is delicious."

He chuckled again, his eyelids lowering by half as he watched me take another drink. "I can't—shouldn't—have any. So I'll have to take your word for it."

"Oh! Do I get to be your liquor sampler at these things? I never drink."

"Really? And you work at a bar."

"But that's just it, right? People who work at Disneyland don't go to Disneyland. When is the last time you watched a football game for fun? To enjoy it?" I glanced at the glass in my hand, finding it half empty.

Maybe I was just thirsty? I promised myself I'd sip the remainder, but I'd be lying if I said the champagne hadn't been welcome. For one thing, the act of talking to and standing close to Rex while he donned this sexy suit didn't seem quite so disruptive to my brain function while I drank champagne. And for another thing, I was no longer feeling angsty or inadequate about my dress.

Social lubricant, indeed.

"I can't remember the last time I watched a football game for any reason other than work."

"Oh, the irony, am I right?" I tipped my glass toward him, grinning because I felt like grinning. "Once something you enjoy becomes a job, you stop doing the thing for enjoyment."

His eyes fastened to my smile. "I still enjoy football."

"Right, just like I—clearly—still enjoy champagne. But it's also my job."

Rex gently relieved me of my second glass, which—despite the earlier pledge to myself—had also inexplicably become empty. "Champagne is your job?"

"Booze is my job." I patted his chest. "And now you are too."

Rex gave me a quizzical grin, his gaze moving over my face as though mesmerized . . . or maybe conflicted. He looked not at all impervious or gruff. He looked . . . real.

Meanwhile, I was experiencing that initial thrill of warmth and euphoria that accompanied being buzzed. A sweet happiness, a cozy sinking and settling into a new reality bordered by possibility and optimism, where everything is funnier and everyone is better looking and happiness seems so entirely within reach.

No wonder turning water into wine was the first miracle in the New Testament. *Jesus for the win!* Or I guess Mary, since she'd asked him to do it.

Rex licked his lips and he opened his mouth. But before any words arrived, we were interrupted by someone tugging on his shoulder and someone else gripping my arm.

"Oh my God! Gail? Abigail McNerny! Cyrus said it was you and it's you!" A medium-sized woman wrapped her arms around me, thereby forcing me to let go of Rex's hand. "It's me! Rachel! Remember? From lunch? We sat at the same table sometimes."

"Oh, oh. Yes. Hi." I nodded profusely, remembering Rachel at once, but not because we'd shared the same lunch table a few times. Rachel McQuaid, the girl I'd swapped seats with at our graduation, so she could sit next to Rex.

"It's okay, I changed my hair." She flipped the ends of her black bob, giggling. "This is my husband, Tom Marie. I changed my last name, so I'm Rachel Marie now. Tom, this is Gail."

I turned to find a tall, nice-looking man with kind brown eyes holding out his hand. We quickly exchanged pleasantries as Rachel Marie explained, "Gail went to high school with us." Then to me she said, "Tom and Rex played ball together in college. That's how we met." She gestured to her husband.

"I see," I said, even though I didn't. Maybe she and Rex had become friendly the summer after our senior year?

She beamed at Rex, then at me. "It's so awesome you two are together!"

"Rachel," Tom said, a gentle rebuke.

"I always thought you two would be cute together. You're both so tall!" She laughed, ignoring her husband and reaching up to tap my shoulder teasingly. "I should've let you sit next to Rex at graduation, but it all worked out for the best. If I hadn't dated Rex, then I never would've met my Tom."

Ohhhh. So. . . Rachel and Rex dated. Oddly, this tidbit did nothing to deflate my champagne buzz. Perhaps because Rachel had truly been a sweetheart in high school. I kinda liked the idea of someone like Rachel ending up with Rex. He deserved a sweetheart.

Tom smiled at his wife indulgently and then it turned apologetic as he faced me and Rex. "So how'd you two reconnect?" he asked, obviously anxious to change the subject away from their origin story.

Rex glanced at me, and I took that as my cue to start earning my one thousand dollars. "Well, it's kind of a crazy story."

Rachel's grin widened. "I can't wait to hear it."

"I'm a bartender at this little place downtown, and—"

"Oh! What's the name? We love downtown Austin. So quirky, right Tom?" Rachel appealed to her husband.

"It's called the Boozy Rancher," I said. "The sign has a cowboy and—"

"Yes! I know that one. Okay, so what happened?" Rachel softly poked at my arm, prodding me to continue the story.

"Okay, so, we were an hour away from closing when in walks this guy." The back of my hand lightly hit Rex's stomach, and I'd planned to withdraw it after the playful gesture. I really did!

But instead, I let it linger, my knuckles moving up and down his shirtfront, and his abdominal muscles. I don't know what possessed me to do it, only that once I started with the knuckle-stomach caress, I couldn't seem to stop.

"So you walked into her bar?" Tom asked Rex, looking delighted.

Rex nodded and caught my errant hand, bringing it to his lips and kissing the back of it. "Yes. I was with a priest and a rabbi," he said stoically.

Tom and Rachel laughed while I struggled to concentrate under the heady burden of Rex's hot, soft lips brushing against my knuckles.

"And the rest is history," I said a little breathlessly.

Rachel made a face of disappointment. "I thought you said it was a crazy story."

"Rachel," came another of Tom's placid rebukes. "Don't you think it's crazy that Rex walked into the bar where she works? That's pretty random."

"I don't think it's crazy," Rachel said, crossing her arms. "Now, if there'd been a bar fight or something."

I snapped the fingers Rex didn't hold and pointed at Rachel. "Great idea. I'll add that to the story. Or there's a robbery!"

"Yes. Add that." Tom laughed. "Rex walks in while you're being robbed and he saves you."

"Or he's being robbed and I save him. *Hmm?*"

"That's good." Rachel nodded, clapping her hands together.

I faced Rex, grinning up at him. "You don't mind, do you darling? If every time I tell this story, I make it crazier and crazier?"

Rex gave my knuckles another kiss, a hint of a smile peeking out from behind where he still held my hand. "Whatever makes you happy, babe."

Babe.

I found myself transfixed. Caught in the very real snare of his pretend term of endearment, and his pretend happy gaze, and his pretend kisses on my hand, and our pretend closeness while his gorgeous hazel eyes pretend twinkled down at me.

A lovely but confused warmth stretched and bloomed in my stomach, coiling and uncoiling, asking the champagne to dance. Our eyes remained locked and the amusement behind his features became something markedly less benign and quite a bit hotter. Or, I guess, pretend hotter.

He's so good at this. Oh my goodness. *Is this what it's going to be like every time we go someplace?* Honestly, Rex fake acting like he adored me felt a lot stronger than two glasses of champagne.

"Aww." Rachel's appreciative sound snapped me out of my stupor, and I tore my eyes from his, blinking our audience back into focus. "You two are the absolute cutest! I am so happy for you both. So relieved to see Rex with someone as awesome as you, Gail."

I managed a smile. But this time I gave into the blush because I was now legit breathless. I couldn't fight the surge of heat cresting over my cheeks while also concentrating on my lungs, keeping myself from panting like—oh, you know—any animal in heat.

"Abby. Not Gail," Rex said, lowering my hand but still holding it. I felt his eyes on me as he added softly, "She goes by Abby now."

CHAPTER 9

"Yes, of course duct tape works in a near-vacuum. Duct tape works anywhere. Duct tape is magic and should be worshiped."

— ANDY WEIR, *THE MARTIAN*

I like to think of myself as a master at non-reaction.

Rex's playful touches, his long, hot looks, his cornucopia of endearments—babe, beautiful, dearest, sugar—had all required me to up my game. For every one of his adorable, sexy, sweet assaults, I'd had to maneuver, evade, and cope until I'd finally settled into a rhythm. I bobbed and weaved, shutting down my heart before it took his pretending too seriously. Several times, I had no choice but to go on the offensive.

He kissed the back of my hand, and I kissed his cheek.

He kissed my cheek, and I kissed his neck.

He kissed my neck, while standing behind me—his warm, solid front pressed to my back, an arm wrapped around my middle, a hand on my stomach—and I excused myself to the bathroom and did deep breathing exercises.

After dinner, Rex stayed with me until I had my coat and my car was pulled around, making me promise to message him in the morning. Slipping into my car exhausted, I exhaled my relief. I then immediately regretted the exhale because my car reeked of vomit on the inhale. Gagging, I rolled down the window and held my breath, freezing air pummeling my face all the way home. I didn't mind, the frigid breeze a godsend, clearing my head and heart of residual heady warmth and replacing it with cold sobriety.

Could I do this again? I had no idea.

Did I want to? Heck yeah.

And thus was my dilemma. As I programmed Rex's number into my phone, as I went to sleep, as I awoke super early and rode my bike to the pottery studio to finish up the cauldron mugs and special orders, as I ate my breakfast at the picnic table outside the studio just past 10:30 a.m., I couldn't make up my mind about what to do.

I needed to call Rex. He didn't have my number, and I promised him I'd call.

If you do this, before you agree, you have to tell Rex about Declan and your divorce. My stomach soured at the thought. But then the sick feeling suddenly dissipated. Perhaps Declan was—for once in his miserable life—the answer.

Yanking out my phone before I could give the matter any more thought, I selected Rex's cell number and dialed.

Yes. Once Rex hears the truth, he'll change his mind about you, and then the decision will be made for you. NICE!

Rex answered on the forth ring. "Hello?" He sounded wary, and I heard metal clinking against metal in the background, he was probably in a gym or lifting weights.

"It's Abby."

"Oh! Hi." He no longer sounded wary. "Did you get home okay?"

"I did. Thanks. So, I'm calling about tonight." I clicked the lid back on my Tupperware and slid it into my food sack.

"Are you coming?" A door opened and closed on his side of the call, the sound of the weight machines abruptly stifled. He must've left the gym or gone somewhere more private.

"First, I need to tell you about me—I mean, I need to tell you something about my past that is likely to make you rescind your offer."

Talking about this subject always made my stomach turn and I was determined to avoid sharing unnecessary details. But I wouldn't avoid the truth or taking responsibility for my stupid decisions.

"O-okay?"

I gathered a deep breath for courage and mentally distanced myself from what I was about to say. "Here it is: I am divorced. My ex-husband was a con artist and stole a lot of money from a bunch of important people. When we divorced, a portion of his overall debts were given to me, and I had to declare bankruptcy. I also had to go to jail for a short while since they thought I was in on the scam, but when they figured out I was just an idiot who'd also been conned, they let me out. I've been paying back the money for going on nine years and I still have two years left."

Unsurprisingly, Rex was silent as he absorbed this. Checking my watch, I gave him a moment, then added around a growing thickness in my throat, "I completely understand if this information changes things. If we were to go through with your plan and get married, my past would undoubtedly come out, and it would look bad for you."

"No. No—wait. Let me . . ." I heard him breathe lightly. "Give me a minute."

"Sure." I pressed the phone to my ear using my shoulder and zipped up my food sack, checked around the table to ensure I hadn't left anything, then meandered back inside the studio. Giving my studio-mate Paul a friendly chin tilt, I walked to my backpack and stuffed the sack inside.

Other than me and Paul, no one else had opted to spend their Saturday morning in the studio. Over the summer, this place would be packed during the weekend. But fall had been unexpectedly—and uncharacteristically—cold this year. I imagined very few people wanted to spend Saturday in an unheated studio space, dipping their hands in chilly water and working to form cold clay.

"Abby."

I straightened, holding the phone with my hand again. "Rex."

"I have questions."

I frowned. "Okay."

"You said you've been paying the money back for nine years?"

"Yes."

"That means you were twenty when you divorced?"

"I was eighteen when I filed for divorce and went to jail for two months," I whispered, turning my back to Paul. "The bankruptcy was settled the year after."

Rex went silent again, but just for a moment. "How old were you when you got married?"

"Eighteen. The marriage only lasted three months."

Even through the phone I got the sense he had a million questions. Something about his pauses felt heavy, like he was weighing his words and they were a ton each.

"You knew about the con?" he asked.

"Nope. I thought he was real." I'd been so colossally, monumentally, breathtakingly stupid and trusting and naïve.

He made an abrupt grunting sound. "We'll discuss it tonight."

That gave me pause. I'd been so certain he would call everything off. "Are you sure? What if we're photographed together? Or someone—"

"Other than your . . . past, is there any other reason you don't want to come?"

"I mean—no. But—"

"Good. I'll text you the address. Oh, and I'm supposed to tell you, the theme is Cowboy-Cowgirl Christmas. Whatever the fuck that means." This last part was grumbled and pulled a smile from me. Rex had always been one who cussed freely. It was usually said on a grumble. Like now.

"I have boots and jeans. No problem. But Rex—"

"We'll talk tonight. See you at six. Sit on the groom's side."

My mouth still open to lodge a protest, the telltale sound of Rex ending the call clicked through to my side. Rearing back, I stared at the screen of my phone, frowning at his abrupt and gruff goodbye.

Actually, he hadn't said goodbye at all, had he? He'd just hung up without giving me the chance to say anything at all. As I frowned at the phone, his promised message came through with the address, but then he sent three others.

Rex: Boots, jeans, and red and green flannel is what I was told

Rex: Hats also ok

Rex: I'll meet you outside the church at 6. Be there

"Well, good luck with the opening!" I scooched to the right side of the back seat, giving Henry an encouraging smile as he pulled up to the curb. "I'm sure you'll do great."

"Hey, thanks Abby." His blue eyes met mine in the rearview mirror and I opened the back door. "And good luck to you too."

Hooking my mouth to the side, I laughed. "I'm going to need it, right?"

Henry also laughed and turned around as I unfolded from the car. "You'll do great. Have more faith in yourself!" he called after me.

I bent down so I could peer into his car one more time. "I will! No more doubting. I'll get those things made for the holiday markets. And I'm so sorry about your cat. After seventeen years, that must've been so hard."

Henry gave me a sad smile. "Hey, what can we do? Life is fragile."

"It is," I agreed, feeling his angst but hoping my commiseration helped in some small way.

His smile brightened as we swapped stares and he gave me a friendly nod, which I returned. I then shut the door, feeling a bit better about everything in general.

"Who was that?"

"Ah!" I sucked in a startled breath, flailing as I spun to find Rex standing directly behind me on the sidewalk. His eyes were focused beyond my shoulder, frowning at the taillights of the Nissan Leaf pulling back into traffic.

"Gosh, you scared me." My hand on my chest, I chuckled as I shook my head, working to dispel the spike in adrenaline.

"Who was that?" he repeated. Rex's hazel glare shifted to my face, two frown lines etched deeply between his eyebrows.

I gulped. "I—what? Who?"

"That guy who dropped you off."

"Oh. His name is Henry."

"A friend of yours?"

"Henry? No. I just met him. He's an Uber driver."

"You just met him?" Some of the sternness leached from his features and was replaced by confusion. "Then how did you know about his cat dying?"

"Because we talked about it in the car." I pulled my fleece-lined flannel closer and crossed my arms against the cold. "It's so sad. I really think his vet's office took advantage of the situation and the fact that Henry is here all alone. If he had more family nearby, I think he'd be able to make decisions with a clearer head. But being by yourself, it's hard to lose any part of your support system, even a seventeen-year-old blind, deaf cat with diabetes and cancer. I mean, I get it, but . . . what? What's wrong? Do I have something on my face?"

I wiped at my mouth because that's where Rex was staring as a ghost of a smile tugged at his lips. I hoped I hadn't inadvertently spittled while I spoke. Owen—the dentist from Fridays at the bar—spittled while he spoke sometimes. I still hadn't figured out how to tell him gently, so he just kept on spittling all over the bartop which I'd taken to covering with napkins upon his arrival.

"You—" Rex's gaze traced a path from my eyes to my nose, mouth, chin, then back up, lips parting like a lot of words were on the tip of his tongue. Ultimately, he just shook his head. "Never mind. Come with me."

Grabbing my hand in his giant paw, he tugged me forward, but my feet stalled as soon as I spotted two women hurrying into the church.

"Oh no." I gestured to the two women walking in front of us. Green tank crop tops with the words *Jason & Amy* in red glitter on the back, blue and green flannel shirts tied around their waists, cutoff jean shorts, brown Stetson hats, and cowgirl boots.

"What's wrong?" Rex looked over his shoulder at me.

"Was I supposed to wear cutoffs? I missed the sexy cowgirl memo." I glanced down at my jean-clad legs, dark red and green flannel, and so did Rex. I gave him an apologetic look as his eyes moved over my long double braids draped over my shoulders.

"No, you didn't," he said, putting his hand on my back and pressing me forward.

"No, I didn't what?"

"Miss the memo."

"I—"

"What I mean is, there was no memo," he said gruffly, looking harassed. "Come."

Guiding me around the side of the massive church to a side door that had been propped open, he closed it behind us as soon as we entered. We then walked down a long, nondescript hallway with peach-colored walls and tight-weave corporate carpet. Eventually, we arrived at what looked like a general-purpose meeting room. It didn't have a conference table but rather a few gray folding tables pushed together in the center of the room with brown folding chairs surrounding it.

Once we were inside, he closed that door too. Then, pulling me around to face him, he let me go. But his arresting eyes held me in place.

Taking a deep breath, he said, "I think I have a way to solve the divorce problem."

That had me standing straighter. "Uh—"

"I can buy the story from your ex through a broker, make him think he's selling it to a paper. That will silence him as he won't be able to discuss it once he's sold it."

I could only stare at Rex as chaotic thoughts ping-ponged in my brain. This was *not* what I'd been expecting him to say.

He wasn't finished. "We'll give an exclusive to the Austin Sentinel after our wedding. I have a contact there who's friendly, and I'll proactively bring it up. Without your ex able to contradict the story, our version of events will be what people hear. Problem solved."

Stepping away from Rex, I shook my head. "I—I don't—" My hands came to my forehead, but then I remembered I had makeup on and dropped them. I didn't want to smudge anything important. "Rex, I don't want you to do that."

"Which part?"

"I certainly don't want Declan to profit from—"

"Other than the money part, which part is a problem for you?" he asked brusquely, reminding me of Kaylee and her mad lawyery skillz.

I could see we were about to negotiate, so I ticked my concerns off on my fingers. "First, you shouldn't have to pay for my mistakes. Second, Declan is a sleazeball. I don't want him making any money off me or you. Third, I don't want you lying to the press to—"

"Would I have to lie?" he cut in smoothly, his gaze straying from my face to conduct a quick sweep of my outfit again.

I glanced down, feeling a prick of uncertainty under his inspection. Fiddling with one of my long braids, I asked, "Is this—are you sure I look okay?"

"Perfect," he said curtly, his gaze—now cool and aloof—returned to mine. "You said you didn't know about your ex's illegal activities, so why would we lie to the press?"

"I didn't know about Declan's lies. I found out when—" A tight band squeezed my chest, and I breathed through it and the memory that caused it, forcing the feelings of bitterness and betrayal down, down, down. Calmly, I started again. "I found out when I was arrested."

He lifted his chin, inspecting me. I couldn't read his expression, but I thought maybe he looked . . . interested? Interest mixed with some empathy? "Do you mind telling me the whole story?"

I glanced at the door behind him. "Do we have time? Aren't you a groomsman?"

He wore boots like me, but also black pants and a white shirt with brown suspenders which did amazing things to highlight the broadness of his shoulders. It was a good look for him.

"It starts at seven thirty, I don't need to be anywhere until seven. We have time."

My stomach cinched itself tight as we stared at each other. I hadn't planned on telling him the whole story, just enough to make it clear how bad he'd look if we pretend married.

Rex's eyebrows lowered a scant millimeter and his gaze grew less careful, less aloof, more open, imploring. "What happened, Abby?" he asked, his voice deep and soft and lacking in all judgment.

Lifting my eyes to the speckled, paneled ceiling, I turned from Rex and meandered into the room. "Well, it's a funny story actually." It wasn't funny. It was tragic and made me look pathetic. *But if the shoe fits.* "I met Declan at the bar. He was a patron when I first started, used to flirt with me—"

"I thought you started at sixteen?" Rex's voice sounded close, like he'd followed me into the room.

I didn't turn. Instead, I walked to the nearest of the folding chairs and took a seat, already weary. "I did. And Walker banned him from the bar because he wouldn't stop."

"Good." Rex picked up a chair and brought it close to mine, sitting directly in front of me.

Working to ignore his steady perusal, I plowed forward numbly. "Declan showed up a few years later. I'd just graduated from high school and was working at the bar full time."

"You were eighteen?"

"Yes."

"And how old was he?"

"Thirty-one."

Rex turned his face away, but not fast enough. I'd caught the flare of disgust behind his eyes, the clenching of his jaw, and my lungs felt too tight.

Stuff it down, down, down.

Crossing my arms, I maintained an unperturbed exterior. "He started coming on days he knew Walker wouldn't be there, and I liked him. He was funny, charming. He asked about me, seemed interested in everything I said, like I was a freaking genius or something." I paused here to send Rex a humorous self-deprecating look.

Rex stared at me, anger persisting in the line of his jaw and the intensity of his eye squint.

I cleared my throat. "When he asked me out, I said yes."

What I didn't share was that—other than Cyrus when we were younger—no one else had ever shown interest in me or asked me out or flirted with me. Declan had been the first person to make me feel smart. Only Rex and one other guy at our high school were taller than me. It wasn't a secret that, by and large, high school boys didn't make a habit of asking out girls who were their height or taller.

"And?" Rex prompted, leaning forward and placing his elbows on his knees. His eyes were affixed to his hands.

"He picked me up in a Maserati for our date, took me to this ridiculously fancy restaurant, then to this amazing club, and we danced all night. I had the best time." I'd had no idea how seductive it could be to be wanted by someone experienced and older, especially someone who seemed so far out of my league. "He said he was an investment banker, and I had no reason not to believe him."

"He wasn't an investment banker."

"Uh, no. He pretended to be one and swindled a bunch of people out of a crap ton of money. But that part is for later. He proposed after three months and I said yes, so we got married."

Rex's eyes lifted to mine, searching. "Why'd you marry him?"

"I thought I was in love and living in a fairy tale," I said, because it was the truth. *See? Stupid.*

He seemed to hesitate before asking, "Your mom . . . she died just after graduation, right?"

"That's right." She'd left me some money and I'd been doing fairly well financially, had savings and a house, before the marriage. After the divorce, the court had sold everything of hers that had any value, leaving me with just photo albums, two handmade quilts that no one had bought at auction, and a few books.

"Did he . . ." Rex frowned, swallowed, then started again. "Did he treat you well?"

"He did. At first, he did." I nodded, thinking back. "But after we were married for a few weeks, he started telling me I should try to be a model. And then shortly after that, he'd host these dinners where he *told* people I was a model, and that made things awkward."

"Why awkward?"

"Well, because I'd contradict him and tell them the truth—that I wasn't—and then he'd get mad when we were alone. Basically, he wanted me to lie about it and pretend to be a fashion model and tried to make me feel bad for not just doing it. He said it would make him look good in front of his business associates and that it was all just one big game, that they expected me to pretend—BS like that."

"What did you do?"

"I couldn't lie." I shrugged, not feeling like any more of an explanation was necessary. "And when I refused, I realized the fairy tale was over and I'd made a huge mistake."

"He wanted to divorce you? Because you wouldn't lie?"

"No. He was too busy by then because his other web of lies had come crashing down. He'd borrowed against fake collateral in order to create a façade of wealth, and then he'd conned a bunch of people into investing in fake companies and startups. He pocketed the money to bankroll his lifestyle and brought in new investors by living more and more extravagantly."

"Shit."

I chuckled. "Yeah. Anyway. I found out when the police came and arrested us both."

"Holy shit."

"And when it became clear I had no idea, they offered me a deal. I would divorce him ASAP and testify against him. If I did so, I wouldn't have to serve more jail time as an accomplice. Ultimately, I didn't have much to offer the prosecution, even though I tried to be super cooperative, especially when I found out he'd been cheating on me the whole time." I paused here to breathe around the same something that always lodged in my throat whenever I thought about being cheated on.

I didn't love him now, I had no residual feelings for him—except loathing—but, for some strange reason, the cheating always choked me up.

Clearing my throat, I continued. "When it came time for the divorce settlement, they gave me just ten percent of his total debts instead of fifty percent, which turned out to be fifty percent of the new debt he'd accrued since we married."

"Fucking hell," Rex said on an exhale, giving his head a subtle shake.

"I declared bankruptcy—since there was no way I could fork over hundreds of thousands of dollars on a bartender's salary. Oh, yeah, Walker hired me back, no questions asked. He's a good guy."

"Did the bankruptcy ruling wipe out the debt?"

I laughed. "Uh, no. That's not how bankruptcy works. I had to pay it back—"

"Pay it back? Pay it *back*?! You weren't the one who—" Rex stopped himself, shoving his fingers into his short hair. "Sorry. Continue."

"They reduced the amount and gave me a payment plan to pay back the creditors and stretched it out over ten years."

"How many years do you have left?"

"Two."

"Fuck."

"It's okay."

Rex chuckled, a sound without humor. "It's really not."

"No, it is. I learned a good lesson and that lesson has likely saved me from lots of misery since."

His gaze flickered over me. "Oh yeah? What's that?"

I shrugged. "Never trust anything or anyone that seems too good to be true."

"Hmm." Rex opted to stare at me and keep his thoughts to himself for several seconds before asking suddenly, "Is this why you don't date?" He winced subtly as soon as the words left his mouth, giving me the sense he hadn't meant to speak them out loud.

Before he could take the question back or apologize, I answered, "It's the main reason, yes. But also, who wants to date a bartender with hundreds of thousands of dollars in debt, trust issues, and too many hobbies?" I chuckled, shaking my head. "I promised myself I wouldn't date anyone until the money was paid back and I was—*am*—debt free. I don't want to . . ."

"What?"

I frowned thoughtfully at the carpet, admitting to Rex what I'd never admitted to myself. "Enter into another relationship where I'm automatically at a disadvantage, where I'm the weaker of the two, with less to offer." I sighed, studying the weird pattern of the short fibers. "Admittedly, being a bartender has made it easier."

"*You* being a bartender has made not dating easier?" He sounded surprised by this. "You must get hit on all the time."

My mouth curved with a slight smile. "People tell bartenders things they wouldn't tell their therapist or their priest. Not a week goes by without a sad sack coming in and spilling their guts about a shitty marriage. The husband cheats on her with a woman half her age. Or the wife leaves because she's in love with someone else—usually his best friend. Sometimes they come in to celebrate their divorce and end up spending the whole evening complaining about what they didn't get in the divorce settlement. It's . . . marriage prophylaxis."

"It paints a skewed picture," he muttered.

I stared at nothing for a moment, sifting through all the sad stories I'd been told during my years behind the bar.

"Why do you do it?" Rex asked quietly, pulling my attention back to him. His head was cocked to the side, his gaze open and searching. "Why listen? Why not just tune them out?"

"Because I've been where they are." I smiled wider. "Walker was my bartender, serving me Shirley Temples because I was too young for alcohol, and he made all the difference. He got me through it by listening. He set me up with Kaylee as a roommate—he knew her mom and made the introduction—so I wouldn't be homeless."

"Abby—" Rex sighed, frowned, shook his head again, opened his mouth, closed it.

I reached forward and grabbed his hand. "It's okay, Rex. It really is. I'm good. I'm very content now with my life. And yes, the stories are depressing, but I know what they're going through, or some version of it, and I think . . ." I waited until he gave me his eyes again before finishing my thought. "I think that makes me the right person to listen."

CHAPTER 10

"Sometimes life is too hard to be alone, and sometimes life is too good to be alone."

— ELIZABETH GILBERT, *COMMITTED: A SKEPTIC MAKES PEACE WITH MARRIAGE*

The wedding was fine.

During the reception, Rex had also been fine. Not nearly as touchy-feely as the rehearsal dinner the night before, but perfectly fine. Once I'd talked myself out of being disappointed by his lack of pretend long, hot looks, pretend playful endearments, and pretend kisses, I'd settled into my placeholder role with cheerful aplomb.

Unlike the event yesterday, several people had braved Rex's *fuck-off-not-now* face to request a photo or an autograph during the reception, which gave me a little thrill each time. I wasn't sure of Rex's feelings on the subject, but I'd thoroughly enjoyed watching people gush about how much they loved and admired him, taking pictures for his fans and making funny faces while I'd snapped the photos, only sometimes succeeding in cracking Rex's granite exterior enough to make him smile.

He hadn't asked me to dance, and I hadn't suggested we do so. As a paid placeholder, I figured it was not my role to have an opinion one way or the other. I'd stood next to him, smiled when appropriate, laughed when appropriate, and refreshed our drinks when the occasion arose, which had given me an opportunity to move around and stretch my legs. He drank nothing but ice water with lime and I'd nursed two glasses of champagne all night.

All in all, this job was startlingly similar to being a bartender or a waitress, except instead of serving multiple customers, I had only one.

Thus, when Rex leaned down and whispered in my ear, "Act like you're tired and ask me to leave," I gave the world a full monty view of my back molars as I yawned and leaned my head on his shoulder, whining softly about having to get up early and needing rest.

Rex placed his arm around my waist and steered us over to the bride and groom to say our goodbyes. Amy looked stunning and her husband couldn't stop staring at her—or trying to snog her on the dance floor—long enough to say much more than, "See you later."

We strolled from the reception room together and didn't separate until we were on the elevator. Once the doors closed, I stepped away from his hold and he let his arm drop. We retreated to the opposite sides of the spacious lift.

Rex leaned against the elevator wall, inspecting me with tired eyes. "You were amazing."

"Thank you, it has pockets," I muttered, the words automatic. I laughed at the absurdity of them, rolling my eyes at myself. "I mean, no problem."

"Thank you."

I fought against the urge to curtsy, instead tipping my head. "You're welcome."

"How you were with the fans, not—" He seemed to weigh his words. "Not getting upset."

"Why would I get upset because you have fans? Heck, I get it."

The side of Rex's mouth hitched, his gaze moving over me. "I bet you do have fans."

"No." I laughed, glancing at the elevator buttons and noting our progress toward the lobby. "I meant, I *am* a fan."

"You're a fan?"

"Of course I am. I'm a fan of yours. I love watching you play football."

"Really?" He cracked a smile and, for reasons unknown, something about the expression made my palms sweaty.

"Yes. Really. Aren't you a fan of anyone? If my hero—which, to many people, you are their hero—materialized at a party and I had the chance to tell them how much they meant to me, I wouldn't care about talking to their date, I'd want to talk to *them*. I can't even say for certain I'd notice if they had a date. When fans see the object of their admiration, they sorta have tunnel vision. You know?"

His eyebrows pulled together, like maybe he was confused, so I added, "Maybe that makes me a bad person—"

"No. It doesn't. You're right. But you're the first woman I've, uh, taken to one of these things who has that perspective."

"Why? What usually happens?"

Now he chuckled, rubbing the back of his neck. "Well, usually, she—my date—doesn't like it, the people who come up and don't seem to notice she's there. My dates don't like being invisible, and I get that. I understand not wanting to be treated like an accessory." He sounded thoughtful, entirely reasonable, and exhausted.

"For the record, since you're paying me to go to these things and I'm here in a professional capacity, I don't mind being an accessory."

Rex's forehead wrinkled and I got the sense I'd said something wrong. I rushed to clarify, "And for the record, even if this were an alternate reality and we were on an actual date, I wouldn't have felt like an accessory tonight, more like . . ." I seriously contemplated the matter and settled on, "Support. I'm here in a supportive role. Tonight wasn't about me, and that's perfectly fine. Not everything—or most things—need to be about me. I don't mind being invisible. But I guess it might also help that, if I had a superpower, I'd choose invisibility."

"You're not invisible," he grumbled, full-on scowling.

"Hmm." I tapped my chin, deciding to lighten the mood rather than address his odd feelings about my preferred superpower. "Then I should add more camouflage to my closet."

That made him huff a little laugh, which had been my goal, and I smiled at my success—both at making him laugh and at making it through the evening without having to excuse myself for deep breathing exercises. It had been a good night, we'd settled into a rhythm, and I felt more confident and comfortable with his proposal than I had yesterday, especially now that he knew the truth about my past.

Which, speaking of—

I opened my mouth to broach the subject when the elevator dinged, cutting me off. A moment later, the doors slid open. Rex—a smile lingering on his face from my joke—put his hand over the pocket door to keep it from closing while I exited and then followed me out, stepping close to my side and wrapping his arm low around my waist.

I was about to peer up at him in question but then caught sight of a few wedding guest stragglers in the lobby. *Ah. I see.*

I wrapped my arm around his waist too, and he glanced down at me, lifting an eyebrow. "You okay to drive?"

"No. I don't have my car, remember? I'm going to call an Uber."

"Oh." Rex frowned at this news, but his forehead soon cleared. "Text me when you get home and let me know how much to reimburse you."

I scoffed. "I'm sure the evening's fee will cover a thirty-dollar car trip."

"No. I want to reimburse you for everything. In fact—" Rex looked left, then right, then pulled me over to a cluster of sofas in the hotel's lobby hidden by a large column and several tall plants. Sitting us down on one of the couches, he faced me. Our knees bumped at his closeness. "Have you decided?"

Unable to hold his hazel gaze, I worried my lip and studied the back of the column. "If it were as simple as what we did tonight, me showing up to support you when you needed, then I would absolutely say yes."

"Why isn't it that simple?"

I closed my eyes. "Rex—"

"I'll pay your ex-husband off. It's nothing."

"I don't want you using your money for that."

He was quiet for a beat. I opened my eyes and found him staring at me.

"What? What is it?" I leaned back a little so I could see him better.

"What if I already did?"

I held very still. "Did what?"

He glanced away. "It's done." I didn't miss how his jaw ticked or the uncompromising severity behind the words. "I paid him off through a broker. He can't say anything, he can't sell his story to anyone else."

"When did you do this?" I'd just told him about Declan this morning! When would he have had the time?

"I got a call just after the wedding ceremony that it was done, but I'd put it into motion this morning. My guy is really good, the best."

I heaved a heavy sigh and covered my face with both hands. "Rex—"

"You underestimate how much I need you."

Making a sound of disgruntlement—mostly to combat the volcanic eruption in my chest caused by his words—I dropped my hands and glared at him. "You do not need me. Four days ago, you didn't even know me. And I really wish you hadn't paid off Declan. I don't like others interceding on my behalf."

"I paid him off for purely selfish reasons."

I'm sure my features broadcasted the intensity of my skepticism.

"Abby, I do need you," he said matter-of-factly, without effect or dramatics. "My job is about hard work, talent, skill—sure. But it's also about what's going on up here." He tapped his temple. "If you and I marry, a whole host of bullshit just evaporates."

A fissure of understanding pushed the scale toward Rex's side of the argument. I assumed by "whole host of bullshit" he meant—at least in part—the sports announcer who'd co-opted Rex's nickname to mean "training wheels for women."

"It's Clarence O'Dea, isn't it? That sportscaster who makes fun of your nickname?" We hadn't discussed the guy yet, but if I had to guess now, looking at the harsh, unhappy line of Rex's mouth and the murderous intent in his eyes, that dude and his constant perpetuating of the nickname perversion had been messing with Rex's head.

"That's part of it," he rasped out, glaring at some spot behind me.

"Mostly, it's about building a team to guarantee success. I'm tired of being distracted by failure."

"Failure? What failure?"

He cut me a hard look. "You know."

"I don't think I do."

"I'm a shit boyfriend."

I found this hard to believe, but it didn't matter what I thought. He seemed to think it was true.

I tried a different tactic and pointed out the obvious. "Not every date needs to lead someplace serious. You can date someone without being committed. Keep things casual and—what?"

He was shaking his head before I'd come anywhere close to finishing. "I don't do that. I don't have time or energy for that kind of fucking around. It's either serious or it's not."

Inspecting him, I marveled at this oddity in his personality. "Who usually breaks up with who in your past relationships? You or—"

"I do."

"Because you don't—"

"I don't have time or energy to burn with someone who doesn't want what I want."

"Which is?" This wasn't me; I didn't push people for information, but a wee little voice in the back of my head was leading the charge. She wondered if maybe, while I stood in as a placeholder for Rex, I could also find him his forever partner. Our former classmate Rachel McQuaid Marie had been right yesterday when she'd said Rex deserved to be with someone awesome.

As he often did, Rex opened his mouth as if words were on the tip of his tongue, but he hesitated as his eyes moved between mine, like maybe I'd judge him for his answer.

"Do you even know what you want?" I asked, hoping the question sounded nonjudgmental.

"I want to be successful."

That had me lifting an eyebrow. "And the women you've dated previously didn't want you to be successful?"

"No, that's not—I don't want to let anyone down."

"Okay . . .?"

He closed his eyes, looking mildly frustrated. "If I'm not enough for someone exactly as I am, if I can't be successful at my job and meet my teammate's needs, successful with my family—my aunt and uncle—and meet their needs, and also consistently be what she needs, there's no point in continuing, is there? But I do *need* someone for events—stuff like today, exactly what you did—in order to maintain success elsewhere."

The picture of who Rex McMurtry was truly, as a human with flaws and peculiar hopes and quirks and strange ideas about the world, came more sharply into focus, and I filled in the remaining blanks out loud, "So you build a team of people you pay to fill the gaps, and you want me to be part of that team."

He nodded, but then his attention flickered to the right, perhaps rethinking our conversation. "Clarence O'Dea is definitely part of it though, what he says about the women I've dated."

"How so? Is it messing with your head?" I thought it might also be messing with his friendships. I couldn't imagine Walker ever being okay with someone saying his wife had needed "training wheels" before marrying him.

"It's not about me, not really. It's—I don't like—" Rex made a sound of frustration. "These women, the ones he's talking about, they're friends of mine, good people. I don't like how he talks about them. He calls me their training wheels—or whatever the fuck." Rex breathed out a bitter sound. "It's degrading and disrespectful. They deserve better."

Unable to stop myself, I leaned over and rested my head on his shoulder, my hand coming to his back to rub soothing circles on the wide expanse. Miraculously, the action felt entirely natural. *If only teenage Abby could see me now, she'd faint.*

But it wasn't like that. Rex was . . . *We're friends.*

At the very least, we were becoming friends, teammates, coconspirators for good (I hoped) and I wanted to help him. Currently, I didn't feel any butterflies, I didn't feel flustered or nervous. I felt only compassion for another person—a flawed, weirdo human—in need.

He sighed, resting his cheek against the top of my head, accepting my comfort. "I want it to stop, for everyone's sake, but I can't make a statement without making it worse. Not yet."

Rex was in an impossible position. If he called out the announcer, Rex would be labeled a crybaby, or "sensitive," and things would just get worse, especially for someone like Rex who relied on his gruffness, *fuck-off* face, and aura of toughness to be effective in the field and for his team. Ignoring Clarence hadn't done any good.

I also saw his point. If Rex were married, presumably the taunting would end, and the guy would have to turn the spotlight of his gross attention elsewhere. But that didn't seem right.

"If we can get Clarence to stop taunting you, that's good. But, Rex, what if he just turns his attention to someone else?"

"I have an idea about that." Rex straightened, forcing me to straighten as well. His eyes landed on one of my braids and he picked it up, rubbing his thumb back and forth over the tied off end. "Once we're married for a few months, the next time I'm asked about it—because they'll always ask me about it until I'm finally able to shut it down—I have a plan."

I nodded, glad we were on the same page. Like me, he didn't want to move the spotlight elsewhere; he wanted to turn this kind of ugliness off completely.

But something he'd just said snagged my attention. "Exactly how long do you see this"—I motioned between us—"lasting? Do you have an end date in mind?"

His stare grew enigmatic—not unfriendly, more like opaque—and he shrugged. "As long as you're willing."

"What if I'm always willing? Are we going to be fake married forever?"

A hint of a smile curved his mouth, and he let my braid drop. "Sounds good to me."

I snorted. "Yeah. Right. Come on, a year? Two?"

"I need your help, Abby. *Your* help. You're not just someone to fill in a gap, you're you. I would never ask anyone else to do this. I need *you*. I trust you, I—" His focus lifted and he captured my eyes. "Will you help me?"

CHAPTER 11

"We are what we pretend to be, so we must be careful about what we pretend to be."

— KURT VONNEGUT, *MOTHER NIGHT*

Halloween came and went, and so did all my special orders for the Etsy shop. I'd been working day and night to catch up from my lost weekend with Rex, not that my bank account had suffered. He'd sent me a cashier's check for five thousand dollars IN THE MAIL! Like a psycho.

After waffling back and forth for a week because it was more than we'd agreed upon, I'd deposited it.

Then I'd paid back Kaylee in full for the money she'd loaned me over the years. It felt good to pay her back. But after living with thousands of dollars in my checking account for two weeks, it hadn't felt good—ultimately—to deposit Rex's cashier's check.

I wanted to help him, but I didn't want his money. I needed to work to pay bills, but I wouldn't be able to work as much if I helped him. And that's where I currently lived—contradictory wants and needs and levels of comfort with my present situation.

The prenup arrived the Monday after Halloween.

Cue tense music.

I opened it, not knowing what it was. When I unfolded the thick stack of paper and read his name and mine together at the top of the page, I stopped, my insides too shaken to comprehend legalese and heretofores and aforementioneds heavily seasoned with a smattering of Latin.

Rex—who'd been radio silent since the wedding—texted me the day after the document arrived, sliding into my messages as though we were friends who sent legal documents back and forth like some friends sent memes.

Rex: Did you read the prenup? Text me any changes once your lawyer takes a look

Rex: Send me a joke

Rex: If you want/have time

I frowned at the first two of his texts. If this was how he messaged his ex-girlfriends—demanding jokes like I was a dancing monkey—then I could understand why he considered himself to be a shitty boyfriend. And yet, for some reason, the third text made me smile and more than made up for the second one.

Abby: I don't have a lawyer. So I'll be out of contact for a while as I go to law school and study for the Texas bar exam

Abby: That last text was the joke

He immediately responded.

Rex: You are hilarious. I wish you were here. If you need a lawyer, pick anyone. I'll reimburse the cost

Well, I didn't like *that* idea one bit. The last thing I wanted was more of Rex's money. But I didn't want to sign any legal document without having it reviewed by someone who was in my corner. So, again, I found myself with contradictory wants and needs and levels of comfort with my present situation.

I didn't text him back and I didn't start cold-calling family law firms. A solution occurred to me later in the afternoon, an obvious one. I tracked down Kaylee at her apartment after making a copy of the prenup at FedEx and blacking out our—mine and Rex's—identifiable information.

"To what do I owe this honor?" Kaylee smiled brightly, not at all perturbed by my unannounced visit.

"Can I come in? I have a friend who needs legal advice."

Pulling off her glasses, she stepped to one side and motioned me into her apartment. Part of me missed sharing a space with her. She was so tidy, and she never decorated for the holidays, which meant I could do what I wanted and enjoy her wonder and awe. As I glanced around at the blank canvas that was her immaculate living room, I made a mental note to bring over a few decorations sometime this week.

"What kind of advice?" She padded over to the open door of her balcony, where she'd obviously been sitting. After the pre-Halloween cold snap, Austin had been experiencing several gorgeous sunny days with highs in the mid-70s.

"It's a prenup." I trailed after her, shaking my head as she lifted up a bottle of white wine. "No, thank you. I can't stay long." I had a whole mess of half-sculpted ceramic Christmas ornaments to paint sitting on my kitchen counter, and a scarf—for Kaylee—I really wanted to finish knitting so I could make a hat for Walker's wife Ramona, color block mittens for my friend Josephine, and so on.

"A prenup." She held her hand out and I passed it over. Unlike me —who'd struggled with the meaning of every paragraph—she placed her glasses back on her nose and powered through the whole thing in five minutes while lounging at her patio table and gulping wine. "Well. . ." She sat back in her chair. "What does your friend want to know?"

"Is it fair?"

She tilted her head back and forth. "It depends. Why is your friend getting married? For love or money?"

I worried my bottom lip before reluctantly saying, "Let's say love."

"Then it's more than fair. She keeps everything she came in with, gives up nothing, cannot be held responsible if the marriage accrues debts. But then gets half the value of any property purchased during the marriage, regardless of her financial contribution to the property. She can end the marriage at any time and he's responsible for all legal fees. In addition, he's settled on her a hefty monthly allowance which can't be reduced over the course of the marriage and grows along with inflation."

I'm sure my eyes were as round as saucers. "What?"

"That's not all. Each kid comes with a dispensation, two million for the first two, and five million for each additional child."

I choked on spit and shock. *Children?!*

"And there are benchmark payments for each major anniversary—five years, ten, fifteen, twenty, et cetera."

Twenty years? What? Surely Rex wasn't planning on this farce lasting twenty years. And . . . kids?

"You look dismayed and you're not even trying to hide it. Interesting." Kaylee tapped her fingernails on her wineglass, her eyes narrowing. "Who is this friend?"

My cheeks puffed out with my exhale, and I croaked, "Can I hire you?"

"Why?"

"Because I need some of that lawyer-client confidentiality stuff."

"Oookay." She smiled, looking at me like I was weird and interesting and amusing. "What have you gotten yourself into, Abby? Some sort of Russian oligarch wants a mail-order bride?"

I laughed without humor. Her suggestion wasn't too far from the truth. "No. A pro football player."

Kaylee chuckled, but then the amusement vanished when I just continued staring at her. "Wait—you're serious?"

"Not a mail-order bride, more like a fake wife. A placeholder. And there won't be any children or five-year wedding anniversaries, I'm sure that stuff is just in there to make the whole thing read more legit."

"You are serious." She appeared winded. "You are being serious right now."

I rubbed my forehead. "Okay, so, remember that guy? The big guy who walked into the bar and I said I went to high school with him? A few Wednesdays ago?"

Saying nothing, she nodded.

"We did go to high school together, and his name is Rex McMurtry."

"SHUT UP!" She jumped to her feet, her wine sloshing in her glass. She didn't notice it spill on the table so she must've been really shocked. "You went to high school with TW McMurtry? Why—when did—why didn't you ever tell me?"

"Sit down." I leaned my elbows on the table and surrendered to the fact that I wasn't going to be able to figure this out on my own. I needed her help. I needed to talk this through with someone. "But first, I think I will take that glass of wine."

I'd left Kaylee's apartment feeling both less and more confused. Less confused because the prenup went above and beyond in protecting me should Rex go into debt or fall on hard financial/legal times. Signing the prenup wouldn't put me in danger, it wasn't a scary document, and I could sign it without fear of harm to my future.

Kaylee had also advised me to take the money, all of it. She'd offered to introduce me to her finance lady who would help me invest it and then I'd finally be out of the financial crater caused by the implosion of my first marriage.

This last piece of advice didn't feel right. I knew Kaylee only had my best interests at heart, but I couldn't dispel the hovering cloud of doom that pressed down on me every time I seriously considered accepting all that money.

I went to work, I went to the studio, I reread my favorite books, I ignored Rex's text messages asking me about the prenup and responded with jokes and goofy memes instead. And still, I couldn't shake the cloud of doom.

A full week after Kaylee's review of the document, I woke up in a cold sweat at 3 a.m., yanked violently out of a dream where the police had come to take me to jail for some reason I couldn't exactly remember, something to do with using illegal glazes on my pottery.

Unable to fall back asleep, I'd set up my sewing machine on my kitchen table and stitched together pieces I'd cut a few weeks ago for a new knitting bag I wanted to make for my friend Jonathan. I'd taught him how to knit last year, and he loved ancient Roman history. I'd found the fabric I was using in the dollar bin at Joann Fabric, head busts of Roman emperors, and snatched it up.

The pinning for the bag went at a snail's pace, however. The only time I wished I had an ironing board was when I sewed.

While I meticulously pieced and pinned and sewed and meditated on my dream about illegal glazes, a notion occurred to me. And that notion became a decision, which then grew into determination, which ultimately settled my mettle, leaving me feeling enormously better.

I wouldn't take any excess money from Rex.

Allowing Rex to pay for expenses like clothes, plane travel, and hotel made total sense. Those were costs I wouldn't normally have accrued. I needed clothes, and I needed to travel places in order to help him in my role as placeholder. It also made sense to accept compensation to cover the days I couldn't work at the bar—since I'd be missing work when I traveled with Rex and went to his events, and I needed to pay my bills—but I decided to accept nothing above what I'd usually make for a day's work.

I realized it was the thought of accepting the "fee," as Rex called it—it was called something else in a the prenup, "allowance" I think—that felt wrong.

When we divorced, Rex could use the money I didn't take to reimburse himself for paying off my ex, I could walk away with a clear conscience, minimal disruption, no strings between us except friendship. I reasoned that helping a friend out of a bad situation, like my friends had once done for me, would be more than enough payment.

Feeling lighter, more able to breathe, I yawned and turned off my sewing machine. I then walked over to the kitchen counter where I'd left the prenup and I signed it. Snapping a photo of the signature page, I sent it via text to Rex.

Abby: I'm mailing this back for your signature today and I'll send you my work schedule for the next month so you can pick a wedding date. Here or Chicago?

As soon as I hit send, three dots appeared on Rex's side of the conversation. Lifting an eyebrow, I checked the clock on the screen. It was 5:45 a.m. He must've been up early to work out or for practice.

Rex: Chicago, in two weeks. I have a charity thing on Friday night I need you for while you're up here

Rex: Assuming that works with your schedule

I smirked. This was Rex's modus operandi, sending a brusque, demanding text message first, then following it up with something more accommodating. I wondered if he realized how gruff the first message sounded after the fact.

Abby: Both days work! And if you have any other events you need me to attend over the next two months, please send me a list so I can ask for the days off

Rex: Richmond game Thanksgiving, wedding second weekend in December. There are more. My agent will share my calendar with you so you can plan

Rex: My agent will always arrange for a car to get you from the airport

My stomach did a little summersault at *Richmond game Thanksgiving.* I knew Rex's team was playing on Thanksgiving in Richmond, I also knew Rex's team was expected to lose. I'd never been to a pro game before, but I imagined there would be nothing for me to do at one of his football games other than enjoy myself. So why did he want me there?

Unless I'm missing something?

Abby: You want me to go to the Richmond game? On Thanksgiving?

Rex: Yes

Abby: How does this work? You'll be playing so I'll be doing what?

Rex: Watching the game

Frowning, I reread his reply several times. I wanted to go, absolutely! But I didn't understand why Rex would want me at one of his games just so I could spectate. And why this game? The request seemed too good to be true and thus excitement warred with unease.

Abby: What do you need me to do while I'm there? I want to go, but why do *I* need to be there? What is expected of me?

Rex: All the players' spouses go and sit together. I need you to be my wife. I already have your ticket

Every muscle in my body tensed, goose bumps of doom broke out over my skin, and some morose, pessimistic part of me had a good chuckle at my expense. Rex wouldn't be there as a buffer or focus of attention. I'd have to try to blend in on my own with the other players' wives while not letting them see how much of a dumb, uncultured hick I was.

Great. Just freaking great.

See? If something seems too good to be true, it always, *always* is.

CHAPTER 12

"'The thing is, I suppose,' he said, 'that one gets into the habit of being oneself. It takes some great upheaval to crack that shell and force us to discover what else might be underneath. '"

— TANA FRENCH, *THE WITCH ELM*

The morning after sending the snapshot of my signature on the prenup, I awoke to a text message from Rex sent several hours earlier.

Rex: Where'd you get that tall table?

Rubbing the sleep from my eyes, I sat up in bed and fired off a response.

Abby: Who dis? No one I know would text me at 5 a.m.

Rex: Your fiancé

Abby: Ohhhhh. Him.

Rex: Yeah. That guy.

Abby: I'll email you the address and phone number of the dealer in Texas. He imports from the Netherlands

Figuring that would be the end of it, I placed my phone facedown on the nightstand. But then it buzzed again almost immediately.

Rex: cc my agent pls

Abby: Why? Is she tall too?

Rex: She'll place the order

Abby: Does she order all your stuff?

Rex: No. Just furniture, clothes, food, airline tickets, gifts, etc.

I smiled quizzically at this information. Did Rex delegate everything to paid employees? How . . . tidy.

Abby: So she's your work wife

Rex: You could say that

Abby: And now you'll have me, so that makes you a bigamous work husband

Rex: Big Work Love 😉

A laugh burst out of me at the unexpected response and winky face. Shaking my head, I placed the phone facedown on the nightstand again and got ready for my day, resolved to push the perplexing conversation from my mind.

❄

Rex: Hey

Rex: You around?

I lifted an eyebrow at Rex's midafternoon text. I'd just arrived at the bar to start my shift and had been counting chip bags in the back. Since today was a Monday, I doubted we'd get a substantive rush at any point this evening; Mondays and Tuesdays were typically used to clean up from the craziness of the weekend.

Abby: Yes. What's up?

Rex: How was your day?

Abby: Not bad. I had a productive day at the studio then biked over to work. Now I'm counting chip bags

I reread my response several times, then decided to add,

Abby: How about you?

Rex: Studio?

Abby: I'm a member of a pottery studio. I make ceramic goods

Rex: Like plates and mugs?

Abby: Yep

Rex: Do you sell them?

Abby: Yep

Rex: Can I buy some?

Abby: Nope

"What's so funny?"

My head whipped up and I found Walker standing just inside the back room doorway.

Glancing between me and my phone, Walker pointed to my cell. "Is that Josephine with more of those TikToks?"

My friend Josephine had charmed Walker by showing him funny TikTok videos over the summer. He wasn't certain what TikTok was, just that it was a social media thing used by "the younger generation."

"Um, no. It's—I'm messaging a friend. Sorry." My phone buzzed in my hand, but I resisted looking at the screen. I'd texted my friends while working before, but for some reason this time it felt different, like I was taking advantage of Walker's leniency.

"No need to apologize." Walker walked toward the office, giving me a puzzled look as he strolled past.

I waited until I heard the door close behind me before reading the new message from Rex.

Rex: Why not? Aren't I ceramics worthy?

Abby: Because my sister wife buys your furniture, clothes, food, airline tickets, gifts, etc. If she wants to buy any of my ceramics, that's fine

I hadn't met or spoken with Rex's agent yet but given how she seemed to manage so much of his life, I hoped we would be friends.

Rex: She doesn't buy my ceramics. I am very particular about those

Abby: Why? Do they have to be giant-sized?

Rex: Yep. And perfectly formed just like the rest of me

I barked a laugh even as my face flooded with heat. *He didn't mean . . . Did he*? Or was I reading too much into the text? *Get your mind out of the gutter, Abby.*

Squinting at his message, I dithered and hemmed and hawed before —on a rush of recklessness—responding with,

Abby: Ego included, obvs

As soon as I sent the text, a weird, tight discomfort settled in my stomach. What was I doing?

Text flirting with Rex, that's what you're doing.

Regret and confusion pressed heavy on my shoulders. Did I want to text flirt with Rex? Or anyone?

I don't . . . think so?

I'd meant every word I'd told him: I didn't date, I didn't want to date, I had no desire to enter into any kind of romantic relationship until the debt was paid off. Maybe we weren't flirting, but the fact that the notion had even entered my brain was troubling.

I shouldn't want to flirt with Rex, or anyone.

Determined to stop thinking about him and our conversations in that light, I wondered if I should add something else, something to dispel the awkwardness I might've just created with my last message. Before I could decide what to say, a new text came through.

Rex: You know it, babe

Rex: Do you want to pick out your wedding dress? Or should I have my agent do it?

Nibbling my lip, I pushed my hair out of my face and tried to focus on his text. One week after signing the prenup, waking up to new messages from Rex was no longer unusual, but it was problematic. Five out of the last seven days I'd awoken from sexy Rex dreams just to find a question from him on my phone, usually asking about my schedule or what I had planned for the day.

After graduating from high school and prior to signing the prenup, the frequency of my Rex-related dreams had severely declined. Maybe an odd one here or there, once or twice a year. But with all the text messages and friendly banter, and him being so freakin' hot when I'd seen him last, the fantasies had made their forceful return.

They were also much more—*ahem*—adult than they had been before.

I'd never felt brave enough to have a one-night stand, figuring—with my luck—I'd end up with a missing kidney at the end of the night, or in prison again, or shipped off to some ice planet as the new bride for a blue alien. But recently, I'd seriously considered finding a guy for some no-strings sex. I desperately needed some relief from the constant barrage of Rex.

My brain mostly clear of the lingering post-dream images, I typed out what I hoped was a thoughtful response.

Abby: Your agent can do it unless you need me to for some reason. Remind her that I'm tall

Rex: You're short

Abby: I am not short

Rex: Shorty

Abby: Keep that up and I'll wear platforms to the wedding, shorty

Rex: I would love to see that

Ignoring the lovely, swirling heat playing with my internal organs, I tried not to smile or think too much about how natural it had become for our texts to veer into flirtatious territory. Then again, maybe they weren't flirtatious. Maybe I was reading too much into his messages. Again.

He is not flirting with you, and you don't want him to flirt with you because you don't want to flirt with anyone.

As usual, I was the one to change the subject and steer the conversation back on course.

Abby: What is the plan for the wedding?

Rex: After Saturday's practice, we'll get married on the stadium field and the team photog will be there to document for media

Rex: Sound okay?

Abby: Sounds awesome!

Rex: And the team will be there

Abby: WHAT? SRSLY???

Rex: Yep. It's all set

Abby: Please tell me you'll be in your football uniform. You can pick out my wedding dress- anything you want- if you promise to wear your home uniform for the wedding

I cringed almost as soon as I sent the text, my fingers flying over the keypad faster than my brain had been able to catch the request or the offer. Ah well. It was done now, and I should've known better than to text first thing in the morning.

I was prone to making an idiot of myself during our morning text exchanges. I grew more circumspect and thoughtful as the day progressed, which helped me not at all. Rex seemed to prefer messaging me in the morning.

Rex: You'll wear anything I want?

Abby: As long as it's not the Squall's mascot outfit, yes

Rex: My jersey?

Abby: And what else?

Rex: Platforms

Abby: And?

Rex: That's it

My face on fire, I sputtered a shocked laugh and lifted my hair off my hot neck.

This was flirting, right?

He was flirting with me. It had been over ten years since I'd flirted with someone who wasn't drunk or almost drunk. I was out of practice, but this was most definitely flirting . . . right?

Or maybe he's just being funny?

I'd been the one to bring up the platforms earlier, perhaps this was him being clever and silly?

Come on, stupid. He's just trying to develop a repertoire with you, break the ice. This isn't flirting.

Bah! I'd thought the word *flirt* so much it was starting to sound strange in my head.

WHATEVER!

My point was, Rex would not flirt with me. He just wouldn't. From his perspective, he was paying me to fake date and marry him. If we weren't friendly and comfortable with each other one-on-one, then we would have no hope of convincing anyone our marriage was real. Obviously, that's all this was, and I needed to stop entertaining crazy thoughts and confusing myself.

Frowning at the phone, I mentally composed several potential responses while successfully talking myself off the crazy ledge. After much debate, I responded with,

Abby: Sure thing, boss

A reminder to myself that's who Rex believed himself to be.

I was only doing this as a favor.

I wouldn't take his money above the necessary costs incurred by helping him.

But he still thought of himself as my boss, and I seriously doubted Rex would ever flirt with someone he considered an employee.

He's being friendly. Not flirting. The end. Stop thinking about it.

I'd just walked into my apartment and flipped on the lights after a late shift when my phone buzzed in my back pocket.

Rex: Are you awake?

Abby: What's up?

I stared at the screen, waiting for a response, and shifted on my feet tiredly. The three animated dots danced and persisted for a full minute. Either he had a lot to tell me, or he'd typed out a message, deleted it, and was typing out something new.

Crossing to the kitchen, I placed my phone on the counter and walked to my wee little pantry to extract a box of shredded wheat. I also pulled out a jar of Nutella. The day had been a long one—a bar fight, a gun pulled, broken glasses and bottles, ambulances, police—and I needed the comfort of Nutella slathered on something crunchy.

Finally, just as I finished taking my first bite, the phone vibrated.

Rex: How was your day?

I stared at his text, replaying the events of the evening. I didn't want to unload on him about my day. That's why Nutella and shredded wheat existed.

Abby: Okay. How was yours?

Rex: Is the car okay? Does it still smell? Do I need to send the guys back out to detail?

Abby: It's fine. Even Kaylee said it smells better than new. How was your day?

Rex: Did you go to the studio today?

Rolling my eyes at his evasiveness, I texted,

Abby: HOW

Abby: WAS

Abby: YOUR

Abby: DAY

Abby: ?

Rex: Fine

What a stinker.

Abby: What did you do?

Rex: Work

Abby: That's it? Just work?

Rex: And text you

Abby: Oh. Then why wasn't your day awesome?

Rex: My deepest apologies. Upon reflection, you're right. It was awesome

Abby: It's important to reflect

The three dots appeared, then disappeared. I thought he wasn't going to respond. But then, just as I'd finished rinsing off my plate and leaving it by the sink to dry, another message came through.

Rex: Goodnight, Abby.

I know it'll sound silly, but for some reason his words felt sad to me. I considered responding with a benign *Goodnight, Rex*, or not responding at all. But an odd urge to cheer him up had me typing,

Abby: Sweet dreams, babe

Rex: 

The smiley emoji made me smile. As I readied for bed, brushing my teeth and washing my face, I wasn't sure which had helped alleviate the day's stress more: the complex magic of Nutella or Rex's simple smiley emoji?

❄

Waking ridiculously early to shower and change for my trip to Chicago, I wasn't surprised to find a message from Rex already on my phone.

Rex: My agent is sending a car for you today to pick you up and take you to your hotel while I'm at practice. Then you have appointments for fittings

Rex had mentioned earlier in the week that I could pack light as the event outfits—for the charity thing tonight and for our wedding at the stadium tomorrow—would be provided upon arrival. Underwear, socks, toiletries, PJs, and flying clothes were the extent of the items I stuffed in my backpack.

I'd packed and repacked my bag multiple times. This was my first time taking an airplane in my entire life and not because I was afraid to fly. I had no idea if I was afraid to fly. I'd never been given the option, until now.

Abby: Will I meet your agent?

Rex: Not this trip. Are you bringing me any perfect, giant mugs?

Abby: I don't have any glazed and fired that match your giant physique

Rex: Bring me one anyway

Rex: A wedding gift

Abby: What are you getting me? (as a wedding gift)

Rex: Literally anything you want. Ask and it's yours

Oh. That was a dangerous thing for him to send so early in the morning, especially after I'd woken up this morning from a sexy dream about the two of us taking a dip in a hot tub. Obviously, requesting sexual favors was out of the question. I decided to ask for something similarly unlikely.

Abby: World peace

Rex: Except for that

Abby: For democrats and republicans to get along and to see themselves as citizens of the same country.

Rex: Or that

Abby: Affordable, reliable internet

Rex: Not that either

Abby: Fine. What will you give me?

Rex: You have to ask and be specific

Rex: I will only do what you ask me to do

Hmm. That read like a riddle. Clearly, my mind was still addled from my lusty dreams.

Abby: A high five?

Rex: Aim higher

Abby: A tall high five?

He didn't respond right away. In fact, he didn't respond for several minutes, so I got up and took my shower, made coffee, got dressed, and he still hadn't responded.

But just as I selected the Uber app to order a ride, a text came through.

Rex: See you soon

CHAPTER 13

"From my experience, honey, if he seems too good to be true—he probably is."

— CANDACE BUSHNELL, *SEX AND THE CITY*

"Every person can be explained by a Frank Sinatra song."

I straightened from the tall column where I'd been leaning and glanced over my shoulder, immediately smiling as my eyes connected with the debonair, piratey features of my old high school pal. "As I live and breathe, Cyrus Malcom."

It had been weeks since I'd seen him last, and his chin was still covered in stubble, not a beard, and that made me wonder if he'd been purposefully keeping his facial hair at this stage of growth to give him a villainesque aura.

His smile stretched and he laughed. "Gorgeous Gail McNerny, you are breathtaking." He stepped close to me and bumped our shoulders together. "Why are you over here all by yourself?"

My smile wavered and I shrugged. "Oh, you know. Lurking." It was the truth, I was lurking, mostly because I didn't know what else to do.

I felt him inspect me before he asked, "How was your flight? You got in today, yes?"

"I did." I wanted to say more, tell him how Rex's agent had flown me first class, and it had been a bit overwhelming. I'd felt super uncomfortable in my big seat thinking about all the people behind us who seemed to be squeezed together in coach. It didn't feel fair, and the unfairness of it plagued me during the entire flight.

But I didn't say any of this because I didn't know what Rex would want me to say.

"Have you traveled much?" Cyrus's question was softly spoken, coaxing. Perhaps he sensed my reticence to share.

"Not much," I hedged. "How about you?" Directing the conversation back to the other person usually saved me from talking about myself.

Cyrus's green eyes seemed to glitter as they narrowed. "I bet you haven't traveled at all. Today was the first time you've ever been on a plane, right?"

My shoulders slumped, and I felt every bit the fraud that I was. "How did you know?"

"I know more about you than anyone else here, and your circumstances." Again, his voice was soft, and his eyes turned kind.

Cyrus knew about my disastrous marriage to Declan, the bankruptcy, the debts. Too embarrassed to ask Walker for help since I'd quit the Boozy Rancher when Declan and I had eloped, Cyrus had been the only person I could think to call when I'd been arrested.

"So, tell me, how was it? How was your first plane ride?" His tone was light and friendly, and he seemed genuinely interested.

"Uh, well, navigating the airport was harrowing." So many people, none of whom smiled.

"But you did it." My old friend gave me an encouraging and deferential head nod. "Soon you'll be a jet-setter."

I chuckled. "I don't know about that."

"Give yourself some credit. It's no small thing flying for the first time on your own. And now, here you are."

"Here I am . . ." He had a point. I'd flown on my own for the first time, dealt with all the unknowns, and I'd survived. I should feel proud of myself for that at least.

That said, I had been enormously relieved when I'd spotted the car Rex's agent had sent to pick me up and take me to my hotel downtown. I'd stayed in hotels before, but nothing as opulent as the room Rex's agent had booked. Upon arrival, I'd spent a few moments wandering around the room, afraid to touch anything. Then, when I realized the time, I set about following the instructions his agent had emailed me the day before.

Leaving my overnight bag behind, I'd walked to a fancy looking shop on the Magnificent Mile and had three dress fittings: a long, formal red silk dress for tonight; a beautiful white dress for our wedding tomorrow at the stadium; and a green tea dress with a flared skirt that ended just above my knee for the wedding we'd be attending together in December. The last one also had a tiny matching hat, and I was grateful for the ladies at the shop who'd taught me how to affix it to my head.

I had my doubts about actually wearing the hat, however. It had feathers. And a wee little veil. And made me feel ridiculous.

"And this dress." Cyrus's eyes lowered as he made a *chef's kiss* movement with his fingers. "You look like art."

"Thank you, it has pockets." It didn't really have pockets.

I ignored the pinpricks on the back of my neck, pleased Cyrus had noticed the dress—because I loved it and thought I looked amazing in it—but the evening thus far had not been a particularly pleasant one. In retrospect, neither had the afternoon after my flight.

The tailor and the saleswomen present for the fitting of the red dress had realized at the same time I had that I couldn't wear my current underthings tonight. Don't get me wrong, the dress was absolutely stunning, I'd never felt so beautiful and sexy, but the material was extremely unforgiving. It didn't play nice with my trusty cotton underwear and bra. I'd taken off both and then the lines looked perfect except my boobs were—*ahem*—a little too boobtacular.

The tailor and lead saleswoman promised to figure out a solution before I returned. I could do nothing but place my trust in their hands.

After finishing the fittings, I'd walked to a spa—also on Magnificent Mile—where Rex's agent had arranged for several beauty treatments: pedicure, manicure, facial, waxing of multiple surfaces (all painful), makeup, hair blowout, yada, yada, yada. They'd also served me lunch which, admittedly, had been nice.

In the middle of a spa treatment, while the technician waxed the hairs at the apex of my thigh (to the left of my cooch), I couldn't help but laugh at myself. I was every cliché from every movie where the uneducated, backwoodsy bumpkin goes to the big city and has herself a makeover montage.

But, I supposed, if I were a fancy lady, I'd be doing this kind of thing on the regular, and therefore no makeover montage would've been necessary. I would be living my life in a state of perpetual makeoverness.

The thought left me feeling oddly numb and adrift, and by the time I'd finished at the spa, I barely had a half hour to jog back to the dress place, agree to wear the new bra, underwear, and stockings they'd procured in my absence, pull on the newly tailored red dress, red shoes, and matching wool coat, and be outside in enough time for the limo to pick me up on its way to grab Rex from work.

And then—the cherry on top of a poo pile—when Rex had slid into the limo, he'd given me an aloof, cursory once-over and nodded politely. Before I could say a single word, his phone rang and he took the phone call, a call that had lasted the entire drive to the charity dinner thing. Now I lurked next to a column on the edge of the room while watching Rex be pulled this way and that by some man who'd claimed him as soon as we'd walked into the gala and who couldn't wait to introduce Rex to some very important people.

"And now you're lurking." Cyrus tsked, cutting into my reflections. His dark eyebrows arched over his pretty green eyes. "That's a damn shame. If you were my fake fiancée, I'd show you off like diamonds."

My stomach dropped. Squinting at my former friend, I whispered, "*Fake* fiancée?"

He nodded once. "Rex told me."

"Told you what?"

"He told me he's paying you to marry him, and he told me what happened the night of Jason's bachelor party, back in Austin."

I lifted my chin, absorbing this information. Given the events of the day, I didn't have much energy to figure out how I felt about Rex telling Cyrus about our agreement.

Then again, I'd told Kaylee. *Yeah. But she's your lawyer. Cyrus is no lawyer, though he might play one on TV someday.*

"You still got a thing for Rex?" Cyrus bumped my shoulder again, his tone gentle but interested. "Is that why you're doing this?"

"I like him," I hedged, my voice too high. I cleared my throat. "Rex is a good guy. He's always been a good guy."

"So that's why you agreed to be his fake wife? Because he's a good guy?"

I shrugged. "And the money." The lie almost caught in my throat.

They were obviously still good friends, and Cyrus would want to look out for Rex, that made complete sense to me. But Cyrus had witnessed firsthand the depth and breadth of my Rex obsession during our freshman year of high school. It was a moot point now, but I didn't want Cyrus thinking I'd agreed to help while secretly harboring some ulterior motive or scheme about hooking up with Rex. That boat had sailed.

In fact, given Rex's non-reaction to me in the limo, I suspected that boat had never been built.

"Oh, right. The money. All that money. . ." Cyrus's words held a hint of mockery. I ignored it, keeping my gaze forward and on Rex. The man who'd absconded with him about a half hour earlier still hovered nearby, but now Rex was standing amid a circle of women and talking to another man who I thought looked familiar but couldn't quite place.

As though reading my mind, Cyrus said, "Alaric Jordan."

A memory clicked into place. "He went to high school with us," I muttered. He'd been the prom king my graduating year and, if memory served, had been good friends with both Rex and Cyrus.

"Yep. Now he's a venture capitalist, splits his time between Houston and Chicago."

Something about the way Cyrus said *venture capitalist* had me glancing at him. A sardonic smile twisted his lips and his eyes sparkled with mischief. "Aren't you going to ask me about my Frank Sinatra song theory?"

I tried to recall what he'd said upon initially coming over to me, but I couldn't. "What was it again?"

"Every person can be explained by a Frank Sinatra song."

"Ah. Yes." I nodded, leaning against the column again. "Well, that is a theory."

"You've always done that."

"Done what?"

Cyrus stepped in front of me, blocking my view of Rex, Alaric, and the others. "When someone says something you think is idiotic, you respond with a factual statement without admitting or denying value. 'That's a theory' or 'That's an idea.' It sounds like a compliment at first, but really you're saying nothing at all, giving nothing of your thoughts away."

I wore a patient smile. "That's another theory."

He looked like he wanted to laugh but instead squinted at me. "Don't you want to know what Frank Sinatra song you are?"

"I'd prefer to know which of Frank's songs you believe yourself to be epitomized by."

"That's easy." He grinned happily, which made him look more like his younger self than the suave movie star he'd become. "'That's Life.'"

"Ha. Ha." I could see that about him. "Good one."

"And you are obviously 'The Lady Is a Tramp.'"

My expression flattened. "Obviously."

Still wearing his boyish grin, he pushed his hands into his suit pants pockets and tilted his head to the side, scrutinizing me. "The fact that you have no follow-up questions illustrates my point perfectly, as it's about a woman who doesn't give a shit what other people think and does whatever she wants."

"That's why I said *obviously*."

"And Alaric is—"

"'My Way'?" I hadn't seen Alaric since graduation, nor had we ever really spoken, but if our former prom king and valedictorian was still anything like the teenage version of himself, the song fit perfectly.

"Yes. Exactly." Cyrus's gaze moved over me approvingly and he laughed; apparently, my willingness to play his game put him in a good mood. Turning around such that he rested his back against the column, he lifted his chin toward the crowd around Rex. "Let's do a few others, shall we?"

"Nah. I feel like it could turn mean and petty quickly."

"Okay. Fair point." He glanced over his shoulder at me. "Then let's only do it to people we like."

"Fine. Who else do we like?"

"Rex."

I stiffened and tried not to sound robotic as I said, "Oh. Yes. Rex."

"What do you think?" Cyrus let the back of his head hit the column.

"Uh . . ." My stomach twisted as my eyes moved over Rex's beautiful body in his beautiful, elegant suit.

With all the texting and jokes and back and forth, I'd thought . . . or I guess I'd hoped . . . *bah.*

I didn't know what I'd thought or hoped, but today, during the entire afternoon spa debacle—as I'd been poked and prodded and pinched and pinned, waxed and cinched and painted—stupidly, I'd thought all the disorder and discomfort would all be worth it when I saw Rex.

Maybe I hadn't explicitly acknowledged the thought at the time, but now, standing here all dressed up in this gorgeous red dress, with my hair in long, thick, shiny waves, and my expertly drawn makeup, and my new lacy lingerie, I acknowledged the truth: I had never looked as good in my life as I did tonight. The afternoon had been fun—all the getting ready and becoming beautiful despite the disruption—until Rex slid into the back seat of that limo and pretended I didn't exist.

"He's a tough one, don't you think?" Cyrus asked, rubbing his pirate stubble.

Rex was a tough one. I used to think he was tough like crusty bread—hard on the exterior with a soft, warm, irresistible center—but I was starting to wonder whether I'd had it wrong. Maybe Rex was tough like boiled, unseasoned flank steak. Just . . . tough.

"I would've said Rex's song was 'Saturday Night (Is the Loneliest Night of the Week),' until just recently," Cyrus volunteered as though I'd asked.

"I've never heard that one."

"It's good, but depressing, about a dude who misses his girlfriend on Saturday nights since that's the night they always went out, but they don't go out anymore because—presumably—they broke up at some point. Where 'she' is every woman he's ever dated."

"Hmm." I didn't know what to think about *that.*

"But that's not him anymore, not since—well—you." I felt his eyes slide to the side and inspect my profile.

I kept my attention forward as I said, "Tramps have that effect on people."

Cyrus laughed, turning to face me again, his eyes sparkling down at me like twin gems. "You are adorable, Abby." His voice was silk and sandpaper.

I shifted back a step as our gazes connected, surprised to discover Cyrus now had game. *Plenty* of game. When I saw him last, he'd been thoroughly without any game, no flirt power, just an abundance of earnestness and an unhealthy habit of wearing his heart on his sleeve. But now, and maybe without even really trying, sexuality and charisma rolled off him in waves.

"So . . ." I crossed my arms, flailing for a subject change under the intensity of Cyrus's magnetic stare, but then dropped my arms to my sides again when I realized how much crossing them drew attention to the generous amount of boobage I had on display.

"*Sooo*?" Once more, Cyrus placed himself in front of me, his hand now on the column at his left, my right. I felt a little boxed in.

"A person's Frank Sinatra song can change?" I finally managed to croak out.

"What?" He blinked, as though confused.

"It's not constant?"

"Ah." He nodded his understanding, pushing away from the

column and coming to stand at my other side. "Of course it can change. People change, and so does their song."

I followed Cyrus's line of sight to the group of people—mostly women—who still stood around Rex and Alaric.

"You know . . ." He bumped my shoulder like he'd done earlier. "He's dated all of them."

"Huh. How about that." I was all turned around, not knowing what to feel, or whether I had the right to feel anything. What a strange, disconcerting hour it had been.

"And now they're all married."

I peered sideways at Cyrus. "Wait, what? Is that true?"

"Oh yes. You know what that means."

"What does it mean?"

He leaned in close to whisper, "Your future husband is probably in this room."

I stared at him for a long moment and then I chuckled, smacking his shoulder with the back of my hand. "Shut up."

"No." He also laughed, caught my wrist, and held my hand. "It's true. All of Rex's ex-dates marry one of his friends."

I tugged my hand away. Cyrus let me go. "That's stupid."

"It's true."

"But—"

"Ask anyone. Hell"—he gestured to the women surrounding Rex—"ask any of them. Every single one of them met their future husband when they were dating Rex or shortly after dating him."

I knew this was at least partially true, that Clarence O'Dea jerk never stopped pointing out how many of Rex's exes married his friends. But still, it couldn't be *all* of them.

"Any woman he's ever been on a date with, the very next person she dates ends up becoming her spouse."

I made a face. "Not every single one."

"Every single one."

"And he just has to go on a date with them? Like, just one date?"

"Yes."

"Since when?"

"Since his very first girlfriend. You remember Emma Cortez?"

I hesitated before admitting, "Yes. I believe they broke up sophomore year because her parents wanted her to focus on school, right?"

"Yeah. Well, she married the next guy she dated, met at Princeton. He's a doctor, she's a lawyer, it's like that. And you know his second girlfriend, uh, what's her name? They only dated for like a month." Cyrus snapped his fingers, his gaze losing focus over my head.

"Jennifer Killigan." I couldn't remember my cousin's daughter's name but knew the names of all Rex's girlfriends in high school. Yes. I'd been *that* person.

"Yes! Her. She and Mark Towers married, and Mark was the very next guy she dated after Rex."

"This is a distressing topic."

"And yet, it's also true." Cyrus pointed to one of the women circled around Rex. "That's Yana. Rex took her to one work thing, one date. And now her wife is Rex's agent. That one? That's Kerry. They dated for two weeks. Her husband is now Kendrick—over there—a friend of Rex's from college. They played ball together. And, see her?"

"Please stop." I turned and walked aimlessly . . . *away*. My heart did weird things and my brain felt too full.

Cyrus's laughter followed me and soon he was at my shoulder again. "Wait, Abby. Come on." He wrapped his hand around my elbow and pulled me through the crowd, leading me onto a vacant—freezing—balcony.

Snow had accumulated on the railing, a full inch, and I wrapped my arms around myself. "Why are we out here? It's cold."

"Of course it's cold. It's Chicago in November." He released my arm and quickly shrugged off his jacket. "Here, put this on."

I accepted it automatically, pulling it over my shoulders. "How will you stay warm?"

"Are you kidding? I'm full of hot air." He stepped back, smirking in a way that looked self-deprecating, but he did not look cold. "Look, we can go back inside in a sec. Are you okay?"

"Yes, of course." *No, I'm not.* "I mean, it's—I thought—I don't know. I guess, I *did* know that a few of his ex-girlfriends and dates had ended up with a few of his friends and acquaintances, but I didn't realize it was every single one of them."

One of Cyrus's eyebrows ticked up as he watched me, but he offered no comment.

"That's . . . that's crazy, right? I feel bad for him. That the press has turned his nickname into the butt of a joke about his personal life. It's —" I wasn't doing a good job of explaining myself, so I slowed down, breathing out snarled emotion and breathing in calm. "It's sad. And frustrating. He is such a decent person—a good human—and I don't understand why it never works out for him."

"Maybe it hasn't worked out because he hasn't dated the right person," he offered with a shrug.

"Yeah. Yeah, that could definitely be it." My eyes lost focus as I recalled once more the complete and utter lack of interest in Rex's gaze when he saw me for the first time tonight, my stomach and heart giving just an echo of the dull, aching pulse I'd felt earlier.

Had I been holding out hope that I was that right person? Not . . . consciously. But after tonight, I wouldn't entertain the hope subconsciously either. And now that I'd well and truly given up, maybe I could be Rex's Rex.

Maybe I could be the girl he "dated" before he met his wife.

"Abby?"

I blinked Cyrus back into focus, filled with newfound purpose. "Do you have someone in mind?"

He stared at me like he'd missed part of the conversation. "Someone in mind?"

Ah. Yes. He had missed part of the conversation since I'd been lost in thought and debating with myself. "For Rex? Do you have someone you think might make him happy?"

Cyrus continued staring at me.

"Because I would like to help. Truly." I crossed the balcony and stood directly in front of him. "It's not too late for me to call off the wedding. If there's someone you think he's interested in, someone who will treat him well, and he's been hesitant to date because of how things normally turn out for him, just tell me what I can do and I'll do it."

As his gaze moved between mine, the side of his mouth curved slowly upward until he breathed a little puff of a laugh. "Uh . . ." He laughed again. "Abby."

"Yes?"

His eyes narrowed though he still grinned. "I don't know," he said haltingly. "I think I've meddled enough as it is. Maybe I should—we should—just let things run their course now." Then under his breath he added, "How does Rex make this look so easy?"

My stomach sunk at his caginess. "But there is someone?" *Maybe Alaric knows?* I doubted Alaric would remember me from high school, but I could still ask.

"Listen to me, you beautiful, sweet, lovely woman. There is no one else." Cyrus gently cupped my hands and pressed them together between his palms. "Stop worrying about Rex. He's a big boy, he can take care of himself."

"But I—"

"Abby."

Both Cyrus and I turned our heads toward the deep voice, finding Rex standing just outside the threshold of the door. Though he'd said my name, his eyes were on his friend, and he looked . . .

Well. He looked pissed.

"Oh, hey there Rex." Unhurriedly, Cyrus released my hands and stepped away from me, wearing an unconcerned smile.

The larger man continued glaring at Cyrus but held his hand out to me. "We should go in for dinner." His voice was monotone, but the slight edge of harnessed anger made my back straighten and my neck itch.

Why was he angry? He'd been the one to leave me the moment we'd arrived to go meet very important people. And now he was angry because I was talking to Cyrus?

Drawing myself up, I opened my mouth to point this out, but then his gaze cut to mine and the words died on my tongue. He looked angry, yes. But there was something else there too. Sadness? Frustration? Maybe something had happened inside the gala while Cyrus and I had been out here discussing how best to help Rex find a lady worthy of him.

Deflated, I pulled off Cyrus's jacket and handed it over to him. "Thanks."

"Anytime," he said, his eyes twinkling with more mysterious mischief. As he glanced between me and Rex, he looked like he might laugh. Just as I made it to the door, Cyrus added, "Seriously, *anytime,* Abby," and then he did laugh.

Rex made some sort of sound in the back of his throat—a cross between a grunt and a loud sigh—and his hand closed around my fingers in a tight squeeze the moment I placed them in his palm. Holding open the door, he guided me inside first, then slid his arm around my waist, pressing me more snugly against his side than I recalled him doing before, his body tense.

I peered up at him, watched his Adam's apple bob with a swallow, his *fuck-off-not-now* expression firmly in place.

"Are you cold?" he asked quietly, not looking at me, his voice a grumbly rasp.

I shivered. "A little."

He brought us to a stop and turned me so that we faced each other, his hand now splayed on the center of my back, hot through the thin layer of silk. The harshness behind his eyes seemed to dwindle as they hooked into mine.

"Do you have a wrap or—or something?"

I shook my head.

His eyebrows pulled together, and I only had a split second to register the concern in his gaze before he pulled me forward and wrapped his arms around me, bringing the front of my body fully against his. My lips parted in surprise as a burst of warm loveliness originating in the lower half of my stomach swirled and pressed outward, meeting and mingling with his heat everywhere he touched me.

I was being hugged.

By Rex.

And it was an experience like no other.

My friend Josephine said my hugs were best because there was just so much of me, so much height and my arms were long. She said it was like being wrapped in a chenille blanket with the added bonus of boobs and perfume.

For the first time, I understood what she meant. There was just so much of Rex. He was so darn big and strong and warm and—yes—it was like being wrapped in a chenille blanket. But instead of boobs, this one had massive biceps and smelled like the warmth of sunshine on a cold day, like heat and cologne, grass and snow, an indescribable dichotomy of everything cozy and brisk.

Dear Lord. I can properly die now. Life will never get better than this.

After a prolonged moment that felt infinitely too short, Rex's hands lifted to my shoulders, slid down my arms, and he pulled away.

"Better?" he asked, ensnaring my gaze again, his voice low and soft and lovely.

"Much," I said, feeling warmer . . . everywhere.

CHAPTER 14

"I'd rather die on an adventure than live standing still."

— V.E. SCHWAB, *A DARKER SHADE OF MAGIC*

"Take the money."

I groaned, splashing an island of bubbles away from my stomach. "I can't take the money."

The hot bath in the giant hotel tub had provided some comfort, as had the bottle of wine I'd indulgently ordered from room service. But when my brain refused to settle and my heart persisted in its sad ache, I'd called my lawyer.

Kaylee was the only one I could talk to about this. She was my friend, and I trusted her judgment. I'd told her all about the day and evening with Rex, what Cyrus had said at the gala and how Rex had—apart from the brief hug—basically ignored me all night. Then, when the gala had ended, he'd asked the driver to drop me off at the hotel and had opted to take a different car home.

"No, Abby. Take the money. For your own good and peace of mind, take it."

"I know you're thinking about my financial future, but taking the money is out of the question." Lifting my hand from the water, I inspected my wrinkled fingertips. I missed baths. My apartment only had a shower.

"I'm not talking as your lawyer right now, I'm talking as your friend. Yes, taking the money, which you agreed to take and which you have earned and will earn, is best for your financial future. But I also think you need to take it because not accepting the money means you're blurring lines that shouldn't be blurred."

"What do you mean?"

"If you take the money, you'll think of Rex as a boss—not a friend with the potential for more—and you'll see him within those boss-like boundaries. Would you care whether or not Walker commented on how pretty you looked in your dress tonight?"

I wrinkled my nose. "I see your point." If Walker ever commented on how pretty I looked, it would weird me out. "But Walker isn't comparable to Rex. I see Walker as an older brother, even a father figure."

"Fair enough, you've known him forever and so, sure, the boss lines have blurred there too. But let me ask you this, what do you see Rex as?"

Lifting my eyes to the ceiling, I ignored the dull ache in my chest and the miserable weight in my stomach. "I had a big crush on him in high school."

"I'm sure you did, along with everyone else. The dude is seriously hot."

"I guess . . ." I heaved a sad sigh. "I'm so stupid."

"You are not stupid."

"You would think I'd learned my lesson, but obviously some frivolous, naïve part of me must be hoping for that fairy tale to come true. That he asked me to do all this because he likes me, but the truth is—"

"He thinks of you as an employee, and he's been very upfront about what he wants and expects. He spelled it out in a prenup, an excessively fair and generous prenup. *That's* why you should take the money. He thinks you're taking the money, he thinks you're being fairly compensated for your time and effort. He probably didn't comment on how lovely you looked tonight because he didn't want to make you uncomfortable, seeing as how you *work* for him."

"You're right."

"I know."

I laughed lightly, feeling both better and worse. "Okay. I get it now."

"So you'll take the money?"

"No. I mean, yes. I'll accept it, but I think I'll donate it."

Kaylee released the world's most obnoxious sigh. "Why are you this way? Why can't you do nice things for yourself?"

"If I take the money for myself, it will make me unhappy. I learned that when I accepted the first check. Other than paying you back, I haven't spent any of it. Having thousands of dollars in my checking account gives me nightmares—don't ask me to explain it."

"I won't. I love you, but you make no sense."

"But you're right. I have to accept the money because that's what Rex and I agreed. I'm being a nincompoop." I nodded at my own assertion, feeling the rightness of it in my bones. "He thinks of me as an employee, not a friend, not anything else."

"What if he did? What if he wanted more?"

"He would never think of me like that."

"But what if he did?"

I considered the question and laughed at myself as the answer became confusingly crystal clear. I was a mess of contradictions: I wanted Rex to notice me, but I didn't want to date him. I wanted his praise and attention and flirting, but no scary commitment or expression of feelings.

"What's so funny?" Kaylee asked.

"No. Not with Rex. He . . ."

"What?"

"We would never be equal. I would always be at a disadvantage."

"Because he's wealthy?"

"No, it's not that," I said, my bones feeling heavier as I relayed the sad truth. "Because I don't trust myself around him. I like him *so much.* And know it's not just the idea of him, it's him. I've gotten to know him. I feel like he could ask me to do anything, ask me for anything, and I'd say yes."

"Yikes."

"I know."

"So, no Rex. But I thought you didn't want to date anyone?"

"I didn't," I hedged.

"But you do now?" A note of hope entered her voice. "You're ready to date again?"

I didn't need to think about the question. I knew the answer immediately, though I was loath to admit anything out loud. The idea of dating someone, putting myself out there, *trusting*, was still terrifying. And as soon as I confessed the truth, I knew Kaylee would start setting me up with her surfeit of single male friends.

And yet, something had changed recently. I'd changed. Pretending and texting with Rex had flipped a switch. A secret, dormant longing had been reignited. I wanted someone to flirt with, to have inside jokes with, someone to share my day and my burdens. *Someone not Rex.*

Haltingly, I said, "I want to take things slow."

She squealed.

"And, it'll have to wait until I'm finished helping Rex." I held up my pruned index finger from the water. "I'm not going to cheat on this fake marriage. Doing so would undo all our hard work, and I feel like dating someone on the side would be super shitty to Rex." He'd never explicitly said one way or the other, but I doubted Rex wanted me dating someone while he and I were fake married, and he said I could end the arrangement whenever I wanted.

What if he *dates someone?*

I forced my throat to work around rocks and shards of glass in shades of envy green at the thought because it wasn't any of my business. If Rex wanted to date someone, good. I was a placeholder, that's it. We'd divorce, maybe they'd get married, and that would be that.

"Fine, don't date until you and Rex are done with the arrangement. But this makes me so happy!"

I laughed. "Why are you so obsessed with me dating?"

"It's more like I'm obsessed with you finally getting over that skidmark ex of yours and leaving the memory of him in the dust where he belongs. I hate that he had so much power over you, even years later. You are the best. And I want to see you happy."

"I'm already happy."

"Okay, *happier*." I could picture her rolling her eyes, but I knew she was still smiling. "I want to see you blissfully, ecstatically, rapturously happy. And free of fear. You deserve it."

We married at the stadium on the fifty-yard line after Rex's Saturday practice in a whirlwind ceremony.

Rex's agent arranged it with the owners and the coaches, and the team photographer snapped pictures of the ceremony. Rex wore the home uniform as promised and I wore my white dress, a gorgeous strapless ball gown with a gathered bell skirt in silk taffeta and a fitted bodice. Surprisingly, Rex's agent hadn't thought about procuring a bouquet, and there were no rings. I didn't particularly care about the rings, but it did seem strange not to swap something during the ceremony. Declan and I had married at the justice of the peace, no one present but us and the other waiting couples. In retrospect, my wedding to Declan hadn't felt like a celebration so much as something to tick off a checklist, but there had been rings.

Today, though, I had no bouquet. Ryan Johnson—yes, the quarterback for the Squalls—handed me a football to hold instead, as a joke. I thought it was an awesome idea, so I did. This seemed to buy me instant credibility with the rest of the team.

At the end of the ceremony, after we recited our run-of-the-mill marriage vows in front of the stadium chaplain, the entire football team, the coaching staff, admin staff, and a few random stadium stragglers, Rex gave me a quick kiss—a speedy and abrupt press of the lips—before I had a single second to anticipate it. He then pressed his forehead to mine, his small, pretend happy smile encouraging my insides to play twister.

Everyone cheered, and you know what? No rings, no bouquet, surrounded by strangers (other than Rex), I felt celebrated. I felt cherished.

It was, by far, the strangest experience of my life. But also one of the most memorable. My smiles and laughter were real, and I felt oddly joyful. I knew it was fake, I knew all the arrangements—from having the team present to the dress that had been chosen for me—had been for the benefit of the media, lending our unconventional nuptials believability, but I loved every second of it. The adventure, the unknown, even the unexpected and disorder.

And I especially loved throwing the football thirty yards like a badass and into the hands of running back legend Trent Komfer. Everyone cheered again.

Congratulations and good wishes were handed out liberally; the photographer must've taken over a thousand pictures; and when it was all over, Rex left to change while I wandered around the football field, grinning as I contemplated my strange life. Or rather, grinning as I contemplated how strange my life had become.

As I reflected on where I was, both geographically as well as where my life choices had taken me, I decided that my life had been missing something for the last decade. Maybe even longer. Maybe my life had been missing something since the very beginning.

I'd needed this.

I'd needed a little excitement, a change in routine, an event to shake me awake from my sleepy existence. Reluctantly, I admitted to myself that a smidge of upheaval every now and again wasn't the worst thing in the world.

"Ready?"

I turned and found Rex standing three yards away. He now wore a finely cut dark gray suit, a light silver shirt, and an ice-blue tie. His short hair was still wet from his shower, he'd shaved, and one of his inscrutable stares was pointed right at me.

Even though it was just us, I grinned and said, "I am ready to depart, husband."

Something flared behind his eyes, the suggestion of a smile tugging at his mouth. "You're going to call me husband from now on, aren't you?"

"I am. Husband."

His smile, though exceptionally small, broke free. "Does that mean I can call you wife?"

I sauntered over to him, tapping my chin, and said, "I think I actually prefer *babe*." Now that I knew we weren't flirting, and we never would be flirting, ease and comfort had replaced confusion and hope. Perhaps, before we went our separate ways, I'd start to think of Rex like a brother, similar to how I viewed Walker.

Still giving me his little smile, his eyes narrowed at my approach. "What? Like the pig?"

"Exactly like the pig." I snorted twice, punctuating the sound by poking him in the chest. He glanced down at my hand but made no move to remove my fingers. "Wait, wasn't the dog's name in that movie Rex?"

His smile widened, but he refused to flash any teeth.

"I always loved it when the farmer said, 'That'll do, pig.' Like, I don't know, everyone wants to be told they're doing a good job by someone they admire and respect, you know? It's a universal theme, I think. Such a wholesome, wonderful movie."

"And that's why you like *babe*? Because it's wholesome?" Rex reached for my hand and wove it under his arm, pressing my fingers to the crook of his elbow as he turned us toward the exit.

"Uh, no." I laughed. "I like it when you call me babe because you make it sound like the opposite of wholesome."

Rex's steps slowed. "Oh?"

"Yep. You make all this pretending fun, Rex." I used a weird voice and an affected accent to keep the mood light. "And if I have to be fake married to anyone, I'm glad it's you."

His smile waned just a little and he deadpanned, "Because I'm so cuddly and approachable."

Without skipping a beat, I nodded. "I'm fairly certain, judging by that hug last night, you are a championship cuddler, husband."

"Is this your way of hinting that you want to add cuddling to the agreement? Because, if so, just say the word, *babe*."

I busted out laughing, withdrawing my hand so I could shove him away playfully. He was so solid, he didn't move an inch. But he did laugh, his teeth finally making an appearance. Rex caught my hand and brought it back to his elbow, trapping it there.

"So what do you want to do?" he asked, sounding happy. Since there was no one else around, I let myself believe his happiness was real. "I have a game tomorrow, but how about dinner?"

"My plane leaves at nine thirty tonight. I should be getting to the airport." I sent Rex—my boss—an apologetic smile. "Maybe next time?"

Once again, his steps slowed, and this time the smile fully vacated his features. "Wait. No. I told Bernadette to fly you out tomorrow, after the game."

"Yeah, but I asked her to change it last night, after the charity thing, so I can get back and have a full day at the studio tomorrow."

Rex's expression seemed to darken, his jaw set, his eyes cutting away.

I studied him, not understanding his reaction. "I'm—I'm sorry. We didn't have anything tomorrow on the schedule. I didn't think you'd care."

He shook his head, his eyebrows pulling together, though he did not look at me. "You're right. It's fine."

I squeezed his arm. "Rain check, okay?"

"Sure." Rex nodded, looking distracted, his eyes on the Astroturf. "When am I seeing you again?"

The Richmond game. At the reminder, the smile vacated my features as well. "Thanksgiving. If I see you after the game, that is."

He glanced at me. "You sound nervous."

"I am. A little."

"Why?"

I shrugged, feeling shy about telling the truth. But then I remembered that Rex was my boss and he needed to know if I was struggling with a work assignment. "I'm a little worried I won't fit in."

"You will. Just . . . do whatever the other wives do."

"Okay."

"You still look nervous."

"I am." I ducked my head.

He brought us to a stop, waiting until I met his searching eyes before saying softly, "Don't be. Be yourself. If they don't love you, they're idiots."

That was nice of him to say.

"So, *will* I see you?" I asked. "After the game?"

"Yeah. All the wives go down to the locker room after, it's tradition, then they leave, then we all meet up again and the whole team has Thanksgiving together." He gave me a barely-there smile. "I've seen you eat, you'll do great."

"Ha ha." I rolled my eyes, but I took a measure of comfort in his reassurance. "Then I should bring my knitting?"

He tugged me forward again toward the exit. "Sure. I believe one or two of them knit, I couldn't tell you who, though."

Now I pulled him to a stop and captured his eyes to make sure he wasn't teasing. "Wait. They knit?!"

He nodded.

I exhaled my relief, feeling immeasurably better. Now *that* completely changed everything.

CHAPTER 15

"The world is full of magic things, patiently waiting for our senses to grow sharper."

— W.B. YEATS

"Hello?"

"Abby, hey."

I grinned. "Who dis?"

"It's Rex."

"Rex who?"

A pause, then, "*Babe*."

"Ohhhhh." I chuckled, a shiver running down my spine. I seriously loved how he—my boss—said *babe.* In the days since I'd returned from Chicago, he'd been calling just as much as texting, checking in throughout the day and sending me *Babe: Pig In The City* memes. "Hello, husband. How are you?"

"Gooood." He sounded good. If I had to guess, he wore a smile. "Did you see the paper?"

That brought me up short. "Uh, paper?"

"The Austin Sentinel."

Oh!

I jumped up from my stool, rushing over to my backpack. I'd left for the studio so early this morning, I'd shoved the paper in my bag without reading it. "Wait, I thought the article was going to be published next Tuesday."

"No. Today. I wanted it done before there was a leak."

Rex sure was efficient.

Apparently, today—the Tuesday after the wedding and not next Tuesday as I'd thought—was the day Rex's interview and our wedding photos would appear. Rex had specifically asked to run it in the middle of the week.

"I haven't seen it yet." I unzipped my backpack and pulled the plastic-wrapped newspaper out. "Was the reporter nice? What did they say?"

"He was nice." Rex's voice contained just a hint of a menacing edge. "If he hadn't been, I wouldn't have done the interview. It's in the sports section, like we wanted."

The paper had wanted to put Rex's interview on the front page, but Rex and I both agreed the article was a necessary evil, a low-key way to share the news of our wedding and broach the subject of my sordid past so we could control the story.

Freeing the newspaper from the sleeve, I flipped to the sports section and reared back. "Hey. That's us." I hadn't seen the wedding photos from our awesome ceremony in the stadium last weekend. Rex hadn't sent me any and I felt weird asking for them.

The main picture for the article was a candid shot taken just after Rex's blink-and-you-would-miss-it kiss. Our foreheads were pressed together, and we were both smiling. "Aww. Look how cute we are, boss," I said, spreading the paper out on the wedging table.

"Read the article when you have the time, but I think you'll be pleased."

I scanned the text quickly and spotted the softball editorial style right away. Local boy football hero returns to small-town Texas and sweeps local girl / lost love off her feet after she endures heartache and tragedy, blah blah blah. "You rescued me?" I smirked at the first sentence of the fifth paragraph.

"Those were his words, not mine."

I chuckled, opening the paper to where the article continued, speed-reading until I got to a surprising quote. I blinked at it, read it again just to make sure I had it right, then cleared my throat to recite the quote. "'McMurtry admits that his wife Abigail was the one that got away, and that he's always hoped he'd find a way to get back to her.' Admitted that finally, did you?" I teased.

I knew it was all fake—just like we were fake—but it still made a squiggle of warmth dance in my tummy.

"I didn't say that," he grumbled. "He paraphrased."

"Then what did you say?"

"I don't remember."

"How convenient."

He grumbled again, something unintelligible, but it did not sound authentically grumpy. I could tell he was still smiling.

"What was that, husband? I didn't hear you."

"I said, Abby is the love of my life."

There was no way he'd said anything remotely close to that, but it was fun to hear him say the words. "Damn straight, you did. What else?"

"Flies love her feet and so do I."

I threw my head back and laughed.

He also laughed, loud enough for me to hear it over the phone.

"Did you talk about how you love my eyes and they were the first thing you noticed about me?" Even though he couldn't see me, I fanned my eyelashes, blinking my eyes several times. "And how you want to lose yourself in their glowing depths?"

"*Glowing depths* makes you sound like an alien. And it wasn't your eyes, it was your hair."

I cackled. Before the trip to Chicago, I would've considered this flirting, but now I saw it for what it was. Like Walker, Rex liked to tease, and that was perfectly fine with me. I also liked to tease. "Is that what you told him? Because it's red?"

"Because you had your back to me and it was all I could see," he said, then added a second later, "And I was hungover."

"You told him you were hungover?"

"No. Read the article."

"Fine. I will." I closed the paper so I could look at the photo of us again. It really was a beautiful shot.

"Are you all set for Thanksgiving? You got your flight?"

"Yep." I traced the skirt of my wedding dress with my index finger. "But your agent's office didn't send through the hotel information."

"Oh, the place is booked full. You and I will be sharing a suite."

My eyes widened. "A what?"

"A suite. It has two bedrooms." He seemed to hesitate. "Is that okay? I should've checked—"

"No, no. That's fine. I've never stayed in a suite with two bedrooms before. It sounds fancy. Totally fine." It was totally fine. Walker, his wife Ramona, and I had shared a hotel room once. This would be just like that.

Except you're both the wife and the employee this time.

Before I could think too much about *that* twisted thought, he said, "There's something else."

"Something else?" I inspected Rex's smile in the picture. It looked genuine, and I had no doubt that it was. He must've been so relieved to finally have it done and over with, and everything settled.

"My—uh—aunt called me."

I looked up from the photo. "Your Aunt Sally?"

"That's right. She wanted your number."

I rolled the edge of the paper between my thumb and index finger, unease settling in my stomach like a snapping turtle. "Oh?"

"Yes. She wanted you to come for Thanksgiving. I explained you'd be in Richmond with me."

"Oh." I hadn't seen Rex's Aunt Sally since my mother's funeral. I liked the woman, she'd always been kind to me. She also had the same fun-loving worldview as Rex's dad but without the short attention span and impatience for anything other than instant gratification.

Rex cleared his throat. "She wants us to come for Christmas too."

"For Christmas? I thought you didn't see your family for Christmas."

"I said I don't see my dad and my siblings for Christmas. But sometimes I do spend part of the week with my Aunt Sally and Uncle Terry."

"I see . . ." My brain was all over the place. I really didn't want to playact in front of Rex's aunt. In addition to being kind and generous and awesome, she was also wicked smart. She'd see right through Rex, and that would make everything awkward and awful.

He was quiet for a beat, then said, "I can tell her you have to work."

I thought about my options. "Do you want me to come?"

"I do."

That surprised me. "Wait. What? You—"

"It would look strange if I were there and you weren't."

I opened my mouth but only a whisper of a noise came out. He couldn't possibly want to spend a day lying to his aunt.

"And if we arrive together—just for one day or one dinner—that should be plenty." His tone remained conversational and completely reasonable. "I can't spare much time, and they know that, so it wouldn't be odd for me to fly in for a day and then fly out."

"They? Who is *they*?"

"Aunt Sal, Uncle Terry, and their friends from the gym."

Rex's aunt and uncle owned a gym in Alenbach where an annual weightlifting competition took place during the first weekend of summer. His aunt had competed every year I'd lived in our hometown and took home the first-place ribbon most of the time.

"Rex, don't you think they'll see right through us? Don't you think they'll see it's fake?" I was glad to be the only person in the studio this morning, it allowed me to speak freely without worrying others would overhear.

"I don't."

"Your aunt and uncle have known both of us our whole lives. And your aunt is smart. Really smart. She'll know right away." I was sure she would.

At least I was certain she'd see through Rex's act, but maybe not mine since it was less of an act and more of a . . . well, a situation.

Rex's Aunt Sally had known about my crush on her nephew when she was my Girl Scout leader in middle school—I was 99 percent certain she had—which would give my part of the deal credibility. And since I truly did like Rex even now, though I no longer held conscious or subconscious hopes after talking the issue through with Kaylee last weekend, I wasn't too worried about Sally suspecting *me* of lying.

"If you pretend convincingly, then there should be no problem," he said, a cross between a grumble and a growl. "I have to go."

"No, not yet. You're either being a snot or purposefully obtuse, boss." I pushed away from the wedging table and paced over to the wheel where I'd been throwing earlier. "I'm not the issue."

"*I'm* being obtuse?" His tone reeked of incredulity heavily perfumed with disdain.

"Yes. Obviously."

"How can you say that?"

"Come on. The charity gala?"

A pause, then, "What about it?"

"You said maybe seven sentences to me all night—which was fine, whatever, I'm not complaining. But you were not a man in love on the precipice of getting married. I was there to be helpful, I know my place, and I know I'm a paid employee. I'm just saying, you can't treat me like an employee in front of your aunt and uncle and then expect them to believe we're newlyweds for real. Especially not during Christmas."

Rex was quiet for a long time. He was quiet for so long, I had time to pace back over to the newspaper, fold it, return to my backpack, and stuff it inside.

Eventually, he said, "Abby, I don't think of you—"

Setting my hand on my hip, I checked the clock on the wall and waited for him to finish his thought. I took off my watch whenever I used the wheel, not wanting to get slip and water all over it.

Rex cleared his throat and started again. "I won't treat you like a paid employee. I'll be . . . convincing."

I shook my head, skeptical. "Think about this very carefully before you agree."

"I have."

"If they suspect you don't have real feelings for me, they'll push you about it. They'll confront you. You'll have to boldly lie to their faces or tell them the truth."

"They won't suspect I don't have real feelings for you," he said, his voice deeper than before, giving me the sense he was losing patience with the conversation, or I'd said something to insult him.

A humorless laugh bubbled out of me at his reaction. "Okay, if you say so." I mimicked his grumbly tone, rolling my eyes, and knowing in my bones that this was a mistake.

He'd been a good actor at the rehearsal dinner before Halloween, but he'd been aloof and distant during the other two events we'd attended together. These wouldn't be friends and acquaintances in a crowded room. This was his family. At Christmas. In a little house. Family always, *always* knows what was real and what was lasting.

And what was not.

"Is there something you want to tell me?"

Still distracted by my phone call with Rex, I stopped in my tracks just inside the door of the Boozy Rancher. Walker stood in my way, blocking any path I might try to take into the bar.

His eyes fierce, his mouth curved in a severe frown, he seemed to be waiting for me to say something significant.

"Uh . . ." The Thanksgiving decorations I'd spread liberally around the bar two days after Halloween looked great. Everything seemed fine, just as I'd left it last night. "You said you were okay with the Leftovers Are for Quitters and Thankful for All You Fuckers signs. Should I take them down?"

"Not the decorations, Abby. Do you have anything important to tell me?"

I glanced left. I glanced right. "No?"

He made a small sound in the back of his throat, his eyes narrowing. "Really?"

"What did I do? Did I do something wrong? I swear I locked up last night."

Reaching over the bar at his left, he picked up the newspaper—

today's paper, opened to the sports section—and lifted it in front of my face. "You're married."

The ground beneath my feet shifted. *Shit.*

I was such an idiot. "Oh. That."

I should've told Walker yesterday, but I'd been putting it off, thinking I had more time until the article published.

"Yeah, Abby. That." Walker lowered the paper, his hands now on his hips.

"Surprise." I tried to force a grin. I failed. Likely because I felt like a jerk. *Shit.*

My boss's usually smiling mouth arranged in a grim line, he tossed the paper back to the bar and reached around me to lock the front door. We still had ten minutes until opening time, so I surmised we were doing this now. *Shit. Shit. Shit!*

Dead bolt flipped, he turned and paced away, putting most of the dining room between us before facing me again. "What's going on? Why didn't you say anything?"

I stumbled a few steps toward him. "It was . . . sudden."

"Apparently. Real sudden. So sudden you couldn't be bothered to tell me."

Yikes. He sounded angry.

My stomach hurt and my head spun as I tried to sidestep lies. "Rex wanted to do it in Chicago. It was very last minute."

"I see." Walker looked at me like he wanted to yell but held it in. "He treating you right?"

I nodded.

"And are you happy? At least tell me you're happy about getting married again."

My conversation earlier with Rex pressed against the back of my skull. I had a headache. "I'm not unhappy."

"You—"

"I'm sad that you seem upset." I darted another step toward my friend and the closest thing I had to family these days.

"Hell yeah, I'm upset."

I winced, crestfallen. "I thought so." *I hate this so much.*

He closed the distance between us, stopping directly in front of me.

"You're like a daughter to me, Abby—if I'd had one early in life. Or a niece. You mean a lot to me, and to Ramona." He sounded so solemn, hurt. "I'm sorry, but I don't understand why you'd go off to Chicago without telling anyone, get married to this guy, and then come back here like nothing happened, saying nothing. Explain it to me."

"It's—I can't—" I closed my eyes and snapped my mouth shut so I wouldn't blurt out the truth. I hated lies. I didn't want to be a liar. And now I felt like a complete idiot for not considering how hard it would be to lie to Walker. *Once again, I am so freakin' stupid.*

"How can I make it up to you?" I asked, my voice barely more than a croak and—DAMMIT—my chin started to wobble.

He made a soft sound. In the next moment, his hands were on my shoulders, and he'd pulled me into a hug. Automatically, I hugged him back.

"You don't need to make it up to me. I mean, it would be nice if—once y'all get pregnant—you tell me before you give birth to the baby."

I heaved a broken laugh, grabbing fistfuls of his shirt and swallowing convulsively. I didn't trust myself to speak, not yet. Walker was just so good and I was the worst. I felt glad I wasn't his daughter. He deserved someone so much better than me.

"I'm upset, but I'll get over it. It's just . . ." His arms tightened. "I don't have much family. I got you, Ramona, Jonas, and Owen the dentist who comes in on Fridays, and that's it."

Now I laughed for real, shaking my head and pulling away to swipe at my eyes.

He didn't let me go far, his hands moving back to my shoulders as his eyes searched mine. "Honey, you matter to me. And that means I want to have a say in your life, not the final word. You do what you need to do, but I want to know about you. Got it?"

I nodded, sniffling. "Okay."

"Good. So." Walker let his hands drop. "Tell me what happened."

"Um." I glanced at the wall behind him. "So, Rex and I have known each other since—"

"Elementary school. I remember. What happened? When did y'all get together? How long have you been seeing each other? What do his parents think? Are they treating you nice? They didn't seem to be there in the pictures."

So many valid questions.

I pushed my fingers into my hair. "His mom passed away our junior year of high school."

"I see. What about his dad?"

"He owns a big car dealership in Alenbach but is semiretired. He and his new wife travel a lot, I think, and since it was sudden, they didn't come." As far as I knew, everything I'd said thus far had been factual.

"Why do you look so . . ."

My gaze cut to his and I found him studying me with perceptive eyes. I tried to look less . . . whatever he thought I looked. "What?"

"Abby, is there more to this?" Walker's voice gentled and his stare sharpened. "Are you in trouble?"

"No! I'm not in any trouble. I'm good. So good. And if I were in trouble, you'd be the first person I asked for help."

His head tilted subtly to the side. "Not your husband?"

"Uhh—right. Rex first. Then you. Then Owen the dentist."

He didn't believe me. "Then why are you here instead of in Chicago?"

"I work here."

His expression morphed into one of intense disbelief. "Really? For how long?"

"What? You want me to quit?"

"What?" He mimicked my tone. "You don't want to live with your new husband?"

I told myself to stop twisting my fingers. "It's kind of complicated."

"Abby, it can't be that complicated. There's only one reason you marry somebody."

"Yeah, you're right. It's—I'm just being difficult. I don't want to leave Austin." Also not a lie, but Walker had a really good point. The next time I spoke to Rex, we'd need to discuss this.

"A man needs his wife. And a wife needs her husband. Y'all shouldn't live apart, not if you can help it."

I scratched the back of my neck, working to keep the tightness from my voice. "Lots of people live apart. And he'll be back. Once the season is over, he'll be back here. In Texas. With me."

Walker's head moved back and forth in a slow movement and his eyes narrowed again. "Nah. Something is going on. Something is off about this."

"I—"

He held up his hands. "And I understand you don't want to tell me what it is. But when you're ready, I am here for you. Understand?"

I said nothing, not wanting to lie and deny anything was wrong or reassure him that all was well. He was right, something was *off.* Namely, I'd married a man for money, was now his employee, and that man was a taciturn grumpypants with massive mood swings who I couldn't seem to stop having sex dreams about.

"All right. I see how it is." His tone grew knowing. "When you're ready, you'll tell me."

"You think so, b—Uncle Walker?" I'd been about to call him *boss*, but somehow that felt wrong after using it so often with Rex.

He tried to flatten his expression, but I saw the twinkle of amusement shining through. "Very funny."

"You prefer Daddy Walkerbucks?"

"Just Walker, thank you." He stepped forward, pulling me into another hug and rubbing my back. "You can tell me anything, Abby. I mean it. You'll always have a place here."

"I know. And if I ever have anything to tell you, I will."

"Good." He pulled back and lifted his chin toward the front door, his hand landing heavy on my shoulder. "Now get to work. The drinks aren't going to make themselves."

CHAPTER 16

"When it comes to judging individuals, I do not like remarks such as 'too good to be true.' They speak as though one is rewarding the nature of evil. Yet, ironically, we still wonder where all the good people have gone."

— CRISS JAMI, *KILLOSOPHY*

"Be with you in a second," I called to the group of three women who'd just entered the bar. When I spotted how many shopping bags they held between them, I pasted a smile on my face and gestured to table seven. "Take that table over there, plenty of room for your bags."

They nodded gratefully and wove through the late afternoon crowd toward the table I'd indicated. Ingrid would likely bitch at me for giving up a five-top for just three people, but she wasn't anywhere in sight, and she could just deal with it.

Stop. Ingrid is awesome. Ingrid won't care. Stop assuming the worst of people. You are not this person.

Breathing out a huge sigh—I was so disgusted with myself—I finished an order of two hot toddies and one spiced cider, then placed them on the pickup station for Ingrid to take. On a whim, I decided to serve the drinks myself, penance for thinking so poorly of Ingrid.

I'd been a real jerk recently and I needed to snap out of it.

Rex hadn't contacted me or responded to my messages since last week, our tense exchange about going to his aunt's house had been our last conversation. No texts waiting for me when I woke up, no surprise calls during the day just to check in, no ridiculous memes making me laugh. True, I'd only texted him once, two days ago, asking him to call me so we could discuss how to handle the whole living apart thing. He hadn't.

I tried to ignore how much his silence bothered me, having to work extra hard to smile and be cheerful with customers and my coworkers as Thanksgiving approached. But it did bother me.

Whatever. He's not my friend. He's my boss. If I did something wrong, he can put it in my performance review and send it to HR.

I assumed "HR" in this scenario would be his faceless agent, who I still hadn't met officially but who had been sending me emails during Rex's radio silence.

She'd been passing along details for future events, sending me outfit options, asking about my travel preferences, and helping me sign up for my very first frequent flyer account. I liked her. Bernadette Loren was clearly efficient and good at her job while also projecting an air of professional friendliness.

I should get an agent.

After my uncomfortable confrontation with Walker, I'd made a point to call all my friends, one at a time, and break the news. No one was upset but everyone was astonished. A few people wanted to buy me wedding presents, and the resultant waves of guilt were overwhelming.

Like Walker, almost everyone had questions I didn't know how to answer, which only served to make me feel like a complete moron *and* a horrible person. Clearly, I hadn't thought this arrangement through. Rex and I needed to talk and hammer out more details, expectations, and what story I should be telling to friends. And this also made me feel like a jerk because now I was apparently a person who strategized how best to lie to her friends.

I hate myself.

Walker had let the marriage thing drop, but he did make teasing—and breathtakingly sarcastic—comments about how being married "sure did agree with me." Likewise, Kaylee and Josephine must've picked up on my irritable mood. They'd ensured I'd asked for tonight off, the Tuesday before Thanksgiving, inviting a few of our friends over to Josephine's loft for a viewing of *The Princess Bride*.

The bell over the door rang again just as I'd finished placing the drinks on table four and ascertaining whether they needed anything else. They didn't. Affixing a bright smile to my face, I faced the front door, and my words of greeting died a quick, messy, painful death on my tongue, the bright smile dimming to a black hole of shock and horror and nausea.

"Declan," I whispered. He didn't hear me, but it didn't matter. The smarmy bastard was looking right at me.

Licking his lips, he meandered forward to the hinged countertop opening which led to the galley, his ice-blue gaze trailing down my body. When his eyes lifted, his black eyebrows had hitched higher, and he—in an intense moment of déjà vu—inclined his forehead toward the back of the bar. He wanted to talk in the back room. *Just like old times.*

Glaring at him, I pressed my hand to my stomach and walked slowly forward, stalling to gather courage. The last time I'd seen him had been in court when I'd testified against him. For ruining so many lives—for completely shattering my youth and faith in humanity—he'd been given just seven years in prison.

The unfairness of it still strangled me, which was likely why I needed to clear my throat before speaking. "What are you doing here?"

"Hey, beautiful. Thank you for asking, I'm doing fine. How are you?" He grinned down at me, his voice equal parts smooth and rough, but the look in his eyes unsettled me, sent a spike of adrenaline from the pit of my stomach up my spine.

"Leave." I sidestepped him and walked into the galley, shutting the hinged countertop before he could follow. My good sense followed and I reached for my phone, calling the security guys with steady fingers. I wasn't going to wait to see if Declan did as I wished, because he never did. Nor could I go to the back to retrieve Walker for help, leaving Declan alone in the bar would be idiotic. Also, something about him felt wrong, desperate.

Where is Ingrid?

"Okay. It's going to be like that?" In my peripheral vision, I watched him turn and lean his elbows on the bartop directly in front of me. "Then let me get right to the point, beautiful. I'm going to need more money if you and Rex McMurtry want that sweet little story he told the paper to remain unchallenged."

Ignoring him and the cold wave of fear spreading to my fingertips, I brought the phone to my ear and waited for someone to pick up.

"You cheated me, bumpkin. You shouldn't have done that to a man who has nothing to lose."

"The only cheater here is you," I muttered just as dispatch answered my call. "Hello? Yes. I'm at the Boozy Rancher and I need a disruptive customer removed."

"If I'd known why someone wanted to buy the story, there's no way I would've accepted that offer." His voice hardened and he leaned closer. "You're going to talk to your husband and you're going to give me what I want, do you understand? Or do I need to speak slower and use smaller words?"

Dispatch confirmed they were sending over a team, said it would be five minutes or less, and I hung up. Glancing at the clock on the wall behind Declan—four minutes and fifty-eight seconds, *I can do this*—I stepped back and crossed my arms.

"Look at me, you dumb hick." He made no attempt to hide his anger or the threatening tone in his voice.

I reaffixed my glare to him. If I fully ignored him, he'd cause a big scene. He hated being ignored.

He lowered his voice, like he was telling me a secret. "Are you still so stupid that you think I'll stay silent about the truth? About the part you played? I'm going to need a lot more money. *A lot* more. The price tag for burying your past just tripled."

I shook my head, saying nothing, because there was nothing to say. I played no part in his schemes and lies. The only thing I'd been guilty of was being too stupid and lonely and trusting to save myself from a con artist.

But I also stayed silent because he was freaking me out.

His gaze slithered over me again and he bit his bottom lip, sucking it between his teeth. "You look good, though. But then, fucking rich, powerful men always did agree with you."

"Leave. Please," I choked out, knowing he detected my fear and not turning to look as I sensed Walker come out of the back room to my right.

Declan's slimy glare cut from my breasts back to mine. "Maybe we can work something—"

"The fuck?" Walker, apparently recognizing Declan immediately, lifted the hinged countertop and barked, "Leave. Now. Or I'll make you."

Releasing a noisy breath, Declan set his glare on Walker. "Fuck off old man, this has nothing to do with—"

Walker had my ex's arm behind his back and his face slammed against the bartop before I could cover my mouth to suppress a yelp. "That's refusal to leave. Now I make you."

Judging by the wide-eyed and slack-jawed expression on Declan's face, my ex hadn't been expecting my typically affable boss to react so swiftly or violently. Nor had I.

Yanking him by the neck and arm, Walker marched Declan to the front and shoved him forward, using my ex's body to push the door ajar, which made the bells ring over their heads. Then Walker followed him out, the door swinging shut just as Declan found his voice to shout a protest.

Acutely, I became aware of a few things at once: the music in the bar, Dean Martin's "Baby, It's Cold Outside," the absolute silence otherwise, and that every set of eyes seemed to swing in unison from the front door to me.

Dropping my hands from my mouth, I straightened my back and lifted both my chin and my voice, "How about a round on the house?" *Courtesy of my prenup allowance.* This seemed like an appropriate use of Rex's money, especially since Declan likely wouldn't have shown his face today if I hadn't agreed to help Rex.

This suggestion was met with a few confused frowns, but mostly a smattering of perplexed laughter and cheerful agreement. I did a tally of what each patron was drinking and moved to deliver on my promise.

Ingrid, suddenly at my elbow, leaned in close and muttered, "Who was that?"

"My ex-husband," I whispered. "I took table four their order earlier. Give me a hand making these drinks?"

"You have an ex-husband?" I felt her eyes move over me as she quickly jumped in to help. "Since when?"

"Since forever ago."

She leaned to the side, peering out the front door. "He's . . ."

I didn't look. "Handsome?" He was still handsome, *really* handsome. Age hadn't diminished his beauty. Blue eyes, black hair, mysterious and sexy once upon a time. Now I saw through all that window dressing to the scary sociopath beneath.

"Yeah," she breathed out her answer. "He looks like a fairy-tale prince or something."

I huffed a humorless laugh. "More like a fairy-tale villain." Clearly, she hadn't heard what Declan just said to me.

Ingrid sent me an apologetic smile as we traded commiserating looks. Her ex-husband—who I'd met just once—wasn't a bad guy, but I knew their divorce had been messy. "I'm sorry. I shouldn't have said that. But if my ex had looked like that guy, maybe we'd still be married," she joked.

I didn't smile. "He cheated on me and sent me to prison."

Her eyebrows shot up and she let out a low whistle, filling three glasses with soda water. "All right then. I retract my statement. If my ex had done that to me, no matter what he looked like, they wouldn't find the body." Ingrid bumped my hip with hers. "You're a better woman than me, Abby. Let me get these to table two and take seven's order. How long have they been here?"

I eyed the women at the five-top who were similarly eyeing us. "Just a few minutes, long enough to see the excitement and know they're getting free drinks."

"Gotcha." Ingrid speed-walked to drop off the gin and tonics and then greeted the three women with their load of shopping bags.

Meanwhile, I finished making the new round, waiting to do the hot drinks last so they wouldn't get cold at the pickup station. I alternated between checking the clock on the wall and the watch on my wrist, balling my hands into fists when they started to shake. *Adrenaline.*

I breathed through it.

Walker had been gone for a while and I hadn't seen the security guys yet. Hopefully Walker had met them outside the bar, they were dealing with Declan, and that's what was taking my boss so long.

But still.

I didn't like that Walker hadn't returned yet. I also didn't like the crazy look in Declan's eyes earlier. And I most especially didn't like that he'd said he had nothing to lose. Going back to my apartment tonight didn't seem like a good idea.

Withdrawing my phone from my back pocket, I sent Kaylee a quick text asking if I could spend the night at her place after the movie and then proceeded to unnecessarily wipe down the bar as the last of the adrenaline left my system.

Abruptly tired, I poured myself a cup of coffee and added two packets of sugar and a whole lot of half-and-half. I needed . . . something sweet, the comfort of hot, creamy coffee. When I finally made it back to my apartment—whenever it felt safe to do so—I'd definitely be opening a packet of bacon.

The bar buzzed with happy conversation as my eyes darted between the tables. Sipping my coffee, I checked the clock on the wall again just as the bell over the door jingled, drawing my attention there. Walker caught my eye and lifted his chin toward the back room, his jaw tight, his eyes worried.

Setting my mug down, I preceded him to the office and he met me there, his hand coming to my shoulder and giving a squeeze. "Are you okay?"

"I'm okay." I wasn't quite okay, but I was getting there.

The worry behind his gaze persisted. "I heard some of what he said, the threat, but what did he want?"

"Money."

He angled his head back a scant inch, absorbing this information. "'Cause you're with Rex now?"

I nodded.

"He must've seen the story in the paper."

I shrugged, not particularly feeling inspired to rehash what had just occurred.

"Take the rest of the day, Abby."

"No." I shoved my hands into the pockets of my apron. "My shift is almost over. I'll stay until Kaylee and Josephine come get me."

"No. Take the day. I already called Rex, he's on his way."

I reared back. "Wait, what?"

"You don't need to stay. Ingrid and I—"

"No, no, no. What did you say?" I shook off his hand. "You called Rex?"

He lifted an eyebrow at me. "Yeah," he said, his tone also implying an *Of course I did.*

"What? Why? Why did you call him?" My heart ping-ponged in my chest as thoughts took similar chaotic actions in my brain. "And how do you have his number?"

"His agent called the bar last week and gave it to me." Walker looked at me like I was crazy. "And I called him because I figured you'd be too shaken up to do it, and if something like this had happened to Ramona, I'd want to know right away."

I groaned, turning and pulling my phone out of my back pocket to check my screen. No messages.

Phew.

Maybe it's fine. Maybe Rex told Walker he was on his way just to get him off the phone. Maybe I—

My phone rang, Rex's number flashing on the screen. I stifled another groan.

"Who is it?" Walker asked.

"Here's a hint, his name rhymes with hex," I muttered, swiping my thumb across the screen and bracing myself for . . . whatever. "Hello?"

"Are you okay?"

Closing my eyes against the discombobulating flare of warmth caused by the sound of Rex's voice after a week of nothing—and the obvious concern within his voice—I gritted out, "I am fine. Walker shouldn't have called you. Sorry."

"Did he touch you?" His voice dropped to the deepest baritone, and something about it made the hairs rise on the back of my neck.

"No. Like I said, I'm fine."

"Bernadette booked you a room at the Four Seasons." Sounds of traffic from Rex's side of the call made me think he was on a street somewhere, and I checked my watch. He should've been at work. "I'll be there by six."

"What?" I shuffled a few steps away from Walker. "No. No you will not be here. It's Thanksgiving in less than two days, the Richmond game—"

"She also arranged a car and security for you." What sounded like a car door slamming shut on his side snuffed out the traffic noise.

I growled my frustration. "No. You are overreacting. You and Walker are both overreacting." Truthfully, I didn't know if they were overreacting. But the last thing I wanted was Rex to fly down here when he had an important game on Thursday. "Everything is—"

"Be at the hotel when I arrive."

"Rex."

"Please."

I sighed, renewed warmth spiraling within my middle at the gentle, beseeching note of the single word.

"Please, Abby."

Holding my forehead with stiff fingers, I growled again before gracelessly acquiescing. "Fine! Fine, I'll be there. Fine."

"Thank you."

"You're welcome."

I figured he would end the call now that I'd agreed. He didn't. I listened to the muffled sounds of traffic and road noise for several long seconds before he said quietly, "I'm really glad you're okay, babe."

His line went dead. I sighed, irritated with myself for the swell of relief and gladness I felt knowing Rex was on his way.

CHAPTER 17

"Nothing haunts us like the things we don't say."

— MITCH ALBOM, HAVE A LITTLE FAITH: A TRUE STORY

A giant meal and a bottle of wine were waiting for me when I arrived in the suite. Upon seeing the items, and after my security detail did a sweep of the room and left to stand outside my door, I promptly burst into tears.

I cried for a good long while in the corner of the room, my back against the wall, while hugging a hotel couch pillow to my chest. But past experience had taught me I couldn't solve much of anything by crying in corners, no matter how essential it felt. I wiped my tears, stood, and strolled over to inspect the now tepid food, determined to set aside the events of the day and eat, at least for a little bit.

Pulling the room service cart over to the couch, I numbly clicked through the available movies until I saw *The Princess Bride*, grumbling about the $15.99 fee for the rental, but paying it anyway. Or rather, I guess Rex paid it anyway, seeing as how he'd arranged for the hotel room.

Spearing a maple glazed carrot that didn't taste like anything, two giant Neiman Marcus bags sitting on the mattress in the bedroom caught my attention. I walked over but I didn't look inside, instead reading the note next to the bags.

Dear Abby,

These should be your size. If you need anything else, just email my team.
-Bernadette

PS (I hope you are okay!!)
PPS Be nice to Rex, he's stressed about the game on Thursday

It was nice of Rex's agent to send stuff since all I had were the clothes on my back.

I hadn't stopped by my apartment for one very simple and alarming reason. The security detail Rex had arranged did a sweep of my apartment complex's parking lot before driving over to get me from the Boozy Rancher. Declan had been sitting in a car, parked in the lot, facing my first-floor porch.

My new security team friends had called the police but suggested I forgo picking up things from my place until morning, just in case he was working with someone and that someone followed me to the hotel. Tiredly, and likely in shock, I'd agreed, deferring to their expertise.

I'd also sent Kaylee a text to cancel our plans as well as my request to spend the night, giving her a truncated version of the afternoon's events. She'd called, but I'd sent it to voice mail. I didn't particularly wish to rehash Declan's visit again. But I did send another text, reassuring her I was fine.

Now, instead of watching my favorite movie in the comfort of Josephine's cozy loft with Kaylee, Jonathan, Nash, et al., I was stuck here, in this palatial suite while I waited for my fake husband to show up and do . . . whatever he planned on doing.

As Billy Crystal declared Cary Elwes only mostly dead, my attention drifted to the bags on the bed again, just visible through the open door to the bedroom. Curiosity abruptly getting the better of me, I paused the movie and placed my napkin on the coffee table before meandering over to the bedroom. Once there, I peeked inside the bags, my forehead wrinkling.

They were stuffed.

Reaching inside, I pulled out shirts and designer jeans and slouchy sweaters in cream and espresso brown, the thick knits soft as a cloud beneath my fingertips. Frowning at the tags announcing that these items were 100% cashmere, I searched for a price tag and found none.

Hmm. Thorough of them to remove the price.

Setting aside the sweaters, I dug around the bottom of the bag and lifted several lacy underthings up, beautiful matching bra and panty sets in black, red, and white. These did have the price tags and I nearly choked as I read the first one I encountered. Five hundred and fifty dollars.

"Holy smokes!"

Absorbed by my new inspection of the lace—searching for gold and diamonds and bitcoins to justify the cost—I almost didn't hear the sound of the lock whirring or the door to the suite opening.

But I did hear the unmistakable sound of Rex's gruff voice as he called my name, and I did feel the resultant disobedient leap of my heart.

Turning from the bags and the bed, I crossed to the bedroom door, gulping in air at the sight of his glorious massive form stomping around the room.

He's your boss. You are his paid employee. You are not friends. This is a business relationship. Do not cry in front of him.

I arranged my face into what I hoped was a benign, placid smile. "Hey, husband."

Rex's head whipped toward me. His hazel eyes wide and rimmed with obvious worry, they moved over my form, giving me the sense he was checking me for injury.

I frowned at his inspection and crossed my arms. "I told you I'm fine. He didn't—didn't—" Words fled my brain and I automatically walked backward at his advance, my heart jumping to my throat. Rex didn't stop until my back hit the wall of the bedroom. He then pulled me forward and wrapped me securely in his arms.

I bit my lip and slammed my eyes shut—*don't cry, don't cry, don't cry*—my throat working to no purpose. I'm not sure how long we stood there in silence, maybe seconds, maybe minutes, but he eventually pulled away and gently cupped my cheeks with his hands.

He didn't say anything, just looked at me and swallowed thickly. Reflexively, I gripped his large wrists and held on, too overwhelmed to do anything but stare at his eyes and the enigmatic intensity there.

And then he whispered, "Abby."

"Rex," I squeaked in reply.

"I'm sorry."

"What for?"

"Your—he threatened you. You had to deal with him on your own."

His words confused me, and I spoke aloud as I tried to untangle them. "He did threaten me, but I wasn't alone. Walker stepped in. And it's not your fault."

Rex's mouth formed a stern line, his fingers pushing into and then sifting through my hair. His eyes followed the movements of his hands. "It is."

My mouth curved upward ever so slightly. "No. It's his fault. Not yours, not mine. His."

"I should've known." A frown marred his forehead as he continued to contemplate my hair with touch and sight, looping it around his fingers.

Goodness, what Rex was doing felt nice. Really nice. Relaxing. Comforting. I almost forgot to be confused by his actions. But then I was confused because . . . Wait. *What is happening? Why is he touching me like this?*

Gazing at him and holding my breath, I watched his eyes drift from my hair to my lips, his hands returning to cup my jaw and gently tilt my chin up.

"You're so . . ." he said, the words unfocused, distracted.

"What?" I whispered on a controlled exhale.

Rex's gaze came to mine, abruptly sharpened, then shuttered. He straightened, removing himself a step, his hands dropping to his sides.

Bracingly, and while ensconced in the thorny weeds of turmoil, I studied him from my place against the wall.

"I apologize," he said, his frown deepening. "I'm—"

"You must be tired," I said, wanting to give him an excuse, as though being tired explained away his preoccupation with my hair and storming in here just to back me up against a wall.

I'll have to think about all this later, when he's not so . . . here.

He gave his head a light shake, still staring at me, something I couldn't label gathering behind his eyes. But then he blinked, and it was gone, replaced with the cold marble façade I used to study so intently instead of my schoolwork.

Rex lifted his chin and crossed his arms, backing away another step. "The guards stay," he said, unmistakable determination behind the dark rasp. He looked every bit the foreboding defensive end who relied on intimidation to get what he wanted.

Perhaps most people would find his posture and tone menacing, but based on the sudden, pulsing ache low in my stomach, my body did not. But my body was also weird, turning on like a lightbulb in the face of his harshness, considering the fact that I'd just spent an hour crying in the corner while holding a couch pillow.

I dropped my eyes to the floor to avoid openly ogling him. "I think that would be wise."

"You do?"

"Yes. I do." I pushed away from the wall, taking the odd flare of lust with me. Crossing to the bed, I focused on placing the items I'd withdrawn back inside their bags rather than obsess about the feel of Rex's fingers in my hair, or how his gruffness and bossy attitude really seemed to do it for me.

"We'll take them to Richmond."

I nodded. "Sounds good."

Rex entered my peripheral vision. I felt his eyes on my profile. "Why are you agreeing so easily?"

I shrugged. "The team you hired said Declan was waiting for me at my apartment building tonight, and it's possible he's working with someone, if he thinks this has the potential to be a big score for him." Folding the sweaters carefully, I set them gently in the bottom of the bag. "I'm the last person in the world who will underestimate him. He's . . ."

"What?"

"Scary."

Rex drifted closer. "He won't touch you."

I didn't respond, because Declan had touched me today, just not physically. In a way, he'd slapped me when he'd called me stupid, picking at a scar not quite healed.

I felt Rex's hesitation before he asked, "Did he? Did he ever . . .?"

"No." I glanced at him, giving him a small, reassuring smile. "You already asked me that, before Jason and Amy's wedding."

Frowning again, this time in concentration rather than sternness, he said, "I know. But we're—we know each other better now."

"You mean we trust each other more?" Reaching for one of the staggeringly expensive pairs of red underwear, I tossed it in the bag.

"I hope you trust me more." Rex's eyes and his frown followed the movements of my hands. "What is all this?"

"Bernadette sent me clothes since I was cautioned against stopping by my apartment." I held up a scrap of black lace and showed him the price tag. "Can you believe this costs over five hundred dollars? I mean, what? Where are the cupholders? Does it come with a condo share in Cabo?"

The two lines between Rex's eyebrows deepened, the slant of his mouth angling down. He dropped his eyes to the bed for a split second, then turned and left the bedroom. "I'll sleep on the couch."

Leaving the rest of the items, I followed him. "You're staying?"

Not looking at me, he nodded.

I leaned my shoulder against the doorframe, digesting this information. "Then you should take the bed."

"No—"

"I'm short, remember? And you're a perfectly formed giant." Turning back to the bedroom, I grabbed the bags from the bed and carried them to the living room. I felt his eyes on me as I moved back to the couch and lifted the cover off my half-eaten dinner.

"No. I will—"

"I'm not arguing about this." I picked up the remote and unpaused

The Princess Bride. "I've had a long day, and I'm already all set up here." I didn't point out that he had an important game on Thursday—a game his team was expected to lose by a lot—and he needed to play his best, and he wouldn't play his best if he didn't sleep well tonight.

"You—"

"Shh." I waved my hand at him dismissively. "I'm not on the clock. Leave me alone, boss. Go sleep."

A dry laugh erupted from him, frustrated but clearly amused in spite of himself. Walking over to me, his tone unyielding, he said, "I'm taking a shower. Then you're taking the bed. End of discussion."

I slept on the couch, he slept in the bed, but neither of us slept well. I knew this for a fact. He'd tossed and turned all night—he was a big guy and the hotel bed had squeaky springs—and I was afraid to sleep since I still struggled with nightly sexy Rex dreams. Rex stopped throwing himself around close to 4:30 a.m., but I never managed to stop my clock-watching.

Bleary-eyed, I shoved out of the couch bed I'd made for myself just after 6:00 a.m. and snuck into the bathroom, wanting a long hot shower more than coffee. I let the tiled room fill with steam as I shucked my clothes from yesterday, which I'd slept in, and left them in a haphazard pile in the corner of the bathroom.

Bernadette had bought me pajamas, but since she'd left the price tag attached to those, I hadn't worn them. I'd never slept in twelve-hundred-dollar pajamas and I didn't think I was ready to pick up the habit. What if I could never go back to oversized T-shirts and sleep shorts after this was all over? I didn't want to ruin myself with unsustainable luxury.

Taking my time under the spray, I did allow myself to use the hotel's high-quality shampoo and conditioner, the French-milled soap, and the complimentary razor blades I'd found under the bathroom sink. Uncertain how much time had passed, but certain it had been a lot, I eventually turned off the water and pulled a towel off the shelf, sighing contentedly as I dried myself.

It was at that point that I realized my sleep-deprived, bleary-eyed error. "Shoot!"

All my clothes were in the other room, still in the bags to the right of the couch. Smacking my forehead lightly, I grimaced as I contemplated my dirty clothes from yesterday, heaped in the corner of the bathroom.

Aw, man!

I didn't want to wear them, not after that high-quality shower. Plus, Rex was probably still asleep after his night wrestling with the bed. *Just go get the clothes, bring them back here, and get dressed. Easy peasy play parchisi.*

Opening the bathroom door a crack, I waited for my eyes to adjust on Rex's form in bed. His back was to me, a sheet covered his bottom half, his massive upper half appeared to be unclothed, but he didn't move. Satisfied, I tiptoed out of the bathroom and bedroom while clutching the towel to my chest, leaving the bedroom door just slightly ajar behind me. I then sprinted on light feet over to the bags next to the couch, flipping on a light as I went.

Luckily, I'd left the underwear and bras on top. It was easy to grab a matching set, a shirt, and a pair of jeans. *I know, I know, I wouldn't wear the pajamas, but I'll wear the clothes? Who told you humans make sense? No one, that's who.*

I haphazardly juggled the items while working to secure the slipping towel. In a rush, I turned and return-sprinted into the bedroom, then screamed as I opened the door all the way. Rex was standing right there and not at all where I'd left him less than thirty seconds ago!

My clothes went flying—apparently, I become a popcorn maker when startled—my shirt and bra landing on his shoulder and stunned face.

"Ohmygosh!" I stumbled a step back, gripping the doorframe, my eyes dropping of their own volition, and that's when I spotted his massive—and I mean *massive*—wood. "Ah! Oh my *gosh*!" I covered my face with a single hand.

No seconds later, literally the moment I'd spoken, the lock on our suite whirred and the door flew open. I spun around, my hand dropping to my mouth, startled all over again as a man and a woman I didn't recognize burst into the room.

Immediately, Rex gripped my hips, and he pulled me behind him, hiding me with his big body.

"We heard a scream," the woman said after a tense moment.

I was tucked close to Rex's bare back, one of his hands still on my hip, and I cringed. My bra was still on his shoulder, and I knew the man and the woman were getting an insane eyeful of Rex's substantial erection. Since I could do nothing about the erection but I could do something about the bra, I snatched the black lace, gripping it close.

"Everything is fine," came Rex's calm but sleep-roughened voice, his fingers flexing on me as his other hand closed the bedroom door a little. "False alarm."

I couldn't see the guards—obviously they were new guards, second shift, who I'd completely forgotten would be standing outside the room —but I heard their light footsteps on the natural stone of the small foyer before the suite door snicked shut.

A helpless groan slipped past my lips. "Ah, God, I'm so sorry."

Rex bent and picked something up. His shoulders rose and then fell as he straightened. And then they rose and fell. And then they started to shake.

I peeked between my fingertips as he turned, realizing he'd picked up my folded jeans and held them in front of his groin, and that he was laughing. Not only was he laughing, he was laughing uncontrollably, full-body laughter, shoulder and belly involvement. Dropping my hand, I made a disgruntled face as I scanned him.

"I thought you were asleep," I offered weakly, smiling despite my embarrassment. "And I forgot to grab new clothes when I went to shower."

Rex blinked down at me through his tears of hilarity, his smile huge and genuine and so blindingly handsome, I was tempted to cover my eyes again. I wouldn't. I'd never seen him laugh quite like this before. I soaked the sight up, racking my brain for a means to extend it, prolong his laugh. Unable to think of anything to say, I simply watched him.

I blame sleep deprivation.

Watching him unfortunately morphed into staring before I quite realized his laughter had tapered, and his smile was waning, and he also stared.

Goose bumps rose over every inch of my bare skin—which was basically all of my skin—and I found myself needing to take deeper and deeper breaths, especially when Rex seemed to lean forward, not exactly entering my personal space bubble, but coming precariously close.

Or was that me? Was I the one leaning forward?

With that uncertainty came a sudden hot flash and I dropped my eyes to the carpet, removing myself a step. "Ah, well, I should get dressed. So—" Stepping to the side, I darted into the bathroom and shut the door behind me. Once inside, I pressed my back against the door and sucked air into my lungs, my head silently hitting the door.

What is wrong with me?

Maybe it wasn't my fault. Maybe he was just too epically sexy and distracting. Maybe—

A soft knock sounded on the bathroom door and I tensed. Briefly wondering if I could simply pretend not to hear the knock, I quickly realized any such attempt would be absolutely ridiculous.

I managed a wobbly, "Yes?"

"Your clothes."

"My—?" I glanced down at my hands. The only thing I held other than the ends of my towel was the black lace bra that had landed on his sculpted shoulder. "Oh! Yeah. Ha ha. I guess I'll need those."

Face flaming, I opened the door a few inches and kept my attention low as I accepted the jeans, shirt, and undies from Rex. *BIG* mistake. As he handed over the clothes, his erection outlined by his gray underwear—still just as large and in charge—came crisply into view along with his washboard abs, thick, muscular thighs, and large man hands. Rolling my lips between my teeth instead of muttering a thank you, I closed the door swiftly and tried to expel the images of his luscious body from my mind.

He is your boss. Boss. Boss. Boss.

Bosses do not have luscious bodies.

Bosses are amorphous stick figures in business appropriate attire.

But I couldn't stop the flashes of jumbled images from this morning—his laughter, his thighs, his smile, his bright happy eyes, his stomach, his—

NO! Stop it. Stop.

Overheated, I pressed a cold washcloth against my neck and forehead. I didn't want to wonder how the day could get any worse because doing so would tempt fate. I instead endeavored to focus on the positive: I was now fully and completely awake, no coffee required.

Mortification was like owning a rooster in the morn—

AH! *No! Don't think about cocks!*

CHAPTER 18

"You think fairy tales are only for girls? Here's a hint - ask yourself who wrote them . . . . Yes, girls want their princes, but boys want their princesses just as much."

— DAVID LEVITHAN, *DASH & LILY'S BOOK OF DARES*

Rex and I ended up flying to Richmond together. How he managed to snag the seat next to mine the day before Thanksgiving, I had no idea. Now here we were, me drinking a Bloody Mary because I'd read somewhere they taste better on airplanes, and Rex drinking water. Always water. So much water.

"I have a question," I announced as soon as the flight attendant placed our drinks down in front of us.

"What's that?" Rex faced me in my window seat, so he didn't see the woman's gaze move over his body appreciatively before glancing at me. I gave her a wink.

She grinned, flushing a little red around the ears.

Rex frowned, glancing over his shoulder, but by then she'd already moved on.

"The night you ended up at my bar, before Halloween." I picked up my vodka drink and sniffed. "Why did you drink that night? You haven't had anything but water since."

"Who were you winking at?" I surmised Rex was staring at the guy across the aisle as he asked this because the gentleman reared back, his eyes wide and a little scared.

I patted Rex's forearm. "Concentrate."

He turned the remnants of a glower on me, and I understood why the dude in 2D looked like he was about to shit his pants. "Was it that guy?"

"No." I laughed at Rex's expression. His scowls were so cute. "Come on, answer the question. Why can you drink alcohol in the middle of October but not now?"

"I can't."

"Can't what?" I twisted toward him while holding my drink, bringing the straw to my mouth.

"Can't drink." His eyes lowered to where I sucked the spicy tomato mix through my pursed lips.

"But you did drink."

"Yes." He breathed in, closing his eyes and turning his head toward the seat in front of him. "But I shouldn't have."

"Ah. A night of sweet rebellion."

"No."

"Then what was it?" I stretched my legs, not feeling as guilty this time for flying first class, especially since I was with Rex. His size made first class look like coach.

"It was . . . nothing."

"Do you often drink even when you're not supposed to?" I felt like I knew the answer, but I wanted him to confirm my suspicion so I could ask my next few questions.

"No. Never."

"And yet you did that night?"

"Yes."

"Why?"

He shrugged, opening his eyes, picking up his water, and mumbling, "Why do you want to know?"

"I want to know what inspires you to break the rules."

His eyes sliced to the side, carrying with them a mysterious heat and weight as they crashed into mine. "You're not much of a rule breaker either."

"No. I'm not. But I did color outside the lines in Mrs. Gold's class, whereas I recall you strictly adhered to line norms, even then."

Rex turned his face toward me again, his big head resting on the highest point of the seat. "What else do you remember about me? From school?"

Uhhhh.

My eyes rounded. I didn't want to lie, but I didn't want to tell him the truth either—which was that I remembered *everything*. "Uh—" I nibbled on the inside of my bottom lip. "Let's see . . ."

"Not much?"

"No. I remember a lot." I tucked my hair behind my ears and crossed my arms. "You picked me for the kickball team even though I could never kick the ball."

The side of his mouth hitched. "You were fast, though. Tommy Vanet was a good kicker, and then I'd sub you in to run if he made it to first."

My lips parted and I made no attempt to hide my surprise. "That was you who did that?"

He'd never been the one to direct me to take over for Tommy, it had always been one of his appointed cocaptains. Apparently, Rex had been delegating even then. And I'd been part of a *strategy*?

Here I'd spent years thinking he was just being nice, picking me for his team because I was a reject.

He nodded, his smile spreading. "Why'd you dye your hair black? It was always black. And short."

I squirmed under the continued weight of his gaze and the fact that he clearly remembered more about me than I'd thought. "I didn't like my natural hair color," I said breezily. "And I thought black looked good, so. . ." I waved my hand through the air so he'd fill in the blanks. "But back to my original question."

"Which was?"

"You—being a person who usually follows the rules—drank to

excess, a very uncharacteristic non-rule-following choice. Why'd you do it?" I brought the straw to my lips again.

Rex's eyes flickered to my mouth. He covered my hand holding the glass, lowering it before I could take a sip. "I don't know why I did it."

"You don't?" I glanced between his hand still covering mine, keeping me from my drink, and his eyes. "Do you often engage in self-destructive behaviors that reliably lead to suffering without knowing why?"

"I have recently," he grumbled, sliding his hand away.

This sent a spike of alarm through me and I leaned closer, catching his fingers before he could withdraw completely. "Wait, Rex. Is everything okay?"

His expression turned flat. "Yes."

"What—what kinds of things—"

"Nothing. It's nothing." He folded his arms over his chest, his hands now hidden.

"Can I help?"

"Uh . . . no." He exhaled a dry laugh.

Restless and pensive, I said, "I'd like to help."

He closed his eyes, turning forward again, and ground out, "I'm taking a nap."

"But—"

"Shh."

My mouth opened in outrage. He'd shushed me!

Yeah, but you shushed him last night . . .

Also, he hadn't slept well last night, but one would never know it given how much energy he'd seemed to have this morning.

Traveling with another person was completely different from traveling by oneself. During my first trip, I'd felt lost walking through the airports in Austin and Chicago, and a little panicked. This time, all I had to do was hold his hand and let him take the lead through security, to the best spots for food, and eventually to the gate.

Rex had been recognized a few times before we left Austin as well as on the plane as people boarded. We'd stopped or paused our conversation for him to take pictures with fans. He was always so gracious about it, but he must've been exhausted.

I decided, even though he'd shushed me, I'd let him sleep. Or that had been my plan, but after finishing the Bloody Mary, my eyes had grown heavy. Suddenly, the next thing I knew, his hand was cupping my cheek, gently coaxing me awake from where my head had somehow come to rest on his shoulder.

"Time to wake up, babe," he whispered, tilting my chin up and back as his long fingers slid into my hair. "Come on, beautiful. We landed."

I blinked at him. He filled my vision but not in focus. My lids felt like sandpaper against my eyeballs. "What time is it?"

"Time to disembark."

A bell chimed somewhere overhead and hundreds of clacking sounds filled the cabin, seat belts being released. I twisted in my seat to look around, stretching my back and my arms over my head as I spoke around a yawn. "Did I sleep for the whole flight?"

"You did," he said, his eyes darting up from somewhere as I faced him, making me look down at my shirt to make sure I hadn't spilled any of the Bloody Mary earlier.

"Did you get a nap?" I asked, frowning at my shirt and finding it clear of spots.

"A little one."

My fingers fumbled with the seat belt. "Then you'll sleep when we get to the hotel."

"Oh? I will?"

I focused on him finally, studying the flat line of his lips paired with hazel eyes that looked both warm and stubborn.

"Don't," I said.

"Don't what?" He reached under my seat and pulled out my bag. "Your book, don't forget it's in the back of the seat."

"You'll sleep and you'll like it." I accepted my bag as he put it on my lap.

"What if I'm feeling inspired to break some rules? Be self-destructive and suffer?" He stepped out into the aisle, needing to duck his head a little because he was so tall. The man he'd glared at earlier in seat 2D seemed to shrink back, finding something interesting to study on the floor.

Tugging on the back seat pocket, I fished out my book and then shoved it into my bag. "Break rules and suffer after the game tomorrow. You have my full blessing."

He grumbled something like "I'll hold you to that" as he extended his hand, and I sent him a questioning look. Rex wiggled his fingers in a grabbing motion. "Give me your bag. I'll carry it."

I made a face. "Then who will carry your bag?"

"Me."

"You will not be my pack mule." I shouldered my own bag and straightened, but not all the way. The thingamajiggers overhead made it impossible for me to stand up. I had to kneel in his seat.

Rex made an exasperated face, which I mimicked, which made him glare at me, which made me glare at him, which made him smile, which made me smile. And then we were just looking at each other and smiling and—

"Excuse me."

We both turned our heads toward the woman standing in the aisle in front of Rex. Kind brown eyes, framed by a generous network of laugh lines, moved between the two of us. "I'm sorry, I just wanted to say, you two are so darn cute."

Rex and I traded looks. I recovered first. "Oh. Thank you. You're so kind."

"How long have you been together?"

"Forever," he said, draping his arm around my waist where I still knelt in his seat.

"I thought so," she said, grinning at me warmly. "Don't take this the wrong way, but y'all remind me of me and my husband. We've been together for forty years."

"Thank you, ma'am." Rex's politeness pulled a wider smile out of her.

"Like an old married couple. So much comfort, so much love. Been together since high school?"

"Preschool," Rex said before I could speak. "She was a fast runner." He gazed down at me with dazzling pretend adoration. "But I finally caught her."

❄

It felt like Christmas the moment we stepped off the plane in Richmond, Virginia. The airport had big Christmas trees in the terminal and near our baggage claim. Sparkly tinsel, blow-up Santas, and angels over mangers abounded. I did a lot of rubbernecking to take in the lights and displays, shivering when we stepped outside even though I wore a heavy down jacket.

Rex just smirked at me and said, “Are you cold, Texas?”

I gave his body a nudge with my body. Unsurprisingly, he remained immovable. “It’s cold here! All sane people who don’t live in Chicago think this is cold.”

His smirk became a grin, and he wrapped an arm around my shoulders, rubbing his hand up and down my arm as we followed our driver out to a waiting—and warm—car. Once we were buckled up, Rex made a few calls while I checked my Etsy messages, reading through a few special order requests. Eventually, the heat in the car made it so warm, I ended up taking off my big jacket and rolling up the sleeves of my new designer T-shirt.

“What are you reading?” He leaned to the side as we inched along in stop-and-go traffic, peering over my shoulder.

I elbowed him lightly. “Don’t read over peoples’ shoulders, husband. It’s rude.”

He didn’t move. “What’s that?”

“Special orders for my Etsy shop. It’s important I check in every —hey!”

Rex snatched my phone and promptly took a screenshot of my storefront. Then he texted it to himself while I grabbed at his hands and arms. We were still stopped in traffic, and I felt our driver’s eyes move over us in the rearview mirror.

“You are so rude!” I thought about unbuckling my belt so I could reach my phone. Instead, I pulled down the strap over my chest until I could put it behind me, allowing me maximum movement while keeping the seat belt fastened. If Rex continued this kind of behavior, I’d be thinking of him as an irritating older brother in no time.

"If I place a special order, do you have to fulfill it?" Even though he was finished sending the text, he continued to hold my phone away.

"No." I grabbed the cuff of his jacket and pulled with all my might. He didn't budge. "Ugh! Why are you so strong?!"

He held still, no longer leaning away and definitely not fighting back, seemingly pleased to just let me claw at his torso as he kept my cell just out my grasp. Exasperated, I did unclick the belt—I know, I know, road safety always come first, but it was the principle of the thing!—and I scrambled over his lap, having to place one knee between his thigh and his door in order to finally reach the phone.

"Ha ha!" I grabbed at it, but my jubilation was short-lived because his massive paw of a hand held it with a viselike grip. I started to laugh, frustrated as I worked to pry his fingers off. "You are the worst."

"Am I?" he asked, and in my single-minded focus, it took me a few seconds to register the question or his quiet, thoughtful tone.

When I did, I looked at him, prepared to make threats against his personal effects—had he forgotten we were sharing a suite? Did he think he'd be safe from retaliation?—but then the threats died on my tongue.

He wasn't smiling, nor was he frowning. He was just looking. His gaze traced along various parts of my face while I straddled his lap. Hair wild, huffing and puffing, my determination to retrieve the phone circled the drain until it disappeared completely, and I forgot why I'd been so dogged in the first place.

The car abruptly accelerated, pushing me into Rex's chest before stopping just as suddenly and throwing me back. I grabbed the front of Rex's jacket for balance while his free hand firmly attached to my back, and our eyes snapped together.

I still breathed hard, but it had very little to do with my earlier struggle. "Don't take what doesn't belong to you," I whispered.

His eyes sharpened and he frowned. "I usually don't," Rex whispered back harshly, sounding frustrated and also winded, his hand sliding from the middle of my back to just above my hip. "But you won't let me buy any of your pottery."

Wait? Is he actually mad right now? I couldn't read him.

"So you steal my phone?" I also frowned. Focusing on indignation would be far preferable to entertaining the butterflies in my stomach.

I have no mental energy for entertaining butterflies right now!

The car moved again, and Rex's hand slid to my other hip, his arm tightening around my back. "You never give me any options," he bit out.

I dug my fingers between his palm and the back of the case, and he finally released it. Hurriedly, I tucked it down the front of my shirt and into the left cup of my bra.

While I did so, his head reared back and his lips parted in surprise. "Did you just—"

"That's right, I did." I grabbed his arm for balance and used it to leverage myself back to my seat, ignoring the heat climbing up my neck. "Now it's safe from your thievery."

I felt Rex's eyes on me just as sure as I felt a snappy comeback pressing against the tip of his tongue.

Whatever it was, he never said it.

CHAPTER 19

"When is a monster not a monster? Oh, when you love it."

— CAITLYN SIEHL, LITERARY SEXTS: A COLLECTION OF SHORT & SEXY LOVE POEMS

"He's an absolute monster out there!" Vanessa Johnson—human rights lawyer, mother, knitter, and wife of Chicago Squalls QB Ryan Johnson—turned over her shoulder to look at me. "Whatever you're doing, keep doing it."

I shrugged helplessly and shook my head, knowing my expression was a cross between a smile and a grimace. "It's not me."

This earned me amused side-eyes from the other wives gathered in the box, with Regina Garcia leaning in close to whisper, "Sure, honey. Keep telling yourself that." She patted my knee, a knowing smile on her lips.

They were wrong. They were all wrong.

Yes, Rex was playing the game of his life, but I had nothing at all to do with it. After our odd and tense drive to the hotel from the airport yesterday, he'd been avoiding me. He'd left almost as soon as we arrived at the hotel and had returned after I'd eaten dinner. Rex had very politely asked how my day was, I'd responded with equal politeness, and then he went to sleep. Leaving super early this morning, he hadn't said goodbye, and I'd relied on emailed instructions from Bernadette in order to navigate to the stadium.

But everyone in the box kept coming over to pat me on the shoulder, thank me for God knows what, and tell me to keep up the good work.

Don't get me wrong, I was having a fabulous time now that I was here and not stewing in the hotel suite. Rex had been correct, the player's wives were wonderful. So kind and welcoming. Quite a few of them knit and before the game started, we had all sat together in a circle, showing off our works in progress or recently finished objects. I loved having shared craft interests with people, it was a shortcut to social integration, ingratiation, and initiation.

As soon as the game started, we all moved to the stadium seats at the edge of the box to watch. I loved how focused they all were, voicing their opinions about plays and calls, standing up to cheer and shout, but not booing. Never booing.

Early on in the first quarter, it became clear Rex was playing a heck of a game. Richmond had been heavily favored to win, but their offense hadn't been able to move past their own forty-yard line, the Squall's defense tearing hole after hole into Richmond's offense and forcing the QB to throw the ball away. By the end of the second quarter, the mood of the Richmond team and fans had completely shifted from excitement to anxiety. Not only had Rex sacked their QB twice, he'd intercepted a pass and ran for a touchdown, putting Chicago on the board 7–0.

"You must be his lucky charm." This comment came from Cordelia Davies, a very prim and proper looking homemaker and mother of five kiddos with an upper crust British accent.

She'd surprised the crap out of me earlier by repeatedly cussing like a sailor. And she was quite . . . vulgar. Not that I'm judging! It just came as a surprise the first time she'd nudged me with her elbow during the second half, right after Rex had made his first sack, and said very seriously, "I hope you're giving him blow jobs for each of those."

Vanessa Johnson had overheard the comment and sent Cordelia a chiding look. "Come on, Cordelia. We want her to like us."

After the third quarter and several more sacks by Rex, Regina had cut in just as Cordelia was offering to send me the name of a personal sex toy shopper. "Leave her alone, Cordelia. She's a newlywed, and you're making her red." Then to me, Regina had whispered, "People are going to tease you because you're new. We all love Rex, and we want to know you. Don't worry about Cordelia. She's so great, once you get to know her. But there's always one in every group, you know?"

I nodded in understanding. Kaylee was that "one" in my friend group, and it was not unusual for her to make all our other girlfriends go from laughing hysterically to grimacing in disgust but also still laughing.

Now it was the fourth quarter and Richmond was still scoreless. The only points on the board had come from Rex's second quarter touchdown. Richmond had possession, and our defense led by Rex had just driven them to Chicago's fifteen-yard line after another sack.

"You are magic, my girl." One of the player's grandmothers patted my shoulder, sending me a maternal look. I'd forgotten her name but didn't let myself feel too guilty about it. There were over one hundred people between all the club boxes our group inhabited, and I'd been introduced to all of them.

Rex had taken some brutal tackles. At one point, while our offense was on the field, the network cameras had switched to the sidelines, capturing a close-up of a cut being stitched up over one of Rex's eyes, blood running down the side of his face. My heart had spasmed at the sight, but I couldn't look away.

The poor guy was battered and bruised, and everyone here seemed to be giving me all the credit for his success.

I gave the grandmother next to me a small smile. "I promise, it's not me. I have no magic. He's the one working really hard."

"Then you keep working him hard," the older woman said, winked at Cordelia, then left before I could process what she'd implied.

Laughing it off—my cheeks flaming—I turned my attention back to the game. The clock had almost run out and Richmond was in a tight spot. They might tie it if they found a way to push through our defensive line, but that wasn't looking likely. They seemed to be holding on by a thread, doing everything in their power just to prevent another turnover. I almost felt bad for them.

The players came to the line, and everyone in the box seemed to go quiet. We just needed the clock to run out and the Squalls would win in a major upset during a nationally televised game on Thanksgiving. I sent a prayer upward that we would do it. After all Rex's hard work and the brutal tackles he'd endured, I really, really wanted this for him.

The Richmond QB hiked the ball and I gasped as he immediately backed up into our end zone. We all seemed to jump to our feet in unison. It all happened so fast, Rex charging into the pocket like a giant, pissed off bear, mowing down Richmond's offense. The QB turned and tried to throw the ball away, but it was too late. Rex sacked their QB for a record fourth time, in the end zone, which awarded the Squalls two extra points, and that was the game.

Everyone in the box went wild, screaming happily, hugging, some people cried. It was madness. And everyone seemed to want to embrace me first. Overwhelmed in the best way, I tried to return as many hugs as possible, smiling so widely my cheeks hurt, but I didn't care. I was so pleased for Rex—pleased and relieved—I completely forgot about the fact that it was tradition for all the wives to march down to the locker room together.

Arms looped with Regina and Vanessa as they chatted excitedly about plans for the rest of the evening, I finally came back to myself and tried to remember what Rex had said about what to do after the game.

Just . . . do whatever the other wives do.

Biting the inside of my lip, I glanced at Vanessa and caught her eye. "Hey, so. This is my first time here. What usually happens when we get to the locker room?"

"Oh, well, usually we're not allowed in the locker room. But for the Thanksgiving game we are. And what happens depends on if we win or lose," she said conversationally. "If we lose, then it's usually pretty somber and we just do our best to cheer them up, reminding them that they have Thanksgiving dinner to look forward to, that kind of thing. Then we all meet back at the hotel, and the evening is usually pretty quiet."

"What happens if we win?"

"Oh, girl." Regina's words yanked my attention to her, and I didn't miss the brightness in her eyes. "Prepare yourself. Gird those loins."

My eyes rounded, but then Vanessa laughed, tugging on my arm. "Don't listen to her. It's not that bad. But just know that, after the game TW played, he'll be feeling like a conquering hero all night."

"Lucky you."

I turned over my shoulder and met Cordelia's eyes. The comment had come from her and she was smiling broadly, her eyebrows wagging. She had her arms linked with two of the other wives I'd met in the box, and they were both giving me friendly grins, like they were happy or excited for me.

I chuckled, hoping it didn't sound anxious. "Oh yeah. Lucky me."

. . . do whatever the other wives do.

Inhaling deeply, I told myself not to be nervous. I would do what Rex had suggested: whatever the other wives did, that's what I would do. I resolved to hang back and watch, study each of them as they greeted their husbands, and make a mental list of how they behaved. Then I would approach Rex and do a mishmash of the other wives' actions. No biggie.

The roar of the locker room greeted us long before we actually made it to the door, and the sound sent a shiver racing down my spine. Watching a game at home had been nothing like watching it in person. But this, being so up close and personal to all of it and about to enter the locker room of my favorite team while they celebrated an unexpected victory, felt totally unreal.

Something in my brain sorta switched off, and I felt a bit like I was watching myself, the moment was so surreal.

"Come on," Vanessa shouted, unhooking our arms to pull me in after her. She turned and said something else, pointing behind me, but I couldn't hear her. It was loud, but it was the best kind of pandemonium. Everywhere I looked people were celebrating, husbands hugging their wives, those without wives hugging each other. Several people had opened bottles of champagne and Solo cups were being filled.

I laughed because their joy was so infectious.

Trent Komfer—the running back I'd thrown a pass to at my wedding—stumbled into me accidentally, turned, and gave me a big hug. They were all still in their away jerseys, and he was sweaty, but I didn't care.

"Congratulations!" I shouted as he released me, and I thought he shouted something like "Thank you" in return. Then he was gone, moving back into the chaos to give and receive embraces from his team and their wives until his spouse made it into the locker room. Spinning in a slow circle, I did my best to keep an eye out for Rex while trying to surreptitiously take note of what the other wives were doing.

There was lots of jumping into arms. In fact, almost all the wives seemed to jump at their husbands. I took a deep breath, inhaling sweat and dirt and cold, deciding that I would have to jump at Rex.

I can do that. I can jump. I'd never jumped at someone before, but I'd seen *Dirty Dancing*.

I watched Vanessa—after she jumped—pepper her husband's face with kisses. Cordelia jumped and then attached her mouth to her husband's, but I looked away quickly when I saw one of her hands snake downward.

Regina jumped, was caught, they exchanged a few words, quick smiles, and then they were kissing. Her husband then turned her back against a row of lockers and rolled his—

Oh. Okay. Look away. I wasn't a prude, but I wasn't a voyeur either.

A plan formed: jump, talk, smile, pepper face with kisses, the end. Rex and I had hugged before, talked and smiled before. He'd given me a quick kiss at our wedding. I reasoned that no part of my plan seemed objectionable or like it might make Rex feel uncomfortable. It was a good, solid plan.

Wiping sweaty hands on my jeans, I spun in another slow circle, this time searching for Rex rather than observing the rest of the crowd. I found him after two more spins, coming out of a newly opened door.

Like everyone else, he was still in his jersey, but unlike everyone else, he wore blue sweatpants instead of his uniform leggings. His features were impassive as he accepted handshakes. But no one attempted to hug him.

I frowned. *Maybe he's injured?* He'd taken a beating out there.

I rethought my plan, removing the jumping part and also the embracing part. I'd just skip to the talking, smiling, and lightly peppering his face with kisses. Eyes on my target, I scooched through the general revelry as unobtrusively as possible, but I was stopped a few times by players who wanted to say hi. I decided to give them hugs if they initiated it first, wanting to be careful just in case they were injured like Rex. All of them wanted hugs.

Finally, I navigated through the sea of rejoicing bodies and just about made it to Rex. I told myself to put on an excited smile but found as I stared at him—he hadn't spotted me yet—my grin came naturally and my heart beat fast with excitement. It might've been strange, but I was so proud of him. He was truly exceptional at his job and clearly both respected and beloved by his team.

My excitement was dampened by worry as I inspected the cut above his eye and the swelling around it. I waited until Rex and the teammate he'd been talking to seemed to be finished and then stepped forward, taking the spot the other man vacated. In the split second before I got there, someone had tapped Rex on the shoulder. He turned partway to lean forward as the man in a long-sleeved polo and khakis said something in his ear.

I waited, uncertain what to do, then felt silly for my uncertainty, yet no less unsure. Did I grab his hand? Arm? Tap him on the shoulder? Jumping at him was off the table. Maybe I could—

Rex turned while I was lost to my internal debate, his eyes widening as they landed on me, like my presence was unexpected, or a surprise. Or maybe he'd forgotten I was at the game?

Uncertainty became a sword of embarrassment, and it pierced my heart. My lungs had trouble drawing a full breath.

We should've discussed this in greater detail. I decided, in that moment, we would map out all future events from now on. I didn't want to be caught in this web of awkwardness again, where I thought

I was supposed to do one thing and he expected me to be a mind reader.

Or he forgets you exist.

However, right now, there was absolutely nothing I could do other than try to act natural and get through this.

"Hi," I said, twisting my fingers because—faced with his inscrutable stare—I forgot what I was supposed to do. "Great game! You were awesome out there. Thanks for the ticket. I had a really good time." I paused to breathe. "Is your eye okay?" I pointed to my own eye. "Do you need to see a doctor? I saw them stitch it up on TV, when you were on the sidelines. You probably need ice. Do you want me to get you some ice?"

Rex swallowed thickly, his mouth opening and closing, his eyes moving between mine like they did so often, looking tense and lost.

My patience snapped.

I wanted to yell at him. I wanted to demand he just say whatever was on his mind instead of glaring at me with the words locked in his mouth. But I couldn't do that, not here, not now, not after his stunning victory and in front of so many of his teammates.

Talking hadn't worked. He hadn't smiled at me yet. I couldn't jump him, and he didn't want ice.

So I said, "Fuck it," and grabbed his face, yanking it down to mine.

Our mouths crashed together in a messy, graceless collision, and that was perfectly fine. I told myself to breathe through my nose without smelling him, hold the pose, and count to ten. It didn't need to feel real, it just needed to look believable to anyone who happened to be watching.

1, 2, 3—

Rex's fingers immediately speared into my hair, coaxing my head slightly back. The pressure between our lips lessened, but they didn't part, and what had started as a dispassionate bumping together of mere skin became something altogether different. He brushed his lips against mine, breathing in my breath before pressing softly forward, a slow caress of heat and silk.

4 . . . 4 . . .

He angled my chin by tugging on my hair, and my lips automatically parted. His body surged forward, his hot tongue dipping in to stroke and taste and tease. My hands dropped from his face to grip the front of his jersey, unthinkingly twisting the fabric tightly in my fingers as Rex's hands lowered to the dip of my waist, his fingers digging into my flesh, pulling me tightly against him.

. . . 5, I think? Maybe 3? Probably 2.

We were kissing.

For real.

I mean, for fake-real.

A real fake kiss that made my head spin and my lungs ache. My entire being pressed closer, restless, and I moaned because nothing had ever felt as essential or exquisite as Rex McMurtry's skillful tongue in my mouth, sliding against and tangling with mine like he was just as starved for me as I was for him, his lips, his body, his hands.

I wanted to drown in him. My lungs burned with need for air, and I told those needy bitches to *wait.* But they wouldn't, and spots danced behind my closed eyes, stupid survival instinct kicking in at the worst possible moment. Tilting my head back, I separated our mouths and gulped in air.

Rex's lips landed on the corner of my mouth and nipped hungrily downward to kiss my jaw and neck, hot breath spilling over the sensitive skin as his lips moved to whisper harshly in my ear, "I still have your blessing?"

I didn't know what he was talking about, but he didn't wait for a response. His hands covered mine and wrenched them from his jersey, lifting and placing them around his neck. His palms smoothed to my shoulders, leaving gooses bumps in their wake, stroking and grabbing slowly down my sides, then around my back until he held two big handfuls of my backside. He squeezed.

My eyes went wide. I was choked by lack of oxygen, astonishment, and an abrupt, aching burst of heat. Rex massaged my bottom and kissed my neck. And not a light peppering of lips. His tongue swirled, his teeth bit, his mouth sucked and sipped and tasted , the ticklish shocks of white-hot heat pooling deep in my lower belly, an unmanageable, almost painful pulse of longing.

I became nothing but sensation, my eyelashes fluttering shut, the noise of the room fading to a hum and competing with the sound of my own heart. Mindlessly, I tilted my hips forward. He made a sound between a groan and a growl, using his leverage on my bottom to press my pelvis roughly against his groin. He rolled his hips. I gasped and struggled to get closer, my nails digging into the back of his neck.

My back arched reflexively, and another inelegant moan slipped out as he used his hands on my bottom to pluck me from the ground like it was nothing at all. My legs automatically lifted and bracketed him. His mouth still working at my neck, he carried me through the open door where he'd emerged minutes ago. My hands moved down to his shoulder pads, then lower to fist in the hem of his jersey, yanking it up.

I needed to feel his skin, to feel him flex and move beneath my fingertips. I needed—

"No, no! Not so fast."

"Save it for later, TW. Coach wants to huddle, and we need to *eat*!"

Someone was next to us. Or rather, a few someones had surrounded us, pushing into the room, grabbing for Rex, pulling at his arms. My eyes flew open and zeroed in on Rex, staring at me darkly, lips pink and kissed, chest rising and falling with rapid breaths. My hands tightened on his jersey, but it was useless, we were being cheerfully pulled apart by the rest of the defensive line, one of whom had put his arm around my shoulders to lead me out of the room.

"Come on, Abby. Where you go, he'll follow. We're hungry."

CHAPTER 20

"There is nothing more deceptive than an obvious fact."

— ARTHUR CONAN DOYLE, THE BOSCOMBE VALLEY MYSTERY - A SHERLOCK HOLMES SHORT STORY

The entire team was staying at the same place. Dazed and confused and hot and bothered, I allowed myself to be guided to a car with the other players' spouses and driven to the hotel. My mind swimming in unanswerable questions, I stumbled to the elevator and realized that the security team Rex had arranged back in Austin was still following me.

"Mrs. McMurtry." One of the dudes—two dudes this time, no ladies—gave me a nod.

I returned his nod, wide-eyed. *My life is so strange.*

They trailed after me to my room and unlocked it for me, gesturing that I should wait a minute for one of them to do a walk-through before I entered.

"Why didn't you do this yesterday?" I asked the guard who still stood with me.

"We did, before you and Mr. McMurtry arrived," he said, his eyes on the door.

"Oh. Thank you."

As soon as the other guard exited, they dutifully took their places on either side of the door. I wandered inside the suite, the door shutting behind me, and placed my key card back in my handmade zippered wallet. I didn't know why I had a key, seeing as how one of the guards would be unlocking the door for me.

Drifting over to the big, white couch, I sat down and absentmindedly pressed my fingertips to my lips, replaying the incident with Rex in the locker room.

That was real, Abby.

I shook my head, frowning and rejecting the notion with every fiber of my being.

No. I am the idiot who didn't think through all the implications of this arrangement before agreeing, who didn't tell Walker or my friends about my marriage until after the fact, and who is now surprised and irritated about the fact that she has to lie to everyone.

I continued shaking my head as I leaned back against the sofa, pressing the base of my palms into my eyes. "Just do the opposite of what you want to do," I spoke to myself out loud.

Did I want to call it off? No. I didn't. I wanted to keep hurling myself over the cliff of upheaval and excitement, ultimately crashing to the murky bottom each time, splintering my heart and ruining my integrity in the process.

My judgment couldn't be trusted. If I thought the kiss was real, it was undoubtedly fake, all for show, for the benefit of his teammates and coworkers. I needed to face facts: I never should have agreed to this, my feelings were deeply involved no matter how much I tried to think of him as a boss, and I needed to call it off. Tonight. As soon as possible.

Gut twisting at the thought, I shoved away from the couch. I refused to feel guilty about letting Rex down. He'd said I could end it whenever I wanted, and the prenup had been explicitly clear on the subject. I just hoped he wouldn't be too disappointed and the divorce wouldn't cost him too much.

You should offer to give him the excess money back. I nodded, liking this idea. I was just going to give it to charity anyway. He could use it to pay for the divorce. After additional debate, I decided I would also offer to stay married for a few more months on paper, but I couldn't do any more events. I couldn't go to the wedding with him in December and I couldn't go to his Aunt Sally's house and lie. It was time for me to stop lying to myself and everyone else.

I'd thought the arrangement was too good to be true. Obviously, it was. End of story. Lesson learned. Again.

Feeling resigned to reality, and therefore better and worse, I dressed for Thanksgiving dinner. If there was an opportunity during the dinner, I'd pull him away and tell him. If not, I'd tell him as soon as we made it to the suite.

Mind made up, I neatly folded the clothes I'd been wearing—things I wouldn't be taking back with me to Austin—and slipped on the brown sweaterdress Bernadette had sent for the dinner. The fitted skirt was shorter than I would've liked, but I liked that it was lined with espresso-colored silk and had long sleeves.

Tugging the zipper up under my right arm, I numbly walked to the bathroom and finished getting ready. Vanessa said she would meet me at six o'clock in the lobby so we could walk in together and I didn't want to be late. I didn't want to make a habit of letting people down.

I exited the suite promptly at 5:45 p.m. and, once more, had forgotten the guards stationed outside. "Oh. Sorry. Shall we go? Or are you going? Or—"

"We'll escort you," the one I'd spoken to earlier said, gesturing that I should lead the way.

I hesitated, looking between them, then extended my hand. "I'm Abby. I'm so sorry I didn't introduce myself earlier." I'd introduced myself to the guards in Austin but had neglected to do so here. However, I'd been distracted or overwhelmed since we'd arrived; I wasn't going to beat myself up about it too much.

The guard shook my hand. "I'm Nicolas. That's Stan."

I turned and shook the other guard's hand, giving them both what I hoped was a friendly smile. "It's so nice to meet you both. Thank you for . . . being here."

"No problem," the one called Stan said, his thick New England accent unmistakable.

"Where are you guys from?" I asked, turning to the elevator.

"We're based out of Chicago—I was born there—but Stan is from Boston."

"South Boston," Stan chimed in, giving me the sense he considered there to be a world of difference between *Boston* and *South Boston.*

Upon arriving at the elevator, I bumped into Nicolas as we both reached for the call button. "Oh! Sorry."

He gave me a tight smile, but his eyes were friendly. "You should let us do that, otherwise we feel useless."

"So, do you like Richmond? Have you ever been here before?" My smile was apologetic as I backed away, thinking to myself that I felt pretty useless too.

Stan looked to Nicolas, giving me the sense Stan wasn't a big talker.

"We've been all over." Nicolas's smile widened just slightly. "How about you?"

"Uh, no. I'm from a little town west of Austin in Hill Country called Alenbach, and my first plane trip ever was just a few weeks ago. This was my second."

"Get outta town." The words burst from Stan and he frowned at me. "You never been anywhere before?"

"Nope." I shook my head, chuckling.

"How old are you?" Stan asked, still frowning. "Twenty something, right?"

"Twenty-eight. Isn't that sad?"

The elevator dinged as I faced the suddenly chatty Stan and I heard the doors slide open behind me.

"Lady, ain't nothing sad about you," Stan said, earning him a sharp look from Nicolas but a laugh from me.

"That's nice of you to say, but you should hear me sing in the shower." I turned to the elevator. "I guarantee you, it's—oh!" I gasped, not finishing the thought, because there stood Rex, a towering presence in his impeccably tailored suit, freshly shaven. He was also looking at Stan similarly to how I imagined he looked at opposing players on the field. You know, all murdery.

I huffed a short breath, struggling to regain my composure. "Rex," I said. "I thought—I thought we were—I was told to come downstairs?"

Somewhere behind me I heard the unmistakable sound of a gulping swallow. Then and only then did Rex's eyes cut to mine, warming and softening considerably.

He held his hand out to me. "Stay here, gentlemen."

I glanced at Nicolas over my shoulder. He was glaring in the direction of Stan, but replied, "Yes, sir."

Hot butterflies swirling in my stomach, I stepped forward into the elevator and accepted Rex's offered fingers. Smoothly, he reached forward and punched the button for the conference level—where the dinner would take place—and then released my hand to slide his around my waist, settling it on my hip as the doors shut.

I couldn't seem to catch my breath, but I did manage to say, "Uh, Vanessa wanted to meet me in the lobby at six for a drink."

His big palm shifted to the center of my back, and he separated us so he could look at me. "How are you?" His face gave nothing of his thoughts away and his tone seemed careful.

"I'm okay." It wasn't a lie. I was okay. I'd made my decision and it was okay and I'd get through it. "But it would be good if we could find a moment to talk. I can text Vanessa and tell her I'm skipping drinks."

He nodded, licking his lips, his eyes moving over me as I pulled out my phone from the little bag around my wrist. Vanessa was one of the first contacts in my text messages since we'd just exchanged numbers today.

Abby: I have to skip drinks, but I'll see you for dinner.

Finished, I slipped the phone back into the clutch and zipped it up, smiling tightly at Rex. "All done."

His hand moved around to my side closest to him, his thumb on my stomach, his eyebrows pulled together slightly. "Are you upset?"

"Upset?"

"With me."

I blinked. "About what?"

His attention dropped to my lips. "Kissing you."

"Oh." I shook my head. "No. No, I kissed you first, and so I guess I should be asking if you're upset with me. But I didn't know what else to do. I had this whole plan of jumping at you—all the other wives were jumping and you told me to do whatever they did"—I gestured wildly with my hands, miming a jumping and grabbing on motion—"but I didn't know if you were injured. Jumping seemed out of the question, so I made a list of what everyone else was doing and decided to do that instead. Hence, the kiss." I shrugged, giving him a you-know-what-I-mean half smile.

As I word-vomited my explanation, Rex stared at me, his eyebrows pulling more severely together the longer I rambled on.

When I finally finished, his hand on my side squeezed me tighter. "Are you joking right now? Is this a joke?"

"No." I swallowed around a sudden lump. "I'm sorry."

"Why are you sorry?" he asked, shifting closer and into my space, gazing down at me like my answer to the question might solve all the mysteries of the universe.

"I guess . . . I'm sorry I kissed you? But like I said, I didn't know what else to do."

He heaved a very, very frustrated sounding breath. "Abby—"

The elevator dinged. The doors opened to reveal two smiling couples. Rex turned away from me, sliding his hand back into place on my hip and clenching his jaw. He guided me backward to allow space for the newcomers while my face flamed, and I gripped my little purse with white knuckles.

I recognized the players but not their dates. Introductions were made, hands were shaken, chitchat initiated. Through it all, I wrestled with tumultuous thoughts while Rex kept his arm along my back, his hand splayed on my stomach, holding me firmly against his side. If anything, this short, uncomfortable interaction had just solidified my desire to call off our agreement. We weren't on the same page. He didn't share necessary details, and I couldn't read him.

The doors finally opened to the conference level after making two more stops to pick up more players and their plus ones. Rex and I were the last to file out and he turned in the opposite direction as the others.

One of his teammates hollered at our backs, "Hey! Where are you going? The party is over here."

"Be there in a minute," Rex replied and navigated us around a corner to an expansive and empty hallway. Not releasing me, he tested three doors before finding one unlocked and then steered me inside. I stepped away from his arm, walked to the center of the small room, crossed my arms, and faced him.

It seemed the moment had arrived for me to call things off. I hoped he wouldn't be angry with me, but what could I do? I wasn't going to keep my decision to myself any longer than necessary.

"Abby—"

"Rex." I held my hand up and closed my eyes, feeling suddenly exhausted. "Let me talk first, okay?"

"No. I talk first. This isn't going to work anymore."

I opened my eyes and felt my eyebrows move up and then down. "What's not going to work?"

"This." Looking at the wall over my head, he cleared his throat. "Pretending."

"Pretending," I parroted dumbly, knowing I should feel relieved that he was ending things first, but all I felt was desperation and despair. "I see."

"Do you?" His gaze darted to mine, then narrowed. The skin around the cut over his eye was purple and blue. "Do you see?"

Ignoring the lead weight in my stomach, I pasted on a brave smile. "It was the kiss, right?"

"No, not the kiss." He cleared his throat. "You can keep the money. I already put a whole year into the allowance account. You don't need to worry about—"

"I don't want the money, Rex. I never did. What did I do wrong?"

"Nothing. You did nothing wrong. You were . . . you are perfect."

"Then why? I won't fight your decision," I rushed to add. I didn't want him to think I planned to make this difficult for him. "I'd like to remain friends if possible."

"That's never gonna happen." He laughed while frowning, the

sound striking me as tortured and miserable. And then his features twisted, and he looked tortured and miserable too.

His statement hurt, but I swallowed it down. "I don't blame you," I said softly, reasonably, my temper pushing against my good sense and desire for calm. "I've been having similar thoughts about ending the arrangement, but I do want to know, why now?"

He glared at me as though I was the source of his misery. "You must know."

"I don't know. If it's not the kiss, then I don't know because you never tell me anything!" I erupted, surprising both him and me. I wasn't finished. "I thought I could do this, but you're right. It's not working. I don't like lying to people. I'm not good at it."

"From where I'm standing, you're extremely good at it. You've been very convincing," he ground out.

I reared back as though slapped. "Is that—is that supposed to be praise? Because it sounded like an insult. Let me put it this way: If I knew why you were calling this off, I wouldn't have to ask. People ask questions because they don't know things. If I just magically knew what you were thinking, I'd open up a sideshow act as the omniscient woman!" Yeah, I was yelling, but—dammit—I was angry. And frustrated.

A fierce storm gathered behind his eyes. "Then let me spell it out for you, babe."

"Please do, husband."

"I want you."

I stared at him and waited. When he didn't continue his thought or add an explanation, just glared at me with defiance, I said, "You want me to what?"

"No, Abby," he seethed. "I *want* you."

CHAPTER 21

"There is no dishonor in losing the race. There is only dishonor in not racing because you are afraid to lose."

— GARTH STEIN, *THE ART OF RACING IN THE RAIN*

It took a minute of me staring, then thinking, then sputtering, then staring at him some more, questioning whether I'd misheard, before his words finally sunk in.

"What? No! I'm the placeholder, not the—the—the *place!*"

His eyes narrowed. I'd obviously confused him. "Placeholder?"

I waved away the question I wasn't going to answer and focused on the giant elephant in the room, twirling on pointe in its pink tutu. "You want me? Since—since when?!" I'm not too proud to admit that I shrieked this question.

A flicker of something like discomfort or guilt dimmed his glare and he clamped his mouth shut.

He's serious.

Oh my God, he was serious.

"I'm sorry, but I need a minute to recover from this deus ex machina moment, Rex. This seems really sudden. Really. Freakin'. Sudden."

"You can't be this blind."

I lifted a finger between us, glaring daggers at him, my temper rising in temperature to a boiling lava pit in the span of a single second. "Don't you dare call me stupid!"

"You aren't stupid. But you're blinder than a bat with its head up its ass."

I threw my hands up. "Then tell me, since when? Since when have you—"

"Since I woke up hungover in your apartment."

Blinking uncontrollably, my spine stiffened. "No. Now *you're* joking."

"You made it so easy," he ground out, his tone hostile and accusing, and it had me wondering whether I had been pushing a sinister master plan all along and I'd just expertly outmaneuvered him without consciously being aware of having a master plan.

But no.

I'd had no plan.

I'd just wanted to help. *And I'd lied for him.*

"What did I make easy?" I asked, entranced and baffled, not knowing whether to laugh or cry.

"Falling," he said, as though *falling* were a different F-word. But some of his temper deflated as he added, "It was inescapable. It was like . . . " He shook his head in a subtle movement. "Falling for you was like gravity."

Every nerve ending in my body seemed to be firing at once. I still couldn't think, let alone wrap my mind around what he was saying. He'd wanted me since that first morning? Then why—

"Then why would you suggest I fake marry you? Why would you tell me this was a business arrangement if you actually wanted me?"

"You said you didn't date."

My mouth opened and closed to no purpose until I finally blurted, "You wanted to date me?"

"Obviously."

"But—"

"But when you shot that down, and Cyrus suggested I ask you to—"

"Wait." I held my hand up again. "Cyrus? This whole thing was Cyrus's idea?"

"He suggested fake dating, getting married was my idea. I thought it was a good thing, liking you so much. I thought it would make the pretending easier."

"You—"

"It's torture. I can't—I miss you." He seemed to swallow the *you* as he stumbled over his words, turning aimlessly, his voice a rake over gravel. "It fucking hurts, how much I miss you, and I don't want this. I can't concentrate. I can't think about anything else."

My ears rang as I studied his strong profile, how the muscle at his jaw flexed and released, the exhaustion in his posture, the cut and bruising over his eye. He looked so unhappy. I didn't understand my own emotions, or what to think. I felt like someone had put me in a cocktail shaker.

But I did know he needed food and rest, and I needed space and time to think. I couldn't think about this now.

I hazarded a step toward him. "Rex—"

"Is there a chance?"

I halted. "A chance?"

"Do you want me?" Tone low and controlled, his eyes cut to mine.

I froze, caught. I wouldn't lie, but I didn't want him to know. What good would him knowing do? We were never going to actually be together.

His eyes narrowed and he faced me fully again. "Do you want to be with me?"

Breathing out a tremendous breath that felt like it originated from the depth of my soul, I pressed my lips together to keep my chin from wobbling. I shook my head.

He studied me for a long moment, as though I were a puzzle, or a bomb he'd been sent to diffuse. "You do. You're lying."

"I'm not lying. I don't want to be with you." My eyes stung and I swallowed convulsively. *You're going to have to tell him sooner or later, Abby.*

He looked so confused. "But you want me?"

Aww . . . fuck.

I cleared my throat to keep my voice steady. "I don't want to be with you because you're wrong about me. If you knew the truth you wouldn't want me."

He blinked, just once, and his expression turned calculating as he prowled a step forward. "You want me, but you think I'm wrong about you, so you don't want to be with me."

It sounded crazy when he said it out loud like that, but it was the truth, and it had merit, dammit!

For every step he took forward, I took one backward. "You said I'm rare. I'm common. You thought I had no wish list, I do."

Rex's eyes widened, his forehead clearing. "You have a wish list?"

I nodded.

"About me?"

I nodded again, grimacing.

He cracked an adorable smile. "What's on it?"

"You're not listening." My heart twisted painfully, emotion clogging my throat. "I've misled you. I've *always* liked you. Always. This whole time. All through school, kindergarten through our senior year of high school."

"You did?" Inexplicably, his smile grew.

My back connected with a wall, forcing me to stop my retreat. "I was a stalker. I stalked you. I was completely unhinged."

Rex paused his advance, his smile wavering. "What did you do?"

"I used to sit across the street from the car wash where you worked."

He seemed to debate this before lifting an eyebrow and asking warily, "Every day?"

"Once or twice a week."

His smile returned, quizzical this time. "So?"

"So?"

"So did you sneak into my room and steal hair from my hairbrush?"

"Uh—no."

"Did you send me threatening letters whenever I dated someone else, making plans to harm me or her?"

"What? No. Of course not."

"You didn't stalk me, Abby." His gaze swept over me like he thought I was cute. "You had a crush on me."

"No. No, I'm telling you, my crush was *massive.* I couldn't talk to you, that's why I had Rachel sit next to you at graduation. I would've melted into a pile of awkwardness and nonsense. I would doodle our name together in notebooks. In shop? Our sophomore year? I used to stare at your bottom!"

"You're telling me right now that you've had a thing for me since high school—"

"Elementary school."

"Fine, elementary school, and that's supposed to be bad news? Are you fucking kidding me with this?"

I couldn't catch my breath. "I'm trying to tell you why I don't—why I'm not—"

He huffed, stalking forward again. "Do you want me, yes or no?"

"It's not that simple." I wasn't prepared for this. I'd meant what I'd said. I was the placeholder, not the place. Rex had a final destination person, I wasn't her.

"It is that simple. Everything else is gravy."

"It's not!"

He halted again, his features heartbreakingly patient.

"You're too good to be true, okay?" I waved my hand up and down, gesturing to his entire person as my voice cracked. "It'll never last."

He winced, just the barest flicker of pain behind his expression. "Don't say that."

"You're all my fantasies. Every single one."

"And you're all of mine." So close now, Rex angled his head, waiting until I gave him my eyes to add, "Abby, I'm crazy about you."

"You're not—"

"I am many, many things, but I am not too good to be true." His expression was an odd combination of soft and stark.

I choked on a laugh, continuing to shake my head. "You are."

"I'm an asshole."

"You're wonderful."

"I'm too gruff. Demanding. Bossy."

"You're brooding and sexy."

He cracked a smile, apparently just *enchanted* by this confession. "Babe, I will prove it to you."

"How can you prove—"

"I love you."

My mouth fell open and an electric shock of hot disbelief followed, holding my lungs in a vise grip. "What? You can't possibly—"

"For God's sake," he growled as though he was nearing his wit's end, and his wit's end was a grizzly bear. "Tell me you want me."

"I—"

"Tell me."

"Stop interrupting!"

He lifted an eyebrow and his lips curved into an almost smirk, like he had me, like my capitulation was certain. He was wrong.

Nothing was simple. I wanted him, but what did that matter? He *was* too good to be true. I'd already lived through one fairy tale that had become a living nightmare, I had no interest in trying to survive another.

Besides that, if the scales of power had been unbalanced with Declan, being with Rex would be ten thousand times worse. Even if he wasn't a famous pro football player and I wasn't a fan, and I wasn't me—broke bartender and serial crafter—I had a long history of being a dummy for this guy.

The sway he held over me, that I'd voluntarily surrendered to him, was staggering. I'd never lied for Declan, not even when he begged and cajoled and threatened, not even when I thought I was in love with him. But all Rex had to do was show up in my bar with his big sweater energy and I'd tripped all over myself to make him happy. To help him. *By lying.*

"What?" he asked, his voice a whisper. "What are you thinking?"

Inhaling a steadying breath, I gestured behind him to the door we'd entered earlier. "I'm thinking, this is what we're going to do: We are going to be logical and reasonable and not let emotions get the better of us. We are going to figure this out so that we can both walk away from here with our friendship intact. And then we are going to—"

Kiss.

That wasn't what I was going to say, but that's what Rex did.

One minute I was gathering the wits he'd dispersed all over this room with his confession bomb and the next he'd stepped into my space, gathered me to him, lifted my chin, and pressed his lovely, hot, persistent lips to mine along with the hard, hot, insistent length of his body.

So of course I moaned and wrapped my arms around his neck and kissed him back like I'd been waiting to do it for decades. OF COURSE I DID!

And when he kept on kissing me, his fingers sliding just under the hem of my short skirt, the demanding, drugging slide of his mouth and tongue and teeth redispersing my wits all over the room, I simply did not have the energy to care.

All I wanted was to be kissed by Rex, to be touched by him, to lose myself in his heat and the roughness of his hands, the starved dance of our tongues and the slippery, sweet taste of him. He was big and strong and intoxicating and everywhere, wrapping his arms around me to lift me off the ground, spread my legs, step between them, and pin me against the wall. And I was an addict for it all.

So when he separated our mouths and demanded, "Tell me you want me," I capitulated.

"I want you," I whimpered, my breath hitching at the biting attentions of his teeth and lips, the demanding roll of his hips, the friction of his constrained erection rubbing just the right spot between my open thighs. It was the truth, but I would've said anything to feed this addiction.

A primal sound rumbled from his chest, intensely pleased and masculine. He kissed and bit my neck as though he wanted to consume me, and I clawed at his jacket, pushing it off. And that's when the door opened.

"Ah! There you—oh! Damn!"

A stream of hot air paired with a frustrated, rumbly growl fell along my neck and shoulder. I closed my eyes, too turned on to feel embarrassment, but I did try to catch my breath.

"Sorry TW. Everyone is looking for you guys. I'd give you more time, but we can't start anything without our game MVP." I recognized the voice as belonging to Ryan, Vanessa's husband.

Rex inhaled deeply, drawing me into his lungs, and then he straightened. As my legs touched the ground, my eyes fluttered open. Our gazes locked and my heart skipped. He wore the stare that I'd previously labeled *inscrutable*, but now I recognized for what it was. He wanted me. This was a gaze of longing.

"We'll be right there," Rex said, his voice flat.

I knew his big body hid me from view, so I tugged at my skirt, pulling it back into place.

"Okay. Okay. All right. But I'll just stand directly outside this door and keep watch for y'all. You know, just in case someone tries to bust in and interrupt this very wholesome, Hallmark moment you two are having."

Despite all the chaos of the day, or maybe because of it, I laughed, sealing my lips together to cover the sound.

Rex rolled his eyes. He also smiled. "Thank you, Ryan."

"I got you, bruh," came the quarterback's response.

Rex studied me and waited until I finished fidgeting with my skirt before pushing his fingers gently into my hair, gathering my face for a soft, cherishing kiss.

"I want to give myself to you," he whispered against my mouth liltingly, like these were words of seduction. "But you have to know, I am a selfish asshole sometimes."

I stared forward at his blurry outline, both petrified by the idea of Rex giving himself to me and amused by this description of himself.

Anything that seems too good to be true always is.

"The question is . . ." Rex's hands slid away. He leaned back and recaptured my gaze, his expression stark. "Will you still want me when you discover I'm not too good to be true?"

If I'd considered Rex touchy-feely at that rehearsal dinner all those weeks ago, I'd been grossly mistaken. That night had been nothing compared to now. *Nothing.*

We sat next to each other at one of many round tables, eight people to a table. In general, each player was allowed to bring one date plus two family members. Accommodations were made for those with more than two children, but most players opted to leave the kids at home. According to Regina, people preferred to celebrate Thanksgiving with their families on Friday or Saturday in Chicago instead of managing all the logistics of traveling with kids. I saw three babies and one toddler and that's it.

The room was beautifully decorated in fall colors, a giant—and literal—cornucopia full of wrapped presents sat along one wall. Regina told me the boxes were empty but were labeled with items the players could sponsor for charities in Chicago, everything from a five-hundred-dollar donation to Toys for Tots to a one-hundred-thousand-dollar donation for all community food banks.

Each table centerpiece was also in the shape of a cornucopia, but this one was made of bread, surrounded by edible rice paper autumn leaves and filled with decadent-looking appetizers: huge green cotton candy grapes, Italian cured meats and cheeses, candied nuts, delicate crackers, pâté, and brie baked in dough.

My mouth watered as soon as I spotted the grapes and I realized I hadn't eaten anything since before the game. I'd been too nervous, and then I'd been too engrossed in Rex's performance to think about food at the stadium.

As soon as we arrived at our table, Rex pulled my seat out and assisted scooting it in, a real gentleman. He then settled his chair as close to mine as possible and placed his hand on my leg, pushing my dress up several inches and curling his fingers so they rested on my inner thigh, a scant distance from my underwear.

I sent him a wide-eyed meaningful look.

His mouth curved in a whisper of a smile and he leaned to my ear, sliding his nose against my neck. "Do you want me to stop?"

Combating a shiver, I whispered back harshly, "Would it matter if I did?"

"It's the only thing that matters," he said. "But you have to tell me what you want before I can make it happen." Then he kissed my neck and straightened, glancing at the menu on his plate like he didn't have a care in the world, his thumb rubbing a lazy circle on my skin.

I tried to read the menu. I couldn't concentrate. Our conversation from earlier was still on repeat in my head, especially the part where he'd told me he loved me. *That* was solid-gold crazy. How could he love me? He didn't even know me. We'd barely spent any time together. Yes, we texted and talked on the phone almost daily prior to just this last week, but . . . love? *Really?*

Also, with his fingers so close to my underwear, his hand so hot, his touch so light and rhythmic, my thoughts couldn't gel. Clearly, I was a glutton for punishment because I didn't ask him to stop or remove his hand. When he finally did as dinner arrived, I was inexplicably saddened by the loss of it.

Conversation ebbed and flowed, but mostly flowed, and I felt content to sit back and observe Rex interact with his teammates and their wives. I wouldn't say I was exactly surprised to discover Vanessa and Rex had gone on one date—a charity gala, like the one we'd attended a few weeks ago—and that's where she and Ryan had met. They'd married just two months later.

"TW was my best man," Ryan said, his eyes sparkling with a rascally glint.

"He's everyone's best man. He's like James Bond, already has a tux for every season and occasion." Xander Garcia, Regina's husband, added with a laugh.

Rex had nothing to say to Xander's teasing, his features arranged in a patient but impassive mask.

"Awfully selfish of you to get married," Trent Komfer said, winking at me. "How are the rest of us supposed to find wives now?"

Regina picked up her wineglass. "It was always hopeless for you, Trent, even before Rex got married and closed up his matchmaking shop. No one wants your ugly ass."

The table burst into laughter. Rex cracked a smile, but it was a small one and didn't quite reach his eyes. I felt someone's gaze on me and turned to find Vanessa sending me an empty smile that seemed to match Rex's. I sent her a warm one in return, working to hide mild confusion.

I liked Vanessa a lot. She was amazing, kind, welcoming, brilliantly smart and breathtakingly beautiful. So even though I wasn't surprised that she and Rex had gone on a date, I was surprised that they'd only gone on *one* date.

"Hey," Rex whispered against my neck, pressing a kiss there, making me shiver. "You okay?"

I nodded, tilting my head back to look at him and whispering in return, "You okay?"

His eyes warmed as they hooked into mine. "If you're okay, I'm more than okay."

"One thing is for sure, we all like TW with Abby." Tearing my eyes from Rex's gorgeous hazel gaze, I discovered Trent had lifted his glass toward me. "Whatever magic you're working, keep doing it."

I scrunched my nose, but before I could reply, Ryan cut in. "Seriously. No offense, you know I love you man, but you're so much nicer these days."

"Almost bearable," Xander said with a teasing lilt. "And he's been so chatty. I got two words out of him last week."

"A miracle," Ryan said with mock sincerity. "A true Christmas miracle."

"But meaner on the turf," Trent was quick to add, leaning over the table to clink his glass against Rex's. "You had that Richmond offensive line pissing their pants by the third, and I love to see that. Abby has to come to all games from now on."

"Next week in particular. Make sure she clears her schedule." Ryan pointed at me. "What are we going to do about Kallahan's offense?"

The conversation turned to next week's game, and I stewed in the perplexing information that had just been shared about Rex.

He'd been quiet all through school, sure. Even now, I wouldn't describe him as a talker, but he'd been fine with me. He talked to me.

Except last week when he was giving you the silent treatment.

A tap on my shoulder had me turning. Vanessa indicated with her head to the exit. "Hey, want to come with me to the bathroom?"

I nodded, placing my napkin on the table and whispering to Rex,

"I'll be right back."

His hand on my chair came to my back, his fingers trailing from my neck down my spine to my bottom, giving me a little pinch as I stood.

I twisted, narrowing my eyes at him.

Rex grinned with teeth, showing no remorse.

Fighting an eye roll, I turned to Vanessa and we both strolled toward the exit. The back of my neck prickled and I twisted again, finding Rex still looking in our direction, his attention firmly affixed to my backside. Heat in my lungs, I huffed a short laugh, feeling less and less guilty for ogling his bottom during our sophomore year of high school.

"I think I've had too much to drink." Vanessa linked her arm through mine. "Do you mind? I thought I was okay until I stood up."

"Yeah, of course. No problem." I squeezed her arm with mine. "I'm very sturdy, lean on me."

"You are sturdy," she said with a smile. "I like you with Rex. I think you're perfect for him."

My grin wobbled. "That's nice of you to say."

"I mean it. He's . . ." She shook her head, suddenly frowning. "He's not easy, is he?"

"I don't know about that. I think he's remarkably easy." I knew she didn't mean the question to be insulting toward Rex, but I felt a pang of annoyance anyway. Maybe Rex didn't find it necessary to be bubbly and charming all the time, but I liked that about him, I always had. I liked his dry wit and unique brand of gruff gentleness.

"Really? See"—she wagged a finger at me—"This is why you're perfect together. Don't get me wrong, I've always liked Rex, he's solid. A real good guy. Regina wasn't wrong when she said Rex had a—a matchmaking shop. I watched him do it for years: date a woman, then pair her off with someone else. He *introduced* me to Ryan at the gala and then sent us home together in the same car." She laughed, her nose wrinkling adorably. "If he weren't so great at football, he'd make a great CEO, I think."

"A CEO? Of what?"

"Doesn't matter. He's one of those individuals who sees the

strengths and weaknesses in people and then knows how to—you know—pair them with someone else who has complementary talents. He's good at putting teams together, getting the most out of people. That's what Ryan says. He's . . . shrewd."

We made it to the bathroom and, miraculously, there was no line. I opened the door and steered us inside, careful not to release Vanessa's arm. With her last sentence, she'd started slurring her words.

"Are you okay?" Turning right toward the sitting area instead of left toward the stalls, I guided her to a sofa and squatted in front of her. "Let me get you some water."

"I'm fine." She shook her head, leaning back against the sofa and sighing. "Just need a minute, I think."

I didn't move, not wanting to leave her alone, and debated what to do. In my opinion as a professional bartender, she was two drinks past sober, which meant she'd be feeling better in two hours if she stopped drinking now.

"Should I call Ryan?"

"No. We haven't even danced yet. He's such a good dancer." Her mouth formed a wistful smile and she chuckled. "He's just too good to be true."

I blinked, startled by her use of the phrase I'd had such a complicated relationship with for the last ten years. "How so?" I found myself asking before I could catch the question.

Vanessa's cloudy gaze drifted over me. "Oh, you know. Like how you feel about Rex. He's perfect for me. He's not serious, like I am. I'm too serious. He makes me laugh, rubs my shoulders. He's such a good dad. And he's so damn sexy, I swear." She heaved a dreamy sigh. "That man."

Her eyes followed me as I sat next to her on the sofa, questions I probably shouldn't ask pressing against my better sense.

"What is it?" she asked, tapping my leg lightly with the back of her hand.

"How did you know he wasn't too good to be true?"

The question seemed to confuse her. "He is too good to be true, I just said he was."

"Then is he not true? How did you know it was real?"

She straightened from her reclining position and faced me fully. “You mean, how did I know I could trust him?”

That wasn’t precisely what I meant, but I nodded. “Sure. How did you know you could trust him?”

A hazy, warm smile took over her features and she cupped my face with her hand. “Oh, honey. You can trust Rex. Is that what you’re asking? Listen”—she dropped her palm to cover my hand and squeezed— “I know it’s scary with all the fame and fans and attention. But none of that matters at the end of the day, when you’re up all night with a sick kid or you have a deadline at work and need him home to parent his children so you can get your job done. It’s just you, the two of you.”

“I know none of that matters in the long run. But how do you know there will be a long run? Rex feels too good to be true, and I—I don’t know how to—”

“That’s the thing. He’s yours. He’s *your* too-good-to-be-true. I think Ryan is too good, but that’s because he’s mine. I doubt other people would put up with some of his more annoying habits, and I think some people would find me intolerable to live with. But we are perfect for each other. We . . . click.”

Frowning, I tried to process what she said, but still stumbled over the simple fact that I couldn’t imagine anyone finding Rex anything but perfect.

“Okay, think of it like this: what’s your favorite dessert?”

“Um, almond cake.”

Her head nod was overexaggerated, likely due to her tipsiness. “Good. Mine is Mississippi mud pie. To me, it tastes too good to be true. Whereas I’ve never been a huge fan of almonds. They’re fine, I’d fry them up with onions and put them in green beans if I wanted to make a fancy vegetable side dish. I wouldn’t want to marry almond cake, but I’d marry Mississippi mud pie tomorrow.”

I leaned back slowly, contemplating her words.

“Everyone has different tastes, and that’s good.” She tried to wink but ended up blinking both eyes, just on a delay, one right after the other. “Rex is your almond cake, Abby. And Ryan is my Mississippi mud pie.”

CHAPTER 22

"I figured something out. The future is unpredictable."

— JOHN GREEN, *AN ABUNDANCE OF KATHERINES*

I wasn't precisely nervous when the evening ended and Rex walked me back to our room, helping me carry plates laden with Thanksgiving food for our guards, but my stomach kept swooping and diving and my dress felt . . . constricting.

So much had happened today, like I'd lived an entire year in twenty-four hours. I felt overwhelmed by the prospect of sorting through it all, especially since it wasn't quite over. Rex and I would be sleeping in the same suite again, supposedly in different bedrooms like last night. But so much had changed since this morning, I was uncertain what to expect when we arrived at our door.

And I still had questions. Vanessa's advice about desserts and men had given me a new perspective, but I didn't understand why Rex hadn't fought for Vanessa instead of pushing her at Ryan. If one of his friends had shown interest in me, would he have sent me off with them? Despite all my other questions, this one seemed like the most pressing.

Therefore, once we were safely in the elevator, just the two of us, and Rex turned to me, I asked, “Why’d you introduce Vanessa to Ryan?”

The question clearly caught him off guard. “Pardon?”

I readjusted my grip on the whole pie in my left hand. I had a plate of mashed potatoes, gravy, turkey, stuffing, cranberry sauce, macaroni and cheese, and green beans in my right. “You took Vanessa as your date somewhere and then sent her off with Ryan.”

“I guess.” Rex had one plate like mine—filled with Thanksgiving food—and carried a bag filled with items from the bread cornucopia.

“Why?”

His focus turned inward. “They seemed to hit it off.”

“But she was your date.”

“Yeah.”

“What do you mean, *yeah*? You asked her there for a reason.”

“I met her through my agent, and I thought she’d dig Ryan.” He shrugged. “He’s a good guy.”

“So you set them up?”

“Sure, if you want to call it that.”

“What would you call it?”

He set the bag down and took the pie from me, placing it on top of the other items in the bag and freeing up my hand. “I’d call it exposure. I wasn’t setting them up, just seeing if they’d hit it off.”

“Did you ever think of exposing me to anyone?”

He lifted an eyebrow, like he found my question ridiculous. “No.”

“Because you can’t think of anyone I’d be a good fit for?”

“No, Abby. I want you for myself.” He sounded a little irritated, maybe even angry, by the question.

I stepped back from that line of questioning and returned to the real issue. “So you really did run a matchmaking service, huh?”

“I don’t know about that.” Rex glanced at the buttons, watching our progress as the elevator climbed.

“Then explain to me why you set so many of your friends up on dates with their now wives?”

The elevator dinged, the door opened, he picked up the bag, and we stepped out. "I think I told you, for some reason, folks always want to set me up—me in particular."

"Maybe they saw you as a challenge?"

"I don't know. Might be. I'd get introduced to *a lot* of women."

"But no mothers," I quipped.

He cracked a grin. "Sometimes I'd get an idea—that a particular woman would be a good fit for a guy I knew. Similar interests, values, that kind of thing. If a woman reminded me of a specific guy I knew, then I'd make sure to introduce them."

"As your date?"

"Yeah. Less pressure that way, for both of them." He guided me around the corner. Nicolas and Stan came into view.

"Interesting."

"But then O'Dea caught on and—" Rex shook his head. "He made something out of it."

"Something gross."

"Right."

"So you stopped."

"Yep."

I sighed. "That's too bad."

"Nah. I was done. I don't have many single friends anymore, just a few guys on the team. And then there's also Cyrus. Alaric. That's it."

We'd arrived at our door and Nicolas had already unlocked it, holding it open for us.

I held out the plate I'd been carrying and pushed it into Nicolas's hands. "Here. This is for you." I then plucked the plate out of Rex's fingers and passed it to Stan. "This is for you. There's a table in the suite. Come in and eat."

The two men frowned at each other, then at Rex.

Rex shrugged. "Abby insists."

I grabbed each of the guards by their upper arms and pulled them inside the suite. "I didn't bring wine, for obvious reasons, but there's pie and bread in the bag. I can also make some mocktails if you're interested, assuming this place has soda and cranberry juice."

Leaving the guys at the table, I crossed to the mini fridge and made a happy sound when I found it well stocked. "How does a mock mai tai sound? I see coconut, cranberry, and OJ. That's my recommendation."

The men looked at Rex again. He gave a single head nod. They turned back to me and nodded.

Placing my hands on my hips, I narrowed my eyes at all three of them. "Don't look at him. I'm the one who asked you the question."

"But he's scary, Abby," Stan said. His eyes then flickered to Rex. "No offense."

"None taken." Rex strolled toward his room, dipping his chin, but not before I saw a pleased smile move over his features.

I grunted, my eyes watching Rex as he disappeared into his bedroom and shut the door. Seeing that the guards were still standing, I pointed to the chairs. "Sit down. Eat. I'll make some drinks."

"Are you sure?" Nicolas slowly pulled out a chair.

Meanwhile, Stan sat hurriedly, lifting the top off his dinner, and dug in using the flatware we'd brought with the food.

"You must be starved," I said, pleased to see his apparent appetite.

"It's not that." Nicolas lifted the top off his plate, sending me a wry look. "He wants to finish before the big guy comes back out."

"Bingo," Stan spoke around a bite of food.

I chuckled, shaking my head and measuring out the cranberry juice. "Everyone calls him scary. He's really not at all."

"He's as tall as a mountain and just ripped apart Richmond's entire offensive line today," Nicolas muttered, spearing a few green beans. "Not that I'm complaining, but I'm not sure why we're here. Someone would have to be insane to mess with you."

"And you're his wife." Stan swallowed and scooped up more potatoes. "You wouldn't think he's scary. It'd be weird if you did."

I made a noncommittal sound and finished with their mocktails, carrying them over to the table just as Rex walked out of his room. Carrying his bag.

My eyes rounded, darting between his face and his bag, and my heart skipped a beat. "Where are—"

"You remember. I have to fly back tonight," he said smoothly, threading his fingers through mine and lifting my hand for a kiss.

My brain stuttered, confusion and disappointment mixing with just a hint of relief.

Rex inspected my face for a moment, then let my hand drop. "I'll call you when I touch down in Chicago."

Before he could move too far away, I turned and hurried after him. "Wait. Wait—uh. Come with me." Grabbing his arm, I pulled him over to my room and inside, shutting the door after us. I faced him and whispered hurriedly, "What's going on? You're leaving?"

He didn't look mad or aloof or upset. He looked . . . concerned. "You need time."

"I do?"

"You do this thing where you don't react in the moment. You sorta stuff it down. Then you think about it and react later."

I reared back. "I—"

He stepped forward and, without touching me elsewhere, kissed me swiftly. I grabbed his shoulders as he moved to lean away, my heart twisting, my breath caught in my lungs.

"I should go. Bernadette got me a flight, but it leaves in an hour and a half."

"Don't go." My fingers dug into his shoulders. "We have separate rooms. You're right, I do need to think about things, but that's no reason to leave."

The side of his mouth tugged upward. "No. You need time. I need to leave."

"Why?"

Rex hesitated, his gaze conducting a slow, careful inspection of my features before saying, "I won't be able to sleep here, with you so close. I learned that in Austin, and last night."

"You could sleep in here, with me—"

"No. You haven't made a decision yet. You know where I stand, and now you need to figure out what you want without me breathing down your neck."

"We'll just sleep," I pleaded. "I promise."

He shook his head firmly, but his smile lingered. "No, Abby."

I let my hands drop and stepped away, crossing my arms. "Why? Because I'm so irresistible? You can't keep your hands to yourself for one night? You're afraid of what? You'll lose control? Is that why?" I punctuated the ridiculous questions with a frustrated huff.

Something shadowy flickered behind his expression and his smile dropped. Or rather, it turned sharper somehow, stark. "Yes," he said quietly. "That's why."

He held my gaze for a protracted moment, everything about him still and serious. I blinked, stunned speechless.

With one more hard look, he turned. He opened the door. He left.

Kaylee dropped into her usual stool but had to tuck her briefcase under the bartop instead of the seat next to her. We were packed.

"What can I get you, gorgeous?" I asked with a wink, already reaching for her martini glass.

"A valium."

"We don't serve that." I poured vodka directly into the shaker.

"Then a martini, I guess." She made a face of distaste at the couple sitting next to her, fiddling with her earring. "It's so crowded in here. Who are all these people?"

The bar had been slammed since the weekend after Thanksgiving, and the relentless pace had continued ever since. This was fairly standard during the busy shopping season. Our placement and close proximity to shops and boutiques meant traffic remained steady from the moment we opened at 2:00 p.m. until we closed up at 1:00 a.m.

"See that guy there." I lifted my chin to a fit-looking fella at table four. "He's an astronaut."

Kaylee frowned at me and then looked over her shoulder. "Really?"

"No." I couldn't hold in my laughter as I added dry vermouth to the shaker.

She turned back to me with an eye squint. "Very funny. I actually believed you for a second. Rex is rubbing off on you, I see." She wagged her eyebrows.

I made a face but said nothing, stalling by shaking her martini. True to his word, Rex had called me last Thursday night—or rather, super early Friday morning—when his plane arrived in Chicago. Text messages were also waiting for me on my phone when I woke up Friday, and he'd continued this tradition of ours all week.

The messages were nothing serious or urgent, just checking in, seeing how my day was going, sending me memes or jokes, or telling me a funny story. I found myself waking up earlier and earlier and sleeping less and less because I was so excited to read his texts. With the cool weather, it felt like waking up to Christmas morning every day.

"I like the decorations this year." Kaylee swiveled slightly on her stool, tilting her head back to peer at the ceiling. "Is that mistletoe?"

I nodded. "I put it over your seat so I could kiss you every time you come in."

Her hand came to her chest and she made a tsking sound. "You are the best, Abby."

Saturday after closing, I'd enlisted the two guards who'd been assigned to my late shift—Mary and Jake—to help me decorate the bar for Christmas. We strung Christmas lights back and forth on the liquor shelves, hung tinsel and mistletoe from the ceiling, and decorated a fake Christmas tree with ornaments I'd either made or collected over the years. I never had a Christmas tree at my tiny apartment; all my ornaments ended up here.

I also switched out our plain white paper napkins with holiday-themed ones that contained cheesy jokes and conversation starters.

Placing Kaylee's drink in front of her, I leaned over the bar and gave her a kiss on the cheek. When I pulled away, she was smiling like she'd won something.

"So, what brings you in?" I turned and pulled two tickets off the order printer, clipping them in front of me as I set to work making drinks for tables seven and eleven.

"Uh, actually, you."

"Oh?"

"Rex called me."

My hand spasmed around a whiskey bottle and I looked up sharply in surprise. "Is that so?"

"Yes. I reminded him that I was your lawyer, not his, but he only wanted some gift ideas for you."

I reared back. "Really?"

"Yes. Really." Kaylee sipped her martini, watching me over the rim.

"What did you tell him?"

"I said I'd send a list. Which is why I'm here. What do you want me to tell him to get you?"

"What?" I was shocked. *Shocked.* Knowing Kaylee, I shouldn't have been, but I was. "Kaylee, that's not right. You know what I want."

She tapped her nails on the surface of the bar. "I'm not telling him to get you socks or a gift certificate to a yarn store. Come on. What do you want? A new car? A kiln? What's that brand you're always talking about? Sloot? Scoot?"

"Skutt." Hurriedly, I made the drinks for tables seven and eleven and set them on the pickup station.

"Yes." She snapped. "One of those."

"I have no room for a Skutt kiln. Besides, they require special electrical, you have to have an electrician come in and do some rewiring. I doubt building management would let me have a kiln."

"Then what do you want that's crazy expensive and that you'd never buy yourself?"

I pressed my lips into a stiff line and walked down the length of the bar away from her and her devious questions, checking on the other patrons and taking my time refilling drinks. I hoped she'd let the issue drop or forget about it by the time I returned.

"So? What? How about some sexy lingerie?" She pushed her empty martini glass toward me and shook her head when I asked if she wanted another.

"I don't want Rex to buy me anything."

"What? Why not?"

"You know why," I replied, harassed. "I haven't decided whether or not to explore things with him."

She frowned with her entire face. "I thought you told me you guys made out in Richmond?"

On Sunday before work, I'd related the whole story of what had happened in Richmond—everything except Rex telling me he loved me—but I'd been very clear that I hadn't made a decision yet one way or the other regarding a future with him. At the time, she'd seem to understand my reasons and had applauded my prudence. Now she wanted me to give Rex a list of expensive gifts to buy me for Christmas?

"We're not dating, Kaylee." I filled a glass with ice and water and set it on her napkin.

She leaned forward and mimicked my tone. "That doesn't mean he can't try to woo you, Abby."

I grit my teeth because she'd hit a nerve. On Sunday, after Kaylee had left, I'd made the mistake of watching Sports NetTV and caught the tail end of Clarence O'Dea's segment on Thanksgiving games.

They hadn't mentioned Rex's nickname or made any jokes about being training wheels for his ex-girlfriends, but Clarence had said, "I think McMurtry stepped it up because his new wife was there."

"You can't be serious," the other announcer said.

Clarence had given his head a quick shake. "If I had a woman who looked like that, in the stadium, watching me, I could sack Richmond's quarterback four times too."

"You're saying he played the game of his life to impress his wife?"

Clarence had raised an eyebrow and seemed poised to respond, clearly with something gross.

The other anchor had quickly lifted a hand to stop him. "On second thought, don't answer that."

"I could *drill* it down for you."

"Hey now, this is a family show," the other man had said and then changed the subject.

Rex had played the game of his life because of Rex. Not because of me. Not because he wanted to impress me or woo me or because I had a magical pussy that had bestowed gladiator powers upon him, as everyone seemed to be implying. We hadn't discussed it, but the whole thing infuriated me.

Presently, exasperated, I walked away from Kaylee, checking the order printer again. It was empty.

Rex had been right. I'd needed time to think things through. Unfortunately, the week since returning to Austin had been crazy. Mary, Jake, and I finished decorating the bar in record time Saturday night, and I made it back to the Four Seasons around 2:30 a.m. That's right, I was still sleeping at the hotel.

According to the guards who'd met me at the airport on Friday, Declan had been swinging by my apartment every day throughout the day and banging on my door. Unbeknownst to him, they'd recorded him each time he arrived, continued recording when they asked him to leave, and then captured his veiled threats as he departed.

I was told it wasn't against the law for him to stop by, just as long as he didn't linger or directly threaten me, but that his behavior pattern painted a threatening picture. It was suggested (and I readily agreed) that I stay at the Four Seasons for the time being while the security company Rex had hired documented Declan's comings and goings.

Once we had enough evidence of his harassment, we could then file for a restraining order. We'd already documented his visit to the bar last Tuesday and him parking outside my apartment later that day. Video footage of him swinging by every day for a week—after being told I didn't wish to see him—should be enough. If he popped up again after the restraining order went into effect, he'd be arrested. That was the plan.

The whole thing made me sad, casting a shadow over the start of the Christmas season. How did people without the means to hire bodyguards and stay at a hotel deal with this kind of harassment? Contemplating it made me sick to my stomach.

Talking to Rex, however, always brightened my day. He hadn't been pushing me to make a decision. In fact, he hadn't brought it up even once. He knew about the situation with Declan, so maybe he didn't want to add to my stress.

Declan being crazy plus sleeping at the hotel plus working every shift since returning from Richmond plus low sleep plus driving over to the pottery studio early every morning to work on inventory for the upcoming Christmas markets, I hadn't had more than a moment to think about a future with Rex.

That's a lie. You think about it and him all the time.

I rolled my eyes at myself.

Okay. Yes. I did think about Rex all the time. But it wasn't quality thinking. It was . . . wishful thinking, and it gave me heartburn.

Last night as I'd fallen asleep, I'd decided to just go for it and tell Rex I wanted to do this for real. Then I'd woken up gasping, heart racing at two in the morning from a nightmare where I'd been arrested for serving gin instead of vodka in my gimlets.

Unable to avoid Kaylee anymore, I meandered back over to her. "Listen. I don't want Rex to buy me anything. Just tell him you don't think it would be a good idea."

She shook her head. "But I do think it's a good idea. What is wrong with you? Why can't you let yourself have nice things?"

"I do—"

"You don't. You feel guilty about it. Every time something good happens to you—or is given to you—you don't trust it. Like you expect it to blow up in your face."

"Maybe because it always does," I whispered harshly.

"Just once. It blew up just once and you're still holding everyone responsible for what Declan did."

If her voice had been any less kind and her eyes had been any less soft, I likely would've walked off in a huff and disregarded her words. But she got to me because I could see she cared.

My throat working, I leaned against the bar with both hands and glanced at the mistletoe above her. "Do you want another kiss?"

"No. I want you to have faith, Abby."

I blinked against a sudden sting behind my eyes. "Faith."

"I want you to have faith in yourself." She reached forward and covered my hand on the bar, giving it a tight squeeze. "Good things can happen to you. You should let them happen to you without being afraid that the big bad wolf is around the corner. And you should believe that you deserve them."

CHAPTER 23

"Surprise is the warrior's greatest weapon"

— ERIN HUNTER, *INTO THE WILD*

Eleven days after returning from Richmond, with all the meticulous documentation completed by the security company and the video footage of Declan's daily visits to my apartment, the court granted my petition for a restraining order and Declan was served that afternoon.

I felt relieved but also scared. I didn't think my ex would take the news well, and I had no doubts he'd disobey the order. He didn't like to be ignored and he'd retaliate sooner or later.

The next day, I woke up to a text from Rex.

Rex: Babe. Call me when you wake up, no matter when

Since the text felt urgent, I sat up against the fluffy hotel pillows and called him right away.

"Abby."

"Hey. What's up?"

"Are you already awake?" Rex was in the locker room, I could hear a metal door opening and closing and the sounds of his teammates.

"I just woke up and saw your text. Is anything wrong?" I peered out the gossamer drapes. The sun was just waking up too.

"Your security team called me last night, they didn't want to wake you since you'd just gone to sleep. Your ex was caught breaking into your apartment last night. They think he was trying to set fire to it. He'd cranked up the gas and had poured gasoline on your futon and carpet."

I groaned, my forehead falling to my bent knee. GREAT! Just freakin' great.

"He's been arrested, and I think it's likely they'll ask that he not be released on bail given the circumstances. He'll be charged with . . . well, a lot. Attempted arson, breaking and entering, breaking the restraining order, and so on."

At this news, I sighed and straightened, trying to look on the bright side. "Well. I guess that's not so bad." I hated that he'd broken into my apartment and poured gasoline on my things, but at least he'd be in prison for the foreseeable future. That made me breathe easier.

"Sorry this happened," he said. The background noise disappeared, I assumed he moved into a quieter room.

"It's not your fault."

"What can I do?"

"Nothing, but thank you for calling, and thank you for the guards and just everything." I lifted my hand and then let it flop to my leg. "I'll stop by before work and check out the damage."

"Uh, that's the other thing. The landlord wants you to move out."

"What?!" My eyes flew open. "Are you serious?"

"Because of the damage to the carpet. He has to replace it and needs the place empty. He said he doesn't know when it'll be ready for you to move back in, maybe after the lease is over."

"That sonofablister." I made a fist in the bedsheets. "He's the worst."

Rex seemed to hesitate a beat before saying, "I have a place in Austin."

My brain stuttered. "You have a place in Austin? Then why did I drop you off at a hotel that afternoon after you crashed at my place?"

"Everyone with the wedding party was staying at the hotel and I didn't want to invite them over to my place. I keep it on the down-low."

I chewed on the inside of my lip. Setting aside the fact that I was now technically homeless, moving into Rex's place in Austin would certainly solve a few problems. As far as everyone else was concerned, our marriage was authentic. And yet, as Walker had pointed out, we didn't live together.

"I guess—" I started, frowned, picked an imaginary piece of dust off the comforter. "Rex, if we are together, I mean, if we start seeing each other. . ."

"Yes?"

"Would we stay married?"

He was quiet for several seconds, then asked, "Have you decided?"

"I haven't," I said mournfully because I felt mournful about it and frustrated with myself. "I'm sorry."

"Don't be sorry. No decisions have to be made right now. It can be as simple as: you need a place to stay and my house is empty."

His response felt like no response at all. Did it make sense for me to move into his place in town? Would he live there too during the off-season? Or . . . wasn't that rushing things?

And you'll have to put your nutty quilt collection into storage, no need to expose him to your crazy.

When my silence persisted, he added, "How about you can pay me the same rent you paid at your studio apartment."

I perked up at this. "You'd be okay with me paying you rent?"

"No. But I figured you wouldn't accept otherwise. And think about the fact that this thing with Declan is my fault. He left you alone before I entered the picture and preemptively paid him off without your blessing."

Despite myself, the uncertainty of my present circumstances, and the bad news of the morning, I smiled. "You know me so well."

"Hmm," was all he said in response. Then he cleared his throat.

"So, listen, about the wedding this weekend. You don't have to go if you don't want to."

"No. No, I do want to. I want to—" I cut myself off before I said *I want to see you* because that didn't seem fair. I didn't want to give him mixed messages. I did want to see him, and after Kaylee's visit to the bar last week, I was 90 percent certain I would agree to give things a try with him. But there was still that 10 percent insisting he was simply just too good to be true and I'd pay the price eventually.

"Okay. Good. It's in Alenbach," Rex said, sounding pleased.

"That's right. I'd forgotten." Bernadette had sent the details over before Thanksgiving along with the outfit, tiny feathery hat included. It hung in my closet at my apartment. I hoped it hadn't been doused in gasoline.

"We'll see lots of folks from high school," he said.

"Yay."

He laughed.

"Nah, it's fine." I waved my hand through the air even though he couldn't see me. "I was quiet, not bullied."

"Good. Glad I won't have to beat anyone up."

"But there was this one guy who I liked, and he didn't even know I existed."

"Sounds like an asshole."

I laughed, and the words slipped out before I could catch them, "I miss you, Rex."

He responded as though he'd been waiting for me to say them, "I miss you so much, Abby."

I closed my eyes and breathed through the thunderstorm of emotions rocking and rolling in my body, making me warm and cold and heavy and light. Likewise, Rex didn't seem inclined to talk, and I thought maybe he was feeling something similar.

Eventually though, he cleared his throat and said, "I have to go. I'm needed on the field. Are you working tonight?"

"Yes. I'm working every night this week. I have the Christmas market Saturday before the wedding, and then again Sunday during the day."

"I'll see you Saturday."

"Okay. See you then."

"Bye, babe."

"Bye."

We hung up and I stared at the screen of my phone unseeingly, feeling oddly light.

For some reason, I didn't like saying goodbye first but never minded that he did. Especially when he called me babe.

Rex surprised me by showing up at my Christmas market on Saturday. He caused quite a stir. To be clear, he caused a stir both at the market and all through my body, which had decided to riot as soon as he came into view.

I stared at him transfixed as I circumvented the table displaying my wares, unable to believe he was there with his sexy hazel eyes and adorable whisper of a grin, looking at me like I'd invented Christmas markets.

"What are you doing here?" I'm sure my eyes had never been larger.

"Do you have any giant, perfectly formed mugs?" he asked, his face as straight as a circle (that is to say, not at all straight).

I threw my arms around his neck and hugged the heck out of him. We didn't get more than two minutes before my table was swarmed. I sold out of everything in record time, but we stayed until all the fans had their photos. Then the car he'd hired—a limo of all things—drove us to the hotel so we could get ready.

We chatted easily the whole way, him telling me about work, practice, upcoming events, and me filling him in on crazy shenanigans at the bar. I didn't even care when he changed the subject after I asked him again what he wanted to do about our marriage. I felt lighter than I had in ages, filling my lungs and heart with buoyancy every time he smiled at me or called me babe.

"Please ignore all the boxes and junk. I finished moving out yesterday, my landlord is being a real turd about everything." I placed my key card on the table by the door and walked to the mini fridge to grab two waters.

Since Declan had been arrested and subsequently denied bail, I was down to just one guard per shift. But Rex had sent Anthony home as soon as he'd arrived at the Christmas market, giving the man the rest of the day off.

"This is all your stuff?" Rex accepted the water I handed over, his eyes inspecting the sum total of my belongings.

Or almost the sum total. "The studio is letting me store my supplies and inventory there, thank goodness. I had to trash the futon, none of the appliances were mine, but I still have my tall table and my quilts. How soon do we have to leave?"

Rex meandered over to my stack of quilts, rubbing one of them between his thumb and forefinger. "Have you given any thought to my place?"

My lungs tightened with something hot. "Uh . . . yes."

"What do you think?"

"I'd like to see it first."

He glanced at me, a smirk on his face. "Afraid it's a dump?"

"No. But, I don't know, I feel weird about kicking you out of your home."

"It could be temporary, if you want. Just until you get another place lined up." He sounded so logical and reasonable about it.

"Okay. You're right. I can't stay here forever." I gestured to the suite. It was three times the size of my studio but felt smaller to me for some strange reason. Or maybe, it simply felt too vanilla. Soulless. Like it was trying to appeal to everyone's tastes by appealing to no one's.

Rex looked around again, and once more his attention landed on the pile of quilts. "Why do you have . . . so many quilts?"

I stiffened. I didn't discuss my quilt addiction with anyone.

Deciding to steer the conversation in a different direction as quickly as possible, I asked, "Why do you have a place in Austin? So you can be close to your dad?"

Now Rex stiffened and seemed to grow very still. His eyes still on my tower of folded blankets, he shook his head. "No."

"How often do you see him?"

"Not very."

"Why? I thought he still lived in Alenbach? Will we see him today at the wed—"

His eyes cut to mine, and there was no mistaking the bitterness there. "I hope not."

Scrutinizing him, I rocked back on my heels. "Do you not want to talk about your dad?"

He shrugged. "There's not much to say. He's a worthless piece of shit, everyone loves him anyway, the end."

I set my water down on my tall table, walked over to Rex, and wrapped my arms around him. His heart beat two times before he returned the embrace.

"I'm sorry. I had no idea you didn't get along."

Rex's throat bobbed and he set his cheek on top of my head. "I don't want him anywhere near you."

"Oh?"

"He'll hit on you."

I tilted my chin back and looked up at him. "He'll hit on me?"

"He always does." Rex's eyes trailed over my face, like he was memorizing it. "He breaks up marriages, doesn't care. He—" He made a face.

"What?"

"Only loves himself and only cares about what people can do for him. He almost cost me my chance to play ball in college."

I gasped. "What?"

"He interfered with the recruiting process, suggested to two of the schools he was open to bribes. Said he'd guarantee I'd take their offer if they paid him off."

"Oh my God!" My arms slipped from his waist, and I pressed my fingertips to my lips. "That's—that's—"

"I hate him," Rex said with a vehemence I'd never heard from him before. "I hate him. How he treats people, like we're all here for his benefit and amusement. He cheated on his first wife with my mother, got her pregnant, then cheated on her. That's all he does, cheat. But he was still my dad, you know? I thought he cared about me, he always used to say how proud he was. But when I found out, when I—" Rex shook his head. His focus had turned inward, and I wondered if he knew where he was or what he was saying. "I can't forgive him. And I hate that I didn't cut him out earlier. I should've known, but I made excuses for him, how he treats and talks about women—locker room talk, boys will be boys bullshit, I can't stand it—how he just cheats and takes. I hate him."

I placed a hand on his arm, and his eyes came back to me, widening and blinking before falling away. I could see he was embarrassed, and surprised. I was also surprised by his overshare, and given the way he avoided my eyes, and the pinkish reddish color spreading up the back of his neck, it had been a scary overshare. Yet I was grateful for this window inside. I thought maybe I understood better why Clarence O'Dea's words and treatment of the women in Rex's life had bothered him so much.

But I didn't do scary overshares. Ever. Not even with Declan, which had been a source of constant irritation for him.

"*Why can't you ever be vulnerable with me?*" He'd complain before listing a litany of ways I had failed to open up: no intimate or embarrassing details, no nude pictures, no sexting. I simply did not do vulnerability.

Looking at Rex now, how the red from his neck now stained the tips of his ears as he swallowed three times in a row quickly, his lips parting then closing, as though he struggled to fill the silence, the urge to also share—specifically to overshare—something personal had me speaking before I quite understood what I was doing.

"You asked about my quilts earlier."

His gaze flicked to mine, his embarrassment momentarily upended by confusion at my statement.

"I collect quilts."

He frowned.

"But not because I like quilts." I shifted from my left foot to my right, my heart jumping up my throat, my brain screaming at me to be quiet. "Ask me why I collect quilts."

"Why do you collect quilts?"

"My mom left everything to me when she died, but I lost most of it when the court ordered me to pay back the debts incurred during my marriage. It was all sold off in an auction, except for a few things—books and trinkets which I was allowed to keep. And two lightweight cotton quilts."

The wrath he'd worn earlier had been completely eclipsed by curiosity. "So now you collect them? Because of your mom?"

I twisted my fingers. "Well, no. Kind of. But, uh, one day, while I was searching for a blanket in a thrift store—I actually needed a heavy, warm one—I came across a quilt with patchwork dancers on the front, in the most godawful orange and pink fabric, the colors brighter than sherbet. And I scoffed at how ugly it was before I noticed embroidery on the back. It was signed, from a grandmother to her only granddaughter, and I . . ." My throat closed up.

"You what?"

"I felt so sad." My voice wobbled, but I pushed through it. "This grandmother had made her granddaughter—her only granddaughter—this quilt, picked out the fabric, probably handstitched it, cared about it, fretted over it, poured herself into it, and then there it was, discarded. In a thrift store. All that love, just given away." *Dammit.* Now I was crying.

Rex shifted closer, a warm smile invading his features. "So you bought it."

"I did. And ever since, I always look for signatures on quilts. If they're signed or inscribed—from mothers, grandmothers, sisters, friends—I buy them." I swiped at my tears with the back of my hands, not knowing or understanding why I was crying. It was so silly, they were just quilts. "I can't not buy them, Rex. They deserve a home. They deserve to give love in the manner in which the creator of the quilt intended."

His hands came to my cheeks and his thumbs wiped the trails of tears from my face. Then he bent and kissed both of my cheeks, the right one first, then the left. His hands remained as he straightened, his eyes shining down at me with admiration. And love.

My heart oddly full, I sucked in a breath and smiled. "And that's why I have twenty-four quilts."

CHAPTER 24

"When life itself seems lunatic, who knows where madness lies? Perhaps to be too practical is madness. To surrender dreams — this may be madness. Too much sanity may be madness — and maddest of all: to see life as it is, and not as it should be!"

— MIGUEL DE CERVANTES SAAVEDRA, *DON QUIXOTE*

Rex had been giving me sexy eyes ever since I walked out of the bedroom wearing my outfit. Once again, I liked everything about it, a sleeveless, green velvet tea dress. Underneath were layers of Christmas red tulle which made it stiffly flare. The scoop neck was a little low, but after that red silk dress I'd worn to the charity gala, this one felt positively modest.

Completing the ensemble were red velvet high heels, black thigh-high stockings, and black velvet gloves. Oh! And that little hat, perched forward on top of my head such that the feathers stuck straight up and the fishnet veil covered just my eyes.

"You are exquisite," he said, giving my shoulder a kiss before placing my winter coat on my shoulders.

"Thank you, it has pockets."

He made a face as I turned, part frown, part smile. "Why do you always say 'it has pockets'?"

"I don't know. Because I think it's funny, I guess." I opened the door.

I wouldn't tell him the truth. People always seemed to get irrationally irritated with me when I confessed that compliments made me uncomfortable. They'd say something like, *Just accept it and say thank you.*

But accepting a compliment—truly accepting it—felt akin to trying to make myself shorter. I could do nothing about being tall, and I could do nothing about the weird, uncomfortable feeling in my stomach whenever someone paid me a compliment. Adding *it has pockets* helped deflect the attention away from the compliment and toward something absurd. Introducing absurdity into uncomfortable situations always helped me feel less uncomfortable.

The same limo and driver from before met us at the hotel and drove us to the venue. I was so caught up in our easy conversation that I lost track of time, and before I knew it, we were at the Alenbach Methodist Church. Rex, for once, was not a groomsman, nor had he introduced the bride and groom. They were in their sixties and members of his Aunt Sally's gym. Rex had known them both growing up and appeared more relaxed than I'd ever seen him, during the ceremony and after, at the start of the reception.

Everyone wore tea dresses in Christmas colors, and I made a mental note to send Bernadette a thank you note. Even the bride's dress was in a similar style, and she wore a little hat with a fishnet veil, only both were snow white.

I'd been to a few weddings in my time, and I felt like this one was by far the best. I loved how the groom gazed at the bride with open affection, how a tear had rolled down his cheek and he swiped it away when she met him at the altar, and how they held hands throughout the entire ceremony. I sniffed against my own tears when they exchanged vows and Rex handed me a handkerchief while also pulling me close to his side for a one-armed hug.

The reception took place in the church hall, which had been decorated for the Christmas season with evergreen garlands, white lights, and red ribbons. Rex's Aunt Sally and his Uncle Terry had been the matron of honor and the best man, so we didn't get a chance to say hi until the receiving line.

"Oh! There you two are! I was keeping an eye out for you. Goodness gracious, Abigail! You are a sight!" Sally pulled me forward for a tight hug but then quickly released me to smack her husband's shoulder. "Terry! TERRY! Look! Look who it is."

Terry gave me a once-over, frowned, and then said, "Who the hell are you?"

Both Rex and Sally laughed, and eventually so did Terry, holding out his hand.

"I'm sorry. I'm a jokester. Of course I know who you are. Welcome to the family. So glad someone finally took this guy off our hands." He gestured to Rex with his thumb and winked at me.

"Now, y'all are still coming for Christmas, right?" Sally sent Rex a hard look, one that actually reminded me of him.

Rex stiffened at my side. "Uh—"

I grabbed his hand and squeezed. "Yes, ma'am. We'll be there. What can I bring?"

"Just bring yourself." Sally waved away my offer to contribute. "But I'll put you to work. I'm counting on you both to help me with the gingerbread houses and decorating Christmas cookies for the bake sale. And are you sure you can't stay the night?"

Before we could respond, Terry piped in, "I'll also need an elf, just for the afternoon. Tamsin Kirkland is pregnant this year and can't fit into the costume. Do you have any elf experience, Abigail?"

I shook my head. "No, sir. But I'm happy to help if I can."

He squeezed my hand—which he still held—and then released it. "Good girl. Now get out of here. You two are holding up the line."

Rex patiently bent low for his aunt to give him a kiss and then guided me to a corner of the reception hall, his arm slung around my waist. "Are you sure you want to go to my aunt's?"

I nodded, and all at once my heart was in my throat. "I do. I want to go."

He lifted an eyebrow. "You'll be okay with the lying?"

Stepping out of his grip, I threaded our fingers together and smiled up at Rex, watching his face intently as I said, "Who says we'll be lying?"

Lips parting, his face went adorably slack with surprise, then brightened with understanding. "Are you—"

Biting my lip, I nodded quickly. "If you still want to give things a try, then I—"

He cut me off with a kiss, his big hands wrapping around my waist and dragging me to him, his tongue seeking mine, his lips and teeth hungry for me. And I felt just the same, my hands mindlessly sliding into his jacket so I could hold on to his rock-hard sides, pressing my body closer, impatient for the feel of his heat, the smell of his skin.

"Oh. Look at you two. Really upping your game."

Someone hit Rex on the shoulder and he—reluctantly, and with an impatient growl—slowly pulled away, pressing his forehead to mine as he opened his eyes. Jaw grinding, Rex turned his head.

Cyrus Malcom stood just a few feet away, green eyes glittering with an amusement echoed in his smirk and the arch of his brow. "So believable. You should be on the stage."

Rex, keeping me pressed to his chest, sent Cyrus a smile laced with irritation and . . . something else. "Didn't know if you'd be here."

"Of course I'm here. The bride is my aunt."

Rex inclined his head just slightly. "Abby, you know Cyrus."

I wiggled my fingers at my old friend, then slid my hand back under Rex's jacket.

Cyrus laughed, looking exceptionally pleased. "Finally figured it out, did you? I knew you would."

Rex continued to glare while smiling, just a little one, and I glanced between the two of them, confused. "What—what did he figure out?"

"That you were the one for him. You made matchmaking look so easy, Rex. But you made it so, so hard." Cyrus's eyes drifted to me, warm and kind. "Congratulations. I'm happy for you. Both of you."

For the third time that day, my eyes pricked with tears. I whispered, "Thank you, Cyrus."

And I thought maybe I understood now.

Cyrus had known how I felt about Rex in school. Then, when Rex had talked to him about me, he'd suggested fake dating me to Rex. Clearly, Cyrus had thought it was time for Rex to have a matchmaker of his own.

Giving Rex another teasing punch, he sauntered away, grinning. I watched him go, then laughed as he reached over his shoulder to give himself a pat on the back.

I turned to Rex, planning to ask him if my suspicions about Cyrus were true, but I lost myself as soon as our eyes connected, floating and drowning in the greenish golden warmth of his gaze.

"We'll go slow," he said. "I want you to trust me."

"I do. I do trust you."

His head tilted to the side, eyes narrowing. "You want to trust me. Big difference."

"Rex—"

"Let me prove it. Okay?"

I glanced at the ceiling and sighed. "Fine. Whatever. But I trust you."

"And we'll go slow?"

Now I narrowed my eyes. "Depends. How slow?"

It was strange to attend a wedding with Rex as his date. I found myself falling into habits I'd created during earlier events: stepping back and saying nothing, inquiring as to whether he needed another drink, offering to take photos when a fan walked up.

Rex kept pulling me forward, asking me how I was when I was quiet, and responding to my offer to fetch him a drink with a glower.

Even in our hometown, Rex received requests for autographs. I wasn't surprised, but Rex's patience seemed to diminish with each person who approached and he unleashed his menacing glare on more than one fan who'd asked me if I minded snapping a picture.

"I told you, I don't mind," I whispered, unnecessarily straightening his tie just so I could put my hands on him and lean close enough for him to hear.

His frown moved around the room. "No more pictures."

"Rex—"

"You're not my fucking assistant, Abby. You're my—" His mouth clamped together at the last minute and a feeling coursed through me, one I couldn't identify, but it made me hot and cold and nervous.

We needed to discuss exactly *what* I was, and what he was, and what we were doing. Now wasn't the time. I'd bring it up in the limo on the way home.

His temple ticking, he snatched the empty cup in my hand. "*I* will go get the drinks. Not you."

"Okay." I lifted my hands as though I surrendered. "But I want extra lime in mine and only three pieces of ice. And make sure they're ice cubes, whole ones, not shaved or crushed."

His brow relaxed, his gaze turning warm as he squinted teasingly. "Anything else, babe?"

"If they're out of lime, I'll take three cherries. And if they don't have three cherries, then just one twist of lemon and no ice."

Making an amused scoffing sound, he placed a kiss on the corner of my mouth and left for the bar. I grinned after him, my eyes tracking him through the crowd and admiring his powerful body in the bespoke suit. The kiss on the corner of my mouth was as affectionate as he'd been since saying he wanted to take things slow.

I'd have to figure out how to put his foot on the accelerator. Now that I'd made my decision, I wanted things to be full speed ahead and his hands absolutely everywhere all the time.

"Abigail."

I turned at the sound of my name, pleased to see Cyrus approaching. "Hello, matchmaker."

He gave me a nod, but his eyes looked a little frantic. "Hey, do me a favor. Don't look, but remember Graham Jefferson?"

"Yes?"

He lifted a disdainful eyebrow, his tone dry and droll. "He keeps breaking out into monologues from Arthur Miller plays and I'm avoiding him. I think he wants me to help him get an acting job. Talk to me for a minute, act really interested in what I'm saying."

I shook my head. "I'm not that good of an actress."

He barked a short laugh, rolling his eyes. "Okay. I walked into that.

But I set you up with the love of your life, the least you can do is save me from Graham's Willy Loman."

My heart skipped a beat as Cyrus said *love of your life*, but I stifled the rebellious organ, inclining my head and widening my eyes. "Oh wow. That's so interesting. I sure hope no one interrupts this very important conversation."

"That's more like it." He breathed out, clearly relieved. "Thanks."

"You're welcome, but"—my eyes darted to the left and I spotted Graham Jefferson staring at Cyrus's back, his posture restless—"unless we keep talking, he's going to look for a way to cut in."

"That's fine. We have plenty to talk about. For example, you putting in a good word for me with Rex. I want to be his best man when you two redo your wedding."

"Oh? You do?" I said lightly, covering another skip of my heart.

"Yes. I do. It'll piss off Alaric. I can't wait."

"Well, you might have to wait a while."

Cyrus took a sip of his drink, a sidecar if I had to guess, and frowned. "Why's that?"

"Rex wants to take things slow."

My old friend dipped his head as his eyebrows rose high on his forehead. "Does he?"

"I think he doesn't want to pressure me or something."

"Huh," he said, like this fascinated him. "Are you getting a divorce so you can date? That's not something you hear every day."

"Rex wants to take things slow, so maybe? Or maybe we should take a break or something so we can just . . . date?."

"But you don't know?"

"He changes the subject whenever I ask." My eyes instinctively sought out Rex, still standing in line for our drinks. He'd been accosted by another group of fans and was posing for selfies.

"Huh," Cyrus said again, rearing back a little, his eyes flickering over me.

"What? What is it?"

He opened his mouth but stopped himself, giving me the sense he was weighing his words. When he did finally speak, his cadence was careful and slow. "Have you ever asked Rex why he got drunk that night? The night he walked into your bar? He's not supposed to drink at all, and usually doesn't."

"Kind of. I asked what was it that made him break the rules and he never answered." I'd wondered about the drinking since, but not enough to push him about the subject beyond our short conversation on the plane to Richmond.

"You should." Cyrus lifted his drink toward me as though to punctuate his suggestion. Then he frowned, huffed, and said, "Actually, I'll tell you why I think he got drunk. Then you can ask him again and see what he says."

I wasn't so sure this was a good idea. "Uh—"

Before I could make up my mind, Cyrus leaned forward and dropped his voice to a near whisper. "It's not that Clarence douchebag guy that upset him—at least I don't think it was. Rex being Rex, he didn't like that the man was disrespecting his friends, I get that, but I don't think that's what pushed Rex to partake that night when he never, *never* does during football season."

"Then what do you think it was?" I asked, too absorbed to wonder again whether it was a good idea.

"I think it was being there with all his friends, so many of them happily married with kids and families. Alaric and I might be the only two guys he knows who aren't married and that's because we'd be shit husbands. But Rex, he's always wanted a family, lots of kids. He wants little league games and ballet performances."

My heart squeezed at the image Cyrus painted: Rex with his own hazel-eyed children, tea parties and teaching them to ride bikes, playing dress-up and coaching sports teams.

"Ah, I see you have similar aspirations." Cyrus's grin was shaded with the barest brushing of mockery. "Good for you. Anyway, I think he drank to numb the envy because—deep down—Rex truly believed it was never going to happen for him."

"He's said that?"

"Not to me." Cyrus placed a hand wide on his chest. "And not because I haven't pushed him about it. I'm enlightened. I talk about my feelings. He listens but doesn't reciprocate. He's a caveman. No wonder, though. Look at his father. But back to my theory."

"Which is that Rex got drunk because he was envious? Of his happy friends?"

"More or less. Envious and depressed because he thought he'd never have a family. His dad and mom really fucked him up, you know? And the irony isn't lost on me. Rex came from a broken home and shitty parents and wants to be a parent and partner, I come from the perfect family, am a commitment-phobe, and think kids are gross."

Ignoring his self-assessment, I pondered this theory about Rex. "I don't understand. Why didn't he think it would ever happen? By his own admission, everyone is always trying to set him up."

Cyrus shrugged. "I don't know what to tell you, but I will tell you this juicy slice of gossip, because I'm guessing you don't know or haven't realized: you are the first woman Rex ever dated where it wasn't someone setting him up. Even in high school, college, and after. All of his dates and girlfriends were setups. I think you even set him up with Rachel, right? At graduation?"

"I—I guess I did . . .?"

"Yeah." His eyes moved between mine, inspecting me. "That means you're the only person he's ever wanted to ask out without anyone else interfering."

I gave him a flat look. "You interfered."

"But not until after Rex said he'd wanted to ask you out and you'd shot him down before he could." Cyrus raised a finger between us, pointing in my direction accusingly. "I only interfered and suggested the fake dating thing because it felt like fate to me, the two of you meeting like that after so many years."

Staring at my shoes, I struggled to process Cyrus's gossip and chewed on the inside of my lip. Rex had wanted to ask me out, I already knew that. But hearing the background and context made it feel more meaningful. And real.

"It was fate," Cyrus repeated. "You and your volcano-sized crush for thirteen years, your ex leaving you with a pile of debt you were still paying off, and then you telling Rex you didn't date. And then him with all this money, finally finding someone he just really *liked* for the first time—no one pushing him, no one setting it up—and needing a date to all his grand soirees. I had to interfere. It was fate. What else could it be?"

Rex tricked me into a false sense of frustration.

After our kiss in the reception hall—which he blithely blamed on the mistletoe hanging from the ceiling—and the one press of lips on the corner of my mouth, all he did until dinner was hold my hand and give my knuckles chaste kisses.

I thought, despairingly, that this was what I could expect from him: weeks if not months of little pecks on benign parts of my skin. The idea seemed intolerable when I felt like I might burst into flames from wanting him so much, especially after my conversation with Cyrus.

Conversations with Rex over the past weeks, things he'd said, seemed to come more sharply into focus. Rex wanted me. *Me.*

Falling for you was like gravity.

Prior to my conversation with Cyrus, I didn't believe those words. I'd wanted to, I was trying to, but I didn't. Until now. And with this new belief in the veracity of his claims came a rush of feelings and desires, all of which were frustrated by the fact that Rex had said he wanted to take things slow.

But then, when we sat down for dinner and he pulled out my seat for me like he'd done at the Thanksgiving dinner, helping me scooch in and then moving his chair close to mine, his hand settled on the bare skin of my upper leg again, just above the band of my stockings, his fingers curling inward to my inner thigh.

My eyes widened, but I didn't look at him this time. I picked up my water glass and pretended nothing was amiss. It was a buffet dinner, so when our table number was called, he stood, retrieved our food, and sat again. He repeated the same movements, only placing his hand higher, his fingertips brushing lightly against my underwear.

Sucking in a shaky breath, I widened my legs to accommodate his fingers, thankful that our backs were to a corner and for the ballooning, long tablecloth that completely concealed my lap.

No one saw or seemed to notice when his hand skimmed even

higher upon returning with our desserts, his pinkie finger moving back and forth over the lace of my underwear just as Rex took a bite of wedding cake. Slowly, I scooched to the edge of my seat, spreading my legs.

"Mmm, babe." He turned his body toward me, lips in a secret smile, his clever eyes sharp. "You need to try this cake."

With the new angle, he shifted his hand, now using his knuckles to press harder and slide up and down.

I shook my head, breathless and likely flushed. "I think I've had too much."

He considered me, his movements stilling, then he made to withdraw his hand. I grabbed it, keeping it in place. "Okay. One bite."

"I don't want to force you."

"No. I want it."

Rex's attention moved over the high color on my cheeks and neck, his irises growing darker. "Or we could get it to go?"

"Come on, Rex. What's your hurry? Stay a little longer. The bride and groom haven't danced yet," Cyrus called from across the table.

Rex turned toward Cyrus, taking his hand with him and draping his arm along the back of my chair.

Finally, I could breathe. And think. And see.

While Rex and Cyrus bantered back and forth good-naturedly, I wondered at myself, why I hadn't asked him to remove his hand earlier —here or during the Thanksgiving dinner with his team. I briefly considered that Rex had wanted it, so I let him because I wanted him to be happy.

But that wasn't at all true. I hadn't been thinking about him. I'd been focused on me. *I'd* wanted it.

Even though his hand placement had meant I'd spent most of dinner on pins and needles, I'd absolutely loved every second of it. I'd loved the excitement. The swooping swirls in my stomach and the deep ache at my center. The upheaval.

What is happening to me? Am I an upheaval fan now? Do I need to add upheaval to my Christmas card list?

. . . No.

I hadn't liked Declan's visit to the bar or having to stay in that hotel room or being forced to move out of my cozy little apartment. I hadn't liked our confrontation in that conference room on Thanksgiving. I could see clearly now that it had been necessary, and I could appreciate what it had accomplished, but just thinking about it, all the confessions and hard truths, it made my heart feel heavy.

Maybe I like some upheaval, but not all upheaval . . . which makes me normal.

"Oh, they're breaking out the DJ." The woman next to Rex leaned around her husband to peer at the back of the dance floor, cutting into my thoughts. "I hope it's all Christmas songs. They said they were thinking about it."

Rex glanced at me, using his arm behind my chair to pull me closer. "Do you want to stay?"

I leaned against him, enjoying the warmth and strength of him. "Will we dance?"

"Do you want to?" He dipped his chin, his voice deep with meaning, echoing words that seemed familiar, "I will only do what you ask me to do."

CHAPTER 25

"Engage people with what they expect; it is what they are able to discern and confirms their projections. It settles them into predictable patterns of response, occupying their minds while you wait for the extraordinary moment — that which they cannot anticipate."

— SUN TZU, *THE ART OF WAR*

We stayed and we danced, but not for long. After three songs, I pulled Rex off the dance floor. He was such an exceptional dancer, watching and feeling his body move against mine was making me crazy.

He must've texted the limo driver while we said our goodbyes. The limo was waiting for us when we walked out of the hall, my arm beneath his jacket around his back, his arm low on my spine and hand on my hip.

As I readied myself to broach the subject of continuing our marriage during the drive home, the limo driver exited the car.

Rex waved him back. "Thanks. I got it, Vincent. Please raise the privacy screen."

"Sure thing." The old man tipped his fingers toward Rex in a salute and returned to the driver's seat.

The privacy window was fully raised by the time Vincent left the church parking lot. I turned to Rex after buckling myself in, deciding now was the time to spell everything out and settle things between us, and his lips caught me unprepared. This time he couldn't blame the kiss on mistletoe, but it also wasn't hungry or needy. It was light and teasing. Infuriating.

I shifted restlessly, lifting my hands to his strong jaw, hoping to encourage him to deepen the kiss. He wouldn't, but his hot palm came to my knee and slid up my leg, encouraging me to spread my thighs. He angled his chin, just out of my straining reach and avidly stared down at me as his hand bunched my dress, his middle finger sliding up and down my center over the lace of my underwear.

"What do you want?" he whispered , his free hand moving up my neck to fist in my hair. "Do you want this?" Rex punctuated the question by pulling aside my panties and rubbing a circle around my clit. But then he groaned, his movements stilling. "Fuck."

"All of that," I said, too mindless to care he'd just discovered how wet I was. His teasing touches at the table had turned me on like a Christmas tree.

I attempted to bring his mouth back to mine, but his neck was so freakin' strong he didn't budge, no matter how much I tugged. Likewise, I squirmed in the seat, frustrated with myself for putting on the seat belt.

"Rex. Rex—I need you. Please," I whined, abandoning his face and neck to slide my open palms down his shirt front, catching my nails on the little white buttons on the way to his pants, and giving the hard length at his groin an enthusiastic stroke with both hands.

He shuddered—a harsh, shaking breath—and abandoned my body to grab my wrists and hold me still. "No."

"Rex—"

"No. You first."

I stopped reaching for him. I mean, who was I to argue with that?

Nodding, I relaxed my arms, my wrists now lax. He positioned my hands on either side of my hips, then unfastened my seat belt. Eyes on me, his mouth curved in a faint smile as he reached under my dress, hooked his fingers in my underwear, and slowly slid them down my legs, encouraging me to lift my hips.

"This is a fantasy of mine, Abby," he said, his lips a hair's breadth from my lips, his voice a rumble. "You're my fantasy." Deftly tucking the red lace in his shirt pocket, he returned his hands to my knees, smoothed them up my thighs, once more bunching my dress, leaving a shock of shivers and goose bumps in their wake, his fingers eventually digging into my bare hips. "Come here."

Lifting me to his lap such that I straddled his legs, my knees on either side of his hips, he then turned his attention to the zipper at my back, pulling it down and unclasping my bra.

His eyes on my lips, he whispered, "Kiss me." He curled his fingers into the straps of my dress and bra, dragging the fabric down on both sides and exposing my body to the cold air, my breasts feeling heavy, my nipples tight.

"Rex . . ." I moaned, my head rocking back on my neck as his gaze lowered to my chest.

He licked his lips, eyes flaring. Withdrawing my arms completely from the dress, he brought my hands to his shoulders before I could touch him anywhere else, pressing them down and instructing, "Don't move these."

Immediately, my nails dug into his suit jacket. I tried to be loose, but my body was strung tight, my sex clenching as the backs of his knuckles softly brushed against the undersides of my breasts.

"Now, you ask me to make you feel good, because I'm the only one who can," he said solemnly, his voice holding a hint of menace, like he enjoyed seeing me so needy and wound up. "And ask nicely."

My hips shifted restlessly over his pants, searching for friction, and I arched my back, offering myself. "Please."

"Please?"

"Please touch me."

He cracked a smile, his eyelids drooping, his thumbs lifting to drag mercilessly over my nipples. "Be more specific."

A little cry escaped me before I managed, "Please make me come."

"Why?" He leaned forward and lifted my right breast with his hand, his tongue drawing a tight circle around the center.

My hips rolled on instinct, and I sucked a breath in between my teeth, my hands spasming on his shoulders. "Because you're the only one who can," I choked out, hoping to God I'd said the magic words because this was slow, painful torture. His eyes on me, his hands, his tongue—all instruments of suffering.

A sinister, satisfied grin claimed his features and he leaned back as though preparing to watch a show, getting comfortable, the back of his neck connecting with the headrest. Caressing a leisurely and massaging path downward to my waist then hips, he gathered the layers of my skirt slowly. My breath hitched, my nails digging into his shoulders again.

"Please . . ." I begged, my eyes fluttering closed against the assault of anticipation. Yes, I am aware he'd barely touched me, but I *needed* him. Begging seemed like the only course of action.

His fingertips traced light circles on my inner thighs, moving so achingly slow I whimpered.

"This is so much better," he said, a secretive smile in his voice.

"Than what?"

"Than the fantasy." With his words, he smoothed one hand around to grab my bare bottom and the fingers of the other dipped inside my entrance.

My high-pitched moan was interrupted by a gasping breath as my eyes flew open. He watched me. Lips parted, eyelids drooping over expanding pupils, the tendons of his neck in sharp relief belying his relaxed posture.

The hand on my backside massaged with greedy, grasping movements. He added a second finger to his invasion, his thumb stroking up to my clit, circling it with slow precision. Needing so much more, I tilted my hips, rocking my body.

"Tell me how much you need this," he demanded, his voice a scrape as his eyes drifted to my breasts where they bounced as I chased his skillful touch.

"I need it. God, I need it so much." More whining, high-pitched confessions tumbled from my lips. I didn't recognize my voice, but the words were undoubtedly true. I was mad for him, and I was embarrassingly close already. The ache in my abdomen hurting so good. "I want you," I added, unprompted. "I need you."

His hips jerked beneath me, his eyes flaring, and he drew in a shaking breath. "God, fuck. Abby."

Suddenly, his hand on my backside had fisted in my hair and he pulled my mouth down to his for a ravenous kiss, his thighs flexing, his thumb and fingers at my center pressing harder, moving faster.

I came apart, just like that, with my mouth gasping against his, needy, mindless sounds of bliss erupting from my chest. He withdrew his fingers all the way just to add a third as he returned, curling the long digits just slightly and pushing the base of his palm against my clit to rub with each inward stroke. I threw my head back, crying out again as a second release rocked through me, the rough friction just this side of pleasurable.

I heard curse words leave my mouth along with his name in high, keening breaths, my hands disobediently sliding up to the back of his head as I anchored myself to him with digging fingernails, riding one shuddering wave of ecstasy after another until a switch flipped and the gratification became overwhelming.

"Stop. Rex, stop. Please. Too much."

He did. Immediately, he removed his fingers and wrapped me in a tight, crushing embrace, his lips coming to my neck to kiss and lavish my skin with his tongue.

It took a long time for me to stop shaking, and for me to catch my breath, and to circle back to earth. But thanks to his languid kisses trailing from my ear to my collarbone, then lower to my breasts, the descent was a gradual one. I felt like I was sinking into a hot bath of his touch, somehow both gentle and demanding.

"*Mmm . . .*" he rumbled, like I tasted better than the wedding cake he'd offered me earlier, his hands grasping my hips. His lips were at my breast sucking, his tongue swirling, his teeth scraping. He muttered something that sounded like, "Worth the wait," and I shivered, suddenly cold.

"Oh, babe." The words were heavily seasoned with an apology. "Are you cold?" Rex made a soft tsking sound, hot breath spilling against my skin, moving his mouth to my other breast and shifting his hand to splay on the center of my back. "Something for me to remedy. Hold on to me. That's it."

With weak arms, I did as I was told as he leaned forward, never ceasing his attentions to my breast. He easily lifted his hips up to peel off his jacket, then settled it on my shoulders without looking up, his fingers moving inside the coat to grip my bare skin and hold me in place so he could continue lavishing me with wet licks and bites.

I swallowed around a renewed swelling arousal, my breath speeding up again. "Rex."

"Shh. Let me finish."

"Finish?" A shaky laugh left me on an exhale, and I arched my back. My mind was a mess, darting in all different directions, but my body caged it, sought to silence it, demanding I do as he instructed.

Ultimately, I did. I sat as still and silently as I could, the only noises in the limo were my labored, hitching breaths and the sounds of him devouring my skin. Eventually, somehow both too soon and innumerable, tortuous moments past my limit, he slid his lips upward.

Holding me close once more, he whispered, "Thank you," against my ear, and I could feel his smile.

This time when I laughed, it was full of disbelief. "*Thank you*? Why are you thanking me?" My blood was still humming, my body's restiveness reawakened, just as intense as before. I needed more of him. I needed his skin and body in a bed so I could touch and taste him like I pleased, just as he'd done to me.

And I didn't want to wait. Tonight. When we arrived at the hotel. Or maybe right now? In the limo?

Rex pushed his fingers into my hair, angling my head back so we could lock eyes while still keeping hold of my body with his other arm. "Thank you for letting me live my fantasy."

My eyes blinked rapidly, and I found I needed to back up another inch so I could see him better. He was serious. *This,* what had just happened, just now, *that* had been a real fantasy for him. One he'd been thinking about, one he'd wanted to experience in real life. With me.

His words earlier, his talk of fantasy and what he wanted me to do, had sounded like nonsense to me at the time, not a script he was following, one he'd already played out in his head. The current look on his face, the primal satisfaction and gratitude, the peace behind his gaze, like I'd scratched an itch that had been an affliction until just this moment, it took my breath away.

"Is that—" I couldn't order my thoughts, so I blurted, "Is that why you rented the limo? Today? Because—" I gestured to the interior of the car and then to my body.

He smiled, showing me his white teeth, his eyes blissful. "Yes."

My jaw dropped. "You were planning this? All night?"

"*Nooo.* No," he said, shaking his head, his tone full of mock innocence. "*Planning* is definitely the wrong word. More like, strategizing. Like chess."

I smacked his shoulder even though I laughed. "You selfish, sneaky bastard!"

He also laughed, moving his fingertips between my shoulder blades to subtly push me forward. "I said *thank you*, didn't I?" Still laughing, he gave me a kiss. "Should I send a note? In the mail?"

I laughed harder at the thought and twined my arms around his neck, resting my chin on his shoulder as I thought about everything that had happened today, all the chess moves I hadn't noticed because I wasn't looking for them.

"You used me to fulfill a fantasy," I said, thinking about the words as I said them and wondering if I should be upset.

"I did. Hopefully now you'll feel more comfortable asking me to return the favor."

My body stiffened, and I grew still as his words sunk in. *He wanted—*

"You won't mind? If I . . . use you like that?" My chest pinged with guilt.

"Not at all. Like I said, I hope you do." Rex's chest rose and fell with a deep breath, his hands moving to untangle my arms.

I leaned back, inspecting him as he reluctantly helped me put my dress back in place and fasten my bra. When I was all covered and zipped up, his expression turned mournful. "I should've had him circle the block a few times."

I started, twisting my neck to peer out the window. "Are we already here?"

"Almost. Hey. Kiss me." Rex's eyes were on my mouth again.

I evaded him. "Wait. Wait a minute. Do you—can you come up?" We still needed to discuss the status of our marriage, whether I was moving into his house, and when, and what that meant moving forward.

"No. I have to get back. My flight leaves at midnight, and I have meetings tomorrow."

I knew he wasn't playing until Monday, so I pushed, "On a Sunday?"

"Yes."

I squinted at him. "Seems unfair of you, to get me all worked up and then leave. And we need to talk about our future."

He picked up my hand and kissed each of my knuckles. "Now you'll want me to come back."

"More strategy?" I asked flatly.

Rex smiled against my fingers. "Of course."

"So now your plan is to seduce me and then leave me hanging until I trust you?"

He tilted his head back and forth, as though considering my question. "Basically."

"That's not very nice."

"I never claimed to be."

A niggling of a notion hurt my heart. Rex didn't think he was nice. He thought he was unapproachable. He didn't think he'd ever find someone.

And I needed him to know how wrong he was.

I squeezed his hand and waited until he gave me his eyes. "But you *are* nice. I know you, I know you're a nice person."

"You don't know me, Abby," he said starkly, with just a hint of dry humor. "If you did, you wouldn't say I'm too good to be true, or that I'm nice. But you'd also know I'd never fuck you over. And you'd trust me when I tell you I'm crazy in love with you."

❄

Knowing about Rex's plan—I'm sorry, his *strategy*—did nothing to inoculate me against it. Or him. Or wanting him so desperately. I became obsessed with checking my phone, my breath catching when I spotted a new text.

I'm pretty sure he knew this because his messages had grown more suggestive since he'd left me last week at the door to my hotel room, exhausted and yet still craving his touch with the heat of a thousand kilns all firing to cone 10.

On Sunday,

Rex: Hope you didn't want your panties back

On Monday,

Rex: Are you watching the game today?

Abby: Yes! Of course

Rex: Naked?

Rex: Please say naked

On Tuesday,

Rex: We won

Abby: I know. Nice tackle in the third

Rex: What do I get?

Abby: What do you want?

Rex: A picture of you

I'd sent him a shot of me at the studio with my hair in a messy bun, wearing a clay-covered smock and crocks. Little did he know, I was working on his Christmas present.

Rex: Sexy

On Wednesday, while I was moving into his house in Austin after Bernadette had arranged for my access and because it was ridiculous for me to keep staying in the hotel,

Rex: I had a dream about you last night

Abby: Was it a good one?

Rex: Very

Abby: Aren't you going to tell me about it?

Rex: I'd prefer to show you next time I'm in town

And then, on Thursday, while I'd been at work, counting the chip bags in the back,

Rex: I miss you

Abby: I miss you

Abby: What are you doing right now?

Rex: Fucking my hand and thinking of you

I'd gasped, shock arrested my lungs as an involuntary pulse of hot longing shot straight south.

He was so . . . so . . . *boorish!*

Maybe he was right, maybe I didn't know him as well as I'd thought. The Rex of my fantasies, the Rex I'd assumed him to be, had always been such a gentleman. But this guy? He cussed more than I'd expected, and—now that I knew him better—the gruffness I'd assumed was a façade had turned out to be a genuine facet of his personality.

Rex was gruff. Blunt. Vulgar at times. But he was also sweet. Thoughtful. Generous. And kind. He wasn't nice, but he was kind. One just had to watch how he was with his fans to know this was true.

Even as I debated with myself how I felt about his crass text and whether I liked it, my mind's eye couldn't help but conjure the image: Rex, lying back, his big body spread out, his muscles flexing and tensing as he stroked himself, completely naked. Or maybe he still had his underwear on and he'd reached inside like it was a secret, and—

"Abby?"

My head whipped up and I stared at Walker, not having the wherewithal to fight against the flames crawling up my neck and cheeks. "I'm sorry. What?"

He raised an eyebrow, a quizzical look on his face, and glanced between me and my phone. "Everything okay?"

"What? Oh. Yes. Mm-hmm. Perfectly perfect." I tried for nonchalance. I totally failed.

"Did you take inventory?"

"Almost finished."

"Okay." His eyes flickered to my phone again. "Just, uh, take your time. A few tables just finished up and cashed out, so if you need a minute, or need to use the office. . ."

"Thanks," I squeaked, my blush now moving higher, making the top of my head hot. "Be right there."

With narrowed eyes and a smile, Walker turned and ambled back to the bar.

I released a shaking exhale.

Abby: I'm at work right now

Rex: I'm in my bed, remembering how wet you were in the limo and thinking about how next time I'm going to come on your tits

I gulped in air, shocked and aroused all over again and supremely irritated. I'd texted him several times over the week, asking for a time to talk so we could sketch out plans for the future. He never had time for a call to get things sorted, but he had plenty of time to ambush me with sexy messages.

I fired off another text,

Abby: How would you like it if I sent you this kind of text while you're at work and trying to concentrate?

Rex: Pics or it didn't happen 😉

I laughed, angrily amused, and shoved the phone into my back pocket to finish counting the chip bags. But I couldn't focus. I messed up two drink orders—which I'd never done—and Walker sent me home to take the remainder of the night off.

If we were in a battle, his strategy was winning. Hands down.

CHAPTER 26

"A life spent making mistakes is not only more honorable, but more useful than a life spent doing nothing."

— GEORGE BERNARD SHAW

The following week progressed in a similar manner with Rex sending me provocative messages, me loving—and feeling confused about—every minute of it, him never having time to talk on the phone. I made a new rule, never check my text messages while at work or during the Christmas markets.

Making matters worse, everywhere I turned in his house was a reminder that he wasn't with me. I'd taken what I'd assumed was the guest room. Pictures of Rex with friends or his Aunt Sally and Uncle Terry were everywhere, decorating the walls along with a few interesting pieces of art. Apparently, he was a mid-century modern fan; the interior of his house was also decorated as such, with a heavy dose of Scandinavian design.

He'd also ordered one of my tall tables, a much longer version, with enough places for eight.

Rex's house wasn't huge, but not many of the homes in the neighborhood were. Comprised mostly of cozy bungalows, Clarksville had a rich, interesting history, was relatively quiet but full of culture, and was extremely accessible to downtown. One bus and I was at the Boozy Rancher, a ten-minute walk and I was at my pottery studio. I couldn't have picked a better spot for my commute, and that almost made up for the uncertainty I felt about staying at his house.

On Sunday of the following week, the night before Rex was due to return so we could head over to his Aunt Sally's for a pre-Christmas dinner, he sent me a text just as I was walking in the door.

My guard followed me in and promptly strolled past with a little wave. Mary had set up camp in Rex's security room. I'd discovered when I'd moved in that Rex had installed a panic room, complete with TV screens broadcasting every possible camera angle around the perimeter of his house.

Before Declan's recent behavior, I might've thought it was excessive. But not now. *Thank goodness that psycho is in jail with no chance at bail.* The prosecutor in the case had called me and said she hoped for the maximum sentence, which meant I wouldn't need to think about the possibility of Declan causing trouble for several years.

It wasn't late, I'd only worked an afternoon shift at the bar, but I was tired. Christmas markets had absorbed my Thursday, Friday, and Saturday mornings and afternoons this last weekend. I'd then completed a shift at the bar almost every night.

Rex: How was work?

Abby: If you're messaging to torture me with another sexiness assault, it'll have to wait until tomorrow. I'm tuckered

Rex: Wish I was there. I'd give you a massage

Abby: I will shut off my phone if you turn that suggestion into something lewd

Rex: You don't like it when I'm "lewd"?

Abby: I love it, but I miss you so much it hurts. Give a woman some peace

Rex: I'll save it for another time

Rex: Miss you

Rex: See you tomorrow

I picked Rex up from the airport Monday morning in the car I shared with Kaylee. She'd flown home to Colorado for two weeks. Mary loitered with me for a time at the airport and we discussed ideas for the screenplay she was writing.

Mary and I had become friendly since she'd been assigned as my full-time guard. We'd even gone out early this morning to get acrylic fingernails together. As a potter, I never had long nails. I loved the way they looked but accidental nail marks in my greenware had convinced me long ago to keep them short.

Over the last week, I'd read some of the script she'd written, impressed with her dry humor and cunning wit. I hadn't told her yet, but when she finished, I wanted to send it to Cyrus.

We'd only be gone for the day, but I hoped Mary had more for me to read when we returned. She wouldn't be following us to Alenbach; Rex seemed to think—and I agreed—that in the unlikely event Declan had a coconspirator, Rex's presence would be enough of a deterrent. At this point, the security company doubted that Declan was working with anyone. But Rex wanted Mary to stay on for the foreseeable future, arguing that it was better to be safe than sorry.

As soon as Rex stepped out of the terminal area and strolled past security, somehow looking even hotter than he ever had before, I ran the short distance to jump in his arms. He caught me. We kissed and kissed and kissed some more, probably making a spectacle of ourselves, but I didn't care. Neither did he if the smile on his face was any indication.

"I missed you *so much*." I wrapped my arms around his neck and squeezed with all my might. "Do you have any bags?"

"No. I shipped everything to my aunt's house. We can go." Rex stole another kiss before letting me go, but not too far. He held on to my back, so my body slid down the front of his. "Fuck. I've missed you," he said on a growly exhale, grabbing my hand and kissing the back of it.

I turned to say goodbye to Mary and blinked, confused. She was nowhere. She'd already left.

I shook off my mild surprise at Mary's disappearing act and led the way out of the airport. I loved that we held hands all the way to the car. I loved that he stood behind me in the parking garage elevator and squeezed my butt. And I especially loved that he'd made a playlist for the car ride over, all Christmas songs.

We chatted easily on the way about this and that. I told him how I'd picked up a Christmas tree for his house and had done some seasonal decorating. "Not a whole lot, I didn't want to overstep, but—"

"Babe. You can decorate it however you want." He shifted in the seat. Even though he'd pushed it all the way back and reclined it, his head still brushed the top, just like it had done that night he'd thrown up in my car.

"It's just a few items to make it feel more like Christmas. I haven't had a tree in ages, my place was too small, and your living room is just the right size. I won't move your things or—"

"However you want."

"But I won't—"

"However. You. Want."

Pulling to a stop at a red light, I squinted at him, my mouth a straight line. "I'm not doing that. It's your place."

"But if you decorate it, it kinda becomes your place."

"Great. Let's talk about this. You said that you wanted to take things slow, right? And now you want me to move in permanently? That's not taking things slow. And are we staying married? You said we would discuss it when I'd made my decision, and I have, and—"

Rex's hand came to my neck and pulled me forward for a slow, dragging kiss. His tongue a whole textbook on seduction, his other hand moving to my thigh and stroking upward. I gasped in his mouth, unthinkingly reaching for him, and the car behind us honked its horn.

I flinched back, realizing belatedly that the light had turned green. I also forgot why I was irritated. In fact, I forgot what we were talking about in the first place.

"How were the markets last weekend?" he asked, the hand that had grabbed my neck now came to rest just above my knee.

We'd been talking about our future and then he kissed me, that's what happened. *He's trying to distract you.* I frowned at the road.

"Oh. Good. Good." My gaze flickered to the blue sedan in my rearview mirror. "I'm almost sold out of everything. The Rudolf mugs were a clear winner. But back to the marriage question—"

"Are you finished with your Christmas shopping?" he asked, his tone making me pause. There was something behind it, a leading question.

I couldn't suss out the trap, so I responded honestly, "Almost. I can't figure out what to make Walker."

"Why don't you buy him something he'd never buy himself."

"Like what? A new jukebox for the bar?"

"Sure."

I snorted. "Come on, Rex." Those things were thousands of dollars.

"Come on, Abby. You have the money."

Ah. I see.

Staring forward, I decided a change of subject was in order and racked my brain for one.

Unfortunately, he wasn't finished. "That money is yours. You can't give it back. And you haven't spent any of it."

I drew in a deep breath. "I know."

"Why?"

"I'm not used to spending money."

"Abby."

"And I like making things for people as gifts. And besides, it's not like I earned it."

"It's yours, as per the prenup—which you signed before we married—it's yours, no matter what."

I readjusted my hands on the wheel. "But we're not really married, are we?"

"Okay. Fine." I could see him staring at me in my peripheral vision. "You don't want to spend it. Then what are you making me?"

"I can't tell you that." Smiling sweetly, I tilted my head to split my attention between him and the road. "It has to be a surprise."

He grunted, but I sensed humor in it. But then he asked, grumpy as a thunderstorm, "What do you want for a hint?"

I cackled. If my hands had been free, I would've rubbed them together. "Ha! Not so fun, is it? Being on that side of things."

"What side?"

"Wanting something and having it withheld."

The hand on my thigh slid higher. "You know I'll give you whatever you want, you just have to ask and be specific." His voice was sandpaper and sin.

My heart thudded in my chest, lava pooling in my stomach as my brain went wild with possibilities. But that was the problem, what—specifically, other than clarification on the plan for our future—did I want from Rex?

He said he loved me and I believed him. Clearly, he wanted me to stay put at his house in Austin, be there when the season ended. He trusted me. He wanted me. He wanted to be with me. He respected me and listened to my opinions, sharing his own and himself freely. He gave me so much without me asking. He treated me like a queen.

So what was it I wanted?

Sex. Lots of sex.

I frowned, batting the thought away. I couldn't ask for that.

"Well?"

Yes, you can. Ask!

I gathered a deep breath, held it in my lungs. Ironically, Bing Crosby's "White Christmas" played over the radio and it had just started to snow, though I couldn't recall seeing any warning in the forecast. My car didn't have snow tires.

"I want to talk about our future," I said resolutely.

"Tell me what you want, not what you want to discuss. We can talk anytime. What can I *give* you?"

Flipping on my turn signal as we merged onto the interstate, I told myself to pay attention to the road instead of contemplating how to ask Rex for sex. But the urge persisted.

Why are you hesitating? He loves you! JUST ASK HIM!

"Abby?"

"I—"

"Be specific."

"I want a fantasy," I blurted, then bit my lip.

He was quiet, a moment that stretched for ten beats of my racing heart before I felt compelled to add, "Like the limo, like what we did. That was one of your fantasies. I want us to—uh—do one of mine."

Rex remained silent for a beat longer before saying, "Well?"

"Well, what?"

"Are you going to tell me what it is? Or do I have to guess?"

Oh jeez. Which one? There were so many. And how far back should I go? *Not too far back, your high school fantasies were tame.* Not only were they tame, but most of them had already happened. Rex had talked to me, we'd laughed together, we'd held hands, he *liked* me.

As I'd grown older, I'd revised those adolescent fantasies and they'd grown up too. Holding hands had become hanging out in his bedroom and kissing, which had become hanging out in his bedroom and him convincing me to take off my underwear so he could touch me, which had become hanging out in his bedroom and him convincing me to take off my underwear so he could touch me and then convincing me to let him—

Goodness, it was hot in here. Right? So hot. I was burning up. Tugging my scarf off, I threw it to the back seat.

"That good, huh?" he asked.

My eyes cut to him and then back to the road. Yeah, I was blushing. In my fantasies, he'd never pressured me or made me feel bad if I'd said no, but he'd been a master at enticing, making me do things I wasn't quite sure about, and then making them so worth any consequences that might come after. But it still begged the question: why did all my fantasies involve Rex convincing *me* instead of me convincing *him*?

That's easy. If he's the one convincing you, then he's the one who likes you more, and it's so much less scary because you're not the one who has to be vulnerable with feelings.

"I want you to . . ." I sucked in a breath, gathering courage. "I want us to pretend we're back in high school, and you have a massive crush on me, and I'm in your room studying, and then you—uh—you coax me in to taking off my clothes and stuff."

OH DEAR LORD! If my face flamed any hotter, I'd be on fire.

Rex shifted in his seat, and I heard him breathe out, then in. "What kind of stuff?" he asked, his voice gruff.

"You know. Touch me. And then"—I struggled to swallow, my throat was as dry as bisqueware—"go down on me like you really, really want to. Like you can't stop thinking about it."

He shifted in his seat again, and I felt a million tiny pinpricks press into my skin at once. But I'd come this far, I might as well finish.

"And then we have sex, because you want to be with me so much, it consumes you." I scrunched my face, grimacing, waiting, and wishing I could take all the words back now that they were out.

Rex's hand lifted from my thigh and gently plucked my right hand from the steering wheel. He brought my wrist to his lips and placed the gentlest of kisses there. And then he said, "Okay."

I chanced a glance at him. He was smiling against my arm, just a small one. His eyes faced forward out the windshield.

"Okay?" I croaked, my eyebrows skyrocketing.

"Sorry. You're right." He gave my wrist another kiss, his smile a little wider. "I should've said, *Fuck yeah.*"

Rex's Aunt Sally had knitted me a stocking.

It hung on a hook along the mantle, right next to Rex's. She didn't say anything, didn't point it out or draw attention to it. But my eyes snagged on it as I surveyed the interior of her living room, absorbing the general splendor of her thorough and impressive dedication to Christmas kitsch.

Santas were in every corner, some danced and sang if you walked by them, some were paired with Rudolfs with blinking noses. She had six trees in the house: a live one in the living room, a fake one in the family room, a live one in the dining room, two smaller ones in the kitchen and hallway, and a fake white one covered in pink glass Christmas ornaments on the landing to the second floor.

I couldn't even begin to absorb the splendor. A huge, quilted advent calendar in the hallway, fake evergreen garlands with holly, twinkling lights, and red ribbon on the stair banister and around every doorframe on the first floor, multiple nativity sets on top of the fireplace as well as a huge blow-mold one in the front yard. A train table had been set up in the family room, already covered in green felt, but the track was only half constructed.

She even had that leg lamp from *A Christmas Story* on the side table in the living room and that bowl of eggnog with the reindeer antlers from *Christmas Vacation*. The woman was a marvel.

"That's a lot of ugly Christmas sweaters." Rex inclined his head toward a stack of knit jumpers on the sofa, lifting an eyebrow at his aunt.

After my embarrassing fantasy confession in the car, and Rex's surprising—but not really surprising—response, he'd changed the subject and did most of the talking. Interesting anecdotes about practice, team intrigue, upcoming events I might want to attend like their annual New Year's party or maybe another football game, this time at the Squall's stadium, dominated the remainder of the drive.

By the time we'd arrived at Sal and Terry's, most of my blush had burned off. However, a residual spark remained, smoldering in my lower belly. Rex knew one of my fantasies now. I'd trusted him with it. All I could do was wait and see what he did with it.

"Well, buck up, buttercup." Sal patted Rex's back. "One of those sweaters is for you."

"Sal—"

"And you'll wear it with no complaints." She grinned at me and winked. My mother had never winked in my life. This was a winking family, apparently.

He heaved a sigh, his eyelids drooping grumpily, but he didn't actually *look* unhappy. Maybe to most people he would. But I knew his unhappy face, and this wasn't it.

"And you'll also wear a smile because we don't put up with this grumpy shit from you, and you know it. Now, be a good boy and help your Uncle Terry with his train set."

"I'm too big to get under the table."

She reached up and cupped his cheek like he was a toddler. "You say that every year and yet you always find a way. Now scoot that tush and be careful with the gold wires, he spent a fortune on those things. Oh!" Sally reached over to the pile of sweaters and withdrew the one at the very bottom. "And put on your sweater. Look festive. It's Christmas, for hootenanny's sake."

Rex glanced at me as though asking for help, or for me to reason with his aunt on his behalf.

I pointed to the family room and raised an eyebrow. "You heard the woman. Move that tush."

Sal burst out laughing. Rex gave a low chuckle and accepted the sweater, pulling off his fancy, designer cable-knit one. He then tugged on an exceptionally bright blue one with snowflakes at the chest, falling snow down his ribs to another band of snowflakes and white hearts around his middle. Even in the garish cotton blend, he still had big sweater energy.

Rex kissed me, mock glaring as he leaned away. "I can see now this was a mistake. You two are trouble."

Sal linked her arm with mine. "Team Trouble is going to decorate Christmas cookies and catch up. Now get."

Without ceremony, Sal turned us toward the kitchen and leaned down to whisper in my ear, "I can't tell you how excited I was when I heard the news. It was like an answer to our prayer. We couldn't be happier."

Since I'd seen Sal and Terry at their friends' wedding a few weeks ago, I'd been marinating in how best to broach or discuss the topic of my marriage to Rex. We were legally married. We were also now officially together. But we weren't *really* married.

"I am so sorry." I swallowed around a lump.

She reared back, frowning at me. "Why are you sorry?"

"It was very last minute, only the team was there."

"Oh, sugar. We didn't expect an invitation. Rex is . . . well, you know." She smiled, but her eyes struck me as sad.

"It's an interesting story if you'd like to hear it," I said the line I'd practiced, a segue to the truth. I refused to lie.

"Only if you want to tell it." We'd made it into the kitchen and she released me. "But if you're tired of repeating yourself, there's no need. All I care about is that you love each other and continue to do so. Now go over to the gingerbread. Do you know how to pipe frosting?"

Relieved and a tad bewildered to be so swiftly let off the hook, I sputtered, "I do. I mean, I can. I don't have professional experience, but I—"

"Sugar, just do your best." She cupped and patted my cheek, exactly how she'd done to Rex in the living room, and turned on her heel.

I surveyed the workspace she'd created and all the bare cookie shapes, deciding to tackle the Christmas trees first. "Any particular design you want?"

"No, no. Just go for it." Sal busied herself with dinner, stirring a pot and then checking on a roast in the oven. "I really do wish you two would spend the night. Or the week. Or two weeks. I have Rex's room all ready, and the snow is really coming down out there."

I looked up from the cookie I'd just started to decorate. "Rex's room?"

"Yep." Sal closed the oven, setting the meat thermometer on the island counter. "You didn't know he has a room here? He moved in with us after his momma died."

I straightened at this news. "Did he?"

"Oh yes. We tried to make his room look just the same, even painted it the same color, and he kept all his furniture. Except, of course, we upgraded him from a double bed to a king-sized one. He was already so big when he was a junior."

"Huh." I frowned at the half-frosted cookie, starting again. "I had no idea." I guess I hadn't been as good of a stalker as I thought.

"Life is so strange, isn't it?"

I glanced up to see her watching me, her eyes moving over me thoughtfully. "You had such a thing for Rex in school, and he was so damn blind. That boy was blinder than a bat with its head up its own ass."

I expelled a laugh at the familiar description, delighted to learn Rex had co-opted this saying from his aunt.

"We can all be blind sometimes," I said diplomatically in light of my recent inability to perceive the obvious.

"Well said." Sal's gaze seemed to turn inward, her tone introspective. "I hope, now that he has you, he'll be more open—or, I guess, comfortable?" She peered at me, presumably to see if I agreed with her word choice. "I hope he'll be more comfortable thinking of us as a place he can come home to. He never really had a home with his parents. His momma moved all the time all over town, never staying in the same house for long, always looking for better, and he never even had a room at my good-for-nothing brother's house."

I stared at her silently, following her agitated movements, and poring over every Rex-related detail revealed.

She picked up a knife and began hacking at celery stalks. "I'm glad he cut my brother out, I am. But we love our Rex, you know? He's so stubborn, doesn't trust it. But he does always come for Christmas at least, that's something. I am glad I don't have to worry about him being lonely anymore, now that he has you. And you"— sighing at the mess she made, Sal lifted the knife in the air and sent me another sad smile—"after your momma died, you just disappeared."

"I moved to Austin. I had a job there."

"Oh right, at the bar. I remember hearing that, but I figured you must've left and gone to college, maybe art school? You were always so crafty and creative."

I'd never considered going to art school. It was odd to hear her suggest it.

"And you were so cute coming over here for Girl Scout meetings, asking if Rex was around and then hiding from him if he was. You never could ask for what you wanted, always taking your pizza slice last and settling for sauceless veggie instead of pepperoni." She chuckled at the memory, abandoning the celery to drain water from a steaming pot. "I wondered if you would ever get over your shyness."

A snippet from my conversation with Rex in the car earlier drifted back to me.

I want us to pretend we're back in high school, and I'm in your room studying, and then you convince me take off my clothes. . .

"I still am. Just a little," I said, working against the heat wave clambering up my chest. "But I think I might be getting better."

CHAPTER 27

"Imagination is everything. It is the preview of life's coming attractions."

— ALBERT EINSTEIN

Oh my—

Was Rex—

WHAT IS HAPPENING?

"You changed," Rex's Aunt Sally said from the doorway behind me.

I'd been sent to check on the guys and their train finagling. The announcement that dinner would be ready in three hours was on the tip of my tongue when Rex had crawled out from under the table and stood to stretch. He still wore his bright blue knit jumper, but he'd changed into—*gulp*—gray sweatpants.

Thin ones.

So now he had BSE and BDE.

Rex gave me a quick once-over, his eyebrow and his lips quirking in unison, and then turned his attention to his aunt. "Yeah. Sweatpants made things easier since I was crawling around on the floor."

"Good boy. I knew you'd figure it out. How's it coming?" Sal came to stand next to me and crossed her arms. "Almost done?"

"We're all finished," said Terry, flipping a switch and bringing the train set roaring to life.

"Oh. Isn't that nice." Sally allowed the engine and cars to circumvent the track three times before shouting, "Okay. You can turn it off now. It's too loud!"

Terry turned it off and immediately started fiddling with one of the buildings.

"Rex, sugar, why don't you show Abigail around the house? So much has changed since she was here last. I know it's last minute, but your uncle and I must run over to Mrs. Leavers to pick her up. She's alone until her son comes, and with all this snow, I'm just worried about her getting over here for dinner on her own. We should be back in about an hour and a half, maybe a little longer."

Terry's head snapped up. "What? Why do I have to go?"

"Because you do. I need protection," she said primly.

"From what?" He seemed truly perplexed.

She scowled at him. "Irritating men."

Rex, behaving like a proper gentleman and dutiful nephew, did as his aunt requested and gave me a tour of the house. I walked behind him, unable to pay attention. I couldn't stop staring at his round, ripe ass. Even when he showed me his aunt's collection of angel figurines, I stood there swallowing my saliva. The porcelain angel's smiles started to look strained—like, *Come on lady, pull it together!*—and their heavenly eyes filled with judgment.

I blamed it on the conversation we'd had in the car, and the gray sweatpants, and the BSE and BDE.

It wasn't until we were upstairs and he opened the door to his bedroom that I was finally able to snap out of it.

"This is your room?" I glanced at him. To be clear, I glanced at his face. This time.

He nodded, watching me.

"This is . . ." It was astonishing. It was the coolest bedroom I'd ever seen.

A train track ran around the perimeter just below the ceiling and big silver letters on the side of the engine told me it was called the Starlight Express. Up high, the walls were dark blue with painted constellations—real ones, mapped out on his walls—that faded into a lighter blue near the baseboards. National Geographic posters had been hung at eye level of various planets and celestial bodies.

"I had no idea you liked space!" I spun on him.

Rex stood in the doorway, leaning against the frame. "I did. I was obsessed with rocket ships and space travel when I was a kid." As he spoke, he pushed away from the frame and shut the door behind him. "I'd given up on all that by the time I moved here, but my aunt and uncle didn't know me very well at that time. They'd known me better as a kid, and remembered I liked space."

"So they did all this to try and make you feel welcome?" I looked around, noticing the furniture finally. He had a large desk free of papers that converted into a drafting table, a king-sized bed with a mission style headboard but no footboard, and a single nightstand with a lamp. "Where's your dresser?"

"It's in the closet, along with a bookshelf." He lifted his chin to the folding doors on the far wall. "Had to move them in there to make space for the bed."

"Because you're so big," I said unthinkingly, talking to myself. "That's why you have no footboard. I sleep on a futon for the same reason."

"Tall people problems." He shrugged, coming to stand next to me.

That earned him a smile. "I thought I was short?"

"I was talking about myself."

"Oh. I see." I inspected the room again, searching for pictures, anything that announced this had been and still was his bedroom. I found none.

"Thanks for coming over to study."

My eyes darted to Rex where he stood next to me. Hovering. Eyes on my lips. Intent.

Oh . . . *Oh!*

"Rex," I whispered, abandoning my inspection of his room, my breath suddenly coming hot and fast. "Should we do this here? I mean —your—your aunt—"

"If you don't tell, I won't," he whispered back, leaning closer and hooking a finger into the loop of my jeans. He dragged me over to his bed. "Come." He'd switched to his normal voice. "Let's study."

I swallowed saliva that tasted like lust and disbelief. *Oh my God. This is happening. This is HAPPENING!*

Of their own volition, my eyes dropped to his sweater, then lower to the front of his sweatpants, and a thrill spun and spun low in my abdomen. The sweats left nothing to the imagination. Nothing. And he was . . . I mean. *Damn.*

I licked my lips.

"Like my sweater?"

I nodded jerkily, then closed my eyes for just a second. I needed to regroup. "Oh yes. It's very . . . bright."

"Thanks. My aunt made it."

We were now next to the bed and Rex gestured to the mattress. "Ladies first."

Taking a deep breath, I climbed on the huge bed and settled on the far side. Rex walked around the mattress to the closet and withdrew two books. I smiled because they looked like textbooks. Returning to the bed, he sat on his side and passed one over, *University Physics, Vol. I.*

Working hard to quell my ridiculously pleased smile at how seriously he was taking this, I accepted the book and leaned back on his pillows, opening it to a random page. Rex lay on his side, facing me, propped up on an elbow and opened his book.

"Oh. Look at that. This is the wrong book. Mind if we share?" Without waiting for me to respond, he tossed his book behind him and looked up at me expectantly.

"Uh. Sure," I said, tucking my hair behind my ears and turning on my stomach to lie next to him, placing the book in front of me and making sure it stayed open to the same page because I'm a complete weirdo and was also taking this seriously—much more seriously than I thought I would.

Both of us on our stomachs, we flipped through pages, and I read them out loud. He'd stop me every so often to point out something he thought might be on the test or to ask if there was a definition for a word in the glossary. We settled into our roles, and my heart stopped beating erratically. I imagined this was what it would've been like if we'd dated during high school or college.

I admired his gorgeous eyes, filling my lungs with this moment of being together, playing together, and having such a good time.

I noticed after a time he began shifting closer to me. I caught him staring at my face twice. The first time, he tore his eyes away and back to the book. The second time, he just continued to stare, and his gaze flicked over my body, his eyelids heavy.

"Are you hot? I am." He promptly stood from the bed and—facing me—removed his sweater, leaving him shirtless.

That's right. *Shirtless.*

My mouth fell open, my eyes hungry as they devoured every dip and valley I hadn't allowed myself to enjoy that morning he'd woken up in my apartment. Rex had light brown hair on his massive, defined chest, a deep V framing his abs, and a happy trail leading into his sweats. I gathered an unsteady breath, too entranced to care that I was staring.

"That's better" he said, drawing my eyes up to his face.

Setting one knee on the bed, he bent and tugged on my sweater at my shoulder. "You should take this off."

Amused, I lifted an eyebrow. "Should I?"

His fingers slid down to my waist and pushed under the hem. "Let me help you, come here." Rex used his strength to pull me up so I knelt on the bed in front of him. Distracted by his sudden manhandling, I lifted my arms as he lifted my sweater and shirt up and off, making me yelp.

"Rex!" I leaned forward and into him, grabbing for my shirt.

"What?" He tossed my garments to the discarded book on the floor, well out of my reach. "You'll be more comfortable without them." Rex's eyes trailed down my front as his hand slid into my hair. "Come here . . ."

I had to brace my hands on his naked chest in order to keep from crash-landing into his face, my breath hitching at the feel of his body beneath my fingertips, my blood turning to fire in my veins.

"We've been studying so hard," he said, just an inch separating us. His mouth then brushed back and forth against my parted lips. "Let's take a break and relax."

"What do you have in mind?" I whispered, entranced by the moment, letting myself live the fantasy.

Holding my eyes, Rex's hands lowered to the front of my jeans, popping the button. I caught his wrists. He smiled innocently.

"This will help you relax." He sounded so confident and reasonable, and I let myself be convinced.

Never looking away, Rex unzipped my pants slowly, like he didn't want to make any sudden movements, and then lifted his hand to push into the waistline of my underwear, leaning forward to give me a soft kiss as his middle finger separated me and gave me a gentle stroke.

"See? Doesn't that feel good?" he asked on a quiet whisper.

I nodded, gripping his arms, my lace-clad breasts brushing his chest with each inhale.

He circled my clit with achingly delicate caresses as though exploring me, his touch tender and loving, coaxing, and I sucked in a shuddering breath. Rex "TW" McMurtry definitely understood the assignment, and he was acing it.

He'd listened, and instead of teasing me, making it lewd, or being boorish, Rex was playing the part of an enamored high school senior, anxious to please the girl of his dreams.

He tugged lightly at my jeans, working them down and over my hips. His hand then lifted to the middle of my back. I barely noticed he'd pushed my pants to my knees until Rex gave me another light kiss and guided me backward, still working me tenderly with one hand while supporting my weight with the other.

My back sunk into the mattress, my legs bent in front of me, my ankles tangled in my jeans. Rex lowered himself next to me, still holding my gaze. "You're so beautiful, Abigail." He kissed my cheek, my nose, the lids of my eyes.

The fingers in my underwear shifted away to grip the fabric. "Can we take these off?"

I nodded, my heart in my throat, and moved to push them down, but Rex was already rising above me, hooking his fingers into the lace at my hips and slowly dragging them off my body along with my jeans. I could only presume he dropped them in the same pile as my sweater and shirt.

His gaze moved over me now, dazedly trailing over my shoulders, my bra, my stomach, and he brought his hands to my knees to separate them, placing a delicate kiss on the inside of my right, and speaking against my skin, "You're so soft." He kissed higher on the interior of my thigh, his tongue coming out to lick me, and encouraging my legs further apart. "You taste so good." His arms moved under my legs and he knelt on the floor, pulling me toward the end of the bed.

"What—what are you doing?" I lifted up to my elbows, watching him drag his lips against the sensitive skin just south of my pussy, his hot breath fanning against me.

"Tasting you," he said gruffly, his eyes colliding with mine over the canvas of my body, his pupils dominating his irises. I sucked in a breath and held it because gentle, tender playacting Rex was gone.

This was real Rex.

A spike of raw arousal had my body clenching deep inside and heat pulsing up from the base of my spine to my neck. His dark eyes on me, he lowered his mouth, closing over my center and French-kissing my clit. The heat in his gaze and the hungry, slippery wet sounds he was making had my head whipping back, my body arching.

I fell back to the bed, the base of my palms pressing against my eyes as a keening sigh wrenched out of me.

"Take off your bra," he commanded, licking me with the flat of his tongue. "Want to see those tits."

With shaking, fumbling hands, I unclasped my bra and pulled it off.

He grunted his approval, then sucked me into his mouth, groaning, the rumble of the sound vibrating through my body. My needy sounds filled the room and my legs began to shake.

"Fuck, you're so fucking perfect. I could fucking do this all fucking day. Don't come yet."

I laughed helplessly, because I was so close. "Don't think I have a choice, husband."

"Oh, *babe*." His chest rumbled again, a deep, pleased purr, vibrating my center, his generous lips and eager tongue joined by a thick finger sinking into my channel, my hips jerking instinctively, my body arching off the bed as the constellations on the walls of his room blurred into stars bursting behind my eyes.

But then he was gone, leaving me dangling just as I'd begun to fly, and my eyes flew open. Rex had stomped to his closet and opened a door, slamming it and barreling back to the edge of the bed. He was fully naked, his cock jutting out and curling upward from a patch of brown hair, thick and big and so damn beautiful, saliva rushed into my mouth. He had a foil packet in his hand and he tore it open with his teeth.

"Oh! Wait," I said around a shiver, lifting my hand. "I'm on birth control."

Apparently that was all he needed to hear because he tossed the foil packet away and climbed on top of me.

"Need you," he said between fast, starving kisses, rubbing the entire length of his erection against the spot he'd frenched earlier. I groaned, reflexively shivering again, my body almost painfully sensitive with the orgasm denied, tasting myself on his lips.

I grabbed fistfuls of his hair and tilted my hips up in offering, and he pushed inside. My head whipped back again at the invasion while his eyes slammed shut, his jaw clenched, the tendons on his neck in relief.

"How are you so perfect?" He sounded almost angry about it as he rocked his hips back and then rolled them forward in a controlled movement.

My breath hitched and my hands flew to his shoulders as he filled me a little more than before, and I felt myself stretch to accommodate him.

He rocked back, pressed forward, again stretching me, hitting something deep inside that made my eyes roll back. "God, Rex."

"Okay?" He asked through labored breaths. "This okay?"

I bit my lip and nodded, my hands sliding under his arms to grab his back, feel his muscles move under my fingertips as he continued to slowly roll his hips, giving me more and more of himself each time.

"You—I'm—" I shook my head, trying to spread my legs wider to accommodate the size of his body. I'd never thought of myself as small until that moment.

He reached behind himself to grab my knees, one at a time, and pressed them back to the mattress, opening me further. I swallowed convulsively as my eyes fluttered and I found his gaze fastened to mine, his brow furrowed.

"Babe. Is this—"

"It's good. So good." How big and hard and rough he was—literally everywhere—was a little overwhelming, a little painful, but so fucking good.

He frowned. Shook his head. "I think you need to be on—"

"No. Trust me." I lifted my head to kiss him. "I love it." I bit his chin. "Don't stop, please." I sucked on the skin of his throat. "Please."

Rex lifted himself up and away, planking over me and searching my face, his cock still entering me slowly, carefully. "Abby, tell me if—"

"I will." I reached up and trailed my nails down his chest, saying again, "Trust me."

He nodded, but the concern in his features persisted, and his movements seemed to grow even softer, his thrusts shallower.

I squirmed beneath him, planting my feet back on the bed, pivoting my hips to encourage him to go deeper.

He stilled, his eyelashes wavering. "St—stop that."

"Then give it to me." I slid my hands to the sharp bones of his hips and tried to force him down. "I want it."

His eyes flared, grew dark. "Oh yeah?"

"Yes."

He pushed forward, thrusting hard, filling me completely, the pressure indescribable.

I gasped, smiling. "More."

His jaw clamped down, his lids lowering, and he withdrew quickly only to return twice as fast, repeating the motion again and again until the bed squeaked and rocked and banged against the wall, and I thought I might die from how unbelievably *essential* it felt. Holding himself on one arm, he reached between us and tapped my clit, then stroked it—slow at first, then faster and faster—maintaining a soft, teasing pressure that soon made me whimper. My release built a fire in my lungs, lava in my veins, until I felt myself fragment into infinite tiny pieces of sharp sensation.

I knew I'd feel it tomorrow—or probably later today—but I didn't care. I'd walk funny for a month if it meant living a moment like this.

Rex followed me without a sound, the movements of his hips becoming unpracticed and selfish, drilling deeply and prolonging my ecstasy, his entire body tight, his thick thighs flexing as my body constricted around his with each of his inelegant thrusts. And then his arms gave out as he rolled to the side and gathered me tightly to his body, his mouth on my neck, then collarbone, my throat, then chest.

My throat closed at the raw intensity of his kisses even as an ache in my chest ballooned. What we'd just done had been profound for me, and I wondered if it—the trust and the vulnerability—had been just as profound for him. I couldn't imagine my life without him now, without all parts of this magnificent man, so gruff and sweet, rough and sexy and perfect. To me, he was perfect.

"I love you," I whispered, not thinking about it, giving myself permission to *feel* it first. "I love you so much."

Rex stilled for a split second, then lifted his head from my chest, his wide eyes moving between mine. "What did you say?"

I smiled, tears pricking behind my eyes for some reason. "Rex McMurtry, I love you."

His eyes grew glassy and he blinked, his chest expanding with a deep inhale. "I'm going to need you to say that every day."

"How about every other day?" I teased, blinking the blurriness from my eyes and laughing so I wouldn't cry.

"Twice a day." He kissed me quickly. "And thirty times on a game day."

I laughed harder and he rolled to his back, bringing me with him. He seemed content to just stare at me, his eyes dazed and hazy, his hands stroking my body lazily. I played with the hair on his head, twisting it and enjoying its texture. Then I kissed his nose, eyebrows, the spot between his eyebrows, his cheeks, and chin. I traced a line to connect the dots of my kisses with a light finger, wondering if my hands could sculpt his likeness and thinking that I'd like to try.

Maybe I'll go to art school and learn.

I pushed away the errant thought, tucking it away for later, much later, because I wanted to be right here, right now, thinking only about us. But then another errant thought entered my mind and I paused in my mapping of his face.

"Do you mind?"

He blinked, his eyes focusing on mine, his hand stilling on my bottom. "Mind what?"

"That our first time was part of my fantasy?"

A sly grin slowly tugged at the side of his mouth and his hand resumed massaging my backside. "Babe, I have a feeling every time with you is going to be a fantasy."

CHAPTER 28

> "Fate is like a strange, unpopular restaurant filled with odd little waiters who bring you things you never asked for and don't always like."
>
> — LEMONY SNICKET

Dinner was a boisterous, unruly affair with lively debates regarding the true story of the Alamo, which Tex-Mex restaurant in Alenbach was best, and arm wrestling challenges.

Rex won all the challenges except the one against me. I kissed him as soon as it started, his hand went lax, and I slammed his fist down on the table. Then I stood and raised my fists in the air in triumph. He didn't seem to mind.

"I heard that Pauline is running against her own son for county dogcatcher." The white-haired Mrs. Leavers whispered loudly to Rex's Uncle Terry, her eyes narrowing into slits. "I hope he annihilates her."

We were all sitting or standing with our pie, chatting in the various rooms—all twenty or so guests—and I couldn't seem to bring myself to stop eavesdropping on Mrs. Leavers. She was so cutthroat. I loved it.

"Me too." Terry nodded. "He's got my vote."

I felt big hands slide onto my hips. A second later, hips brushed against my backside. Rex leaned down to kiss my cheek, then neck, then he nuzzled and bit my ear. "Can I get you anything?"

"I'm so stuffed. I couldn't eat another bite." I turned and smiled up at him, the ground shifting a little beneath my feet as I swam in his eyes.

He took my plate, kissing the corner of my mouth and then licking it. "You missed some frosting, right there," he teased, stepping back.

I smacked his bottom as he left, wrinkling my nose at him and chuckling. He was so cute.

The hairs on the back of my neck prickled and I glanced around, watching as a few sets of eyes dropped the moment I made eye contact. They then seemed to swap stares with each other, many accompanied by smiles and headshakes. I didn't feel self-conscious about it, this had been happening all night. Sal had explained that folks weren't used to Rex being so outwardly affectionate.

"You mustn't think anybody minds, it's just strange to see." She'd bumped my hip with hers as she, Terry, and I had worked on the dishes while Rex had cleared the table earlier. "I think it's wonderful."

"So do I," Terry had piped up.

Presently, I smiled at anyone who was still making eye contact and the room fell back into easy conversation. Or in Mrs. Leavers's case, vicious conversation.

Most people left around seven, citing growing concern about the snow. Terry accompanied Mrs. Leavers home, telling Sal to sit down and rest as he pulled on his coat. They bickered, but they sure were sweet together.

I finished up in the kitchen with Rex while Sal had a rest. Sounds of the *Great British Baking Show: Holiday Edition* sounded from the other room.

I passed Rex a bowl to dry, dunking my hands in the sink to wash the next dish. "I don't understand you, Rex. You make no sense."

"How so?"

"Your aunt said you never come home, only for Christmas. If I had a bedroom like yours, a place to come back to and people who loved me like Sal and Terry, I'd be here every chance I got." I glanced at him and found his expression thoughtful.

Rex's eyes lost focus and his chest expanded with a deep inhale. He said nothing for a moment, then, "They're too good to be true."

I almost dropped the dish I'd been washing. "I'm sorry? What did you say?"

His smile wry, his gaze sharpened on me. "When I came, they were so nice, and . . . attentive. Interested. They wanted to see my report cards and hardly asked me about football. It was weird."

"You mean, when you moved in? After your mom passed?"

He nodded. "I've known them all my life, as my aunt and uncle, and they were nice then. But I wasn't allowed to spend much time with them. My mom had sole custody, and Sal is my dad's sister, so . . ."

I frowned, unfortunately understanding his meaning without further explanation.

Turning off the water, I faced him. "So why don't you visit them now?"

"They still seem too good to be true," he grumbled.

I laughed, rising up on my tiptoes to give him a kiss. "You are the cutest, do you know that?"

Rex set down the dish he'd just dried and wrapped his arms around me. "No one, in my entire adult life, has ever called me cute."

"Except me."

His eyes lost a little of their focus and turned soft. "Except you."

We gazed at each other, much like we'd done earlier in his bedroom until we had run out of time. Just before the guests had arrived, I'd taken a quick shower and changed back into my clothes. Moments later, Terry and Sal had returned with the perfidious Mrs. Leavers.

Looking at Rex like this now, sharing these sacred moments of mutual love and trust were as close to heaven on earth as I'd ever experienced in my life.

"Maybe we both deserve some too-good-to-be-true people in our lives," I whispered, like it was a secret.

His attention dropped to my lips and he grinned. Then he kissed me, soft and slow, making me dizzy and warm. And when he finished,

I sighed, so happy I didn't know how I could contain it. It was too big for me. *It's Rex-sized.*

"I love you," he said.

"I know," I said.

He lifted an eyebrow. "You're not going to say it back?"

"I already said it three times today." I slid my arms from his neck and cackled, returning my attention to the sink.

Rex pinched my bottom and I yelped, showing him my hands covered in suds. "Don't make me retaliate, you know I will."

"Truce." He laughed, a rumbly, happy sound that gave my heart wings. Then he had to ruin the moment by saying, "Hey. We should get going soon. The plane leaves at midnight."

My heart lost its wings. Sal had said earlier that she wished we could stay, and so did I.

"What? What's wrong?" Rex leaned against the counter and searched my face.

"It's just, I wish I could stay."

Rex reared back and frowned like he was surprised. "You want to stay?"

"I do. I mean, I barely finished decorating the gingerbread cookies, and there's loads more to do, plus the sugar cookies. And she said she was making peppermint bark, I've never made that. And Terry mentioned needing help at the Santa house. He's short on elves, and I thought maybe I could see if one of the costumes fit."

As he examined me, the severity of his frown increased. Taking a deep breath, he opened his mouth to say something.

Feeling compelled, I interjected before he could. "I know you can't stay—you have that game on Wednesday, so obviously we need to get you back to Chicago. But I don't need to work this week, and I've been working every day for over a month. I'm tired. I don't get a chance to decorate gingerbread houses and craft holiday ornaments with friends. Your aunt *knits*, Rex. She does colorwork." I gestured to his sweater with a soapy hand. "I've always wanted to learn how to do colorwork."

Rocking back on his heels, his frown easing but not completely disappearing, he nodded. "Then you should stay," he said quietly.

I smiled. "Really?"

He nodded. "And I'll come back, after I'm done in Chicago."

My smile widened and I'm sure I looked like a kid who'd just uncovered indisputable proof that Santa was real. "Are you serious? You'll come back here? We can spend Christmas Day with your aunt and uncle?"

He nodded again, a whisper of a smile on his lips, but I noticed it didn't reach his eyes.

Now I frowned, examining him as I turned from the sink and grabbed a towel to dry my hands. "What's wrong?"

His lips twisted and he glanced behind me to the wall. "Oh, you know. I was hoping for a ride to the airport."

"I can still drive you."

Rex's aunt walked into the kitchen and made a beeline for the fridge. "What are y'all talking about? And does anyone know if there are any tamales left or did Richard leave with them?"

"I was just telling Rex that if your offer is still open, I'd love to stay here for the week with you and Terry."

She clapped her hands together. "Oh! That's so wonderful!" Sal crossed over and pulled me into a hug. "We'll make gingerbread houses and get a jump start on the Christmas cards for next year. I always do my paper crafting a year ahead."

I felt a little light-headed with glee at the mention of paper crafting. "Do you happen to have a Cricut?"

She leaned close, giving me a saucy grin. "I do. And a new vinyl stencil roll. We could silk screen T-shirts if you want."

A sound of blissful anticipation tumbled from my lips. So much crafting, so little time. Best day ever. *Maybe I can stay two weeks . . .*

"Stay as long as you want and come back whenever you want. That's my only rule," she said as though reading my mind. Then she backed out of the kitchen.

I sighed as I stared after her, wondering if a more perfect Christmas ever existed.

Rex left by snowplow an hour later.

For a moment, I thought he'd have to stay. Despite all the talk about snow, I hadn't realized exactly how much had fallen. In an average year, Austin never received more than a dusting. But in Hill Country, the fluffy white flakes weren't as unusual. That said, this much snow this fast was definitely an anomaly.

I was grateful that Mrs. Leavers's nephew owned a snowplow business for Rex's sake, but as I knitted next to Sal that night while watching the British overachieve at baking, I fretted after he left, feeling like maybe he'd been upset with me, or disappointed in me somehow for staying with his aunt instead of going back to his house in Austin and waiting out the week there.

It's not that he didn't kiss me before he left, or that he didn't say he loved me and tell me he'd see me soon—he did all of that. It was . . . a feeling. Something about the dullness in his eyes, how they didn't hold mine for longer than a few seconds, like looking at me was difficult.

"She can't make an Italian meringue like that!" Sal gestured to the television and released a disgusted sigh. "She'll make it rubbery, and it won't separate the layers of lemon curd. Good God, people. Get it together."

If I hadn't been so distracted by unease, I probably would've joined her heckling, especially when one of the bakers didn't roll their fatless sponge the MOMENT it came out of the oven, and then were surprised later when it cracked. *Amateurs.*

"Sugar, is that your phone?" Sal leaned forward, twisting her neck from side to side.

Startled from my tumultuous thoughts about Rex's mood during his departure, the sound of my phone ringing abruptly reached me. I jumped up. Jogging to where I'd left my bag by the front door, I dug around inside for my cell and frowned at the number. Swiping to answer, I brought it to my ear.

"Hello? Bernadette?"

"Thank goodness you answered. I've been trying to get Rex for the last fifteen minutes."

I checked the time on my phone, it was just after ten. "Why? What's wrong?"

"Just tell him there's been a change of plan with the flight out. I managed to get you on that Learjet like he originally wanted. It's waiting for you when you get to the airport, so don't check in with the airline."

I felt my face scrunch in confusion. "I'm sorry, Rex isn't here. He left for the airport two hours ago."

Silence, then the line crackled, and then a broken, "—not with him?"

"What?"

More silence, and then, "You decided not to go?"

"Decided not to go?" I echoed, walking into the living room and ignoring the dancing Santa in the corner. It suddenly flickered off as all the lights in the house went dark. Then, a second later, everything came back on.

"—you were coming back with him, to Chicago, for the week. I got the jet. My team got everything all set up, though Rex had to call in a few favors for the Mulaney tickets tomorrow, but—"

"Bernadette, I don't know what you're talking about. He never asked me to go to Chicago with him." And as soon as the words left my mouth, the truth hit me.

He was going to ask! He was going to ask and you interrupted him. You wanted to stay here.

Sinking to the couch as my heart lodged in my throat, I rubbed my forehead and said, "Shit."

The line crackled, and Bernadette said something I missed. Then there was silence.

"Hello? Bernadette? Are you there?" I jumped to my feet, doing some mental math. Maybe it wasn't too late. Mrs. Leavers's nephew would be back by now, maybe I could take the snowplow into Austin and we could catch the plane together, and then—

The lights in the house went dark again as I pressed the phone to my ear, waiting for Bernadette to respond. She didn't. The line went dead. And when I looked at my phone screen, intent on calling her back, I had no service.

CHAPTER 29

"Do not be afraid; our fate
 Cannot be taken from us; it is a gift."

— DANTE ALIGHIERI, *INFERNO*

Sal turned on their massive generator before we went to bed, but my cell service didn't return all night and all through the next day. It was like living in ancient times, with mead and beheadings and blacksmiths.

Except, I really just meant no internet or cell reception.

I didn't enjoy myself during paper crafting time. Or stenciling and screen printing time. Or even gingerbread house making time. My car was still snowed in—it was still snowing!—and even after I dug out both my car and the driveway with Sal's help, Mrs. Leavers's lazy nephew wouldn't come over and plow the street. He said it was too icy.

I'll murder him and frame Mrs. Leavers.

I felt conspired against, like after one blissfully perfect day, the universe had remembered that the only kind of upheaval Abigail McNerny received was the yeast infection in the vagina kind. (I didn't have one, but based on my luck I figured it was right around the corner.)

I needed to talk to Rex. I couldn't talk to Rex. It was driving me bonkers.

Terry and Sal were so kind when I explained what happened, Sal in particular seemed to understand my stress.

But Terry had said, "Oh. Well, that'll teach you. Next time let the man talk."

I did not find this amusing. Neither did Sal.

What could I do? Stress bake.

I made German stollen and fruitcake, yule logs and mince pies, bourbon trifle and pecan rolls. I ate half of the trifle before Terry found me and carted me up to bed, drunk on trifle and remorse. He promised to wake me up as soon as either the internet or cell connection came back online.

When I woke up on Wednesday—Rex's game day and Christmas Eve—communication methods hadn't returned and I wondered if I could expect wolves to come and pick over my bones before dusk, because what else could possibly go wrong? What? Else?

"The internet is back!"

I stiffened over the intricate gingerbread house tin roof I was making with edible silver foil spread over chocolate bars, eyes wide, afraid to believe my ears. But then the sound of the TV coming on had me jumping into action.

I raced to my phone, which I'd kept charged, and waited, chewing on my thumbnail until the heavenly sound of chimes announcing new messages.

Rex: Bernadette called, said she talked to you. Don't worry about it. Have fun with Sal

Rex: Are you mad at me?

Rex: I didn't ask because you deserve the Christmas you want

Rex: Just found out Hill Country has no cell reception or internet. When you get this, tell Terry to turn on the generator. Stay safe

Rex: Be back later than I thought, last minute thing

UGH!

I gripped the phone to my chest for several seconds, mentally processing his messages and breathing deeply through my own special brand of stressed out. Then, I started typing,

Abby: We just got reception back just this minute. Rex, I am SO SAD I didn't go to Chicago with you. If you'd asked, I would've gone in a heartbeat. I didn't know it was an option. A Christmas with you is the only Christmas I want. Please, please call me when you get this. I know you're playing today, and I'm cheering you on from here. I love you and can't wait to see you

Without thinking too much about it, I hit send and held my breath for reasons unknown. When I realized it was silly to hold my breath, I started breathing again.

"Oh! I got the game. There's Rex." Sal's voice carried to me from the family room, and I jogged to her side, searching for him on the screen.

He was there and playing and safe and fine, and here I was, twisting myself into knots of German stollen and drowning my sorrows in bourbon.

WHY AM I THIS WAY?

Heaving a breath, I flopped back on the couch and chuckled at myself, feeling like an idiot. But then, as I watched the game, catching glimpses of Rex's stern face, I got a little mad and resentful.

He should've asked me to go. Why didn't he ask me to go? Didn't he know I would prefer to spend a lifetime with him in the North Pole rather than literally anywhere else without him, even if crafting were outlawed in the North Pole?

And, on that note, why hadn't I asked him if I could go to Chicago for the week? Why did I need to be asked? He was my husband, wasn't he?

Shut up, he is. It's legal, so it's real. That's how the world works.

What was wrong with us?

Gritting my teeth, I stood, prepared to make an announcement—that I was sorry I'd been a complete killjoy, but I would be spending the rest of the day crafting and enjoying myself—when words flashed on the TV screen and made my announcement catch in my throat.

Rex "TW" McMurtry Joins Clarence O'Dea and Jim Johnson Tonight After the Game!

"What?" I sat down again, rereading the words. "That can't be right." Rex would never go on that guy's show. Never. Never ever. He hated that guy.

My phone still in my hand, I sent Rex another message.

Abby: You're going on O'Dea's show? Is that why you're going to be late?

I didn't know if he'd answer, if he'd have time after the game, before his appearance, but something about this smelled yeastier than a . . . loaf of bread.

"I still don't get it." Sal brought her bowl of fresh kettle corn over to the sofa. Kicking up her feet, she reclined on the couch. "Why would he go on that awful man's show?"

"I don't know," I said, pressing my hand to my knee to keep it from bouncing. I was nervous. Rex's team had lost their game, he hadn't texted me back, and now he had an appearance on Clarence O'Dea's show.

I hated that he'd lost, and I kept having crazy thoughts, specifically that they wouldn't have lost if I'd been there. This made no sense. At no point would I have suited up and gone in, I wasn't the twelfth player, and I didn't have a magical pussy—as evidenced by the fact that right after the first time Rex and I made love, his team lost. If anything, my pussy was cursed.

"I hope he punches him in the face." This came from Terry as he sat next to Sal and tried to swipe some popcorn from her dish.

She smacked his hand away. "I do too. He deserves it. Now, if you want popcorn, there's plenty in the kitchen. Help yourself."

He grumbled but didn't stand, instead opting to add his feet to the coffee table next to Sal's.

A commercial for tractors wrapped up and the opening music to O'Dea and Johnson's show on Sports NetTV reached a crescendo, the graphics flashing across the screen, super snazzy and loud. I braced myself, needing to press a palm against my knee again to stop my nervous twitching.

Clarence O'Dea's stupid face came on the screen, and I felt my lip curve into a sneer.

"Welcome everyone to Time Out," he said, launching into his spiel. He talked about this and that, and then finally announced that Rex would be on the show. He paired this information with a smarmy grin for the camera and said, "Should be interesting, so stay tuned."

Segment after segment followed, each of which were a slog of O'Dea's tasteless jokes followed by Johnson's uncomfortable laughter. Then, finally, they announced Rex! And there he was, strolling out, wearing a suit, his face arranged into a marble mask.

I stood, connecting my palms as though in prayer and pressing my fingers to my lips. *Why is he there instead of here?* If Rex had left right after the game, he would've been in Austin already. Didn't he want to get back to me as quickly as I wanted to get back to him?

"TW, honor to have you here," Johnson said, looking like he meant it. "Can we talk about that Thanksgiving game against Richmond? What a performance."

"Hold up, hold up, hold up." Clarence raised a hand, looking back and forth until he seemed satisfied the camera was focused on him. "I think we probably need to clear the air first." He sounded mockingly contrite, and the camera panned to Rex.

Rex's eyes were not on Clarence. They were inspecting his own fingernails. He looked bored.

"So I know I've been hard on you, and everyone knows I like to tease. So I appreciate you *finally* coming after all those invitations we sent. I thought maybe you held a grudge, couldn't take a little good-natured, all in good fun ribbing. So the question is, TW, is it all water under the bridge?"

Rex squinted, glaring at Clarence, saying nothing.

"Well?" O'Dea pressed, smiling.

Rex cleared his throat and opened his mouth to speak.

Clarence cut in before Rex could, which had obviously been his plan all along. "Or should I say, is all *Training Wheels* off the bride?" Laughing at his own joke, Clarence looked to Johnson as though expecting him to be laughing. "So *have* you hung up your training wheels, Rex? Did your wife make you? She's a Hooters waitress, right? And if so, how will all the remaining single women out there learn how to be good wives?"

Hooters waitress?! Did he think that was an insult? WHAT A PENIS HEAD! Hooters waitresses were incredibly hard workers and made gross men feel better about themselves all day long. They were basically Mother Teresa in leg-colored tights.

The camera didn't cut to Johnson, so we had no idea what the cohost was doing, but the camera did cut back to Rex.

And Rex was smirking.

"Uh oh. Here we go." Sal handed Terry her bowl of popcorn, licked her fingers, and leaned forward, her elbows on her knees. "One way or the other, Clarence O'Dea is going to regret his own birth after this."

Rex cleared his throat again and faced O'Dea. "You're talking about real people, Clarence. Real women, good people. You're disrespecting them to their families on national television on Christmas Eve, and you've been disrespecting them for almost two years."

Clarence's smile dropped into a perverse line, and he rolled his eyes, shuffling his papers and making a big show of tapping them against the desk. "Okay, well—"

"You've done a lot of talking about this, now it's my turn," Rex cut in and the camera returned to him, cutting Clarence off. "Other than not speaking up sooner, I have no regrets about my choices, my conscience is clear. I hope the same can't be said for you. I hope you recognize your lack of honor and that it disgusts you. It disgusts me. But if you don't or can't, if you think this—disrespecting women on national television—is okay, you don't deserve to be sitting in that chair." Rex stood, unclipping his microphone, and adding just before he tossed it down, "And shame on anyone"—his eyes swung around the entire studio, landing on where Johnson sat at the end—"who helps you stay there."

Sal, Terry, and I stared at the TV as Rex strode off the set. I was . . . shooketh. And so proud. And so damn impressed. It was just so Rex. He didn't argue, he didn't insult Clarence or scream at him or belittle him. He got straight to the point, sparing as few words as possible to make that point, and then left.

"Oh my good Lord," Sal said, blinking at me with wide eyes. "That was—"

"Bad. Ass." Terry passed the popcorn bowl back to Sal and stood. He paced the room. "I couldn't be prouder of our boy if he'd won the National Model Railroad Association's Model Contest."

"Well said, Terry." Sal placed the popcorn on the table and stood to give him a high five. "I feel like I need to celebrate. How does some champagne sound to you, Abby?"

My mind was reeling. I nodded dumbly.

She moved for the kitchen, but struck with a sudden idea, I reached for her wrist. "Wait. Wait. Do you have any gold thread? Or gold-colored wire?"

"Uh, I think so." She glanced at Terry. "We have extra gold wire from the train set, I think?" Terry nodded and she turned back to me. "How much do you need?"

A swell of nervous anticipation and restless certainty had me shifting from foot to foot. "I don't know yet. But I'm also going to need a crochet hook, the smaller the better."

CHAPTER 30

"Let gratitude be the pillow upon which you kneel to say your nightly prayer. And let faith be the bridge you build to overcome evil and welcome good."

— MAYA ANGELOU, *CELEBRATIONS: RITUALS OF PEACE AND PRAYER*

While Sal helped me hunt down everything I needed to make Rex his impromptu Christmas present, I texted him.

Abby: HOLY CRAPACANNOLI!!! YOU WERE SO AWESOME!!!

Abby: I am so proud of you!

Abby: You are getting laid tonight

Abby: So much getting laid. All the getting laid

Abby: Ring ring—Who's there?—Rex. But he can't come to the phone right now because he's about to get laid

When he didn't answer any of the texts after fifteen minutes, I decided to stop staring at my phone and get to work.

After I finished, Sal and I knit for a bit while continuing to rave about Rex on the show. Rex didn't text.

Terry and I fiddled with the train set, trying to add a log loader. Rex didn't text.

I took a shower and slipped into his bed naked, holding the phone tight to my chest so I would feel it the moment it buzzed, and just as I was drifting off to sleep, Rex texted.

Rex: Today was a game day. Where are my 30 ILYs?

I smiled so big my face hurt.

Abby: I love you. You get the rest when I see your face

Abby: Not on a TV or any other screen. In person.

Rex: I'm on the plane. Can't wait for you to see my face

I checked the clock on my phone—11:47 p.m.—and decided I would stay up reading about the raku method of glazing pottery until he arrived. It was thrilling, but I must've nodded off because something woke me. A sound maybe, now long over and gone. But whatever it was, I found myself fully awake and realizing with a start that someone—Rex—was behind me, his body naked, his fingers curled around the curve of my hip, his muscled chest against my back.

His hand moved, sliding down my leg and then moving to the interior, lifting and pulling it slowly up until my legs were separated and the top one lay along his thick, muscular thigh.

"Abby," he whispered in my ear and my heart exploded, my giant smile returning.

"Rex."

He kissed my neck, languid, hot licks and bites. "Say it."

"I love you."

His chest rumbled with his happy sound, his hand skimmed up my side to the front of my stomach, higher, palming my breast.

I released a ragged breath and said again, "I love you."

He kissed my shoulder, then bit the top of it as his fingers plucked at my nipple. My breath came faster, my bottom pressing against his groin. He slid his palm down my stomach and between my legs, stroking me.

"I love you. I love you. I love you." My words were more air than sound.

Rex's hot breath spilled over my neck, sending spikes of heat low to that deep place only he had touched, down my thighs to my toes. His length pressed insistently against my ass and he tilted his hips slightly away. I felt his hand move between us and then his erection was between my legs, the length of him rubbing my center.

I panted, reaching behind me and gripping his forearm. He was everywhere and he was so big. The push of him behind me, the strength of him almost overwhelming.

"I needed you," he muttered, and the words sounded mindless, like they spilled out of him.

I nodded, repeating more *I love yous* and losing count. He grunted in response before shifting up behind me and positioning me on my stomach, my elbows angling up my upper torso. Rex climbed behind me, spreading my legs wide, his big hands falling to the mattress on either side of my shoulders to brace himself above as his chest pressed against my upper back.

Oh God, oh God, oh God.

I'd never had sex like this before. I felt so . . . defenseless.

I didn't have a moment to think past my excitement and trepidation before Rex entered me, his muscular stomach pressed against my bottom, one hand at my hip while the other supported his weight behind me.

I moaned, my head falling forward as he moved, in and out, in and out. I felt stretched and heavy, completely at his mercy, my fate in his hands, and it felt amazing. So amazing. Instinctively, I tilted my hips back, my bottom rising in the air, and I heard him curse, a long string of profanities and praise.

"You are too good to be true." He laughed the words, though they were without humor. If anything, he sounded a little bitter about it, winded, like he was out of breath, his hand moving and massaging my flesh, my thigh to my bottom, to my back, side, and shoulder. He gave my neck a squeeze, pushing me down fully to the mattress, my elbows trapped beneath me.

"Is this good for you? Do you like how this feels?" he asked against my ear, his fingertips dancing over my back.

I nodded, whimpering out more *I love yous* as my hips shifted restlessly, the feelings of being so full and touched so deep inside clogging my throat.

"I need—I need to see you," he said, sounding frustrated. In the next moment, he'd withdrawn completely, and I lifted up, searching for him, my hand reaching. Seconds later, he was next to me on the bed, and he'd picked me up by the hips, arranging my body so that I straddled his hips.

I reached for his length and squeezed, and said, "I love this."

A breathy laugh rumbled out of him, his eyes flashing dark, his hands sliding to my breasts, the pads of his thumbs scraping against my nipples. "Then put it inside you," he said gruffly between clenched teeth, his thighs flexing beneath my backside.

Rising on my knees, I positioned the head at my entrance and sunk down, my breath shaky as I took as much of him as I could before rising up and trying again and again and again until I was fully seated.

Rex's hands slid to my hips, his attention fully focused on where our bodies joined, his muscles of his stomach rigid. My breaths were hitching moans and gasps. His breaths were ragged, eventually sounding tortured and labored the longer I swayed above him, pivoting my hips to ensure my clit stroked his length with every forward and backward motion.

Gaze frantic, jaw tight, his fingers dug into me and then released to grab the sheets. "Fuck. Fuck, Abby. I can't. You have to st—I'm going to—I'm so—You're too—" Rex's head pressed back against the pillow as I tried to decipher what he wanted through my lust-filled haze. And then he was coming, silently. I continued to move, picking up the pace as I watched him, enraptured, tearing the sheets from the bed with straining muscles and tight fists, his mouth open, his beautiful body before me, like my deepest, darkest fantasy.

I didn't care that he'd come without me. I only cared that he was here, with me. My sexy Tex Rex. All mine. Naked.

When he'd finished, his chest rising and falling like he'd run a hundred miles, I slowed until his hands came to my hips to hold me still. In the next moment, he'd slid his hands up to my neck, fisting them in my hair and rolling me under him. He kissed me, deep and fast, soft and slow, his arms embracing me tightly as he caught his breath, his skin pressed to mine, his heart decelerating from a gallop to a meander.

"You have seven more," he muttered, slurring his words.

"Pardon?"

"Seven." He leaned back, hovering over me, eyes warm and drowsy. "Seven more I love yous."

"You were counting?"

"And you owe me an orgasm."

I chuckled. "I owe you one, husband?"

I saw something flare at my use of the word *husband*. "Yes. One of yours." His sleepy smile became less sleepy, his fingers finding my breast, massaging it, weighing it. "And we're not sleeping, babe, until you give me what's mine."

I don't know what time it was Christmas morning when I finally woke up, but the sun was up, and Rex was still asleep next to me. I spent a few minutes blinking awake. Then, remembering my plan for this morning, I stole out of bed, trying not to shiver as I picked up the box I'd borrowed from Terry last night, and then slid back under the covers.

I proceeded to stare at my husband like a creeper, waiting for him to wake up so I could give him my present. Well, one of my presents.

His giant, perfectly formed mug was back in Austin under the tree I'd put up at his house. He'd have to wait for that one.

Counting his freckles and eyelashes, I'd just moved on to tallying up his scars when he shifted and stretched. His hands came in contact with my body and his eyes flew open. Wide and confused quickly became drowsy and happy as he reached for me.

I evaded him, shifting away. "Good morning, Rex."

His smile deepened, eyes narrowing on me. "What are you doing?"

"Watching you sleep. The stalker in me will never die."

His sleep-roughened laugh was so sexy. "Good. The stalker in me honors the stalker in you."

He reached for me again and I placed the box in his grasping hands, then tucked my fingers under my chin, greedy for his reaction. "Merry Christmas. Open it now."

Rex looked between the plain square brown box and me, lifting an eyebrow. "What is it?"

"Open it." A nervous flutter, one of doom and fear and not deserving, tried to weasel its way into the moment. I banished it, told it to never return.

Blinking a few times as though to focus his eyes, he propped himself up on an elbow and opened the box. He blinked again, rearing back, his eyes cutting to mine. "What—are these rings?"

I nodded excitedly and scooched forward, plucking my simple crocheted gold ring out of the box and slipping it on my left ring finger. "I made them last night. Mine fits, because I could measure it, but I have no idea if yours does. I used Terry's hands as a guide, but your fingers are much bigger. I can remake it!" My grandmother's diamond would now stay firmly on my right hand.

Rex didn't pick his ring up, but he did shift closer and into my space. And when he spoke, his voice was rough and gravelly. "Why are you giving me a ring?" Rex gazed down at me like my answer to his question might solve all the mysteries of the universe.

"Because I love you, and I want to be your wife, and I want you to be my husband."

His throat worked as his suddenly glassy eyes moved between

mine. "Abby—" My name emerged like static, and he swallowed again.

"I kept asking you what our future was going to be, I kept wanting to discuss it. I kept pushing for an answer. But then when you left and didn't ask me to go with you—" I lifted my fingers to his lips to keep him from interrupting. "I understand why you didn't. But when you didn't ask me to go with you, I tied myself up into knots of worry, irritated with you for not knowing—or trusting—that wherever you are is where I want to be."

He moved like he was going to grab me. I sat up, pulling the sheet up with me. "But then it occurred to me, *I* could've asked. Actually, I could've just told you. So I'm telling you now, Rex. I want you to be my husband. I want to be your wife. I want to have a life with you, children, dogs, cats. Maybe some chickens or a fish. No peacocks. They're bastards."

A laugh burst out of him that was almost silent but still shook the bed.

Placing my palm on his cheek, I pushed my fingers into his short hair, loving the texture, loving everything about him. "I'm telling you what I want. I'm being specific. And you always said, whatever I want, if I ask for it and am specific, you'll give it to me. So . . ." I gestured to the box in his hand. "Put it on."

Rex stared at me, his gaze as soft and sharp as starlight. He'd been fighting a smile, but he finally surrendered to it, showing me all those gorgeous teeth he never shared. Glancing down at the box, he picked the ring up, and I held my breath as he slipped it on his left ring finger. It fit.

Gaze returning to mine, smile still in place, he asked, "Are you finished? Is there anything else you want?" He narrowed his eyes, *still* smiling. "Be specific."

Fighting the urge to leap into his lap, I tapped my chin thoughtfully. "I want more fantasies."

"Done."

"And I want to move to Chicago with you."

His smile slipped and his forehead furrowed. "Are you sure? Are you sure you want to—"

"It's what I want," I said decisively, pointing a finger at him.

Rex's brow cleared, but his smile remained small as his eyes grew serious. "Abby, you must know, I would do absolutely anything for you. Anything." His voice had gone rough again and he cleared his throat. "Please. Never leave me."

My heart cracked open, and I jumped on top of him, pouring the contents of my heart into the kiss, saying, "Never," with each separation and smoothing my fingers over his perfect face.

"Husband. You are not training wheels, and I am not a placeholder. Okay?"

He nodded solemnly and gathered my cheeks in his palms, his eyes turning hot, purposeful. "You are my place, Abby," he said firmly. "Never doubt that I will always be yours."

A PEEK INTO CHRISTMAS FUTURE – 5 YEARS LATER

"All the world is made of faith, and trust, and pixie dust."

— J.M. BARRIE, *PETER PAN*

"Stop pulling that poor woman under the mistletoe and put on your sweater." Sal waved a spatula at us that dripped tomato sauce all over the floor. "Oh, well, shit," she said, noticing the dripping sauce and huffing. "Let me go get a paper towel." Grumbling, she stomped back into the kitchen. "TERRY! Get me a paper towel!"

Rex and I tried to keep our laughter as quiet as possible, our heads coming together as we fought against it valiantly.

"That's the third time she's done that," Rex said, his shoulders shaking. "We need to get her a dog."

"Agreed." I lifted to my tiptoes and kissed my handsome husband on the cheek, not wanting to tempt him with another kiss on the lips as I pulled off my coat and folded it over my arm. "How's Wyatt doing? Did he eat his lunch? When did you arrive? Are you tired? I missed you."

Ignoring all my questions, Rex stepped back, his eyebrows

launching into his hairline as his gaze dragged over me. "What are you wearing, woman?"

I glanced down and sighed. "It's an elf costume."

"A what?"

"An elf costume. I finally did it. I finally helped out at the Santa dance party." I pointed behind him to the couch. "You better put your festive sweater on before she beats you with her saucy spoon."

Backing up, presumably so he didn't have to remove his eyes from my body, Rex took in my red velvet boots, red-and-white-striped stockings that had to be thigh-highs because nothing else was ever long enough for my legs, and green velvet dress that would've been a normal length on anyone shorter than six foot one.

I placed my hand on my hip. "Quit staring and put on your sweater. It has gingerbread men on it, and it matches Wyatt's." Turning, I hung my coat and hurried to the kitchen, grinning at my baby boy's chubby smile.

"He had spaghetti and then I cleaned him up and put him in his sweater. Now he's working on a cookie," Terry announced, bouncing our son on his knee. "Sal even changed a diaper with no help."

Picking up my sweetie, I avoided his grasping fingers and brought his neck rolls to my lips for a bunch of smacking kisses. "I've missed you. I've missed you," I sang, giving him all my love for the afternoon I'd been out, and inhaling deeply.

Wyatt and I had visited Walker for a day before driving over to Alenbach. Both Walker and Ramona had commented wistfully on Wyatt's "new baby smell." It might be weird, but I loved how he smelled, and I dreaded the day his baby smell faded.

Happily, Walker was quite amenable to accepting free tickets to football games, so I still saw him during the season and then more often when we were in Austin during the spring. Splitting our time between the two cities worked for now, but when Wyatt started kindergarten in a few years, we'd have to pick one or the other.

I couldn't quite make up my mind but was leaning towards Chicago. Declan was up for parole soon-- he'd been given four years—and I had no idea what to expect when he was released. Possibly, he'd leave us alone. Then again, if we made things easy for him by staying in Texas, maybe not.

"Aww. Look at my gingerbread boys!"

I turned at the exclamation and found Sal with her hands together, smiling brightly at Rex. "I'm so glad I made those matching sweaters."

"I'm not a gingerbread boy," Rex said flatly. I was about to chastise him for being so grumpy about the sweater when he turned his head to me, winked, and added like he was James Bond, "I'm a man, a gingerbread man."

I pressed my lips together to keep from laughing, but I did roll my eyes to the ceiling. "Anyway. Let me go get out of this outfit so I can help with dinner." Giving Wyatt one more sniff, I passed him over to Terry's waiting arms.

"Don't worry about it. Take your time, and I'm happy to lay him down for a nap. But did you have fun? Being Santa's helper?" Terry asked, holding Wyatt's cookie for him.

"Yeah! It was fun." I backed up toward the doorway. "And I liked the idea of a dance-party Santa instead of the sitting-on-a-stranger's-lap Santa."

"That was my idea," Terry piped in, lifting his hand.

"That's right. Nicely done, Terry." I gave him a deferential head nod. "I salute you."

Sal lifted a sardonic looking eyebrow, her eyes dropping to my red-and-white stockings and short, green velvet dress. "The elf girl costumes were also his idea, so don't give him too much credit."

Terry and Sal's bickering followed me out of the kitchen, making me chuckle, and I jogged up the stairs. But then, hearing footfalls behind me, I glanced over my shoulder.

Rex was following me, his eyes on the back of my legs.

"Oh, hello." I spun as I made it to the landing, careful not to disturb Grandma Sal's white Christmas tree with the antique pink glass ornaments. "Can I help you?"

Without stopping or replying, he grabbed my hand and led me down the hall to our room. As soon as the door closed behind us, he pushed me against it, his hands fastened to my backside, and his mouth covered mine.

"What are we doing?"

"Fantasy time." He rolled his hips.

"Rex," I said, his name a gasp, my body forcefully ready for whatever he had planned. As usual.

"Babe."

"Wait."

His hand fit between us, cupping me over my underwear. "Please. I need you."

He was so bad. He knew I'd do *anything* he wanted if he said please. But then, he'd do anything I wanted if I asked and was specific.

"Your aunt and uncle are downstairs, right now, and so is your son."

"I assure you, Grandpa Terry will run interference with Wyatt, he loves it, and no one will be surprised if we're late to dinner. It's been ages since I had you."

"It's been three days."

"Like I said, ages." He pushed aside the scrap of fabric between his hand and my body, sliding the tip of his finger inside me and then withdrawing to give me a featherlight stroke.

My legs shook.

Rex dipped his mouth to my neck, hot breath mingling with mine, a detonation of goose bumps racing everywhere. "You work so hard." He kissed the juncture of my neck and shoulder, scraping his teeth across the skin. "Let me help you relax."

"I'm convinced." My shaking hands moved to the zipper on the side of my dress.

"No." He stayed my movements and brought my wrists to his mouth for soft kisses. Holding my eyes, he whispered darkly, "The elf outfit stays on."

My lips parted as heat swirled low in my belly. "Wha—?"

Giving me a devilish look as his fingers hooked into my underwear, he kneeled, and he tugged down the fabric. "Everything on but these."

I fought my grin, but it won in the end, my fingers sifting through his hair, my hips tilting forward in offering. "Defiling one of Santa's elves will put you on the naughty list, *husband*."

Lifting my skirt like he was unwrapping a present, he licked his lips. “Oh, I’m counting on it, *babe*.”

The End

Subscribe to Penny’s awesome newsletter for exclusive stories, sneak peeks, and pictures of cats knitting hats. Subscribe here:
http://pennyreid.ninja/newsletter/

ABOUT THE AUTHOR

Penny Reid is the *New York Times*, *Wall Street Journal*, and *USA Today* bestselling author of the Winston Brothers and Knitting in the City series. She used to spend her days writing federal grant proposals as a biomedical researcher, but now she writes kissing books. Penny is an obsessive knitter and manages the #OwnVoices-focused mentorship incubator / publishing imprint, Smartypants Romance. She lives in Seattle Washington with her husband, three kids, and dog named Hazel.

Come find me -
Mailing List: http://pennyreid.ninja/newsletter/
Goodreads:http://www.goodreads.com/ReidRomance
Facebook: www.facebook.com/pennyreidwriter
Instagram: www.instagram.com/reidromance
Twitter: www.twitter.com/reidromance
Patreon: https://www.patreon.com/smartypantsromance
Email: pennreid@gmail.com …hey, you! Email me ;-)

OTHER BOOKS BY PENNY REID

Knitting in the City Series

(Interconnected Standalones, Adult Contemporary Romantic Comedy)

Neanderthal Seeks Human: A Smart Romance (#1)

Neanderthal Marries Human: A Smarter Romance (#1.5)

Friends without Benefits: An Unrequited Romance (#2)

Love Hacked: A Reluctant Romance (#3)

Beauty and the Mustache: A Philosophical Romance (#4)

Ninja at First Sight (#4.75)

Happily Ever Ninja: A Married Romance (#5)

Dating-ish: A Humanoid Romance (#6)

Marriage of Inconvenience: (#7)

Neanderthal Seeks Extra Yarns (#8)

Knitting in the City Coloring Book (#9)

Winston Brothers Series

(Interconnected Standalones, Adult Contemporary Romantic Comedy, spinoff of Beauty and the Mustache)

Beauty and the Mustache (#0.5)

Truth or Beard (#1)

Grin and Beard It (#2)

Beard Science (#3)

Beard in Mind (#4)

Beard In Hiding (#4.5)

Dr. Strange Beard (#5)

Beard with Me (#6)

Beard Necessities (#7)

Winston Brothers Paper Doll Book (#8)

Hypothesis Series

(New Adult Romantic Comedy Trilogies)

Elements of Chemistry: ATTRACTION, HEAT, and CAPTURE (#1)

Laws of Physics: MOTION, SPACE, and TIME (#2)

Irish Players (Rugby) Series – by L.H. Cosway and Penny Reid

(Interconnected Standalones, Adult Contemporary Sports Romance)

The Hooker and the Hermit (#1)

The Pixie and the Player (#2)

The Cad and the Co-ed (#3)

The Varlet and the Voyeur (#4)

Dear Professor Series

(New Adult Romantic Comedy)

Kissing Tolstoy (#1)

Kissing Galileo (#2)

Ideal Man Series

(Interconnected Standalones, Adult Contemporary Romance Series of Jane Austen Reimaginings)

Pride and Dad Jokes (#1, coming 2022)

Man Buns and Sensibility (#2, TBD)

Sense and Manscaping (#3, TBD)

Persuasion and Man Hands (#4, TBD)

Mantuary Abbey (#5, TBD)

Mancave Park (#6, TBD)

Emmanuel (#7, TBD)

Handcrafted Mysteries Series

(A Romantic Cozy Mystery Series, spinoff of *The Winston Brothers Series*)

Engagement and Espionage (#1)

Marriage and Murder (#2)

Home and Heist (#3, coming 2023)

Baby and Ballistics (TBD)

Pie Crimes and Misdemeanors (TBD)

Good Folks Series

(Interconnected Standalones, Adult Contemporary Romantic Comedy, spinoff of *The Winston Brothers Series*)

Totally Folked (#1)

Folk Around and Find Out (#2, coming 2022)

Three Kings Series

(Interconnected Standalones, Holiday-themed Adult Contemporary Romantic Comedies)

Homecoming King (#1)

Drama King (#2, coming Christmas 2022)

Prom King (#3, coming Christmas 2023)

Standalones

Ten Trends to Seduce Your Best Friend (coming 2022)

Made in the USA
Columbia, SC
02 January 2023